Identity

ALSO BY G.M. FORD
FROM CLIPPER LARGE PRINT

Black River
A Blind Eye
Red Tide

Identity

G.M. Ford

W F HOWES LTD

This large print edition published in 2009 by
W F Howes Ltd
Unit 4, Rearsby Business Park, Gaddesby Lane,
Rearsby, Leicester LE7 4YH

1 3 5 7 9 10 8 6 4 2

First published in the United Kingdom in 2009
by Macmillan

A CIP catalogue record for this book is available
from the British Library

ISBN 978 1 407 44114 6

Typeset by Palimpsest Book Production Limited,
Grangemouth, Stirlingshire
Printed and bound in Great Britain
by MPG Books Ltd, Bodmin, Cornwall

FSC
Mixed Sources
Product group from well-managed
forests and other controlled sources

Cert no. SGS-COC-2953
www.fsc.org
© 1996 Forest Stewardship Council

To my editor, Lyssa Keusch,
for keeping the faith.
Thanks doesn't cover it,
but it will have to do. Thanks.

IN THE DESERT

In the desert
I saw a creature, naked, bestial,
Who, squatting upon the ground,
Held his heart in his hands,
And ate of it.
I said, 'Is it good, friend?'
'It is bitter – bitter,' he answered;
'But I like it
Because it is bitter,
And because it is my heart.'

—STEPHEN CRANE

CHAPTER 1

Nobody saw it coming. Although, for reasons unknown, unexpected events always seem to bring forth some well-meaning soul who swears he remembers an uncertain slant of light sifting through the trees that morning, or some fearful and fecund odor wafting in the morning breeze. Not on this day, however.

No . . . October 16 was just another cloudy fall morning, a harbinger of nothing more unusual than winter, a gentle reminder provided by nature in the days before the relentless rains return to wash Arbor Street clean of other seasons.

Yes . . . this was the same Arbor Street which had once aspired to grandeur, when, a century earlier, affluent merchants and manufacturers had erected elaborate Georgian mansions along the northern part of the Hill, each edifice grander than its predecessor, as the newly wealthy sought to upstage one another in the all-too-common manner of self-made men.

A century later, what a frozen-fish fortune once procured for the Jensen family had been reincarnated as Harmony House, a long-term residential facility for physically and developmentally challenged adults. Over the strenuous objections of the hastily formed Arbor Street Citizens Committee, the state had purchased the decaying mansion, cut back the shrubbery, renovated the interior, installed an elevator, ramped and handrailed everything in sight, and then painted the whole thing a single shade of dull green.

'Monkey-shit green,' as Shirley liked to say.

Shirley said a lot of stuff, most of it funny as hell. Thing was, nobody but Paul could understand her horribly impaired speech, and since Paul had never been known to utter so much as a syllable, Shirley's witticisms were pretty much destined to remain an inside joke. That Paul was somehow able to hear words where others could not, that he laughed at her jokes and followed her orders, had long since been chalked off as miraculous, like the way Benny the dog could hear thunder coming from a long way off.

At the end of the walkway, Darl stood with his hands thrust deep into his pants pockets. Darl had a problem with decisions. He just couldn't pull the trigger. Couldn't decide whether to go left or to go right. Left alone at an intersection, he'd stand there until either the cows came home or the cops rustled him up and brought him back to Harmony House because his name and address were sewn into his clothes.

As Paul wheeled Shirley along the walk, he smiled, or maybe grimaced. With all that scar

2

tissue on his face, it was hard to tell. Looked like somebody had crushed the front of his skull with a crowbar or something, pushed everything back so far it was both a wonder he was alive and a mercy he wasn't tuned to the same channel as the rest of humanity.

The state of Washington had estimated his age to be between twenty-five and thirty at the time he was discovered, lying near death in a railroad car down behind Western Station. Some bureaucrat had named him Paul Hardy, after a nephew who had died during childbirth. That was seven years ago, so these days Paul was probably somewhere in his midthirties, a strapping two-hundred-twenty-pound block of concrete who spent his days working for Ken Suzuki, a local landscaping contractor. While Paul could not actually be taught anything per se, he could, with a bit of patience, be introduced to simple tasks. Sometimes you had to show him more than once, but once he got it . . . you know . . . 'take that bag over there and put it in the pile' . . . once he got it, he was an absolutely tireless worker. Had to be led away for lunch. Funny thing was . . . after lunch . . . you had to show him all over again.

As the wheelchair rolled along, a gust of wind rumbled overhead, shivering the branches, separating the dead from the dying as it sent yet another batch of leaves twirling downward to the moist earth, where ancient roots had corrupted the sidewalk, pushing the stones upward at odd degrees and angles, until passersby were obliged to walk on the grass strip between the sidewalk and the curb or risk breaking an ankle.

As they came alongside the first van, Randall stepped back onto the sidewalk. Paul was forced to wheel out to the right, toward the little wire fence separating the sidewalk from the front yard. The sound of Paul and Shirley approaching snapped Randall's head around. His habitually furrowed brow was more deeply pleated than usual. His square lower jaw worked his gum at a speed unattainable by better adjusted members of society. By the time his brain processed the picture of Paul and Shirley and decided these were people he knew, he was already patting himself down, looking for gifts and offerings.

Ms Willis said it was a self-esteem problem that made him give things away when confronted by strangers. She said he was like everybody else; all he wanted was to love and be loved, but anybody who'd ever watched Randall strip to the skin trying to gain favor with strangers harbored serious doubts as to just how mainstream Randall could be considered.

Shirley's anxiety concerning seating proved accurate. The sound of the sliding door brought them running. All of a sudden the moment was at hand, and nobody wanted to be left behind. Ms Willis arrived with Darl in tow. Carman and Roger held hands as they picked their way across the wet grass. That's when Eunice Ponds came

4

trotting out to say she'd changed her mind about wanting to go, and why was she always the one got left behind and why were we bringing old blind Mrs Dahlberg anyway, wasn't like she could see anything, and why didn't we take her instead, at which point, she staged a tantrum right there on the sidewalk in front of God and a couple of neighbors out walking the dog.

Took half a box of tissues, a promise of ice cream from Mrs Willis to put out the fire. As Eunice took her first grudging step back toward Harmony House, onlookers made it a point to spread themselves thin, lest some posture or gesture unwittingly rekindle Eunice's embers of resentment.

The thinning of the crowd created a line of sight which sent Paul leaping away from the van, rushing up toward Shirley and the cantilevered section of sidewalk above his head. Shirley turned her head toward the sound; her good hand worked the joystick for all she was worth, but gravity was not to be denied. Her ruined voice squawked like a jay as the wheelchair bounced over a crack in the cement, turned down over the grass, and rapidly gained speed as it headed for the street.

Ten yards away, Helen Willis stifled a sigh and pulled at the seat belt with both hands. Darl's excitement made it impossible for him to sit still, so instead of waiting patiently as she helped him with his belt, he squirmed around in the passenger seat as if his pants were on fire, turning the task of buckling a seat belt into something akin to a game of Pin the Tail on the Donkey. The stifled sigh suddenly escaped.

She'd been through it a million times. All the different people she might have turned out to be. Lying there in the darkness with only the sounds of her mother's incessant snoring for company, she'd recall how she'd left the Convent of St Mary for the purpose of tending to her mother. All they had was each other. If Helen didn't make the sacrifice, who would?

A week after her mother's funeral, Helen stood on the front walk of the house where she'd always lived, pinching a pair of letters between her trembling fingers. The first had been a government form letter informing her that her mother's Social Security and disability benefits were hereby terminated and 'oh, by the way, sorry about your loss.' The second was from Victory Bank and Trust informing Helen she had forty-five days to vacate the house, which, as it turned out, was being held in trust by the bank until such time as her mother's death, at which time the residence reverted to Helen's long-dead father's heirs somewhere in eastern Illinois.

And so when an old family friend had pulled a few strings and gotten her the job as assistant director of the newly commissioned Harmony House, she'd jumped at the opportunity. When it turned out the duties of the assistant director consisted of housekeeper, groundskeeper, and all-around chief cook and bottle washer, Helen was undeterred. From her first day on the job, she felt she'd made the right move. Something about helping others was at her core. Something about the way these people loved her. How they made her feel.

At least, that's what she told herself. That was her get-out-of-bed-in-the-morning story, that life-long saga of pride and pluck in which she was always the heroine, the story where her choices were willful, where all loose ends were tucked away and cold regret was not welcome at the door.

Whatever the story . . . it worked for Helen, and when, seven months later, Harmony House director Jonathan Chabot had keeled over dead on the back stairs (an embolism, they said), Helen had inherited the directorship, initially as an interim position, and later, when things went on without a hitch, as the official director.

She used her shoulder to push Darl down in the seat and then lunged across his lap. On this, the sixth or seventh attempt, the buckle hit the clasp on a fly and snapped into place. She slid back onto her feet, let out a long breath, and dusted her palms. As she closed the van door, a collective intake of breath snapped her head around. A sharp cry rose above the rustle of the wind. Shirley was rolling down the sidewalk.

A moan rose in her chest. Without thinking, she began to move, running along the gutter, in the space between the tires and the curb, rolling her ankle at one point, hopping, then limping along, favoring the sprain and wailing as she cleared the end of the van just in time to see Shirley flash by.

She watched in horror as the speeding wheelchair launched itself over the curb. Not one of those modern concrete curbs either, but a full-blown chunk of granite over a foot tall, the kind they used back when the houses were built. Helen Willis threw out her arms as if to somehow cushion the collision. She fully expected the chair to come down at a severe angle and then topple over onto Shirley's face. She held her breath as the chair bounced hard on the tiny front wheels, cartwheeled sideways for a moment, and then miraculously righted itself without seeming to lose momentum. She heard the screams and cries of the others rise to a crescendo as the chair rolled out into the street; she forced herself forward in the seconds before Paul flashed through her field of vision, parallel to the ground like a cruise missile, flying like Superman until his fingers hit the handles and his knees hit the street with one of the most dreadful sounds Helen Willis had ever heard.

Paul's weight swung the chair in a half circle. The wheelchair stopped on a dime, leaving Paul hanging from the handles amid the sighs of relief and the squeals of appreciation. After that, everything happened in slow motion.

A ragged cry rose from Shirley's throat. The sound must have meant something, because Paul turned his head in time to see the car bearing down on him. The chorus swallowed its tongue as Paul heaved the wheelchair away, sending Shirley rocketing toward the curb. He had time to get one hand on the street and was struggling to regain his feet when the chorus emitted a mournful sigh.

Paul turned toward the Lexus, his eyes searching the tinted windshield for relief . . . except the driver didn't see him. White teeth flashed as the driver spoke into the cell phone. He was still chatting away when Paul ducked his head and disappeared beneath the front bumper of the Lexus with an ear-shredding scream.

CHAPTER 2

Helen knelt at Paul's side after they'd pulled him from beneath the car. She'd gagged as one of the EMTs folded Paul's face back down where it belonged.

She'd ridden in the ambulance with him. Watched as the technician worked to stabilize Paul's vital signs inside the aid car, engine roaring, light bar flashing, the *whoop whoop* of the siren clearing the way as they covered the three or so miles to Harborvista Medical Center, bouncing and screaming across the crest of the hill, rocketing toward whatever hope of survival Paul Hardy might still have.

Her suspicions were validated when a full trauma team met them in the driveway. She climbed out and stood aside as they worked to save his life. Above the hiss of traffic, she heard a whispered 'holy moley' as Paul's head came into view.

They were rolling him off now. Helen got to her feet and began to follow. The only member of the crew not wearing scrubs peeled off and started her way. Younger than Helen, flowered blouse, fawn-colored wool pants. She introduced herself.

The name went in one of Helen's ears and out the other. Started with a *B* maybe.

'Mrs . . .' It was a question.

'Willis . . . Helen Willis.'

'Are you his . . .'

'Mr Hardy is a ward of the state. To the best of my knowledge, he has no living relatives.'

The woman made a note on the clipboard she carried. 'Do you happen to know if Mr Hardy has medical insurance?'

'Through the state,' Helen answered. 'Very basic.' Helen watched as the double doors at the end of the hall opened and closed. The bed, the staff, the rolling, clattering forest of IV stands, moved as one and then disappeared from view.

'Where are they taking him?' Helen asked.

'To ICU. They're trying to stabilize his vital signs.'

'Is he . . . ? Will they . . . ?' She couldn't bring herself to finish the sentence.

The woman put a firm hand on Helen's shoulder. 'I'm not going to lie to you, Mrs Willis,' she said. 'It's touch and go.' She paused. 'He's in very serious condition.'

Helen thanked her for the candor. 'If they save him—' She stopped. '*When* they save him,' she corrected herself, 'are they going to be able to do anything about . . .'

Helen took a pair of deep breaths and pointed at her own face. 'You know.'

The woman expelled a long breath of her own. 'Whatever it takes to save his life and get him back

11

on his feet. After that . . .' She shrugged. 'The kind of work Mr Hardy is going to need is generally considered discretionary.'

'The state considers toothpaste discretionary,' Helen said. 'I have to fight them tooth and nail for every little thing my people need.'

'It's not just the state,' the younger woman said. 'Your health insurance company . . . my health insurance company . . . when it comes to plastic surgery, there isn't an insurance company on the planet wants to pay for it. They claim it's not "health related."' She made quotation marks in the air. 'They insist it's "not a medical necessity."'

Helen fought to remain in control of herself. 'The people who decide these things . . .' she began. The woman took her gently by the elbow. Helen's voice took on a bitter quality. '. . . these are the same people whose kids are wearing braces on their teeth and whose wives are getting a little nip and tuck every five years or so in order to look young,' she groused. 'I can't believe . . .'

The woman guided her back through the swinging doors. The noise level increased threefold. The muted whir of electronics, the clank of metal against metal, multiple conversations, the grunts and groans of the two dozen assorted souls waiting for help. After a moment the sounds melted into a single musical note, jarring and out of tune, like the big finish of some atonal symphony.

Helen interrupted her tirade and looked around.

'You can wait here,' the woman said, offering a

12

padded institutional chair along the nearest wall. 'But . . .' she cautioned, 'it's probably going to be a while. You might be better off leaving your name and number with the ICU desk. They'll give you a ring whenever there's something to report.'

Helen thought about it. 'He doesn't have anybody,' she said finally.

'You sure?' she asked Helen.

'He's alone,' she said again. 'He shouldn't wake up with nobody here.'

The other woman nodded her understanding, patted Helen twice on the shoulder, and disappeared back into ICU surgery.

Over the next three hours, Helen went outside twice for air. On the first occasion, she stood in the circular drive and watched the bright orange sun as it spilled down over the distant mountains, her mind blank of everything other than postcard platitudes about setting suns and faraway peaks. Second time the sun had been swallowed by the jagged mouth of the mountains and the air held a promise of impending weather.

Helen shivered and wondered again if anybody was any more alone than her Paul Hardy who wasn't even Paul Hardy. If anybody . . . That's when the doctor came out.

Five o'clock shadow. Late thirties, hair just starting to go gray around the edges. Big white hands that seemed to have a life of their own. He didn't seem to be interested in offering one as a greeting. 'Paul Hardy?' East Coast accent.

Helen got to her feet. She could feel herself vibrating. 'Yes.'

He made a slight sideways movement with his head. 'He's alive,' he said. 'We've stabilized his vital signs.'

Wasn't until that moment when Helen realized she'd been holding her breath.

'He's going to make it,' she gasped.

He held up a long white finger. 'That's not what I said. I said he's alive. That's all.' He waited for the message to sink in.

'But . . . you know . . .' Helen began.

'He died in there,' the doctor said. 'Three times.' He relaxed his face. 'I thought for sure he was gone.' He met her eyes. 'We see a lot of this stuff. We kinda get a feeling for what's gonna happen next. You could see it in everybody's eyes. They all thought he was a goner.' He shook his head. '. . . but that SOB just kept coming back.' He smiled. 'Guy's strong as an ox.'

'Can I?' she began.

The doctor made a rude noise with his lips. 'Be serious.' He frowned. 'He's out of it.' He cut off her objections. 'The only exciting thing Mr Hardy's going to do between now and morning is to die.' He checked his watch. 'Come back around nine A.M. If he's still alive in the morning. Well then . . . who knows.'

14

CHAPTER 3

Asked to explain her unnaturally accommodating manner, Helen Willis would have related the tale of her personal moment of epiphany, how rounding the corner of Harding Avenue and Broadway on her way to Mass one misty morning, she'd spotted a bumper sticker on a blue Volvo station wagon. It read: YOU'RE ONLY AS GOOD AS WHAT PISSES YOU OFF.

How, two hours later, she couldn't recall a thing about morning Mass. Not even the subject of the sermon. Instead of listening, she'd ruminated her way through the forty-five-minute service wondering how a two-dollar message tacked to a rusty car bumper could have affected her so deeply. In the end, as she always did, she attributed it to God. She reasoned that walking to Mass was part of the religious experience and that the message on the back of that car was surely as important and as divinely inspired as anything Father Crowley might have uttered that winter morning.

On this particular morning, however, Helen Willis was as close to pissed off as she got. The frosted glass door read: SURGERY ICU. In smaller letters, down at the bottom: *Authorized Personnel Only*. Helen Willis straightened her arm and sent the door flying back against the wall with a crash, revealing a brightly lit room, maybe fifteen by fifty, its gleaming white floor running along the front side of three operating theaters. The nearest doctor was up to his elbows in red. Helen turned away.

From the corner of her eye, Helen watched as a stocky Hispanic woman in a green smock walked her way. 'Jew can't be in here, lady. Jew got to . . .'

Helen stepped farther into the room, allowing the door to hiss closed behind her.

'I'm looking for Paul Hardy.'

The woman untied the upper half of her surgical mask and let it drop down over her chest. 'Lady . . . jew got to see the people upstair . . .'

'The people upstair . . .' Helen felt the hot blood in her face. She took a deep breath and started over. 'The people upstairs said he was down here.'

'Jew got to—'

'No,' Helen interrupted, louder this time.

'Jew—'

'They finally come out and tell me he's back in surgery. Now I've been sitting around here for . . .' She checked her watch. '. . . for over two hours . . . getting the runaround . . .'

She sputtered to a halt. The woman had walked off down the hall and disappeared.

'I've wasted the whole day, and I'm not going

16

anywhere until I see Paul Hardy. Period. End of story,' she said to the empty hallway. She felt better for having said it and then foolish for having felt better.

A minute passed and then two. What had seemed to Helen's ears to be silence was, in reality, far from it. The constant whir of machines filled the low end of the sound spectrum like a drone string, a dirge running like a stream beneath the muted chorus of rhythmic electronic beeps and buzzes and squeals sending their drumbeat messages through the sterile unmoving air.

A lopsided panel of yellow light appeared on the floor at the far end of the hall. The woman in the smock reappeared, closing a door behind her. She'd tied her face mask back into place. When she stepped forward into the light, her brown eyes shone like a deer in the headlights. She gestured with her head for Helen to come her way and then, instead of waiting for Helen to arrive, began walking toward her. She turned her shoulders and walked right past, jerking a thumb back the way she'd come. 'Last room,' she said over her shoulder. 'Jew no sterile. Jew stay outside.'

Helen had a question she couldn't quite put into words. She stood in the hall with her lower lip searching for a word. The woman disappeared from view. Other than the trapezoid of light at the far end, the rest of the rooms hummed and beeped behind tightly drawn shades. Helen squared her shoulders and marched forward.

In the last room the shade had been raised. What the four of them reminded Helen of was one of those NASCAR pit crews on the racing programs Darl liked to watch on Saturdays. Everybody with a job to do. Everybody doing his job with fanatical precision. Each member allocated a certain amount of space and a certain period of time in the tightly choreographed dance taking place before Helen's eyes.

Helen's eyes moved to the figure on the bed. She checked the hands. It was Paul all right. No doubt about it. Oxygen tubes ran from his nostrils. Half a dozen other IV leads had been attached here and there to his arms. Three times around his head and the eye sockets suddenly came into view. The eyes were closed, the eyelids bruised a deep purple. Suture lines ran from his eyes like rays from the sun. God . . . how many . . .

A collection of monitors hung from the ceiling. She could hear the soft beeping of his heart rate and the periodic whirring sound as his blood pressure was taken automatically. They had him sitting up and strapped to the bed. The head was enormous. Size of the Jack in the Box guy. The mound of bandages were bright red here and there, tinged with pink along the edges most other places. She stood and watched as each piece of gauze was carefully unwound and dropped into the waiting metal tray for disposal. When the gauze stuck, Helen brought a hand to her throat and winced.

Her movement caught the attention of the nearest doctor. He looked her way and held up a latex finger, as if to say *wait a minute*, and then went back about his business.

The unwinding of the gauze moved upward. They'd completely shaved his head. His skull was covered with a thick brown stubble. The tape came to an end.

Down below, they'd cut the bandages loose from behind Paul's ears and were gently loosening the entire mask at one time. Inch by inch the blood-stained bandages were separated from the skin below, using forceps to loosen troublesome sections, until the whole piece could be pulled free.

Helen gasped; it was as if an unseen hand had straight-armed her in the chest, driving the air from her lungs and rocking her a full step backward. What she had presumed to be the bulk of miles of bandages was, in truth, Paul's head . . . swollen almost beyond belief, the size of a basketball, the seams oozing and oily along the suture lines.

Her dismay penetrated the reinforced glass. The same doctor turned his head and took her in. He said a few words to the other people in the room, pulled off his latex gloves, and deposited them in a trash container. He removed his hood and face mask, said a few more words, and then pulled open the door and stepped out into the hall. A pair of Day-Glo-green Keds were the only thing visible beneath the monogrammed brown surgery gown. JERRY, it read in gold.

He was young and blond and handsome. Maybe thirty-five. Built like a swimmer. Kind of long and lean with ropy forearms and thick wrists. Whatever he did for exercise, he did it a lot. He cast a quick sideways glance into the room and then back to Helen. 'We forget sometimes,' he said. 'We see this stuff so much it's like we lose track of how alien it all must look to the public.' He stuck out his hand. 'I'm Jerry Donald,' he said.

Turned out he was *Dr* Jerry Donald. Head of what he called 'the big man's post-op posse.' Seemed they'd stayed behind for an extra day in order to check the sutures and make the first change of the dressings. They were scheduled to catch up with the big man and rest of the crew tomorrow morning in North Lake Tahoe, for the purpose of performing a complete lift on a personage whose name he deemed to be sufficiently famous as to preclude mentioning. He said he was sure she understood.

He was wrong. 'Stop,' Helen said finally. 'What in goodness' name are you talking about?' She pointed in at Paul. The crew was busy wrapping his distended head. 'What's happened to him? Why is . . . why is his head like . . .'

He opened his mouth to speak, but Helen quashed him with a restraining palm. She took a pair of deep breaths and then steepled her fingers. 'No . . . no . . . Let's go back to yesterday.' She

20

gestured toward Paul. 'I left this man fighting for his life yesterday evening. I come back to find he's back in surgery.' She let the statement hang in the air.

'I can't speak to the specifics of that,' the guy said. 'All I know is somebody called Dr Richard . . . we were down in Portland . . . all we had was an hour to get everything ready.'

'Who's this Dr Richard?'

He seemed taken aback by the question. 'Dr Lenville Richard.'

Helen narrowed her eyes. 'Where do I know that name from?'

The guy shrugged. 'Magazines maybe. He's on TV quite a bit.'

'What kind of doctor is he?'

'Plastic surgery. He's—'

Helen slapped her side. 'Of course . . . the guy who works on the movie stars.'

'That's the one.'

Helen held her breath and frowned. 'I don't understand.' she stammered. 'How can this be? This is impossible. Who authorized this? Paul's a ward of the state.' She stopped and let her words fall to the floor. 'If anybody thinks the state's going to pay for something like this . . .' She sputtered again. 'Well . . . they've just got another think coming. I'm certainly not going to be the one who—'

'I'm not in the loop on the financial end of things, but—'

Helen was rolling. 'I cannot and will not be held responsible for—'

'—I heard it was the driver.'

Helens brow furrowed. She folded her arms across her chest.

'The guy who hit him,' Dr Jerry Donald added.

'The driver?'

'That's what I heard. They said he was a software tycoon or something. Felt so bad about what happened, he started making calls. Found out Mr Hardy didn't have the wherewithal to pay for this kind of thing, so he jumped in on his own. Paid for everything.'

Helen looked back into the room. Two men and a woman, same monogrammed hospital gowns and matching surgical accessories. They were wrapping clean gauze round and round Paul's enormous head. Donald anticipated her next question.

'You're looking at something like a half a million dollars' worth of craniofacial surgery in that bed,' he said. Helen's open mouth and incredulous expression encouraged the young man to continue. 'The old injury made it tough,' he said. Helen nodded. 'His whole . . . I mean the whole front of his skull was . . . the CT scan didn't really convey how massively compressed the front of his skull was . . . how the sinuses had been crushed behind the orbits. We spent three hours picking old fragments out of his frontal lobes.'

Helen winced and looked aside.

'How the first injury didn't kill him is a mystery to me,' Donald added.

'They said it was a miracle. Said he should have been dead.'

'They were right.'

She pointed at the glass. 'What's all that around his eyes?' she wanted to know.

'That's why the big man's getting the big bucks,' he said with a sardonic grin. 'I'm not sure the technique's ever even been thought about before, let alone performed.' He smiled again. 'That's how Dr Richard decided to get to the fractures in the upper jaw and in the orbits. It was amazing. Medical-journal material for sure.'

When Helen failed to react, he went on. 'He had no forehead left.' He cut the air with his hand. 'Nothing.' He paused for effect. 'Dr Richard had to use a split calvarial graft.' The sound of his own words stopped him. He patted her shoulder. 'Okay,' he said. 'It's like this. The skull has three layers. Essentially, it's a hard layer on the outside, a soft layer in the middle, and a third . . . sorta hard layer on the inside.' He waggled his hand. 'Not as hard as the layer on the outside, but harder than the stuff in the middle.'

When Helen nodded her understanding, he continued. 'We split off pieces from the outside of his skull to make him a new forehead. The calvarial graft will give him a lot of protection up there.' He gestured back toward Paul. 'Interestingly enough, as I was plating it down, I

23

could see the frontal lobes already expanding back to their normal size. I mean . . . right before my very eyes. Like the brain had just moved into a larger apartment or something.' He shook his big handsome head. 'I've been in this business nine years and that was the damnedest thing I've ever seen.'

'Wow' was all Helen could think to say.

'The new bone has a very different curve compared to whatever he may have looked like before the original injury. Should give him a very strong appearance.' Again he anticipated her next question. 'We were working blind here,' he said. 'Usually we have a picture or something, a photo of what the person used to look like, or wants to look like, a picture of his father, or, God forbid, some movie star he wants to resemble . . . you know . . . something, some idea of what the patient's got in mind.' He waved a hand in the artificial air. 'Here . . .' He gestured at Paul. '. . . here we were flying solo. This . . .' He motioned toward Paul with his head. '. . . this is a brand-new person, somebody who never existed before . . . straight off the assembly line.'

He touched the area around his own right eye. 'Not only did we move his eye orbits closer together to make up for all the little fragments we had to remove, but he's got a whole new fore-head.' He grinned. 'It's a damn good thing Mr Hardy here doesn't have a wife and kiddies or anything.'

'Why do you say that?'

He leaned in closer. His voice took on a conspiratorial edge. 'This surgery . . . this is new ground here. This is where science meets art,' he said. 'A few months from now, not even his mother would recognize this guy.'

CHAPTER 4

Suzuki Landscaping was the sole holdover from the mansion era of Harmony House. Ken Suzuki reckoned it was thirty-five years this April he'd started doing the yard work, back when the house was still grand and belonged to a family named Bryant, who'd made a fortune in the moving and storage business and who had more kids than even they could count.

Helen watched as Ken finished up washing his hands in the kitchen sink. For a while, early on, Helen had felt certain it was just a matter of time before Ken made a move on her. Dinner and a movie or maybe a walk in the park. It made sense. They were about the same age. Single. They obviously liked each other and enjoyed the time they spent in each other's company.

She'd considered taking the initiative herself but found that something in her background made anything that forward . . . anything that liberal . . . well . . . they had names for girls like that, didn't they? . . . and so Ken Suzuki and Helen Willis had settled into the friendly confines of middle-aged kindred spirithood.

26

She handed him a wad of paper towels and watched in veiled amusement as he first straightened and then separated the towels, which he then arranged in a neat pile on the counter, before first drying his palms, then the backs of his hands, and finally each finger separately. Helen had to turn away to avoid seeming impolite.

She'd often wondered whether Ken's ultra-fastidious nature was innate or whether it was the reaction of a man born in a Japanese internment camp. She'd wondered whether a proud man like Ken felt a special need for perfection as a result of what happened to his parents. The way they'd never been able to forget the twenty-six months they'd spent sweltering on the Gila River, as Ken put it . . . without privacy . . . without hope . . . without honor. And then coming home to find another family living in their house and discovering there was nothing they could do about it and how the experience had somehow tainted the rest of their lives, as if they were cursed or had neglected some detail which had led to losing everything, some subtle oversight of the soul which Ken Suzuki was going to make damn sure he didn't repeat.

Outside the kitchen window, Paul Hardy wiped his brow with his sleeve, shoveled the last of the remaining soil into the hole he'd dug earlier this morning, and set the shovel aside. They watched as he got down on his knees. The newly planted Japanese maple basked in the spring sunshine as

Paul lovingly worked the soil with his hands now, pushing here and patting there, making sure the dirt was tight enough to keep it upright in the winter winds but not so tight as to cramp the development of roots.

'He's way different than he used to be,' Ken Suzuki said.

'He still spends most of his time downstairs on the exercise machines.'

'That's not what I meant.'

Helen's heart quivered. 'What then?'

'You don't have to show him things more than once anymore.' Ken sensed her discomfort and looked her way. 'You noticed?'

'I've noticed,' Helen said, averting her eyes and hoping Ken would let it go at that. The change in Paul Hardy was not something with which she was at all comfortable, probably because she couldn't come up with a suitable explanation. Any notion of miracles had been forever thwarted by having gotten to know the miracle makers. Over the past several months, Jerry Donald and his 'post-op posse' team had stopped by Harmony House three times to check on Paul, to adjust this and to rearrange that. Last time, a month or so ago, they'd removed the final bandages and then layered away the last of the suture lines, revealing a rugged-looking, blue-eyed . . . stranger.

'He's funny about it, though,' Ken Suzuki added.

'How's that?'

'If he sees you noticed . . . he tries to cover it up.'

28

'Goes back to acting stupid.'

'Yeah.' Ken finished with his hands and deposited the damp towels in the recyclable container under the sink. 'I asked him if he was ready to come back to work. Maybe make a little cash.'

Helen cocked an eyebrow at him. 'And?'

'And he pretended he didn't understand.'

Helen made a doubtful face. 'He's been through a lot . . .' she began.

Ken Suzuki was having none of it. 'He understood me. I could see it in his eyes. There's a flicker in him . . . something that was never there before.'

'He's still the same old Paul,' Helen soothed. 'Mrs Dahlberg knew who it was the minute he walked in the room and that old woman's stone blind.'

Ken Suzuki started to speak but Helen beat him to it. 'He and Shirley are tight as ever,' she scoffed. 'He's still the only one understands what she's saying.'

'I'm not *saying* he's a different guy or anything, Helen. He's still the only human being I've ever met who can walk around with a ninety-pound bag of concrete in each hand. I'm just saying he's not completely out of it like he used to be. There's something back there now. And—' He stopped, seemed to have a brief conversation with himself, then pulled out his invoice book and started to write up the pruning job.

'And what?' Helen elbowed him gently in the ribs.

Ken Suzuki pretended not to notice; he kept writing.

'And what?' she said, louder this time, bumping him with her shoulder.

Ken stopped. He let his hands fall to his sides. 'And whatever's back there . . . for whatever reason . . . he doesn't want anybody to see it.'

A silence settled over the kitchen. Ken finished his invoice. Helen promised to submit it for payment that afternoon. They shared a humorless laugh about how long it would take the state to pay up.

Out back, Paul was watering the maple. A pair of Ken's workers suddenly appeared, their forest-green coveralls covered with wood chips. One still wore his ear protection. The other had dropped them down to neck level. The pair had been working out front, feeding the pruned limbs into the steel jaws of a chipper. Neck level used his hands to simulate turning a steering wheel.

'Looks like we're ready to go,' Ken said. 'I'll come by middle of next week and see how it looks. Maybe ask Paul if he wants to work.'

Helen patted him on the shoulder. 'He just needs to get settled in again.'

Helen said it, but she didn't believe it. Ken was right. Some fundamental aspect of Paul had changed. How could it not? she asked herself. How could someone who's been through what he's been through not be changed by the experience? It was one of those situations where her

30

intellect told her one thing but her instincts told her another.

She followed Ken Suzuki down the steps and out into the backyard. Paul was wrapping the hose around the green metal holder mounted on the back of the house. He didn't look up as they passed. His aura seemed to press in upon them as they walked along the back of the house.

'Spring has sprung' popped out of Ken's mouth as soon as they rounded the corner. The pair gratefully made small talk all the way back to Ken's truck. She waved him good-bye and then turned and walked up the front steps, only to find the door locked and her pockets devoid of keys. She rang the doorbell. Nothing. Repeated the process and got the same result. Banged the big brass knocker. Ditto.

'Damn,' she said, retracing her steps down to the sidewalk before turning left, the opposite way, around the north side of the house. A legion of once-golden daffodils, now gone white with age, pushed their pale faces up through the rich brown loam. The century-old iris plants, running the width of the house, were beginning to bloom.

Paul was closing up the garage. She watched as he locked the side door and pocketed the key, a task with which he could not ordinarily have been trusted. He felt her presence and turned his gaze in her direction.

She gave him a wave and a smile. 'Paul,' she called. 'The tree looks beautiful.'

31

In the seventeen years since Helen had come to Harmony House, Paul Hardy was the only resident she'd ever cared for who was totally unresponsive, which perhaps explained her tendency to talk to him as if he understood what she was saying, in spite of the fact that he obviously did not. What else was she going to do? Ignore him? Treat him like he wasn't there?

Paul pushed his hands deep into his pockets and walked her way, head bent, looking silently down at his own shoes, just like always. His flowing hair had not been cut since the accident, nor had his beard. Another six months, Helen thought with a smile, and he'll look like one of those rock-and-roll guys from Texas.

She moved forward to meet him. Her skin tingled in the rapidly cooling air. She threw a hand onto his shoulder. 'You did a *great* job,' she began. As they crossed the yard, she kept it up . . . about how good the tree looked and what a good job he'd done cleaning up after the job, all the while flicking what she imagined to be sly glances his way, surreptitiously trying to see if Paul understood what she was saying.

As they approached the back stairs, she was saying, '. . . fifty years from now people will be sitting under that tree . . . they'll . . .'

Suddenly Paul Hardy stopped walking. When Helen turned her eyes his way, she shuddered. The close-set blue eyes no longer looked inward. For the first time in seven years, he met her

32

gaze . . . and in an instant, she knew Ken Suzuki had been right. Whoever this was . . . The thought stopped her. She searched for something to call him and realized her conscious mind had no way of dealing with anyone or anything it couldn't put a name to . . . especially a big, powerful anyone or anything standing four feet away staring holes in her deeply furrowed forehead.

She brought a shaky hand to her throat. 'Paul . . .' she began.

'My name isn't Paul,' the stranger said.

CHAPTER 5

Helen Willis sat on the edge of the mission-style divan she'd ordered from the Pottery Barn catalog, her face ashen, her breathing shallow, her knees still weak and unresponsive. Only Paul's great strength had helped her negotiate the back stairs and then the elevator.

Paul stood just inside her room, leaning back against the door, his eyes locked on Helen. 'You okay?' he asked finally.

The voice sounded as if his throat was lined with leather.

'I . . . why I . . . I don't know what—' She stopped and sipped at the glass of water Paul had fetched from the sink. The blood was rising so quickly to her head she thought she might faint. She allowed her skirt to fall down between her knees. She brought a hand to her forehead. Felt like she had a fever. She picked up a dog-eared copy of *The New Yorker* from the adjacent cushion and began to fan herself. 'I had no idea,' she offered finally. 'When did you . . . I mean . . .'

He held up a hand and cleared his throat. 'As soon

as I woke up in the hospital, I knew something was different,' he said.

'What was that?' Helen continued to fan herself.

'I could read. The signs on the wall. The numbers on the screens.' He massaged his throat and continued. 'Took me a couple days to figure out what was so different.'

A chill ran down Helen's spine. *Different* was indeed the operant word. And Paul wasn't merely *different* than he used to be. Oh no. Brand-new face notwithstanding, this was a whole *different* person. A stranger, someone about whom she knew nothing. About whom she knew even less than she'd known about the unresponsive, enigmatic Paul Hardy. At least the old Paul had been predictable and not prone to surprises. 'But . . .' she began, 'you remember your life here.'

'All of it. From the day I came here to the moment the car hit me. I remember how kind you always were to me. How you always made sure I was included in everything.' He smiled.

Helen felt her shoulder muscles relax. She exhaled hard and put the magazine back on the cushion. She raised a questioning finger and opened her mouth to speak.

'I bet I can guess what you want to know,' Paul said in a playful tone.

'What?'

'You want to know how come, if I remember all of it, then why didn't I seem to know what was going on around me? How come I didn't respond to anything.'

Helen nodded her assent. 'Exactly,' she said.

He pulled his other hand from his pocket and showed his palms to the ceiling. 'I don't know either. It's hard to explain. It was like I was there, but I wasn't . . . like I was . . . I know this sounds weird, but it was like I was working on a problem the whole time. Nothing else meant anything to me except figuring out whatever it was I was trying to figure out.' He knocked on the side of his head. 'Nothing else got in or out.'

'And you don't remember what *that* was.'

'Strange, huh?'

'What about before you came here?'

'Nothing.'

A nearly imperceptible slant in his eyes suggested he might not be altogether forthcoming. 'Nothing at all?' she pressed.

He looked away. 'A name,' he said.

Helen waited. He folded his arms and looked uncomfortable.

'Wesley Allen Howard,' he finally said.

'That's all?'

'That's it,' he said. 'One night, about a week after I woke up in the hospital . . . right before I went to sleep, the name just came to me. It's been in my dreams ever since.'

'And you think that's who you are?'

'I don't know. Right now it's just a name that came to me.'

'That's all? Just a name?'

He hesitated. 'Palm trees,' he said. 'When I dream of the name, I dream of palm trees.' He waved a hand slowly in front of his face. 'You know . . . kind of like swaying in the breeze.'

Helen sat back on the couch and smoothed her skirt. 'Does anyone else know?'

'Just Shirley,' he said. 'I've been practicing my talking with her.' A wide smile cracked his face. 'Except Shirley does most of the talking.'

The both laughed. 'You should smile more often, Pau—' She stopped herself. 'I don't quite know what to call you anymore.'

He shrugged. 'I guess Paul will have to do for now.'

'For the time being, I think we should keep this to ourselves.'

'I think maybe Ken suspects,' he said.

She nodded knowingly. 'We talked about it,' Helen admitted. 'You know . . . in your top drawer—'

He stopped her, patted the right front pocket of his jeans. 'The money . . .' he said. 'I found it.' He sighed. 'Nine thousand dollars.'

'It's what you made working for Ken.'

'That's what I figured.'

'He always paid you the same thing he was paying the rest of his men. Not a penny less.'

'He's that kind of guy.' He allowed himself an ironic smile. 'I tried to put it in the bank.'

'And?'

'And . . . you have to *be* somebody to put money in the bank.' The smile disappeared. 'You have to have ID. A Social Security card. A driver's license. Things like that. Otherwise . . .' – he raised a disgusted hand – 'you get to carry cash.'

'You want me to hold it for you?' she asked.

He nodded. 'Might as well,' he said, pulling out the wad of bills.

'Take some for yourself,' she said.

He peeled off half a dozen twenties and then handed the rest of the roll to Helen. 'I need to know about myself,' he said.

'I can tell you what I know,' Helen offered.

Took all of a minute and a half before she was out of info and a strained silence settled over the room.

Paul broke the spell. 'That's it?'

Helen made a rueful face. 'That's it,' she repeated.

Another silence and then he wanted to know, 'What's next?'

She met his intense gaze. 'That's the sixty-four-thousand-dollar question now, isn't it?' She sighed and then stared off into space. The sound of raised voices filtered up from below. Helen stiffened and looked first at her wristwatch and then at the door.

Ten minutes until dinner. Saturday nights it was Mrs Forbes cooking until seven-thirty and Mr Hallanan helping out with the supervision till nine. Unlike some of the others, Mr Hallanan took no prisoners and could, if necessary, be trusted to handle dinner without her.

'I don't know what's next,' she said after a while.

His face said it wasn't the answer he was hoping for.

'What do you want to happen next?' she asked.

'I guess I want to find out who I am.'

This time a full minute of silence passed.

'Let's think about it,' Helen said. She lifted four fingers to her temple. 'This has all happened so fast. I'm just not sure what to do.'

'Me neither,' he said. 'But if I knew who I was, I'd at least know where to start looking.'

'Looking for what?'

He thought about it. 'For myself, I guess.'

'You're right here.' She pointed at his boots.

He pulled his eyes aside and ran a hand through his long brown hair.

'For who I used to be.' Annoyed, he cut the air with the side of his hand. 'For the person I was before I came here.'

'You think he's still out there somewhere?'

Again her question gave him pause to wonder. 'His story's out there somewhere,' the man she'd known as Paul Hardy said. 'Somebody was living a day-to-day life, doing something for a living every day . . . and then what? . . . Seven years ago, he just ups and disappears and nobody notices? . . . Nobody calls the police? Everybody he knows just goes on with their lives and forgets about him?' He looked to Helen.

Her face was as hard as stone. She offered nothing in the way of agreement.

He waited a beat and then nodded, giving himself the validation he'd sought from Helen. 'His story's out there somewhere,' he said with great conviction. 'I know it. I can feel it inside of me, and I'm going to find it.'

'And if you find it? What then?'

'Find what?'

'Whatever it is you want to look for.'

He seemed startled by the question. 'I don't know,' he blurted. 'I haven't thought it through that far.'

'Maybe you should.'

The barely audible sounds of voices and falling feet dented the silence.

Helen checked her watch again. 'It's dinnertime.'

Paul stayed where he was. Helen got to her feet and met his intense gaze. 'We'll work it out together,' she said. 'We'll do what's best for you.'

Apparently that pronouncement was good enough for the stranger. All in one motion, he bumped himself off the inside of the door, turned around, grabbed the knob, and let himself out.

'Paul,' Helen said.

He looked her way.

She walked to the steel door at the far end of her room and pulled out a ring of keys. 'Might be best if you took the back stairs,' she said, opening the door.

He nodded his agreement and crossed the room to her side. He stepped into the semidarkness, grabbed the handrail, and disappeared from view.

40

She stood and listened to the sound of his feet descending stairs.

Dinner was meat loaf, mashed potatoes, and baby peas with apple crisp for dessert. It was also uneventful, which was fortunate because if it hadn't been, Helen probably would have missed whatever it was that went wrong, as her preoccupation with the matter of Paul Hardy was nearly complete . . . what did he say? . . . Wesley Allen Howard?

By 9:40, Helen Willis had locked up the ground floor, turned on the alarm system, and taken the elevator back to her rooms. By ten, she'd changed into her warm-weather nightgown, completed her evening bathroom ritual, and was seated in front of her iMac, her glasses perched at the tip of her nose, her fingers typing.

She tried them all: Google, Lycos, Zabasearch, Peoplefinders. All Search Engines, Whitepages, and every other search engine she could find. Who was it said that too much prosperity was bad for people in the same way that too many oats were bad for a horse? Tolstoy maybe? Anyway . . . Wesley Allen Howard was all over the place. Three . . . four . . . maybe five hundred hits. An hour later all she knew for certain was that finding the right Mr Howard was going to require a substantial narrowing of the field.

Frustrated, she went to bed.

CHAPTER 6

They arrived just after breakfast, rolling onto Arbor Street in a trio of rented Lincoln Town Cars, two black, one silver, eight passengers in all, everybody sporting sunglasses to ward off the morning fog. No loose talk, no slammed doors, all economy of motion and singularity of purpose. First pair out of the cars made its way up the driveway, past Ken Suzuki's truck; a moment later another quartet split up and melted into the shrubbery on either side of the house, all but the small man, all but one wearing an overcoat and sporting one of those little radio earpieces with the pigtail of wire disappearing beneath the collar.

The exception was the tiny gentleman in the gray summer-weight suit. Nice conservative maroon tie, no sunglasses, no radio in his ear. He shifted his weight from foot to foot and looked distractedly out at the street as the weight lifter standing on his left rang the front bell, waited, and then rang it again. When ringing failed, the big guy tried banging on the big brass door knocker, lifting the ring from the lion's mouth and slamming down hard.

Eunice Ponds opened the door. She was still in her white terry-cloth bathrobe and fuzzy blue slippers. 'Yeah?' she said.

The big guy yanked the door from her hand and pushed it wide open. Eunice let out a yelp. In a flash, Benny the dog came sliding around the corner, his nails scraping for traction on the wood floor. Forty pounds of multicolored mutt began to show his teeth and bark in earnest. The hair on the back of his neck rose up like a mottled cowlick. His nails chattered on the floor as he alternately charged and retreated from the strangers.

In a single deft movement, the big guy shoved Eunice aside and punted Benny the dog into the middle of next week, whence Benny then scrambled to his feet on the second bounce and, without looking back, three-legged it in the direction of the TV room, tongue lolling, his breath coming in ragged gasps.

Unlike Benny the dog, however, Eunice was not so easily deterred. As a matter of fact, single-minded tenacity had pretty much been the story of her life up till then. While most people are able to make a distinction between the things that merely cross their minds and the things appropriate to act out, Eunice wasn't wired that way. Once Eunice got a bee in her bonnet, it wasn't going away until she acted upon it; no matter

43

how malicious or mean-spirited the action might be, Eunice wasn't giving up on the idea until either it reached fruition or she died in the attempt.

Eunice was eight years old when somebody first got an inkling that all was not well in Decatur. Problem was, despite her chronological age, she still acted as if she were five . . . a particularly malicious and narcissistic five at that. By the time she was ten, it seemed pretty much certain five was as good as it was going to get. Kind of like one of those 'most likely to succeed, homecoming queen' types who peaks in high school and spends the next fifty years in free-fall ennui, disappointed in themselves and in everything else they encounter along the way.

As doting first-time parents, Milton and Doris Ponds had deflected the first suggestions of developmental deficiency as being, at best, anecdotal and, at worst, maladroit. So convinced were they of their daughter's normality that they'd eventually hired a lawyer to help them fight the local school district's designation of Eunice as developmentally disabled and as such as a 'special ed' student. They lost.

Five more years and three more children, upon whom Eunice enthusiastically heaped both physical and psychological abuse, had eventually, however, disabused Doris and Milton of any conspiratorial notions. Milton's bold proclamations about how no child of his was going to ride the 'little bus' to school faded to stony silence.

If the unending parade of cuts, burns, bruises, and abrasions that regularly appeared on the younger Ponds children did not sound the alarm bell, the children's steadfast refusal to name their older sister as the culprit . . . despite the best efforts of countless teachers, guidance counselors, and child psychologists . . . finally put the fear of God into all concerned.

As if by providence, just as Milton and Doris found themselves facing the unenviable task of deciding what to do with a 'bad seed' (as Milton liked to say), the family fell victim to what local fire authorities labeled a 'suspicious' house fire, a tragedy that not only left them standing on the front lawn watching everything they owned turn to soot, but provided the final impetus for securing a suitable environment for Eunice, one which provided both the sort of supervision she required and the opportunities for professional counseling she deserved.

'Ooooooh,' Eunice wailed. 'You pushed me.' She drew back her fist and punched the guy right in the middle of his solar plexus with sufficient force to immobilize the vast majority of her fellow citizens. Not this gorilla, however. He never even blinked. When he caught her second punch in his black-gloved hand, Eunice balled the other fist and raised it to shoulder level. He smiled and twisted. And then twisted some more until something went pop in her wrist, something sounding like the snapping of a Popsicle stick. A shriek rose from Eunice's throat. She banged her knees on the hard stone floor, her face purple with pain, her howl of agony rattling the rafters.

'No' was all gray suit said.

The big guy threw Eunice's injured hand back at her as if it disgusted him.

Lying on the floor now, her cheek pressed hard to the flagstones, Eunice assumed the fetal position, cradling the injured wrist, sobbing into her kneecaps and howling like an air-raid siren.

Down at the far end of the hall, the double kitchen doors burst open. Helen Willis was patting her hands dry on her apron as she strode to the front of the house. Ken Suzuki held a piece of buttered toast in his right hand. The sight of Eunice writhing on the floor opened his eyes so wide he looked Caucasian.

Helen jogged across the floor and dropped to the floor next to Eunice, who continued to bear-hug her knees and cry. After a series of hugs and soft entreatments proved ineffective, Helen scrambled to her feet. She put her hands on her hips and confronted the strangers. 'What happened here?' she demanded.

Gray suit waved a disdainful hand at the wailing figure on the floor. 'This person attacked a federal officer,' he said. His voice was soft. His diction

46

clipped and certain as if he'd gone to pronunciation school or something.

The squeak of the kitchen door announced the arrival of Mrs Forbes. Helen waved her forward. 'Take Eunice out to the kitchen,' she directed. 'I'll be in there in a minute.'

Together, after a coupla tries, they managed to lever Eunice to her feet. Her tear-stained face was contorted nearly beyond recognition as she shuffled across the foyer and down the hall, holding her injured wrist before her like an offering. Mrs Forbes stayed at Eunice's side, offering a grandmotherly arm thrown around her shoulders and a calming whisper that everything was going to be okay.

Helen Willis turned back toward the front door. She pointed with a trembling finger. 'Get out,' she yelled, stamping her foot. 'I'm calling the authorities.'

Gray suit sneered at her. From the inside pocket of his suit jacket, he produced a small handful of paperwork and a black leather case. He flopped the case open about an inch in front of Helen's face. Gold badge and plastic ID card. National somethingorother.

'We are the authorities,' he said, snapping the case closed.

Helen pushed the case away from her face. Blood roared in her ears. 'Let me see that again,' she demanded. He ignored her.

The big guy spoke softly into a tiny microphone

47

attached to his collar. Helen bellied in closer, but before she could open her mouth, four more men burst into the foyer.

Gray suit twirled a finger. 'Everybody in . . .' He looked around. Pointed a buffed fingernail back across Ken Suzuki's shoulder, over at the front parlor, the only room in the house reserved for formal occasions. 'Put them all in there,' he finished.

Two headed up the stairs. Another pair pushed past Helen and Ken, following Mrs Forbes and Eunice toward the back of the house. The sound of pounding feet beat an unpleasant rhythm, a sound Helen Willis had never heard before, a sound more common to war zones, she thought, and then, inexplicably, her mind wandered to one of her favorite books. She envisioned Anne Frank hiding in that dank annex, imagining her anxiety at the sound of boots on the stairs, then the cold steel terror of the man with the gun.

For some reason, the recollection emboldened her. She turned quickly toward Ken. 'Call the police,' she said with as much command as she could muster.

Her bravado wasn't enough. One look at Ken Suzuki told her she was going to have to make the call herself. Ken stood like a Buddha carved in stone, fear in his eyes and granite in his feet. You could see it. Ken had been rounded up before. Ken wasn't taking any chances here. He made a face at Helen. Shook his head in caution.

Helen was having none of it. She shouldered her way past the big guy and started for the phone in the parlor.

'By all means,' gray suit said. 'Call the *po*-lice.' He put the accent on the wrong syllable and then smiled at his own little joke.

CHAPTER 7

Helen was halfway to the parlor when she encountered Carman Navarre and Dolores Hildebrand, both of whom were being herded into the front room by one of the agents. Carman tugged at Helen's dress. Helen stopped and put a hand on her shoulder. Carman was short and squat, a Down-syndrome victim and one of the most universally pleasant souls Helen had ever met. Nearly fifty years before, a police officer had found Carman wrapped in a hotel towel and stuffed in a garbage bin down in Long County. Unlike, say, Darl and Randall, whose grip on reality was at best tenuous, Carman was generally on top of things . . . as long as you weren't in a big hurry for her to get there. Carman was slow to process information. She got things right, but took quite a while to do so.

The agent sought to hurry them along. He reached for Carman, but Helen batted his hand away. 'Don't you dare touch her,' Helen said. 'Don't you dare.'

Satisfied she'd deterred him, at least temporarily, she turned her attention back to Carman. 'What is it, Carman?' she asked.

Carman leaned in close. 'Somethin's wrong with Benny,' she whispered.

'Like what?'

Carman shrugged. 'He went down in the cellar and won't come up.'

'He was limping,' Dolores piped up.

Suddenly the air was alive with strained voices and the sound of moving feet. They'd rounded everyone up and were herding them downstairs. The elevator door slid open. Paul wheeled Mrs Dahlberg toward the front room. Shirley rolled herself along in their wake. Darl and Phillip were both agitated, a state which each man handled in a completely different manner. While Darl just kept winding himself higher, until he required sedation, Phillip, when overstressed, went thumb-sucking catatonic. Helen took a moment to soothe each man as he passed.

At that moment Mr Hallinan walked up the front steps and into the foyer, five minutes early for his morning shift, as was his habit. Helen Willis hurried to his side. 'Mrs Forbes is in the kitchen with Eunice. I think she . . . Eunice, that is . . . may need to see a doctor.' He started to hurry off. Helen grabbed his sleeve. 'Benny's in the basement. I don't know what the problem is, but Carman says he won't come up. She thinks maybe he's hurt somehow.'

Jacob Hallinan was a man of few words. He immediately hustled off toward the kitchen, pulling the keys to the van from the hook in the hall on his way by.

'How many?' the voice came from behind her. When she turned, she found herself closer to the man in the gray suit than she cared to be. She took a step back. 'How many what?'

'How many residents?'

'Twelve,' Helen said. 'Not counting staff.' The minute it was out of her mouth, she regretted telling him anything at all.

'How many computers in the building?'

This time Helen didn't answer. Instead she turned on her heel and hurried into the front parlor. Everybody was sitting down except for Darl and Randall, both of whom were too excited to be still. Darl was so agitated he just kept muttering under his breath and turning in small circles. Randall was trying to appease Carman with a gift of his slippers. Carman pinched her nostrils, making the 'stinky' sign. Dolores laughed and turned her face aside, whispering something to Mrs Dahlberg, who was sitting in her wheelchair beneath the Art Deco floor lamp.

Three of the assistants counted the crowd.

'Twelve,' one of them said to the others, who agreed.

Same guy pointed at Paul. 'He's the only one who's even close.'

Gray suit only shook his head. 'No. Not him.'

Helen pulled open the center drawer of the sideboard. She came out with a yellow legal pad and a green golf pencil. 'I want your names,' she announced. 'Every one of you.' She waved an angry pencil. 'And your badge numbers . . . or whatever kind of numbers you damn people have.'

The words caught in her throat. She couldn't remember the last time she'd cursed in public. Didn't matter, though. The big guy caught her by the shoulder, welding her to the floor like a butterfly pinned to a board. She tried to step out from beneath the weight but could not move. 'Don't you dare . . .' she shouted. And then, in an instant, Ken was there . . . coming like a line drive, using his velocity to bump the big guy off balance. The lessening of the weight bearing down on her shoulder allowed Helen to step away.

Ken used the opportunity to insert himself between Helen and the big guy. He stood firm, the very picture of defiance, his eyes ablaze, his chin thrust out like a lance, his fists balled at his side, all rigid and primed to go off like a stainless steel spring. The air hummed with tension. If not for Ken giving away a hundred or so pounds to the gorilla, the smart money might have been laid on Ken, on the theory that self-righteous indignation will carry a body a long way. As it was, badass as Ken might have been feeling at that moment, he never stood a single chance in hell.

The weight lifter reached out and grabbed him by the front of his shirt. A couple of buttons popped as he was lifted completely off the floor. His attempts to kick and flail fell pitifully short. Another button popped and fell to the floor, where

it bounced twice and then rolled under the uphol-
stered bench, where people took off their shoes.

'No,' gray suit said again.

The big guy hesitated a beat and then set Ken
Suzuki back onto his feet. Ken shuffled backward
like a boxer. Gray suit stepped into the breach.
He directed his voice at the assembled multitude
in the front room. 'Thank you for your assistance in
this matter,' he said. 'At this time we'll need you
to return to your rooms.' The gorilla whispered
instructions into his collar mike.

Took some of them longer than others to grasp
what was wanted of them. But as was their nature,
once they understood the request, they cheerfully
acquiesced.

Took a full five minutes before everybody but
Helen and Ken were shuttled upstairs. When Helen
cast a glance up the stairwell, she saw Paul Hardy
standing at the railing looking down at her. A kind
of raw electric energy ran between the two of them.
She quickly looked away. 'Again,' said gray suit.
'How many computers in the building?'

She held out the legal pad. 'I want your names
and—'

He cut her off. 'It's up to you,' he said. 'We can
do this the easy way or we can do it the hard way.
You choose.'

Ken moved up close to her elbow. She could
feel Paul's gaze raking her from above and desperately wanted to look up. She steeled herself.
'Where's your warrant? I want to see a warrant.'

54

'We don't need a warrant. This is a matter of national security.'

The words sent a shiver down her spine. She looked back over her shoulder at Ken, whose anger had turned to confusion. 'How could anything . . . how could these people have anything to do with . . .' she sputtered.

'How many computers?' he asked again, his full lips articulating each and every syllable. When she again failed to answer, he sighed and pointed at the weight lifter. 'Toss every room,' he said. 'Bring anything you find down here.'

Helen reached out and put a hand on his sleeve. 'No . . . no . . .' she said.

'Well?'

'Four. Three in the TV room and one in my apartment.' She slapped her sides in frustration. 'How could any of these people have anything to do with a matter of national security? I just don't understand. It's absurd.'

'Perhaps you'd like to save yourself the aggravation of having us take your computers with us.' He held out a sheet of computer paper. Helen took it in her hand and read it. Three words. Her knees turned to jelly. It felt as if her spine had been removed. Ken darted forward and threw an arm around her waist, preventing her from sliding to the floor. She brought a hand to her throat and took several deep breaths.

Gray suit stepped in close again. 'Do I take it from your demeanor that you know who was doing this casting of nets on the Net?' Again he smiled at his own wordplay.

'I . . . it was me. I was—' she stopped. Gray suit turned his head one way and then the other, looking at her like the old RCA dog. Indignation rose in her throat.

'What right do you have to be looking at what I do on my own personal computer? What gives you the right to invade my privacy—'

'Tut-tut,' he interrupted. 'Really,' he scoffed. 'You really must disabuse yourself of this personal privacy fetish. It's so retro.' He held up a beautifully manicured finger. 'First of all, our forefathers never mentioned the word.' He paused to let his words sink in. 'No-where in the Constitution does the word *privacy* appear.'

Helen opened her mouth to speak, but he wasn't finished. 'Secondly, in the age of international terrorism . . .' – he drew brackets in the air with his forefingers – 'you know . . . post-9/11 . . . well, in that world personal privacy turns out to be the price of security and . . .' – he wagged an amused finger her way – 'and you would be amazed how many of your fellow citizens are delighted to make the exchange.'

'You listen to me—' Helen began.

He put his face right in hers. 'And thirdly . . . you need to divest yourself of the notion that you have rights here.' His breath smelled of licorice and stale coffee. 'I can take this house apart piece by piece and leave it lying on the ground.'

He gestured toward Ken. 'I can hold the two of you for as long as I please . . .' – he made a gesture of dismissal – 'without a warrant, without habeas corpus, without having to explain it to a living soul.'

He flicked the piece of paper in her hand. 'Would you care to explain this?'

'It's just a name,' she said. She started to say it. 'Wesley Al—'

He put a finger to her lips. 'No,' he said again and then laughed in her face. 'You haven't been listening, have you?' He smiled and then directed himself to the weight lifter. 'Bring her. Bring her computer. Check with the staff as to what they'll need in order to continue in her absence . . . then—'

Ken stepped in. 'What absence? She's not going anywhere with you. I'm calling my attorney. You just—' and one of the assistants had him by the elbow and was dragging him backward. Ken pulled his elbow free. Another agent grabbed his other arm. 'You fascist bastards are not going to—'

And then one of the agents had Ken in a choke-hold and was pulling him to the floor. Ken hacked and gagged and clawed at the forearm as he was brought to his knees, mouth agape, eyes bulging from his head.

Helen moved his way, screaming, 'Stop it! Stop it!' as she tried to step around the weight lifter to get to Ken. She was a step slow. The big guy took a slide to the left and let her run into his chest. Helen bounced off and took a step backward.

It was her worst nightmare. The knock on the door. The Kafka moment where you were accused of something and nobody would tell you what it was. The system gone wild in a universe gone mad. Maybe that's why her resolve slipped. Why she lost it for a second and looked up, the heaven-ward glance as much to confirm the reality of the moment for herself as it was to see whether Paul was taking it all in. He was. His eyes met hers. She stretched her lips and mimed a single syllable word. 'RUN,' she mouthed.

The good news was that Paul picked it up on the first try. The bad news was that the gorilla picked up on it, too. As King Kong made a dash for the stairs, with a pair of agents hard on his heels, Paul bolted off down the hall and out of sight.

CHAPTER 8

L ike most grand houses of its era, the Jensen Mansion had a set of what were known as 'service stairs,' a narrow zigzag of treads and risers at the extreme back of the house, running from basement to attic, a contrivance designed to provide the staff easy access to all floors and at the same time to keep the hired help out of the public sphere as much as possible, particularly inasmuch as both Winnie Jensen and Harriet Garrison had preferred to maintain the illusion of running the mammoth house on their own, gracefully as it were, without ever so much as breaking a sweat.

Paul had the urge to lock himself in his room and pull the covers over his head, but got sane on the fly and sprinted for the door at the end of the hall, a door that was always locked from the inside . . . always . . . except he'd left it open last night when he'd come down the back stairs from Helen Willis's room. He said a silent prayer, grabbed the knob, and turned. The metal fire door opened, and Paul stepped inside. He slid the bolt closed and waited, listening as the voices began to work their way in his direction, rattling door-knobs, demanding people open their doors, screaming questions and directions as they checked the ten rooms lining the second-floor hallway.

Like a fox harried by hounds, his instincts sent him to ground, propelling him down the narrow stairway toward . . . toward . . . whatever. He had no idea what lay below. No idea if there was an exit. For all he knew the stairs went all the way to hell.

What he knew for sure was that whatever was happening here had something to do with the name Wesley Allen Howard, the sound track to his recent tropical dreams. He'd heard what Ms Willis had said. Seen the little man put a finger on her lips as if to suggest the words themselves were somehow criminal.

Three switchbacks down, he came to a small landing. The air was thick and filled with dust. Felt to Paul like nobody'd stood in that spot for a long time. Like the air had waited too long and had lost its vitality. A rusted metal plate on the inside of the door read: ONE. He reached for the knob.

A floor above, somebody pounded on the fire door in frustration. He heard someone shouting for a key, then came another booming kick on the door. Paul allowed himself a thin smile. The state had installed the doors when they'd renovated the house. They were heavy and made of steel, intended as fire barriers in an otherwise wood-frame structure, and, as state law mandated, were kept locked at all times.

He eased the first-floor fire door open a crack. Voices . . . voices raised in anger . . . filled with indignation . . . punctuated here and there by the guttural sounds of struggle. He applied his eye to the crack and found he was inside the little room just outside the kitchen, the one Ms Willis used as an office.

In grander times, the room had been a walk-in pantry, a central point along the service stairs where the day-to-day demands of the household could be met with great dispatch. These days it was a jumble of paper and files and cardboard boxes, wedged in and around the antique secretary Ms Willis used for a desk. The room was nearly black.

Paul waited, hoping his eyes would adjust. Took a full minute for the edges of the clutter to become visible. Sounds of strife filtered through the door.

Paul crept forward, placing his feet carefully among the clutter. The closer he came to the door, the louder the sounds of struggle became. He could pick out Ms Willis's strained voice from among the chorus of voices, some speaking, some screaming, coming from the direction of the foyer.

Above the din, someone was shouting, 'Where's the key?' over and over.

He cracked the door. A rusted hinge groaned as the door swung open a quarter inch, but he needn't have worried, the river of noise flowing from the front of the house washed the sound away. He was looking directly up the hall toward the foyer, where Ms Willis lay facedown on the floor, her hands manacled behind her back. The little man in the gray suit knelt at her side. He put his face right up to hers. 'Don't make us get a crew in here,' he was saying. 'We'll tear this place apart if we have to.'

Helen Willis turned her face away. 'Go to hell,' she said.

Paul couldn't see Ken Suzuki but he could hear his voice ranting about his rights . . . something about 'due process' and 'probable cause.'

'I should think you'd have more regard for the peace and well-being of your . . .' – he searched for a word – 'your *charges*,' he finally decided upon.

This time she didn't even bother to tell him where he could go. She tried to sit up, but a restraining hand from her antagonist prevented her from doing so. 'Don't touch me. Don't you dare touch me,' she shouted.

Gray suit laughed at her righteous indignation and stood up. He dusted off his palms. The gorilla stepped into the picture. He bounced a set of keys up and down in his hand, then picked them up by the big brass ring and waved them in the air.

'The desk in her room,' he said.

'Get Abrams and Taylor out of the backyard,' the small man ordered. 'Two men on each floor. One in the stairwell, one out on the hallway. Flush him out and then bring him to me. We'll take all three of them with us.'

Paul's body went cold and stiff. His sanctuary was about to become a trap. He watched in horror as another pair of agents arrived in the foyer. The big guy barked orders. Paul eased the door closed and began to back out of the office when his elbow caught one of the piles of cardboard boxes, sending a box thumping to the floor at his feet. A wave of running feet rolled his way.

Throwing discretion to the winds, Paul turned and ran, forgetting that he was under the stairs, forgetting the angle above his head. On his second stride, within easy reaching distance of the fire door, he blasted his forehead into the bottom of the stairs, dropping to his knees, nearly rendering himself unconscious. A muffled cry escaped. He felt vomit rising in his throat. His vision swam. He held his head in his hands and rocked back and forth. The palm trees came again and the beach with the yellow sand, and this time blurry figures, one in the foreground, the other in the distance. They seemed to be beckoning to each other. The voices grew louder and drew closer.

He groaned and massaged his forehead with both hands. His vision pixilated. The beach scene disappeared. Only blackness filled his head. His eyeballs felt as if they would burst from the sockets and fall onto his shoes. A great roar filled his ears. His head throbbed with a pain such as he had never experienced. He held his breath and scrambled deeper into the office on his hands and knees.

His mantle of darkness disappeared as the outer door was jerked open.

'Get him,' someone barked.

Paul had thrust the top half of his body into the stairway when somebody made a dive at him. His pursuer landed mostly on the floor but managed to get his fingers entwined in Paul's belt. Instinctively, Paul kicked like a mule. A hollow thump was followed by a grunt and a slackening of the grip at his waist.

Paul crawled forward. As he crossed the threshold, he heard the sound of angry voices, felt fingers tearing at the pocket of his jeans, felt the pocket begin to give way and then rip off altogether, sending him rocketing into the landing, where he braced his back against the wall, put both feet on the door, and pushed as hard as he dared.

The effort made his head feel as if it would surely explode. The arm in the crack of the door stiffened. He heard a cry of pain from the other side of the door. He gritted his teeth, bowed his back, and pushed harder. The cry from the other side of the door rose in pitch like a skyrocket, reaching a crescendo as the forearm snapped with a dry crack.

The sound of splintering bone and the howl of agony that followed caused Paul to ease off just enough for the awkwardly dangling arm to be pulled back through the crack in the door. The door banged shut. The screams took on a deeper sound, almost like a chant, as Paul dove forward and shot the bolt. Again, his consciousness threatened to desert him. He groaned in pain. The loud booming brought him around.

Somebody was kicking the door hard now, using both feet, he imagined, shaking the whole house as they sought in vain to batter the metal fire door into submission.

Paul scrambled to his feet and ran up the narrow staircase. His head throbbed as he burst through the second-floor fire door and ran headlong down the hall, mouth agape, in full flight without having the slightest idea where he was headed. He could hear the sound of feet on the central stairway. He skidded to a stop, and, for a second, resigned himself to fate. He was about to be apprehended and taken into custody . . . and for what? . . . for dreaming a name . . . for dreaming of a beach and palm trees swaying in the wind?

Shirley's door swung open. She sat in her wheelchair wearing a blue bathrobe. 'Here,' she said in a voice not unlike the sound of tearing sheet metal.

Paul ducked through the door; Shirley bumped it closed with her wheelchair, reached out, and shot the bolt. The hall was filled with noise.

'Under the bed,' she squawked.

Without thinking, Paul did what he always did, which was whatever she told him to do. He dropped to his knees with his head threatening to burst at the seams; he lay on his stomach and wiggled all the way back against the wall, where he could hear the sounds of his pursuers now. Terror ran through his body like an electric surge.

'They're—' he stammered.

'Shhhhhh.' Shirley shushed.

He could hear her rustling about, see the wheels of her chair as she rolled around the room, with the voices coming closer now, until he heard the snap of the lock and the sound of the door swinging open.

A pair of shiny black shoes appeared in the doorway. Paul held his breath waiting for the shoes to move his way, but they didn't. They never moved from the doorway.

'Uh . . . uh . . .' a deep voice stammered. 'No . . . uh . . . I'm sorry. I'll be . . . sorry.' The voice seemed to fade into the distance. The shoes disappeared. The door closed. Paul could hear raised voices coming from the hall. The door opened again. Four black shoes this time. 'I told you,' a new voice admonished. 'We've got to . . .' it went on. 'Ooooh . . .' The voice sounded as if its owner had swallowed something that refused to go down. 'Sorry . . . uh . . . we'll be . . .' The door closed.

'Better hurry out of here now,' Shirley said.

To anyone outside the room, Shirley's voice must have sounded as it were some industrial noise. Not to Paul, who, once again, did as bidden, crawling out from beneath the bed and pushing himself to his feet among the collection of dust bunnies he'd swept out from under the bed with his body.

Shirley sat in her chair facing the door, her back turned to Paul. She'd dropped her bathrobe and was sitting there naked to the waist. From the rear, her skin was translucent and hung in folds and pleats from her ruined body, her twisted skeleton clearly visible through the skin, like some ancient mummy. From the front . . . from the front, Paul could only imagine.

She twisted her head and gave Paul what, in Shirley, passed for a smile.

'You shoulda seen their faces,' she squawked.

'You didn't have to . . .' Paul began.

She jerked a thumb at the window. 'Not all of 'em are gonna be that squeamish,' she said. 'You better go out there. That's as good as it's gonna get.' She winked at him. 'Good luck.'

Paul pushed open the window and looked down. The back porch roof was about ten feet below. He squeezed through the opening, one foot and then the other. Then turned around and held the windowsill for a moment before casting his fate to the winds and letting go.

CHAPTER 9

Must have been pure adrenaline kept him glued to that spot on the roof, because just about the time he allowed himself a deep breath and figured he didn't hear anybody in hot pursuit, he began to slide off. Slowly at first, hands scratching and stretching for a hold, then gaining momentum as he surfed across the slate, felt his feet poke into thin air, and then, with a shout stillborn in his throat, he entered free fall for maybe a second and a half before crashing down onto the back stairs, driving the air from his lungs and sending a hot iron of pain shooting up his left leg. And then *bang* . . . he somersaulted backward into nothingness . . . until the beach and the palms and the sand and the two guys appeared in his head and he could see that it wasn't a Frisbee being tossed back and forth as he'd imagined but a radio-controlled airplane swooping and diving overhead and . . . or was the plane flying on its own and the remote control box was . . . no . . . couldn't be . . . that was crazy.

He lay with his cheek nestled up to the cold concrete of the walk. He croaked and wheezed for breath, dry-heaved a couple times, and then lay in a heap, rocking slightly, hiccuping air . . . until the heaves returned, and he pushed himself to his knees and yakked up a small pool of yellow bile.

His head felt as if somebody'd driven a steel rod in one ear and out the other. He groaned, lowered his face close enough for the odor of his own discharge to straighten him right back up. One foot beneath him and then the other. He wiped his mouth with his sleeve and then wished he hadn't, as the act allowed his brain sufficient time to process the pain screaming up from his ankle.

He hopped on one foot and looked around. The backyard suddenly seemed enormous, the fence miles away. He put the toe of his injured foot on the ground for balance. Pain lanced through his lower leg. He bent at the waist and massaged his ankle.

He groaned and then dropped to one knee. That's when he heard the shouts.

'There he is,' someone yelled.

When he looked up, a head and a pair of dark-clad shoulders were sticking out of Shirley's window, pointing at him and yelling for backup.

Paul struggled to his feet and limped across the yard toward the back fence, an unadorned cedar-planked affair separating Harmony House from the big green-and-white mansion on Howser Street, a house and yard with which Paul was quite familiar as the owners were longtime customers of Suzuki Landscaping.

Paul pushed off his good ankle and managed to propel the top half of his body up onto the top of the fence, which rocked and swayed from the addition of his weight and the power of his momentum. Using his heavily muscled arms, he hoisted himself up and over, landing on one foot in the soft bark of the cut flower garden that Paul had, last summer, helped to build. A deep growl scattered his thoughts like litter.

Then he remembered. The big white German shepherd with the bad attitude. Used to follow him wherever he went in the yard. What was its name? Something about . . . and then it came to him. 'Blanco,' he said, holding out his hand. The dog put his teeth away, ran his pink nose over Paul's knuckles, and wagged his tail. Paul patted him on the head a couple of times and then limped across the yard as quickly as he was able.

He made it to the rear gate and was lifting the latch when he heard somebody scrambling over the fence behind him. Unfortunately for his pursuer, so did the dog.

The guy probably would have been all right if he'd been quicker with his feet or better yet hadn't tried to kick the dog in the head at all. As it was, Blanco sidestepped the flying shoe and bit the guy in the crotch. A high-pitched yowl rose above the rush of wind in the trees. As Blanco lowered his hindquarters and began to shake his head from side to side, the pitch of the scream rose to operatic heights.

Paul closed the gate and limped out toward Howser Street. He could still hear aria al castrado wafting through the trees as he hooked a quick left and gimped it south beneath the canopy of century-old oaks, festooned now with new-grown leaves, glowing ad-glow green in the sun and quivering like virgins in the breeze.

He crossed the street, moving diagonally toward the big gray stone house halfway down the block, another of Ken's customers, whose name he could not recall. He'd rounded the corner of their porch when he heard the squeal of tires and the roar of an engine. He ducked between a pair of massive rhododendrons whose tightly folded purple blossoms threatened to explode their spring encasements. He stood motionless as one of the black Lincoln Town Cars came roaring by, squealing all the way to the corner and turning left, running back toward Arbor Street in a cloud of burning rubber.

Paul moved along the side of the house, crossed the yard, and stepped through the gate. He found himself in a wide unpaved alley running the length of the block. Here on the true crest of the hill, the backyards of the mansions did not abut one another.

Instead, the practical needs of the households were serviced by a communal alley running along the rear of the dwellings, providing surreptitious trash collection, ease of delivery, and ample space for garages, in many cases spacious garages which had once, a century ago, housed the last remains of the horse-and-buggy era, a mews, as it were, where the care of both animals and of leather coexisted in ironic harmony in those halcyon years before the advent of the internal combustion engine.

Paul leaned back against the thick ivy and caught his breath. His head throbbed to the rhythm of his heart. A dull roar filled his ears, and for the first time since he'd regained consciousness in the hospital . . . for the very first time . . . he wished he could go back to who he was before . . . the shuffling specter they called Paul Hardy, the un-responsive guy so completely lost in his own little world of half thoughts and repeated phrases as to render himself virtually invisible, a state that at the moment held great appeal.

His ankle was on fire as he hustled north along the alley, working his way up the hill toward the bright lights of Landon Street, a place where he thought he might be able to lose himself in the crowd. He got about a third of the way down the alley when the sound of an engine snapped his head around in time to see the silver Town Car slide into view, its tires churning up a maelstrom of dust, closing the distance in a big hurry.

The speed at which the car was approaching greatly limited Paul's options. He dodged to the right, into a shallow indentation in the brick retaining wall, throwing his back hard against a pair of green Dumpsters, as the car slid to a halt about a foot in front of his face. From within the massive cloud of dust, a running figure appeared. The apparition circled the front of the car, arms extended in the combat position, gun pointed at Paul's face as he stiff-legged his way over to where Paul stood.

The barrel of the gun looked as big as a tunnel. 'Don't move!' the guy yelled over and over. 'Don't move!' He held the gun an inch from Paul's face. 'Turn around!' he shouted. When Paul didn't move, the agent reached out with his left hand and tried to move him manually. Paul stood his ground. The guy mashed the gun barrel into Paul's forehead. He repeated his command to turn around. Again Paul ignored him.

And then Paul Hardy seemed to relax, almost to resign himself to his fate. He smiled, and then he reached up and slapped the weapon aside as it if were a fly, sending the automatic flying end over end through the air, banging off the fender before finally falling to the ground, where it discharged on impact.

That's when everything seemed to go slow motion. The agent froze. The grip on Paul's shoulder relaxed. He cast a quizzical look Paul's way and then used the hand he'd had on Paul to search the back of his thigh. That the hand came back red seemed to puzzle the guy no end. He dropped to one knee and allowed a low moan to escape his throat. A sticky-looking pool of blood was forming on the ground. The agent's eyes

73

bulged at the sight of his own fluids seeping into the ground among the patchwork of oil stains. His look of astonishment changed to something more akin to fear.

Then his G-man training took over. He pivoted on his knee and made an all-out dive for the gun. Paul jumped completely over the straining body. He clamped a boot onto the stretching arm and kept adding pressure until the G-man stopped straining to reach his weapon and began to yell, 'Okay . . . okay!' over and over, at which point Paul bent and picked up the automatic and then released the guy's arm from beneath his boot.

The black steel felt hot in his hands. The feel told him he'd had one of these in his hands before. He looked down. On the ground, the G-man had pulled off his belt and was applying a tourniquet to his upper thigh. Paul reached to help but the guy cringed out of reach.

'Your radio thing work?' Paul asked, pointing to his own ear. The guy didn't answer, just kept twisting the belt tighter and tighter without ever taking his eyes from Paul. 'Better call yourself some help,' Paul said.

The guy started to reach for his collar and then hesitated, as if Paul's suggestion might be some kind of trick, a ruse designed to get him to do something stupid as an excuse to injure him. His hand wavered in midair.

Paul nodded down at the guy's leg. 'That's pretty ugly,' he said. 'You better call for some help.'

The guy's eyes were locked on Paul's as his hand crept to his call button.

'Agent involved shooting,' he said. 'This is fourteen seventy-three. Agent down, requiring emergency personnel.' He kept his gaze glued on Paul. 'I'm . . .'

'You're in the alley between Howser and Bradley. Three hundred block,' Paul quickly added.

The G-man frowned and cleared his throat, then repeated the location into his microphone. Somebody on the other end must have asked for a clarification because he sighed and started over with the 'fourteen seventy-three . . . agent down' stuff and went through the whole thing again, talking slow and loud and speaking clearly, like there was an idiot on the other end of the line. By the time he finished talking and looked up again, Paul was gone.

CHAPTER 10

The desk sergeant looked like he hadn't moved in a month . . . like under the uniform, he might be covered with bark. The facial expression said he'd seen it all; the boatload of flab hanging over his belt said he'd managed to inhale a few meals while observing life's rich pageant.

He rocked himself off the stool, scowled, and then leaned his badge out over the counter. 'Lemme see some ID,' he said to the little man in the gray suit.

The little guy used an exaggerated sweep of the arm to pull a black leather case from the inside pocket of his impeccably tailored suit jacket. Using only one hand, he flopped the case open and was about to similarly snap it closed when the big cop reached down and plucked it from his fingers.

He brought the ID up in front of his red face and held it there for a long minute before lowering it to the desk. The little man reached for his case, but the cop pulled it back out of reach. 'And you want me to what?' he asked.

Gray suit told him again . . . slower this time, like he was talking to a child. The cop winced at the guy's tone of voice. 'I'm gonna have to bounce it by the watch commander,' he said.

The little man opened his mouth to speak but the cop waved him off. The matter wasn't open to discussion, his big hand said. He extracted a handheld radio from among the menagerie of cop equipment hanging from his Sam Browne belt. He brought the black box to his mouth and pushed the button with his thumb.

'You there?'

'Ramey,' squawked the static voice.

'I need you at the desk,' the big cop said.

Ramey didn't bother to answer. The radio clicked silent. The cop returned it to his belt. 'How many?' he asked.

The little man gritted his perfect teeth and told him for the third time. 'Two.'

'Where are they now?' the cop asked.

The little guy seemed relieved. At last they were covering new ground. 'Outside in the car,' he answered, tilting his head toward the street.

A nearly inaudible electronic buzz was followed by the sharp snap of a lock. From a door built into the wall behind the booking desk, a uniformed officer stepped out into the lobby. A sergeant, Hispanic, maybe five ten, nearly as wide as he was tall. Every bit as kinetic as the desk officer was languid. A few more cop decorations and he risked being mistaken for a rear admiral.

'So?' he snapped.

The desk officer handed him the ID case. Ramey looked it over like there was going to be a test, then, seemingly satisfied, handed it back to the man in the gray suit, who made another show of feline grace as he stashed it inside his jacket.

The cop's thick black eyebrows met in the center of his face like ardent caterpillars. 'So?' the sergeant said again.

'Sergeant . . . ?'

'Ramirez,' the cop said. 'Sergeant Hector Ramirez.'

Gray suit opened his mouth to speak, but Ramirez cut him off. 'And you need what from us?'

With an air of bemused forbearance, gray suit went through it again.

'And you want the SPD to lock them up for you?'

'Yes.'

'On what charges?'

'Interfering with a federal officer.'

Ramirez held out his thick hand. Gray suit looked down into the leathery palm and cocked a quizzical eyebrow in an almost comical gesture that was from hours of practice before the mirror.

Ramirez answered the silent question. 'Paperwork,' he growled.

'We don't require paperwork,' the little guy said.

The two cops shot each other a quick glance. Ramirez's eyebrows ended their kiss. 'The prisoners are foreign nationals?' Ramirez ventured.

'No.' Gray suit pulled a couple of pieces of plastic from his pants pocket and dropped them on the desk. Photo IDs. Driver's licenses.

Ramirez picked them up, shuffled from one to the other and back before handing them to the desk cop, who extracted a pair of half-glasses from his uniform pocket before reading the documents, front and back. Another glance flew from cop to cop.

'They're outside, you say?'

'Yes.'

'Bring them in,' Ramirez said.

Gray suit hesitated for a beat, as if testing the wind for irony. Discerning none, he tried to read Ramirez's face but found himself looking into the unblinking gaze of a stone idol. The little man put on an air of bemused resignation as he turned and headed out the precinct door. On either side of the double doors, filthy windows ran from knee to ceiling. On the right, the windowsills were black, blistered by long-ago cigarettes and littered here and there by half a dozen magazine carcasses, twisted and torn, separated from their once-glossy covers, pages dog-eared and cemented together by substances best left unimagined.

On the left, a thirty-year-old jade plant meandered, long and leggy, out of hand, its arid stalks twisting in every imaginable contortion, filling the grimy windows with its thick leathery leaves, furry beneath a quarter inch of dust.

Sergeant Ramirez spoke into his collar radio. The desk cop stifled a smile. A minute later, a trio of uniformed officers arrived through the door behind the desk. Two men and a woman, their eyes full of questions that didn't have to wait long for an answer.

Both front doors opened. The sounds of the street mingled with the dust and the desperation as a pair of men in dark overcoats led a pair of manacled prisoners into the precinct. The man in the gray suit brought up the rear. He was wiping his hands with a crisp white handkerchief as he shouldered his way through the double doors.

The prisoners were middle-aged. A Japanese man and a Caucasian woman, both in their late fifties or thereabouts. Both looking defeated. Her hair had come loose from the clip at the back of her head and was blowing about in the breeze. The man tried to pull away from his captor but failed. Both looked up at the same time. Both of them tried to speak. The cops behind the desk flinched in unison. Both prisoners had a piece of silver duct tape sealing their mouths.

Ramirez blanched. His hand shook as he pointed. 'Take the prisoners to separate interview rooms,' he said. 'And get that goddamn tape off of them.' He turned his attention to gray suit. 'Keys for the cuffs.'

Nobody moved until it got real awkward. Finally the little guy gave a nod and one of the overcoats stepped forward to drop a set of keys into the female officer's outstretched hand. After that, everything happened at once.

Two of the officers led the prisoners away. Gray suit and his minions turned to leave but found the doorway filled by a pair of massive SWAT officers, boots, helmets, body armor, and all. A futile attempt to flank the pair made it plain: nobody was going anywhere, anytime soon.

'Have a seat, gentlemen.' Ramirez gestured to the battered collection of chairs lining the room. 'Nobody's going anywhere until we get this thing sorted out.'

Gray suit's face was the color of oatmeal. His voice was a whisper as he began to protest, 'We are federal officers and pursuant to the Patriot Act of—'

'Have a seat,' Ramirez repeated, louder this time. 'I'm calling for an A.D.A. We'll let the D.A.'s office work their magic on this thing.'

'I had an officer shot this afternoon. At this moment we are—'

Ramirez stiffened his spine. He jerked his thumb over his shoulder. 'Was one of them the shooter?' he asked.

'No.'

The cop waved disgustedly. 'Then have a goddamn seat.'

'Me and my mother never got along,' she said. She caromed a gaze off the mirror and caught

Paul's eyes. 'Two strong personalities, I guess,' she added with a wan smile. 'That's probably how come Mona and I always get in each other's faces.' She waved a safety razor in the air. 'Mona owns the shop. Her daughter, Sue, and I . . . we run the place. Mona just comes in every afternoon to collect the cash and bitch about anything she can think of.' She waved the razor again. 'Her and me go at it like cats and dogs. Good thing I've got some vacation time coming. It's been getting bad lately. Another week or so and I'd be telling her where she could put her shop and then I'd need to find another job, which wouldn't be easy since I wouldn't have a reference from my last job.' She pretended to check the room. 'I use Mona's certificate number,' she said in a low voice, and then stepped back to admire her work. 'Soon as I close up tonight, I'm out of here. Gonna go back home and try to reconnect with my parents. Already got the car packed and ready to roll. Good-bye.'

Paul watched her from the corner of his eye. Her hair was three separate shades of red, none of which existed in nature. She was dressed like a cartoon character, something between Raggedy Ann and the Cat in the Hat. All kinds of multicolored beads all over her, some of which looked like they might be made of candy, an impossibly short denim skirt over red-and-white-striped leggings, knee-length boots laced up the front.

She bent close again, working her way slowly

around Paul's left ear. 'I never shaved a guy's face before,' she said. 'I've like, you know, shaved myself in all the . . . you know, all the places where girls do that kind of thing.' She wiped a spot of shaving cream from his cheek with a small pink towel. 'Hell . . . I even shaved my head once back in high school . . . back when Sinéad O'Connor was all the rage, but . . .' She rinsed off the razor and stepped back again. Satisfied, she pulled a larger pink towel from a shelf beneath the counter, wet one corner in the sink, and used it to remove the remaining daubs of white foam.

'Okay now,' she said. 'Gonna turn you round here and we'll see how your hair came out.'

She swung the chair in a one-eighty, then pumped one of the chair's handles several times, lowering the chair until Paul's neck slid into the indentation in the sink.

'Your neck was any bigger we'd have to wash your hair in the back room, like we do with some of the *real* big girls.' She pulled his hair out from beneath his head. 'You're gonna need to slide down a little.'

Paul grabbed the arms of the chair and pushed. When he opened his eyes she was looking down at him. 'You're not much of a talker, now, are you?' She smiled and turned on the water in the sink.

'Depends,' Paul said.

'On what?'

'On who I'm talking to, I guess.'

83

'I'm Brittany.'

Paul closed his eyes. The silence rose above the rush of water. She put her hand on her hip, waited a moment, and then leaned in close. 'This is the part in the conversation where you tell me your name,' she whispered in his ear. His eyes popped open.

'Hi, Brittany,' he said. 'I'm . . .' He hesitated. 'I'm Paul, I guess.'

'You guess?' She started to laugh, but caught herself.

'It's a long story.'

'You don't know who you are?'

'Not exactly.'

She began to run his hair under the rushing water. 'How's the temp?' she asked.

He said it was fine. She began to rinse the excess dye from his hair, separating the strands and holding them under the running water, keeping at it until all traces of dye disappeared and the rinse water ran clear.

She wrapped a pink towel around his hair and sat him up. 'I used to think I was adopted,' she said. 'I just couldn't believe I was part of that family of mine. I thought I was like a princess or something, got sent down the river and got lost, got picked up by this crazy bunch of farmers.'

She spun the chair again. This time she left him facing the mirror. She rubbed the towel around his head and then pulled it away. 'Whoever you are . . .' she began. 'Whatever your name is . . .

you sure don't look anything like the mountain-man type who walked into the shop an hour ago, I can sure tell you that.'

She was right. The clean-shaven young man in the mirror was a complete stranger to him. She'd cut most of his hair off and dyed what was left black . . . jet black . . . raven's-wing black. She ran a comb through it, working out the tangles.

As she moved around to his right side, she felt him stiffen.

'You don't like it?' She sounded hurt. She put a hand on his shoulder. 'We could do something else.'

He didn't answer. Beneath her hand, he was trembling. When she looked down, his eyes were fixed on the mirror. She turned and looked over her shoulder. The impending dinner hour had thinned the mall traffic. Coming down the central aisle were a pair of official-looking types in black overcoats, each working one side of the aisle, shouldering people out of the way as they moved from shop to shop, looking around inside for something and then popping back out.

'Coupla Nazis,' she said as they moved closer.

For a second it felt as if he was going to rise from the chair, but it was too late. One of them poked his head in the door. He took in the scene, walked over and stared at Paul, and then checked the back room. 'Hey, hey!' Brittany shouted. 'No customers back there. That's off-limits to . . .'

If he heard her, he didn't let on. A single smirk and he was gone. They watched in silence as the pair made their way out of sight. The trembling beneath her hand began to subside.

'You know those guys?' she asked.

'No,' he said.

She eyed him sideways.

CHAPTER 11

Fact of life number one: sooner or later, they all walked out. Men of all sizes and shapes, races, creeds, and political persuasions . . . no matter . . . next thing she knew, they were packing their things and heading for the door. Some took longer than others; some left angry; some left sad. Whatever . . . they left.

The only constant . . . the only commonality among that collection of dismal departures was the parting salvo . . . that final self-justifying line in the awkward seconds before the slam of the door. It was like they'd all gotten together and written the damn thing down. Like it was in some index somewhere where you could look it up under *P*. 'Parting shot for Kirsten Kane.' Always include the word *control*.

Maybe that guy Artie Gold said it best . . . not surprising since Artie made a living writing speeches for the mayor. Artie'd lasted less than a week and was the only relationship Kirsten could recall that remained unconsummated. Not that they hadn't tried, mind you. Problem was, they got off to such a bad start and never recovered.

Partway through their first physical liaison, just about the time they'd moved from the couch to the bedroom, right about the place where most couples began to confuse love and lust, Kirsten and Artie'd gotten into a spirited screaming match, an unfortunate digression which had quickly wilted the ardor of the occasion. On his way out, Artie had opined to the effect that a few days living with Kirsten was like being swallowed by a beast.

Everybody knew it, too . . . the whole damn county building. Kirsten Kane sheds suitors the way lizards shed scales. What in hell is wrong with that girl anyway? Wasn't like she was fat or ugly or anything. Matter of fact she was tall and seriously put together and altogether a dish of the first order, which probably explained why every new male hire felt a need to make a run at her prior to unpacking. What remained unexplained, however, was the rapidity with which they were expended.

Wasn't like it was something new either. She'd been that way in high school. That's how a beautiful woman got to be thirty-seven years old without ever having been married, a state that, if one were to judge from the attitude of her parents, friends, and coworkers, constituted a statistical anomaly of such rarity as to rival winning lottery tickets and two-headed calves.

Back in the day, she'd attributed the phenomenon to callow youth and her own overly developed sense of self. She'd told herself she just wasn't *needy* enough for men her age and had consoled her wounded pride with the notion that she'd find her soul mate somewhere down the line, that Prince Charming was still out there somewhere, and all she had to do was go about her business and sooner or later their star-crossed paths would intersect.

Twenty years later was a whole different deal. The older she got and the further up the office ladder she climbed, the less appropriate her state seemed to be. By now, nearly everyone in her life had reached out and tried his or her hand at matchmaking only to pull back a bloody stump. Predictably, whispered allegations of dykedom still circulated. Women wondered if perhaps Kirsten's affairs were not invariably unsuccessful because they were merely a ruse to throw observers from the real scent of her desires, a notion that, not coincidentally, provided both an easy answer to the whys of Kirsten's curtailed love life and also, in some left-handed way, validated many of their own most oft-regretted and painful choices.

Men . . . for some of them anyway, it was easy. It was an 'ergo.' Any woman who was crazy enough to reject their amorous intentions must surely be a lesbian. What other answer could there be? For others, the image of Kirsten and another similarly endowed woman rolling around naked and sweaty in the throes of passion was simply more than their repressed libidos could manage to encapsulate.

For her part, Kirsten had decided to give the whole thing a rest. She was telling her friends she was 'in remission' from men, making it sound as if the breed were a carcinogen from which she had, by extreme measures, temporarily been cured of men, all of which probably explained why she got the call . . . a call that normally would have fallen to a junior member of the staff, somebody fresh faced and eager to please on Sunday. But, face it, everybody knew she wasn't going anywhere these days. Everybody from the custodians to the D.A. himself knew she'd be home watching the Nature Channel and not primping in the bathroom, readying herself for some big date.

The first ring of the phone startled her, reminding her how seldom it rang lately.

She picked it up. 'Kane,' she said into the mouthpiece.

'You free?' The voice pulled her feet from the coffee table and sat her up straight. Although they dealt with each other on a daily basis, both face-to-face and over the phone, District Attorney Bruce Gill rarely called her at home. Rarely . . . like in somebody must have died . . . like in she was fired or something.

'I'm here,' she answered.

'I need you over at the North Precinct ASAP.'

There it was. No request about it. Get your ass over there.

'What's up?' she asked.

He told her everything he knew. Right away, she could tell he was peeved. The more annoyed he got, the higher the pitch of his voice. This time on a Sunday night in the spring, Bruce and Katrina Gill were invariably headed out and the Honorable Bruce Gill didn't like business interfering with his social life.

She held the phone away from her ear. He was squeaking about a meeting they'd had last week . . . like it was something she could forget. The day Gill made the front page by refusing to round up a bunch of Middle Eastern types just because the FBI wanted them rounded up. You had to give the guy credit; he recognized the knuckles of opportunity when they knocked. His one-liner about how he wasn't arresting anybody 'just because his middle name is bin' had gotten him above the fold from coast to coast, and made him the darling of every wild-eyed liberal in the country, not to mention conveniently providing a pedestal whence he'd orated that the residents of *his* city should not and would not have their rights abridged in any way by any federal agency whatsoever.

She gazed out the window while Gill used the occasion to warm up his speech for next year's gubernatorial campaign. Shards of sunset lit the tops of the clouds as they slid sideways across the sky; pulled long and thin by a following wind, they moved due north, resolute and arrowlike on their express flight to Canada. In the street below, yellow pulsing lights bounced frantically around the buildings. A crowd had gathered on the corner by the wine merchant. She pressed her face against the glass, but from nineteen stories up, she couldn't make out what was going on. She hated the feeling of being left out. Hated it more than anything.

'I'm on it,' she said finally, cutting her boss off midplatitude.

'All right, then, take care of it,' he huffed, and hung up.

That he offered no instructions spoke to his faith in her professional ability. That he offered no apologies . . . well . . . whatever that spoke to was something she didn't want to think about. She pushed herself to her feet, stretched, groaned long and loud, and then padded off toward the bedroom.

Night rolled silently over the horizon, hunching shoulders and pulling chins down into collars in the minutes before the overhead lights hissed to life, one by one flickering for a moment before drooling their X-ray light onto the pavement below. A cold wind rode shotgun to the darkness, swirling the street debris into a trash tornado, flapping stiff awnings like flags, and ruffling the torn posters tacked to the telephone poles, where a million staples, old and new, bristled in the low orange light like iron quills.

Dinner was long over. Paul was on his third cup

of cocoa, and the waiters were sweeping the floor. He checked his wrist as if he were wearing a watch, wondered where that habit came from, and then took another sip from the white mug curled in his elbow.

An hour ago, his pursuers had entered the restaurant for the second time, annoying the staff, walking among the tables and checking faces. Both times he'd calmly looked up from his plate and met their gaze. Both times they'd continued their search elsewhere. Second time around he'd mused as to how an inability to recognize oneself seemed to pretty much preclude the possibility of other people recognizing you also.

Jalisco was the only place on Landon Street he'd ever seen. Ms Willis used to bring them all up here on Saturday afternoons for lunch. The staff would set up a long table back along the kitchen wall where they could all eat together without bothering other diners, the more delicate among whom sometimes objected to the bohemian table manners of certain housemates.

Without willing it so, he'd found himself ensconced at a familiar table near the back of the restaurant watching passersby on the sidewalk. Wasn't so much he felt at home as it was he had no idea where else to go. He heaved a sigh, sat back in the chair, and looked around. The restaurant was nearly empty. He swiveled his head and checked the place out. Like everything else in his life, Paul remembered it in general terms but had never zoomed to the specifics.

For instance, he'd never noticed the walls before, never noticed the once-bright murals, festive and tropical but covered with an inch of grime now . . . the señoritas, the serapes, the bullfights, and the bougainvillea . . . and the beach scenes and the palm trees wavering in an imaginary breeze.

He closed his eyes and the recurring scene was waiting . . . right there on the inside of his eyelids . . . the beach, the green water, the two figures, and something gleaming white cutting back and forth across an azure sky. He could smell it now . . . the salt air . . . the oceanic odor of renewal and decay. He lowered his inner eyes, looked along the golden beach, past the distant figure where his vision had always stopped before, and then . . . in the distance, nearly obscured by the haze, he could see a line . . . a needle wavering in the rising heat rays . . . but a line nonetheless. He strained for perspective. Something rode on top of the line like a head on a pin. He narrowed his inner eyes. A tower. The wavering apparition was a tower of some sort. Like the kind of thing you saw at an . . .

'We're closing up.' The waiter stood by his side. His face said he was sad but the rest of him said he wasn't. Paul dug in his pants pocket and came out with a twenty. The waiter snapped up the cash and the check and hurried over to the register. In less than a minute he was back, carrying the change on a small wooden tray. Behind them the lights in the kitchen went out. Out on the sidewalk, another one of the waiters was readying the steel security gate.

Paul left the change on the table and got to his feet. His legs were stiff from sitting as he shuffled out onto the sidewalk. The steel security gate accordioned its way across the front of the space. He watched as the waiter locked it in place, pulled down the overhead windows, and locked the door.

The swirling wind sent icy fingers down his collar. He shuddered, hugged himself hard, and then rubbed his hands up and down his bare arms in a vain attempt to create a little warmth. Landon Street was nearly empty. Across the road, above the arcade, the lights of a tattoo parlor threw bright squares onto the sidewalk below, illuminating the half-dozen people waiting at the bus stop. SLAVE TO THE NEEDLE, the sign in the window said. Something in the air spoke of rain.

Paul started left, then changed his mind and went the other way, up toward the far end of the street, where, behind a temporary chainlink fence, the construction crews were building yet another set of condos. He stuffed his hands in his pants pockets as he crossed Harrison Street and walked along the front of the Presbyterian church occupying the corner of the block. He could hear singing coming from inside. He kept walking.

CHAPTER 12

He made her skin crawl. She wasn't sure why, but something in his manner raised goose bumps all over her body. She rubbed her hands together, took a deep breath, and made a point of modulating her tone of voice. 'Mr . . .' she began.

'Van Dusen,' he filled in.

She suppressed her gag reflex. 'Mr Van Dusen . . . my boss, Mr Bruce Gill, the district attorney of Queen Anne County . . . Mr Gill has made his position on matters of this nature quite clear.' She felt herself slipping into her courtroom oratory mode and tried again to relax, but her revulsion for the little man kept her throat tight and her spine stiff as steel. 'This county . . .' she began again, 'insists that any law enforcement actions taken within the confines of the county be . . .' She held up her index finger. 'One . . . coordinated *ahead of time* with the local PD.' The little man opened his mouth to protest, but she silenced him with a second finger. 'And two . . . *must* be accompanied by all the paperwork neces-sary for the actions required.'

'This *is* a matter of national security.' He practically whispered it. Every hair on her body stood on end.

She shuddered. 'How would that be?'

'I'm not at liberty to discuss that,' he said with that smarmy reptilian smile that made her want to punch him in the mouth.

She pulled out her notebook and flipped to the back. 'Wesley Allen Howard,' she read. When she looked up, his face had taken on some color.

'I'd be very careful with that if I were you,' he hissed.

'And why is that, Mr Van Dusen?'

He rolled his eyes to the ceiling in disgust. 'I'm not at liberty to say.'

Kirsten Kane snapped her notebook shut and got to her feet. 'According to Ms Willis, all she did to become a threat to the American way of life was to run a people search on that name and the next thing she knew you and your little band of thugs appeared on her doorstep.' She held up a restraining hand. 'I know . . . you're not at liberty.'

He got to his feet, shaking his head as if disappointed at a child. 'We've wasted far too much time on this silliness,' he announced. 'If you would be so kind as to return the prisoners to our custody, we'll make other arrangements.'

She couldn't help herself. A short dry laugh escaped her throat. Apparently, the little man's arrogance knew no bounds. 'You really don't get it, do you?' she snapped. Before he could answer, she went on, 'Since this seems to be so difficult for you to process, let me make this county's position clear. Ms Willis and Mr Suzuki are tax-paying citizens of this county, well-known people in our community, and as such are going absolutely nowhere with you unless and until you provide us with a federal warrant for their arrest, at which point, *our office* will review the charges and in the event we find the accusations warranted we will instruct the appropriate *local* law enforcement agency to make the arrest. Until such time . . .' – she paused for effect – 'I think you and your merry band should consider yourselves fortunate not to be cooling your collective heels in a cell . . .'

He was sneering at her again, making a little chortling sound in his throat. She had to take a step back to keep from belting him one. She continued, 'In a cell, charged with kidnapping and assault and a raft of other charges I haven't had the time to think of yet.' She pointed at the door. 'Now collect your little robots out there and get out.'

He straightened his shoulders inside the Italian suit. 'You haven't heard the last of this,' he promised. He shook a finger at her. She wanted to break it off. 'This will come back to haunt you,' he said.

'I'll sleep with a night-light,' she assured him.

He stopped at the door and turned back her way. 'I had two men injured in the line of duty today.'

98

'One's been treated and released.' She swept a hand through the air. 'Surely you're not holding Ms Willis and Mr Suzuki responsible for the neighbor's dog.'

'I had a man shot today. He's in critical—'

'His condition's been upgraded to stable,' she snapped.

'We have a suspect in the shooting.'

'That's not the story we're getting from the hospital,' she said. 'Your agent claims the gun went off while he was struggling with one of Ms Willis's residents. He told officers the gun fired on impact with the ground.' She was talking to his back now. Little SOB walked away while she was still talking. She gnashed her teeth in frustration. The door hissed closed. She took a deep breath and looked over at the black glass panel along the west wall of the interview room. She made a 'come here' gesture.

A moment later Sergeant Ramirez pulled open the door and stepped inside.

'Guy's thick as a brick,' he said.

She held up a hand and turned her head aside, as if to say she was unable to express her feelings about the man. 'Can we find a unit to give Ms Willis and Mr Suzuki a ride back to Arbor Street?'

Sergeant Ramirez said it wouldn't be a problem.

'Have them check the street. Napoléon there isn't going quietly on this thing. I'd be willing to bet he's got a couple of his minions lurking around in the shrubbery somewhere.'

99

'And if he does?'

'Send them on their way. If they give the officers a hard time, if they come back after you've braced them off the first time, run them in.'

Ramirez smiled for the first time. 'It would be my pleasure,' he said.

'Have the neighborhood unit check in on the facility first thing in the morning. I don't want those people bothered again.'

'Those idiots have got one of the residents on the run,' he said. 'What about him? We can't just leave him out there.'

She checked her watch. 'According to Ms Willis, the guy's severely disabled. We ought to be able to find somebody like that. He's probably scared to death.'

'Not to mention freezing his ass off,' Ramirez said. 'I got a description. According to Ms Willis, he's wearing nothing but a T-shirt and a pair of jeans. It's getting real raw out there.'

'Check the neighborhood.'

The sergeant nodded. 'We'll keep an eye out for him.'

Paul watched it all go down. They'd ditched the trench coats in favor of blue windbreakers and had downsized the Town Car to a more innocuous Subaru Outback, but right away Paul recognized the one who got out and peed on the maple tree. The guy was too big to forget. He and his partner were sitting half a block south of Harmony House

100

with the engine running when the city police cruiser came by for the first time. Paul watched the silhouettes slouch in the seats as the black-and-white slid by, watched as the cruiser continued up Arbor Street and turned right onto Slayter Avenue.

From his outdoor vantage point, Paul heard the cruiser's engine roar to life, and then a moment later, heard the sound of squealing tires and then the roaring of the engine once again. As the sound faded, he turned his attention back to the parked car. They hadn't heard a thing and hadn't moved a muscle. He smiled.

A minute and a half later the cop car slid around the south end of Arbor Street and screamed their way, engine aroar, light bar ablaze, before sliding to a halt just behind the parked Subaru, allowing the cop in the passenger seat to step out and approach the car with minimal exposure.

The inside cop directed a powerful searchlight beam at the driver's window. On the inside of the window, a flattened palm tried to block the invading white light. The outside cop kept his gloved right hand on the butt of his gun and used his left to knock on the window. The palm disappeared, but the window stayed up. He knocked again.

'Could you roll down your window, please?'

On the third knock, the window slowly slid down. The cop bent at the waist and said something to the driver. The inside cop was outside now, keeping the vehicle between himself and the Subaru. Paul crawled through the dirt on his elbows, all the way to the far end of the porch, where he pressed his ear against the lattice and strained to hear. Still, he couldn't hear what either of them said for the next couple of minutes. He tried holding his breath but that didn't work at all. Didn't matter, though, because, at that point, somebody hit the adrenaline button.

The cop had stepped back from the window and pulled his gun. He assumed the combat position, legs slightly bent, gun held before him with two hands. 'Get out of the car,' he boomed. 'Keep your hands in sight and exit the vehicle NOW.'

The window went back up. The cop repeated his command, louder and more threatening this time. Nothing happened until the passenger door swung open and the weight lifter stepped out onto the grass divider.

'Keep your hands where I can see them,' the cop screamed. 'Turn your back to me and get down on your knees.'

The big guy proffered an ID case.

'Drop it,' the cop bellowed.

The big guy held both hands high and allowed the case to fall open. 'Drop that on the ground,' the cop ordered. 'Turn your back to me and get down on your knees.'

The big guy said something Paul couldn't hear. The world seemed to stand still. That's when the second police cruiser arrived. No lights this time, just a screech to a halt and a new pair of cops aiming shotguns at the Subaru over the top of their police car.

After that, things went fast-forward, didn't take but about five minutes before the pair of them were cuffed and stuffed into separate patrol cars. Another minute and the police cars were gone. All along Arbor Street the status quo returned. Blinds snapped closed. Parted curtains fell back into place.

Paul elbowed himself around in a half circle and crawled back the other way, back to the removable piece of lattice, where he let himself out onto the side lawn and stood up, stifling a groan and shaking his cramped legs back to life.

Before the cops ever showed up, he'd already decided what he was going to do next. He was going to rely on his new look to protect him. Instead of sneaking around to the back door, or tossing pebbles at somebody's window, he was going to walk right up to the front door and ring the bell. If he got caught sneaking around the bushes, he was toast, no doubt about it, so why not try the old 'hide in plain sight' trick. He told himself the same thing he'd told himself when they came into the restaurant: If I don't recognize my own face in the mirror, there's no reason they should either.

Half expecting a shout to ring out or the silence to be broken by the slap of running feet, he moved quickly across the street. As he walked beneath the glare of the streetlights, he noticed the thick layer of dust covering his T-shirt and the front of his jeans. He stopped and brushed the dirt from the front of him as best he could and then moved on down the walk to Harmony House, whose windows were blank and silent and whose outside lights were turned down low.

He hesitated for a moment and then mounted the front stairs, tripping the motion detector, sending the unrelenting glare of the porch light down onto the boards. He stood and looked around, listening again for signs of pursuit, but Arbor Street had gone to bed. Even the dogs were silent. Only the rustle of the night breeze in the trees caught his ears.

He rang the bell and waited, knowing that, this time of night, Ms Willis would answer the bell. He waited and then rang again, trying to stand still, trying not to look guilty of anything, trying to look like he belonged, a thought which forced him to realize that he didn't belong, not there, not anywhere, that he was adrift on the planet, without roots, without a home. In some odd way, the thought caused him to become aware of how cold he was and sent an uncontrollable shiver rolling down his spine.

He was still trying to control his shaking when the curtains parted. 'Yes.'

Her electronic voice came from the little black box mounted above the front door.

'It's me,' he said.

A frozen moment passed. He shook until his teeth chattered like castanets.

'Come closer,' she said.

He took a step forward and nearly put his face against the glass.

She pulled the curtains back and looked into his eyes. He heard a gasp followed by the snapping of locks and the rattling of chains. The door clanked open. A hand reached out and jerked him inside. He stood and watched as she secured the door. When she looked up, her eyes were wide with fear. She whispered, 'Are you crazy coming here? They could be—'

'They were,' he interrupted. Her mouth snapped shut. He told her what had transpired in the street.

'There're probably others.'

'I need my money,' he said. 'And maybe some clothes,' he added.

A hundred questions died in her throat. Instead, she nodded and hustled toward the stairs, beckoning for Paul to follow.

'Hurry,' she said as she mounted the stairs two at a time with Paul hard on her heels. The commotion had not gone unnoticed.

Eunice, Carman, and Dolores stood on the second-floor landing in their nightclothes. All along the hallway doors were open. At the far end, Randall stood on the carpet runner, still fully dressed, rubbing his eyes. Shirley had rolled herself to the far side of the hall for a better view. Even blind old Mrs Dahlberg had found her way to the corridor.

'Everybody get back to your rooms,' Helen said.

Nobody moved. 'NOW,' she bellowed, and then covered her mouth with her hand. The only person who moved was Dolores, who, instead of returning to her room, went tripping down the stairs.

She turned to Paul. 'Get what you need from your room,' she whispered. 'I'll meet you back here.'

Paul watched as she hurried past a dozen frightened eyes, pulled her keys from the pocket of her robe, and unlocked the fire door. When she disappeared from view, Paul opened the door to his room and stepped inside. She'd left the light on for him. The sight of the meagerly furnished space where he'd spent the past seven years, and which, as he saw it now, he was unlikely to see again, brought him to tears.

He blubbered once, swallowed the lump in his throat, and then wiped the hot tears from his eyes before walking over to the closet, where he pushed his only good shirt and pair of pants aside and grabbed the green Suzuki Landscaping jacket from the hanger.

He was still shaking so bad it took him two tries to get his arm in the sleeves. From beneath the bed, he pulled a black Nike gym bag with a big white swoosh on the side. He filled the bag with socks, underwear, three clean T-shirts, and a pair of leather gloves he'd gotten for Christmas. He turned to leave. Shirley sat in her chair in the doorway. He walked over and put a hand on her bony shoulder.

'I'll miss you,' she squawked.

'Me, too,' Paul said.

A tear ran down her face. And then another. And then a torrent began. She swiped at the tears with her good hand but missed. The sound of running feet pulled his eyes from her.

Ms Willis stood in the hall; her hair had escaped the pins and was falling into her face. Paul stepped around Shirley without removing his hand from her shoulder. Ms Willis handed him the big wad of bills, which he stuffed into the pocket of his jeans.

Dolores came running up the stairs, her eyes wide with terror. 'There's people in the yard,' she whispered. 'More than one.'

Helen Willis picked up the hall phone and dialed 911. After calmly explaining the situation to the dispatcher, she walked to the electrical panel at the top of the stairs and turned on the outside lights, illuminating the grounds like a shopping mall.

As Helen started back to Paul, something amiss caught her eye. The tall glass door to the fire extinguisher compartment hung open. The extinguisher was in place. The fire ax, however, was missing. Helen looked around. Eunice was backed into the corner of the hall trying to make like she didn't have a clue as to what was going on.

Helen knew better. She held out her hand. 'Give it to me,' she said.

Eunice looked confused. 'What?' she said.

'Give.'

'They pushed me,' Eunice said.

'Now.'

Eunice brought the ax out from behind her back. Helen Willis plucked the bright red ax from Eunice's thick fingers. 'I know,' she soothed. 'They weren't nice, were they?'

Eunice scowled and shook her head.

'You're going to have to let me take care of this one,' Helen Willis explained.

Helen and the ax were gone down the stairs before Eunice had a chance to protest. A minute passed before Helen returned, breathing heavily and still carrying the ax. 'I don't see anybody,' she announced. She turned to Dolores. 'You sure?'

Dolores bobbed her head up and down.

'Go to the basement and wait,' Helen said to Paul. 'When it's safe to go, I'll turn out the yard lights.' She stepped forward and wrapped her arms around him, ax and all. When she stepped back her eyes were filled with tears. 'Good luck,' she said.

Paul bent at the waist and kissed her on the cheek. 'Thanks for everything,' he said. 'I don't know if—' he began. His voice cracked. He shook his head.

'I know,' she said. 'Go find yourself.'

Paul turned and started down the hall. Pulsing red and blue lights began to dance around the walls. 'It's the cops,' Carman said. The front doorbell rang.

Paul reached the far end of the hall and the door to the service stairs, where Randall stood wide-eyed in the doorway. He was removing his shoes and trying to hand them to Paul as Paul stepped around him. As he moved into the opening and began to close the door, he felt Randall's hand at the pocket of his jacket and slapped it away. Paul closed the metal fire door, locked it, and headed for the basement, the front doorbell chiming in his ears.

CHAPTER 13

Fifteen minutes later, the outside lights faded to black. Paul wasted no time. He let himself out into the backyard; crouching at the top of the stairs, he listened. The distant whoop of a siren and the barking of a neighborhood dog were the only sounds. The cold night air found its way to his neck. He zipped the jacket, picked up his bag, and made his way out to the street, where the acrid tinge of violence still floated on the breeze.

Arbor Street had seen all the excitement it could stand for one night. The houses were dark and cinched up tight as Paul walked straight across the street and cut through a narrow alley between houses. He paused and cast a backward glance at Harmony House, hoping to weld its jagged silhouette to his memory. Only Shirley's light was on. He could see the top of her head in the window. He waved, knowing she couldn't raise her arm high enough to wave back, then stepped into the alley and disappeared from the other-worldly glow of the streetlights.

He was headed west toward the interstate, toward the freeway entrance Ken took whenever they had a job in the south part of the city. He was heading for that dirty half a block right before the freeway began, the place where ragged panhandlers and eager hitchhikers stood shivering on the sidewalk with sodden handmade signs. He remembered Ken saying how he wished he could help them out with a ride but how it wasn't safe to pick up hitchhikers anymore. Too many weirdos out there.

At one point, thinking he heard a car, he stepped deeper into the shadows of an apartment-house doorway. He waited. Turned out to be a gentle breath of wind stirring the leaves in the trees. He went on, moving faster now, nearly jogging.

Overhead, a full moon sat fat and sassy in the sky. The low clouds had thickened and filled with rain, a fickle reminder that ol' man winter hadn't bolted town quite yet, but lay just around the next corner, alert and ready to pounce.

He could hear the distant roar of the highway. The *blat blat* of a truck's jake brake tore the air to pieces. Diesel fumes filled his sinuses. He took a deep breath and swallowed. This was where things got hairy, where he finally had to abandon the back alleys and take to the streets like a big boy. The buildings were larger here, store-fronts, apartments, and condos, no single-family houses, no back alleys, no cover.

He hurried to the end of the block and peeked around the corner. The buildings and lights of downtown popped into view, shimmering and glimmering in the cold night air, headlights and taillights moving everywhere at once, the bodily fluids of the great beast.

He was a block uphill from the bridge over the highway. A quarter mile of stark, arched concrete whose sides were topped with fences designed to protect unwary drivers from falling objects. From here on it was pure luck. If there were enough of them . . . if they wanted him bad enough . . . if they caught him on the bridge . . . well then, they got him, pure and simple. If he got lucky, in a half hour he'd be in another area code, every bit as lost to them as he was to himself.

Go south. That was his whole carefully wrought plan. Go south. If he hadn't been so afraid, he'd have laughed. It seemed like an eternity since the trench coats had pushed their way into the house this morning. Seemed like he hadn't had a second to think and all he knew for sure was that the scene in his head, the beach, the tower in the distance, the men in white shirts . . . he had no idea where it was located . . . or, for that matter, whether it existed anywhere outside of his head . . . but . . . but if it did, he knew damn well it was somewhere south of where he was now.

He waited for the light two blocks uphill to change and then stepped out onto Sylvain Street. A steady stream of traffic moved downhill in his direction. He started down the incline. That's when he spotted the Town Car coming up the hill.

Paul kept walking. There was no turning back now. He let gravity pull him down the hill, his feet slapping on the concrete as he broke into a run. The car's window slid down. Paul and the driver made eye contact as he flashed by.

The guy behind the wheel tried to move over into the left lane but nobody would let him in. He momentarily hit the brakes, as if to stop and jump out, but the tandem metro bus to his rear wasn't having it. He had no choice but to continue on up the hill.

Paul let fear and the incline propel him forward, running full out now across the narrow frontage road that paralleled the freeway, out onto the bridge, which he felt certain he could cross before the Lincoln could manage to negotiate the narrow maze of one-way streets and get turned around.

As the river of traffic on his left become a trickle, he checked over his shoulder and then bolted across all four lanes to the uphill side of the bridge. He was slower now, his legs leaden and spent, his hips threatening to burst from the sockets as he crested the arch of the bridge and started down the other side . . . down toward the low-rent condos on the corner of Sylvain Street and Barlow Boulevard.

His breath was ragged. He sounded like a locomotive as he jelly-legged it around the corner . . . exhausted, slowing nearly to a stop and then picking up the pace again as he approached the corner. His nose had begun to run. As he ran, he wiped it with his sleeve.

A fast walk was all he could manage now. His body burned. He was ashes as he turned the corner.

All he wanted to do was breathe when he heard the sound of tires pulling to a stop on his left.

He dropped his bag. Something in his soul told him to fight. Told him that going along with these people would somehow be the end of him. At that moment it didn't matter who he was or who he wasn't. All that mattered was the animal will to survive.

He balled his hands into fists and turned to face his attackers. A guttural growl began to rise in his throat. His vision began to cloud with fury. A long thin scream reached his ears and then began to fade. He turned toward the approaching sound. The scream was coming from the brakes of a battered blue VW Bug as it ground to a stop along the curb. The passenger door flopped open.

'Hey, big fella.'

The voice sounded familiar. The city lights showed the car packed to the headliner. He bent at the waist and peered into the little car. It was her. The girl who'd cut his hair. What was her name? Brianna? No . . . Brittany. That was it. He was far too spent to talk. She mistook his grimace for a smile.

'Where you headed?' she asked.

All he could manage was a shrug. He checked the street, but they were alone.

'Want a ride?'

Without answering, he plucked his bag from the sidewalk and eased himself into the passenger seat. He pulled the door closed. 'Let's go,' he wheezed.

CHAPTER 14

His driving was shaky. Deputy assistant cabinet members didn't drive much. In the city, on his own time, he used cabs. Otherwise he always had a driver. But not today. Today he held the wheel with both hands, making little corrections, trying to keep his wife Christine's Cadillac between the lines. His first thought was that the steering must be faulty. He made a mental note to call for a service appointment. By the time he'd driven five miles, he'd reevaluated and correctly ascribed the problem to 'operator error.' In his business, correctly identifying the problem was essential to operational success.

The exit was hard to miss. Private freeway exits in suburban Maryland pretty much screamed for attention. All the sign said was NSA EMPLOYEES ONLY. In case you made a mistake, they gave you plenty of room to turn around and your own little entrance back onto the freeway. If that wasn't enough to send you on your way, well then, since 9/11 anyway, it got real complicated for you after that.

Even for a man in his position, a wearisome series of protocols was required to gain entry. Botching any of them would get you a lengthy interview with the Secret Service. Hell . . . he was already cheating. He had the sequence of interior turns and access codes written down. The page lay open on the passenger seat. He wondered how many agency rules he was violating by having committed the codes to writing. Triple figures probably. Years ago, a long-running joke said the initials stood either for 'No Such Agency' or 'Never Say Anything.' He recalled how, about ten years ago, the *Baltimore Sun* had outed NSA once and for all, by pointing out that the long-denied agency was the second largest user of electricity in the state of Maryland. Twenty-one million dollars' worth of power usage managed to raise more than a few eyebrows. Combined with surreptitiously taken aerial photographs showing roughly eighteen thousand parking spaces surrounding the bunkerlike facility, the story made it clear that whatever the agency was doing in the way of electronic surveillance, they were doing a lot of it.

He was still marveling about how long the ten-mile trip from D.C. seemed when the exit sign came up. He used his right hand to fold the directions and return them to his jacket pocket as he wheeled off the freeway and up the tree-lined drive to the first guard gate. He could tell the Marine in the booth recognized him even though the last time he'd been on the grounds was before the kid had been born. He felt better.

Twenty minutes later, he knocked softly on the office door marked DEPUTY DIRECTOR, a designation reflecting the highest perch a civilian could attain within an organization always headed by a general or an admiral. He didn't wait for an answer. He grabbed the steel handle and pushed open the door.

Ronald W. Jacobson, deputy director of the National Security Agency, got to his feet and ambled out from behind the desk as his visitor entered the room. He smiled and extended a hand, then used the hand to pull the other man into a brief embrace. 'Bob,' he said as they hugged and then stepped back to admire the view. 'How nice to see you.' His tone made it sound like a surprise visit, rather than a cryptic request that he drop everything and come on down this morning.

Somewhere on the far side of fifty, Jacobson had a thick head of salt-and-pepper hair and a grip seemingly designed to drop you to your knees. Unlike Bob, who had softened considerably around the middle, Jacobson looked like he had always looked, like an ex-Special Forces op, a lean, mean fighting machine, like he used to be so fond of saying, two hundred pounds of airborne hell, the kind of guy who got himself down to Quantico twice a year on his own time, just to work out on the shooting range, not because his present position required any such certification, but simply because he was that kind of guy.

Jacobson gestured toward the black leather chair to the left of his desk and then returned to his seat. Still smiling, he started in on the social protocol. 'How's Christine . . .'

They tripped their way through the obligatory social chatter. An air of tension hung in the room.

'Your note . . .' he began. 'Sounded pretty dire,' he half joked. He ran his eyes around the room in an exaggerated manner. 'Maybe we ought to take a walk.'

Jacobson laughed a humorless laugh. 'Wouldn't do any good,' he said. 'Trust me.' He spread his big hands. 'Nowhere to run, nowhere to hide.'

'The technology's gotten that good, has it?'

'You don't want to know,' Jacobson assured him.

He twirled his finger in the air. Jacobson got the message. 'This room gets electronically swept every morning. This morning I had them make an extra pass,' he said. His hard black eyes moved over his visitor like ants over a Popsicle.

'We've got a problem,' Jacobson said.

'Interesting pronoun.'

'I knew you'd think so.'

'You know what Mark Twain said about pronouns?'

The banter made Jacobson uncomfortable, made him feel like he was being played with. He kept himself bland. 'No. What did he say?'

'He said pronouns were like kisses. When bestowed indiscriminately, they tend to lose their meaning.'

Bob smiled. 'Last time we spoke, you were sending your oldest boy to camp for the summer and were feeling guilty about it.'

'He's a junior at Harvard.'

'So how can "we" have business.'

'It's old business,' Jacobson said.

'How old?'

'Back at the beach.'

'Really?'

'It's been updated.'

'How's that?'

'The name Wesley Allen Howard came up.'

'Came up?'

Jacobson sat back in his chair, laced his fingers across his washboard middle, and took his visitor in. 'Someone ran an Internet search on the name.'

'Someone who?'

'A woman who runs a group home for retarded adults.'

Bob straightened in the chair. 'And why would she be doing that?'

'They found one of her charges in a railroad car. Seven years ago. Damn near dead with the front of his head caved in.' Jacobson's chair squeaked as he sat forward. 'He's been living in a group home for adults. A complete goner. Didn't speak. Didn't know shit from shoe polish.'

'And then?'

'He got hit by a car.' Before his increasingly anxious guest could ask another question, Jacobson went on. Told him the whole tale of plastic surgery and recuperation. 'We've got a couple of photos of what he used to look like when he lived at the home, but nothing of his present appearance.'

'Nothing?'

Jacobson reached into his top drawer and came out with a manila file folder. He slid it across the desk. His guest used a fingernail to flop the folder open.

Bob winced at the picture inside. 'Jesus,' he breathed. 'That's not going to be of much help.'

'Not, it's not.'

The air in the room was thick as motor oil.

'We can't take a chance here,' Bob said.

'No, we can't.'

'The time frame is scary.'

'Yes, it is.'

'No matter what it takes . . .' Bob let the sentence trail off.

'Indeed.'

'You're already at risk here.'

'I'm waist-deep in somebody else's swimming pool.'

'We have to know.'

The deputy director nodded his agreement.

'What do you need from me?' Bob asked.

'I need the Bureau to keep out of this. But it can't look like—'

'It's their pool you're wading in.'

'I know.'

'I'll see what I can do.'

'You've got the clout. Make it happen.'

His guest sighed and looked out the window, out over the acres of cars to the dark circle of woods beyond. 'I'll make a few calls.'

'I'll keep you posted from this end.'

'What have you got in mind?

Jacobson told him. 'Just like the old days,' he said.

'Except these days we're public figures.'

The visitor got to his feet. 'This gets out, we're going to be a hell of a lot more public than we care to be.'

'You still live in the same place?' Jacobson asked.

Bob frowned at the personal nature of the question but said he did.

'Still walk to that little coffee shop for coffee and a Danish every morning and then grab a cab from there.'

The visitor's spine stiffened. He knew better than to ask, so he nodded.

'We need to talk . . . I'll meet you there.'

'Have you been—'

Jacobson cut him off. 'Same as everybody else in the upper echelons of government, Bob, nothing more, nothing less.'

Bob shook his head. 'Let's hear it for George Orwell,' he said, turning to leave.

'And, Bob.'

He swiveled his head back toward the desk. Jacobson was as close to a smile as he got.

'Maybe you ought to leave those directions you've got folded up in your jacket pocket. I'll see to it they're properly disposed of.'

CHAPTER 15

The dream was old and tired. At least he thought so. In a mind where the remembered and the imagined slept in the same bed, it was hard to tell if anything under the covers could be considered real.

Problem was the whole scenario read like something out of a bad novel. The house was old and stood alone on a barren hilltop. The dream was already under way when he arrived. They already had her. The rank smell of decay already assailed his nostrils. He was in pursuit and in a panic when the dream opened and he found himself confronted by a family of . . . what to call them . . . hillbillies was as close as he could get . . . a clan of hillbillies who owned the house, degenerate and dirty, their speech so slurred and archaic as to be indecipherable, they never lost a step in their relentless pursuit, as he ran from room to room, following the fading timbre of her voice, down trapdoors in the floor, through secret openings in the walls and every other horror movie contrivance, all of it to the beat of their great pursuing boots pounding on the wooden floors behind him.

Often as not these days, he was able to rouse himself from the terror, although he remained unsure as to how he managed to do so. It was like he somehow reached out from the land beyond and gave his own shoulder a shake. A voice in his head would say, 'Hey, man . . . we're there again. In that dream . . . Wake up . . . Wake up . . .'

The hand was gentle this time . . . 'Hey hey.' Was that *her* voice? he wondered as his heart began to push burning blood through his veins.

'Come on now. You got to . . .'

His eyes popped open. He stared straight ahead. In the distance, a dim yellow sun was either setting or rising, he couldn't tell which. Steel-wool clouds pressed against the light like a dressing on a wound, allowing only thin glints of the sun to escape around its uneven edges. To his right, sparse vegetation rolled by the dim reflection . . . by the . . . he lifted his hand and touched it . . . by the window. To his left . . . to his left . . . what was her name again? Brittany. That was it. Brittany drove with one hand and gently patted his shoulder with the other. He sat up in the seat and ran both hands over his face. He swallowed a hundred questions and looked around again.

'My granddaddy would have said you were 'shakin' like a hound dog passin' a peach pit." She pulled her hand from his shoulder and put her attention back on the two-lane road in front of her. 'I don't know what in heck you were dreaming about, but it wasn't good, I can tell you that.'

It was new country, like no other land he could recall having seen before.

'Where are we?' he asked.

'East of the mountains.' She sensed his confusion. 'You been asleep for hours, man. Ever since we left the city.' She pointed out the windshield and yawned. 'It's darn near morning.'

He rubbed his eyes and looked around the car. Other than the seating area, the car was filled nearly to the roof line. His legs were little more than a dull ache. He tried to stretch but didn't have the room. He poked around with his hand, found the lever, and tried to put the seat back. Felt like he was crushing something. He stopped.

'We're gonna have to pull in for gas real soon here,' she said, tapping the dashboard with a multi-colored fingernail. 'We'll get out and rearrange things. See if maybe we can't get you a little more legroom.'

He nodded his appreciation.

'You know. Everything happened so fast, I never asked you where you were headed.'

He thought it over. 'I'm headed wherever you're headed,' he said finally.

She cast him a questioning glance. 'You drive?' she asked.

'A car?' he asked.

She burst out laughing and then, just as quickly, choked herself off. 'I don't mean to be impolite,' she said, waving a hand his way, '. . . but I'm telling you, man, you truly are a stranger in a strange land.'

Blood began to rise in his face. 'How so?'

She checked to see if he was kidding. 'You serious?' she said.

He assured her he was.

'Well, let's see . . .' She brought a fingernail to her chin. 'You've got no idea what your name is . . . no clue as to where you're going. You never been out in the desert before. You don't know if—'

'I can drive' was out of his mouth before he thought about it.

'You got a valid license?'

'Why?'

''Cause it's a long way, and I'd like a little help with the driving if I can get it.'

'What's a long way?'

'Alabama.'

'What's in Alabama?'

'I told you . . . my family.'

He began to pat himself down. Nearly as he could tell, his pants contained nothing other than the roll of money in his right pants pocket. Then he got around to feeling up the jacket and discovered a lump on the left. He slipped his hand inside and pulled out a battered brown wallet.

She was watching the road now. ''Cause if you don't have a license and we get stopped for something . . . I mean like that's the end of the trip right there. They'll sure as shootin' take you and the car and leave me sittin' there on the highway somewhere.'

He used his thumbs to pry open the center section of the wallet. No money, just a folded-up piece of white paper, which he extracted.

She was still talking. ''Cause I'd rather do the driving myself than have that shit come down. That's the last thing I need. I'm thinking this is . . .'

The paper was stiff, the creases folded tight and flattened, as if it had been a long time since anyone had opened whatever it was. He handled it gently.

'. . . a pivotal period in my life. You know where a person . . . you know, puts childhood behind and . . .'

It was a birth certificate. Polk County, Arkansas, thirty-seven years ago next month. Randall Michael James, son of Harold P. James and Elvira Ann Scott. And then it came to him. Randall. It was Randall's wallet.

'. . . you know, kind of strike out anew and . . .'

Poor guy must have stuffed it in the jacket as Paul was heading for the back stairs.

'. . . gotta mend a few fences back home before I can . . .'

The remainder of the wallet contained a tattered Department of Social Welfare ID card, a Queen Anne County Library card, and a Hollywood Video rental card, all in Randall's name.

'. . . that is assuming they can be mended.' She heaved a sigh. 'I've been gone a long time.'

She looked over at him. Sadness filled her eyes. 'Been years since I talked to my family.' She sighed again. 'We parted on real bad terms.' Her eyes rolled in her head. 'About as bad as terms can get.'

He sat back in the seat. The horizon was flat. A dirty sun was rising. 'So . . .' he began. 'What is it you're looking for? What's back home that's not someplace else?'

'Home,' she said. 'You know what they say about home.'

'No place like it' was out of his mouth before he thought about it. He searched for something else to say but came up empty. He covered his eyes with his hands. He could feel something or maybe someone inside of him, someone who knew there was no place like home, but who always stayed in the shadows, someone who—

Her voice hit him like a slap in the face. 'So . . . what am I gonna call you?'

His head swirled. 'Randy,' he said after a moment. 'Call me Randy.'

'You sure?'

'I'm sure,' he replied.

'Okay, man, then it's Randy you are.'

He allowed himself a wry smile. 'It's that easy, is it?'

She snapped her fingers. 'Just like that.'

The sun was a hazy halo on the horizon. Infrequent trees and low-growing thorns dotted the barren ground here and there. A blue-and-white sign announced an impending rest area.

A minute passed before the mercury vapor lights became visible.

'So how come you left home on such bad terms?'

''Cause I was young and stupid.'

He watched as she went back over it in her mind. He wondered how accurate the movies of memory were, wondered if the pictures became increasingly self-serving with the passage of time, as the stories themselves became more and more embedded in the fabric of our being, to the point where the line between fact and fantasy disappeared altogether, and it was the telling that mattered rather than the facts.

The rest area flashed by. She was somewhere else.

'I was weird,' she said after a minute. 'Every little town's got one, and I was it.'

The sound of her own voice seemed to encourage her. 'I just didn't want what the rest of them wanted.' She threw a quick glance his way. 'You're supposed to grow up, marry somebody else from the county, and start popping out fat little babies.' She heard her voice getting brittle and took a couple of breaths. 'Not that there's anything wrong with any of that, mind you.' She waved a hand in the air. 'It just wasn't for me.'

'What was for you?'

'Anything but that,' she snapped.

'And your family didn't approve?'

She laughed. 'Wasn't a single solitary thing about me they approved of,' she said. 'They hated the

128

way I looked, the way I dressed . . . they hated my friends.' She waved a hand again. 'You name it, they hated it.'

'So you left?'

'Might've been better if I had. Problem was, I finally gave in. I just couldn't stand being the outcast anymore,' she said. 'I was gonna marry Danny Leery. I cut my hair . . . cut off my nails . . . Mama ordered me a dress from a catalog. I was really gonna do it. Don't ask me why.' She shook her head in disbelief. 'I just wanted to be loved, I guess. All I knew was Airhart, Alabama, and my family,' she said. 'I spent my whole adolescence telling myself and anybody who'd listen how much I didn't give a shit and then it turned out that I did.' She read the question in his eyes. 'The closer the big day came, the crazier I got. Then somethin' in me just snapped,' she said. 'Thursday before the Saturday wedding, I finally lost it. Danny and me already bought furniture, moved the stuff into a house on his daddy's farm. Relatives from all over Alabama were fixin' to pack and head for the wedding.'

'And?'

'And I walked into town that Thursday morning and I got on the first bus that showed up at the Trailways station.'

'No kidding.'

'I got on that bus and never looked back.' She said it like it had long been rehearsed. 'Later that day I called home . . . you know, so's they wouldn't think anything bad'd come to me. My papa answered.'

'Yeah.'

'He hung up on me.' She swallowed hard. 'Said I wasn't his daughter anymore.'

A faded billboard announced BIG HARVEY'S TRUCK STOP, YUM! YUM! a mere thirty-nine miles distant. A pair of eighteen-wheelers roared by in the opposite lane, shaking the little car with the power of their passing.

'What about you?' she said, without taking her eyes from the road.

'What about me?'

'I showed you mine.' She smiled. '. . . so to speak, anyway. It's your turn. Guy don't know his own name gotta have a heck of a story.'

'It's not much of a story.'

'Why don't you let me be the judge of that.'

He told her everything he could remember.

CHAPTER 16

Kirsten Kane set the phone receiver down and leaned back in her chair. She pursed her lips, closed her eyes, and began to rock. After a few minutes, she sat forward and pushed herself to her feet. She was halfway to the door when her phone began to ring. She ignored the call and stepped out into the hall.

The offices hummed with the muted buzz of low voices, of keyboards clipping away and messages being sent and received. At the end of the hall, his door was closed, usually a sign he was in a meeting. She kept walking anyway.

Gene Connor, his private secretary, smiled as Kirsten approached. She set her phone back into the cradle and folded her hands on the desk in front of her. She was fifty-seven and had been Bruce Gill's right hand since he was a fledgling lawyer. Divorced and comfortable that way, she had twin sons, Aaron and Harlan, who were in their final year of Princeton Law.

'He with somebody?' Kirsten asked.

Gene shook her Margaret Thatcher hair.

'He's alone,' she said. 'Desperately trying to get someone on the phone.'

Kirsten was slightly taken aback by the unsolicited information. Gene Connor took the 'private' part of private secretary quite seriously and generally provided little or no information above and beyond what was absolutely necessary. One courthouse wag suggested it was easier to get through to Jimmy Hoffa than to Bruce Gill.

'Really.'

'You,' she said with a bemused grin.

Kirsten returned the smile. 'I take it I can go in.'

She made a sweeping movement with her hand. 'By all means,' she said.

Her phone rang. She picked it up. 'Office of the district attorney.' She gestured Kirsten onward with her eyes. 'I'm afraid Mr Gill's in a meeting right now. Would you like to leave a message or can I connect you to his voice mail? Yes. Yes. Thank you very much.'

The door read BRUCE W. GILL. Underneath: DISTRICT ATTORNEY. Underneath that: QUEEN ANNE COUNTY painted in gold. By the time Kirsten pulled the door open, Gene had fielded and disposed of yet another caller.

'Just the woman I wanted to see,' he said as Kirsten crossed the carpet and sat down in the green leather chair.

'Gene says you were trying to reach me.'

'You're not answering calls these days?'

'I was on my way here.'

132

'Apparently great minds do think alike.'

'Guess who just called me.'

He leaned out over his desk. He smiled his real smile, not the photo-op special, but the grin that escaped when he was actually amused. 'Pray tell,' he said.

'The U.S. attorney's office.'

'Really?'

'Seems they have an opening in the Bay Area that would be just perfect for me.'

He pushed out a low whistle. 'Expensive place to live.'

'They'd be tripling my present pittance,' she said.

'There's a great breakfast joint down by Washington Square.'

'I'll remember that.'

'Quite an honor.'

'I'd have to start the first of next week.'

He spread his hands in a gesture of surrender. 'I can't imagine what it would be like around here without you . . . but I sure as hell won't stand in your way.' He got to his feet and offered a congratulatory hand.

She stayed seated. 'Something about it doesn't feel right,' she said.

He gave her a wolfish grin and eased himself back into his chair. 'Which brings us to the reason I was looking for you a few minutes ago.'

'Which was?'

The grin got wider. 'Guess who called *me*.'

She checked him for irony and came up empty. 'You're kidding.'

He shook his big head. 'The Democratic National Party.'

'Really.'

'Seems all of a sudden they want me to be more of a player. They didn't come right out and say it, but they danced around a promise that the president might see his way clear to campaign for me next election year. Might even find a place for me in the AG's office.'

'Wow,' she said.

'They need me in Washington for the next few weeks' – he made an expansive gesture – '. . . to talk about my future with the party.'

'Just like that?'

'Out of the wild blue yonder.'

'These are the same people who are always trying to get you to tone it down.'

'The same folks.'

'The same folks who've been all over us like white on rice about our unwillingness to cooperate with government thug squads.'

'The very same.'

'What's wrong with this picture?'

'I'm thinking somebody wants the two of us diverted for a while.'

'Diverted from what?' Kirsten asked.

'Gotta be that affair with the' – he snapped his fingers – '. . . the house thing . . .'

'Harmony House.'

'Yep.'

'What do we do?'

He thought it over. 'I'm thinking we sit tight and wait to see what happens next.'

'Always a good plan,' she said.

'Always.'

'See.' Helen pointed at the computer. The expression on her face said, 'I told you so.' Ken pushed his glasses to the end of his nose and leaned in closer to the screen.

'I don't see any difference,' he said.

'The column on the right.'

'Dates.'

'Birth dates.'

Ken sat back in the chair. 'Oh' was all he said.

'Don't you get it?'

'I see how it's going to help, if that's what you mean. What I don't get is what it is you think we're accomplishing by all of this.'

'Maybe we can help him.'

'Help him what?' Ken asked.

'Find himself.'

'Find Paul?'

'There *is* no Paul.' She waved an impatient hand. 'That's the whole point.'

'And you think we're going to be able to help him by finding this Howard guy.'

'Find the right Wesley Allen Howard and you'll find Paul.'

'I thought there was no Paul?' he said. Before

she could answer, he said, 'It's not like you were going to be able to keep him around here much longer. One way or another, he was about to go. Either he was going to set out on this quest of his on his own, or somebody was going to find out he didn't belong in this place and the state was going to send him packing.' He showed his palms to the ceiling. 'What's the difference? Either way, he's gone.'

'Because . . .' she sputtered. '. . . because I don't like being pushed around. I don't like being hand-cuffed and dragged off to jail. Because I don't—'

'So this is about you,' he interrupted. His voice was sharp.

The tone brought her up short. 'If you don't want to help . . .' she began.

'I just want to get the ground rules straight,' he said quickly.

'The ground rules are that I want to find out what's going on here, dammit. I want to know how an Internet search could possibly bring that bunch of crooks to my door.'

He sighed and made eye contact. 'People's so-called rights are mostly an illusion,' Ken said. 'Soon as things get tough, rights go out the window.'

She opened her mouth, but the look on his face swallowed her objections. Pain had taken root in his black eyes. All the stuff with his parents . . . the relocation camps . . . losing everything . . . all of it . . . didn't take Dr Phil to figure it out . . .

their recent indignities at the hands of the government had loosened the cork in his bottle. His normal reserve had evaporated. He was more vulnerable than she'd ever seen him. She put a hand on his shoulder and left it there.

Ken leaned forward again. He gestured toward the screen. 'And this is with everything factored in?'

'Everybody between thirty and forty, male, Caucasian named Wesley Allen Howard.'

'There's . . .' He scrolled down the page, and then again and again. 'There's two hundred seventy-three names,' he said finally.

'Apparently it's a pretty popular name,' she said.

'Ya think?' he joshed.

'I can't think of any other way to pare it down.'

'Me neither.' He shook his finger at the screen. 'And that's assuming this is all of them. It's not like the Internet is a perfect source or anything either. There could be another few hundred of them out there, for all we know.'

'What we're really looking for is somebody who was reported as a missing person about seven years ago.'

'Is that public information?' Ken asked.

'I don't think so.'

Helen Willis folded her arms across her chest and stared out the window.

'We could call them all,' she said finally.

'And ask them what? Are you missing?'

'We could . . .' She paused.

'Think about it,' Ken said. 'If they answer the

phone, then they're not the person we're looking for. If they don't answer . . .'

'Then maybe . . .'

'Then maybe they're on vacation,' he finished.

'You're so negative.'

'What I am is realistic.'

She walked back and forth in front of the windows. A winddriven mist hissed against the windowpanes, creating an impressionist landscape of dots and blots and wavering edges.

Ken got to his feet. 'You've narrowed it down as much as possible. I don't see how anybody could do better.'

'Unless we got some help.'

'From who?'

She didn't answer. Instead she crossed the room, all the way to the sink at the opposite end. 'We could approach it from two directions at once,' she said.

Ken ambled her way. 'How so?'

'We could try to find out if anybody by that name was reported missing in that time period.'

'From the whole country?' He shook his head.

'And I've got this,' she said.

'This what?'

She pointed to a pint glass on the windowsill. 'This.'

The glass was old. The Coca-Cola logo on the side was beginning to fade. Half an inch of clear liquid filled the bottom. She tapped it with the tip of her finger.

'What about it?' Ken asked.

'The other night. The first time he ever spoke to me. Paul . . .' She made a face. 'I don't know what else to call him.'

'What about the other night?'

'He helped me up here. He got me a glass of water.'

Ken's eyes narrowed. 'You're thinking finger-prints.'

She nodded.

'That's not something we can do without official help either.'

'I've got an idea about that,' she said.

'I'm all ears.'

She told him.

'It's worth a try,' he said.

'First thing tomorrow.'

'Okay,' he agreed. 'First thing tomorrow.'

CHAPTER 17

He awoke to the sound of water. He imagined the gentle patter of rain on the roof above his room, the whistle of wind in the eaves, and the scrape of spring branches on the shingles. He smiled and nestled deeper into the covers. After a minute, however, the noise didn't sound quite right. He opened his eyes, and then he recalled how they drove all the way to Alabama. Thirty-three hours straight. He remembered checking in to the cheap motel in the wee hours of the morning when she just couldn't drive anymore.

He pushed himself up on his elbow and looked around. Cinder-block walls painted a dull gray. The nightstand between the beds was scarred with ancient cigarette burns. The windup alarm clock read 7:35. The air smelled of old sweat and new mildew. He pulled his feet from beneath the covers, swung them over the edge of the bed, and set them down on the orange shag carpet.

The shower stopped running. He could make out the muted sounds of Brittany moving around inside the bathroom. She was humming to herself.

140

He found his jeans and his socks on the floor and slipped them on. He was bent over tying his shoes when the bathroom door opened. She had a towel wrapped around her head and another around her body. The former appeared to be a good fit. The latter exposed nearly as much as it covered. He found himself staring at the gentle curve of her hip.

'Oops,' she said when she saw him sitting on the edge of the bed looking at her. 'Gimme a second here,' she said, pulling the towel closer around herself.

He redirected his attention to his shoelaces. He heard the towel drop and then the swish and rustle of fabric seemed to fill the room. Something in the sound warmed his innards. He attributed the sudden beads of sweat on his forehead to the hot moist air still rolling out of the bathroom. He rescued his shirt from beneath the bed, keeping his eyes averted as he buttoned up. His green Suzuki Landscaping jacket hung from a hook by the door. The black Nike bag sat on the floor beneath the jacket.

He pushed himself off the bed and walked over to the bag, rummaging around inside until he came out with a toothbrush and a nearly flattened tube of toothpaste.

'You done in the bathroom?' he asked.

'Sure,' she answered. 'Go ahead.'

By the time he came back out, she was standing at the foot of the nearest bed dressed in a pair of

141

jeans and a tight black T-shirt. A white arrow pointed upward. The bold lettering read MY EYES ARE UP HERE. She'd washed all the dye from her hair and cleaned the outlandish makeup from her face. 'Whadda you think?' she asked.

'Looks good,' he offered.

She was picking at her dirty-blond hair. 'I almost didn't recognize myself in the mirror.'

'I like it,' he said.

'Really?'

'Yeah. You look pretty.'

'I figured . . . you know . . .' She waved a hairbrush in the air. '. . . no sense making things any harder on the home folks than necessary.'

'They know you're coming?'

'Uh-uh,' she said. 'They knew I was coming, they'd probably move.'

The joke fell flat. She looked away.

He returned to his bag, replaced the things he'd taken out, and zipped it up. 'They'll be happy to see you,' he said.

'Don't bet on it,' she said, stuffing yesterday's clothes into a white plastic supermarket bag and then tying the handles together.

The notion of being unwelcome stopped him in his tracks. The idea had never occurred to him. Without his realizing it, his dream of returning to find his former life was wholly presupposed upon the assumption that the people he'd left behind would be every bit as glad to see him as he would be to see them. The possibility that he would be

142

turned away at the door sent shivers down the back of his neck. What if his sudden reappearance was an unwelcome intrusion into a new and satisfying life. What if the new life was preferable to the old and nostalgic reminders were unwanted. The prospect of rejection bounced around inside his skull like a steel ball bearing, clouding his vision, reducing him to slow motion as he shouldered his way into the jacket.

'Folks where I come from are real good at holding a grudge,' she said. She picked up the assortment of mismatched bags she'd brought inside. She raised her eyebrows. 'You ready to go?' she asked.

He nodded and picked up his bag.

Clouds of steamy breath preceded them onto the sidewalk in front of the room. The sky was a watery blue and devoid of clouds. In the distance a jagged mountain range showed its teeth. She unlocked his door and then circled the car and unlocked her own.

The roar of a tandem rig pulled his eyes out toward the highway and the café on the other side. She started the car. The *swish, swish* of the windshield wipers sounded like a jazz drummer's brushes playing counterpoint to the rattle of the engine. On each pass, the wipers pushed aside a microthin fan of moisture. Took a full ten minutes of swooshing back and forth before they could see well enough to cross the highway.

Rory's Café was jammed with truckers, tiny

butts and big guts, long wallets attached to their belts with chains. Down vests and soiled cowboy hats filled the dozen and a half stools running along and around a worn Formica counter. The service break was flanked by a pair of glass pie displays, where apple, cherry and pear, boysenberry and lemon meringue, coconut cream and a multitude of others competed for the gullet.

The front wall was lined with red booths whose venerable plastic cushions had been torn and taped and torn again until they resembled modern art. At the far end of the café, down by the restrooms, a couple of guys were on their feet, scooping up the check and dropping bills on the table for a tip. Brittany pointed and they headed that way.

It was the kind of place where everybody more or less knew everybody else and strangers were a matter of some scrutiny. The newly reincarnated Randy James heard the decibels of dialogue dim and felt the eyes poking at them as they made their way to the empty booth. Soon as they sat down, things went back to normal.

Brittany slipped out of her jacket and tossed him a menu. Before he could set it down on the table, a short Hispanic man appeared. He smiled and then wiped everything on the table, plates, glasses, cups . . . everything into a gray plastic tub. A final swipe with a damp rag and he was gone for as long as it took to find and deliver two fresh glasses of water. From behind the counter, a voice promised, 'Be right with ya.'

In the booth behind Brittany, a quartet of what appeared to be locals erupted in gales of laughter and prolonged table slapping. The water giggled in the glasses. From the sound of it, they were drunk. Either again or still, it was hard to tell which.

'You're not eating?' he asked when things quieted down and she'd made no move toward a menu of her own.

She made a face. 'I'm not much on food in the morning,' she said. 'But coffee . . . man, I got to have me some coffee.'

And she did . . . most of a pot, if he had to guess, sipping away contentedly while he put down eggs sunny side up, bacon, hash browns, and toast. He drank one cup of coffee and washed the rest of it down with water.

The new Randy picked up the check.

'I'm gonna hit the loo,' she said as they got to their feet. 'I'll meet you outside.'

He stood for a moment watching the sway of her hips as she pushed her way through the doors, then got in line to pay his check and was on his way back to the table to leave a tip when Brittany came out sauntering through the swinging door. She smiled at the sight of him, and he got that same feeling the sight of her wearing a towel had given him. She put a hand on his arm and was about to speak when a flannel-clad mountain blotted out the view.

One of the drunks from the adjoining booth had

wobbled to his feet. Fifty maybe, running hard to fat, his narrow red eyes nearly closed. Big wet lips hid a collection of brown rotted teeth. 'Butcha see, honey,' he announced with a glance over toward his friends, '. . . *my* eyes are right there . . . right there on them nice titties of yours.' He reached out for her nipple with his thumb and forefinger as if to give her a pinch. His lips were pursed and making sucking sounds.

She slapped his hand away. 'Get lost,' she told him.

From behind the counter, the waitress jumped in. 'Stop it, Morris, you hear me?'

His friends in the booth were yakking it up, pounding on the table and spitting all over one another with glee.

'Oh, come on, baby,' Morris slurred. 'Doan be that way.'

She tried to force her way past him, but he reached out to stop her. She tried to brush his arm aside but couldn't budge it.

The waitress was leaning across the counter now. 'I'm telling you, Morris. I'll call the sheriff on the whole bunch of you. Don't you think I won't.'

'Shut up, Donna,' he slurred without looking her way. She headed for the kitchen at a lope. Morris reached again for Brittany's nipple. His lips were making sucking noises again. That's when the newly christened Randy hit him square in the mouth, sending a cascade of spittle, blood, and brown teeth arching out over the three mounds of mold still sitting in the booth.

The place was quiet enough to hear the sickening sound Morris's face made when it hit the floor on a fly. Needless to say, Morris stayed down, his eyes closed, his ruined mouth agape, drooling blood onto the tile floor. After a moment he began to snore.

His pals, however, had other ideas. Unfortunately for them, the story of their lives, once again, intervened. As usual, their timing was atrocious. They struggled to their feet just in time to confront reinforcements from the kitchen. Five guys wielding an assortment of kitchen utensils, the cadre led by a bald fellow in a stained apron clutching a metal baseball bat with both hands. 'Get outta here,' he shouted. He waggled the bat at the curled figure on the floor. 'Take him with you and get the hell out of here,' he ordered.

The drunks made a brief show of manliness before two of them slung Morris's limp arms over their shoulders and lifted him off the ground. The third ran ahead and opened the doors. The toes of Morris's boots slid along the floor as he was half dragged, half carried toward the door.

The guy with the bat wasn't finished. He followed them out, pounding the head of the bat into his palm as he shouted, 'You guys learn how to behave like civilized human beings, maybe you come back. Till then, I don't want to see none of you in here no more. You hear me?'

The one holding the outside door shot him the finger on his way out. Brittany slipped into her jacket and zipped it to the throat.

147

'You okay, honey?' the waitress wanted to know.

Brittany assured her she was all right. Her shaking hands told another story, but nobody wanted to prolong the incident by asking twice. By the time the guy with the bat returned, a couple of the kitchen crew were swabbing the floor and resetting the table. The conversational level of the place was beginning to return to normal.

'Sorry,' bat said. 'Those guys are a bunch of drunken idiots. Sorry you had to—' He stopped talking and pointed to the floor. 'Over there,' he said to the guy with the mop, pointing out the jagged remains of a tooth hiding under the nearest stool. The guy picked it up and slipped it into the pocket of his apron.

The same hushed scrutiny that had ushered them in now ushered them out. Outside, the temperature had risen five degrees or so in the past half hour. Once they'd descended the three steps to ground level, Brittany thrust her arm through his. They ambled arm in arm toward the car. 'Thanks,' she said briefly, leaning the side of her face against his arm. 'I appreciate what you did in there.'

He shrugged. 'What else was I going to do?'

She laughed. 'And while I'm at it . . . I want to thank you for being a gentleman last night.' He frowned and opened his mouth. She took him by the elbow and pulled him along. '. . . not that I'm God's gift to men or anything . . .' she continued, 'but half the guys on the planet would have tried to jump my bones soon as we took off our clothes in the room last night. The other half would have waited till morning. Thanks for being nice about it.' She shook her head and made a disgusted face. 'It's a hell of a world when the only guy you know who isn't weird doesn't know who he is or where he came from.' She sighed as they walked along. 'Probably shouldn't surprise me,' she said. 'These days nobody wants to fuck anymore anyway. Everybody wants to hang you upside down and paddle your ass or something weird like that.' She slashed the air with her free hand. 'Everybody's so jaded.'

He felt blood rising in his body again. He looked straight ahead and nodded.

They were at the car now. She opened his door. His eyes followed her around the car, watching intently as she slipped the key into the lock and pulled open the driver's door. She looked up and captured his gaze over the top of the car. She'd gotten over her rant and was smiling now. 'I'm against violence, you know.' He waited for the lecture. 'I'm always telling people violence doesn't solve anything,' she continued. Her eyes twinkled in the slanted light. 'But it sure as hell solved that little problem, now, didn't it?'

They shared a hearty laugh as they got back into the car and drove the fifty yards to the Texaco station next door. 'I'll get the gas,' he said. He handed her a twenty-dollar bill and stepped out onto the asphalt; he twisted off the gas cap and pulled the nozzle free of the pump. He waited. Finally, twenty bucks and Brittany convinced the attendant to turn on the pump.

Brittany returned and began running a dripping squeegee back and forth across the windshield, pausing here and there to use a little extra elbow grease on particularly stubborn bug carcasses. He watched as she leaned against the glass, smiling to himself and settling against the side of the car. The morning sun warmed his face as he waited for the pop of the handle to signal full. What his ears caught instead was the pop of gravel under a tire. He turned toward the sound.

A Dodge pickup truck jerked to a halt just outside the pump area. Great splashes of yellow mud nearly obscured the copper-colored paint. He heard the rasp of the emergency brake and watched as the front doors swung open together, bouncing on the hinges as the two flannel mounds stepped out onto the tarmac, one carrying a heavy open-end wrench, the other hefting a three-foot length of tow chain with a big brass lock decorating the end.

They hadn't come to chat. They moved at him together, raising their respective weapons as they closed the distance between themselves and their imagined antagonist. The brass lock made a whirring sound as the guy twirled it around his head. Above the low shuffling of their boots, he heard Brittany drop the squeegee, heard the fear in her voice, and she ran his way, chanting,

'Come on. Come on,' and hurrying along the side of the car.

Instead of retreating to the car, however, Randy walked the other way, moving directly at his attackers as if determined to hasten his own demise.

For her part, Brittany was sufficiently transfixed by the bone-crunching potential of the chain to fail to notice the hose and nozzle trailing from her companion's hand. Wasn't until the hose ran out and the safety cable began to hiss from the gas pump that she slid to a stop and closed her mouth. Might have been better for the guy with the chain if he'd done the same thing. Instead, he opened his mouth to sneer just as Randy sent a high-powered river of gasoline directly at his face.

The effect was staggering. The power of the stream pushed the gas down his throat. He first bellowed and then whinnied through his nose like a horse, before tossing his breakfast onto the ground. The puddle of puke failed to break his fall. He collapsed and began to roll around in his own discharge, retching and choking and hacking, writhing in agony.

The other one took just a second too long to process the information. When he looked up, the whole world was the pressurized stream of gasoline flying toward his face, sending a wave of brown liquid over and around his head, filling his eyes and mouth, soaking his clothes, sending him reeling, separating him from the wrench as he brought his hands to his face.

He fell to his knees, threw his face into his cupped hands, and howled. The third guy poked his head around the side of the cab. He was still holding Morris's head in his lap. Looked like he was deciding what to do next. Whatever it was apparently didn't include getting out of the truck.

Randy turned on his heel, replaced the hose and nozzle. He dusted his hands and walked along the driver's side of the car. 'Get in,' he told her over the car.

She stood there with her mouth open. Looking back and forth between Randy and his attackers. 'Get in,' he said again.

He didn't have to tell her a third time. The attendant appeared in the doorway carrying a fire extinguisher. Randy started the car.

'Keep the change,' she shouted out the window.

The guy smiled and gave the okay sign.

Randy popped the clutch and floored the accelerator. They went roaring onto the highway in a dusty *whooosh*.

CHAPTER 18

The VW's front tires bounced off the curb. She blinked herself back into the moment and looked around. Dumbfounded, she pulled up the emergency brake and shut off the car.

'What day is this?' she asked.

'Wednesday, I think,' Randy said.

'What in hell has happened here?' She checked her watch. 'Ten o'clock on a Wednesday morning and the place looks like Ground Zero.'

Randy suddenly recalled an old science-fiction movie. One of those scenes right after the aliens have killed just about everybody in town except the handsome young football star and his cheerleader girlfriend. He could see their faces and hear the eerie organ music, but try as he might, neither the title nor the circumstances under which he had seen the film would come readily to mind. When the movie ended, so did his recollection, as if the memory was a solitary image floating in a sea of ebony ink.

He blinked and looked around again. Reese's Hardware, for rent. Dixie Diner, for lease. South

County Auto Parts, NAPA, available. Pack and Pay, make offer. New Price. It went on and on. The once-prosperous main street of this backwater town had been reduced to a quarter-mile stretch of empty storefronts, both sides of the street, desperate, dusty, and decaying right before your eyes. At the southern extremity, an American flag flapped in the front of an ancient Texaco sign. Directly in front of the VW, a red-and-white circle of neon glowed: OPEN. Hadley's Sweet Shop. That was it. Everything else was closed up tight.

Brittany stepped out into the street. She bumped the door closed with her hip and then turned herself in a long slow circle. By the time she took it all in, Randy stood across the car from her, stretching his arms toward the sky and groaning.

'Damn,' she said. 'When I left . . . this here was the big time, the bright lights.'

'We in Airhart?' Randy asked.

'This here's Thurston.' She pointed in the direction of the gas station. 'Airhart's five miles that way. Nothing there except another gas station and Millie's Market.' She made eye contact. 'Millie's doubles as the post office.' She pointed to a red brick building on the other side of the street. Randy nodded his understanding. The sign had long ago been removed, but the outline of the cursive script remained etched on the bricks. TRAILWAYS, it read.

'Everything's gone,' she said.

'Wal-Mart.' A deep, booming voice pulled their

154

attention back toward the sweetshop. An elderly black man in a starched white apron leaned against the doorway with a broom in his hand. 'Come in here about seven years ago. Took 'em about a year and a half to run everybody off. Ain't no competing wid them for price, and as bad as things around here is, they's no blaming people for buying on the cheap neither. Y'all get behind in your payments, you start living offa inventory, and next thing you know you got no inventory.'

'You're still here,' she said.

He smiled. 'I own the building,' he said. 'Ain't gotta make nothing but the utilities and the taxes.' He narrowed his eyes. 'You one of the Harris girls, ain't ya?'

She smiled. 'Yeah,' she admitted. 'I am.'

'Alma, right?'

She cast a quick look over at Randy. 'Yes, sir.'

'One that run off and left ol' Danny Leery at the altar.'

The smile disappeared. 'Yes, *sir*. I'm the one.'

'He's right up on the hill,' the old man said.

'Excuse me?'

'State consolidated all its offices a while back. Put 'em all up in the ol' high school building. Danny works up there. Does the DMV and issues permits, lookin' out for the county records, you know that kinda stuff. You want anything official done in this part of the county, you got to see ol' Danny.' He beckoned them forward. 'Come on in,' he said. 'Got just about anything you could ask for. Got me an espresso machine. Got wi-fi. I'm diversified is what I am. Gotta be flexible when things get bad,' he said as he turned and disappeared into the store.

'Alma?' Randy mouthed.

Brittany took a deep breath. 'Brittany is . . . you know sorta like my city name. I mean . . . think about it, can you see anybody back where we just came from being named Alma?' She shook her head in frustration.

'Who am I to talk?' Randy asked.

'No kidding,' she said, rummaging around behind the driver's seat until she came out with a silver laptop. 'Might as well check my e-mail,' she said with a shrug.

He followed her inside, where it was cool and dark. Hadley's was an old-fashioned ice-cream parlor, all stripes and squares and shiny stools. The kind of place modern designers were always trying to recreate but never quite managed to capture.

Alma ordered a double espresso, Randy a chocolate milk shake. As the old man shuffled back around the other side of the counter and Alma logged onto the Web, Randy excused himself and walked toward the restrooms. Actually it was a restroom, one of the unisex variety.

On his way back to the table, Randy hooked a leg over a stool. 'How long you been doing this for?' he asked the old man.

The old man poured chocolate milk into a stainless-steel cup. 'Me personally?'

156

'Unless there's some other kind of "me."'

The old man smiled. 'Fifty-seven years.'

'Long time to do anything.'

He dropped three scoops of chocolate ice cream into the cup with the chocolate milk.

'Used to be a lot more fun,' he said. 'Used to be a little movie theater right down the street there. Every kid for miles around'd come in for the Saturday matinee.'

He slipped the cup into the milk-shake machine and pushed the button. He walked over next to Randy. In the harsh overhead lights, the old man's skin was nearly as gray as his hair. 'Soon as the picture was over, they'd all run over here.' He waved an expansive arm. 'I'd have 'em all over the sidewalk out there.'

He flicked his bloodshot eyes in Alma's direction. 'She back to stay?' he asked.

'I don't think she knows,' Randy said.

He looked Randy up and down, 'You and her . . .' he started.

'Just traveling together.'

He lowered his voice and leaned in close. 'I'm askin' 'cause, you know . . . Danny . . .' He looked up at Randy. '. . . you know, the one she left . . .'

'I know the story.'

His eyes took on a conspiratorial cast. 'You was to ask me, I'd hafta say he was still carryin' it for that girl.'

'After all these years?'

'Some things don't change.' The old guy put the

157

period on the sentence with a nod of his head and then turned to the espresso machine.

Randy levered himself back onto both feet and rejoined Alma at the table. She was intent on the screen, pecking away at the keyboard.

'So . . .' he said, 'who's looking for you?'

She shook her head sadly. 'Not a soul,' she said. 'I've been gone three days and nobody's even noticed. It's like I was never there at all.' She stopped typing and looked at Randy. 'See, that's why I wanted to leave. The city's so impersonal. You're gone three days and it's over. Somebody else slides right into your place and nobody knows . . . hell, nobody so much as cares you're gone.'

His failure to respond pulled her eyes from the keyboard. 'Sorry,' she said. 'I wasn't thinking.'

He shrugged and looked out the window.

'You're gonna find what you're looking for. I know you are.'

'Been a long time.'

'You're going to find it.' She reached over the table and put her hand on his.

The tension was relieved by the arrival of their order. Randy handed the old guy a twenty while Alma typed with one hand and sipped coffee with the other. Randy found the milk shake too thick to drink and began spooning it contentedly into his mouth. The old man returned with the change. 'Everything all right?' he asked.

They told him it was. Several minutes passed

158

before she looked up from the keyboard. 'There's a whole lotta Wesley Allen Howards,' she said. 'All over the country. Seems like it was a pretty popular name for guys your age.'

Randy's spine stiffened; he dropped the long spoon into the tall glass and then reached out and twirled the laptop his way. She'd typed the name into something called Peoplefinders. Three hundred twenty-seven hits.

'You okay?' she asked.

'That might not have been a good idea.'

'What?'

'Typing that name. You know . . . putting it out there on the Web.'

'Why not?'

He told her about Helen Willis.

'Are you sure that's all she did?'

'No.'

'It was probably more than just looking up a name.'

'You're most likely right.'

She stopped talking and shut her computer down.

'Might be a good idea if we got out of here,' he said. 'Just in case.'

'You really think . . . you know . . . whoever these people are . . . you think they could . . . you know, some podunk place like this . . .'

'I'm probably just being paranoid,' he said.

She agreed and got to her feet. Randy left a tip on the table.

'No need to run off,' the old man said.

'Thanks for everything.' Randy waved on his way out the door.

She rested her arms on top of the car. 'Maybe we oughta back-track to Hollis . . . you know . . . maybe get a motel for the night. Start fresh in the morning.'

Randy remained silent. Fleecy clouds moved slowly across a pale blue sky. The double line of elm trees running along both sides of the street had begun to bud, sending out little patches of lime-green leaves high among the branches.

'Whadda you say?' she prompted.

'It's your trip.'

'Hey,' she said. 'I'm looking for a little feedback here. Help me out, will ya.'

'You nervous?' he asked.

She started to object but had a change of heart. 'A little . . . yeah.'

'You came a long way for this moment,' he said.

She set her jaw and grudgingly nodded her agreement. 'Might as well get it out of the way, huh?'

'Might as well,' he said.

They drove in silence. Up the length of Main Street, the vacant storefronts looking on with accusing eyes, up past the gas station and a couple of ancient clapboard houses, before the town petered out altogether, giving way to patches of thick forest surrounding hardscrabble farms, gaunt livestock, and a palpable sense of despair.

Couple miles down the road and she pulled the car to the shoulder. At first he thought it might be a silo of some sort, the way it poked into the sky.

'That's the Methodist church,' she said. 'When I was a kid, we walked there every Sunday morning, all of us, rain or shine.' She stopped and looked over at Randy. 'That was before . . . that was when Mark was still alive.' She turned her attention back to the building, bisected horizontally, like heaven and hell, wooden shakes on the top half, planks across the bottom. What must have once been the bell tower had little louvered windows all around, allowing the pealing of the bells to call the faithful to worship.

To the left of the church, a smaller building leaned precariously under the weight of an all-encompassing green vine.

'Kudzu,' he said.

She turned her attention his way. 'You know kudzu?'

He nodded.

'Where from?'

He shrugged. 'Right now, my memory doesn't have a "where" or a "when" or anything else. I keep remembering more and more things . . . movies I've seen, song lyrics . . . stuff like that, but nothing is connected to anything else. They're all just floating around in there by themselves.'

'Gotta be someplace around here,' she said. 'Someplace in the Southeast, 'cause I've been

161

pretty much all over the country, and far as I know, that's the only place it grows.'

'Who's Mark?' he asked.

'My older brother,' she said. 'Got killed in the first Gulf War.'

'Sorry.'

'Me, too. We were real close. We used to—' She stopped herself. She squared her jaw and then her shoulders. 'Let's go,' she said after a moment.

Just about the time the car got rolling again, she downshifted and turned left into a long gravel driveway. Newly plowed fields ran along both sides of the road, rows of brown dirt stretched for nearly as far as the eye could see. The smell of the earth filled the air inside the car. The air was alive with insects.

In the distance, a mighty stand of trees hovered over a clutch of buildings. Two minutes later, she brought the car to a halt in front of a white frame farmhouse. A pair of massive barns towered. A blue Ford pickup and a white Honda Civic were parked out front.

Randy watched as she steeled herself and then got out of the car. He followed her out of the car and then stayed put. A skinny blond girl, her eyes squinting in the afternoon sun, opened the door and peered out. She turned her face back over her shoulder and shouted back into the house.

'Grandma,' she called. 'I think you better come out here.'

Alma walked halfway to the house and stopped

162

in the grass. In the doorway, the girl was replaced by a middle-aged woman in rimless glasses and a patchwork apron. She was drying her hands with a baby-blue dish towel as she came down the pair of concrete steps leading to the front door and stood on the patch of lawn.

'Mama' was all Alma said.

The woman stopped in her tracks. The dish towel fell from her hands and lay in the grass like a wounded bird. She blinked several times. Without warning, tears began to roll down her face. 'Thank you, Jesus,' she said.

CHAPTER 19

She wheeled the VW out of the driveway with a bit too much throttle. The car bounced out onto the two-lane blacktop with a bang. The engine rattled twice and then stalled, leaving them sitting crossways on the pavement. Didn't matter, though. In both directions, as far as the eye could see. County Road 14 was stone empty.

'What's the big hurry?' Randy asked as she twisted the key and tried unsuccessfully to coax the car back to life.

'Papa comes home tomorrow.'

'So?'

'So . . . he's probably gonna take one look at me and send me packing.'

The engine turned over, caught for long enough to maraca the car, and then died.

'He's going to be just as glad to see you as everybody else was,' Randy scoffed.

'You don't know my papa.'

'You'll always be his little girl. That's how papas are. Stop worrying about it.'

The engine came to life with a knock and a shudder.

'You could have stayed back at the house,' she said, revving the engine.

'They were starting to ask me questions.'

She grinned. 'That's how they are. They're used to knowing everything about everybody. No strangers around here.'

'Yeah . . . except I don't know the answers to the questions.'

She laughed. 'That would have been interesting, now, wouldn't it?' She reached over and patted him on the shoulder. 'Besides . . . it's Wednesday,' she said.

'So?'

'So . . . I have to find him.'

'Your father?'

'Nooooo, dorkus . . . Danny.'

'You sure you're up to this?'

She sat up straighter. 'I gotta be.'

'Couple hours ago, you were scared your own family was going to throw you out. Now all of a sudden you're ready to face a guy you left standing at the altar.'

'If there's anybody I owe an apology, it's Danny. He was my sweetheart since the eighth grade and I . . .' She slowed the car and looked over at him. 'I've gotta make this right.' She put her eyes back on the road and seemed to consider her own words for a moment. 'At least as right as I can.' She banged a hand on the steering wheel. 'I've gotta walk out of there today feeling like I did everything I could to apologize for what I did . . . for the pain I caused him.'

'I was him . . . I'd still be pissed.'

'I wouldn't blame him if he punched me one.'

He thought about telling her what the old man in the soda fountain had told him, that this Danny Leery guy still carried a torch for her, but decided against it. She'd already made up her mind, might as well let her go through with whatever she was planning to do. He didn't feel like it was his business to be changing the whole nature of the reunion. If the old man had wanted her to know, he'd have told her.

By the time they'd blown the dust from the car, they were back in Thurston. She drove past the sweetshop and turned left at the next intersection . . . School Street, of all things . . . riding second gear up a long tree-lined incline until a long brick building came into view. She turned left into the parking lot. The afternoon sun had warmed the pavement, sending gentle heat waves rising like apparitions into the air. Spring weeds sprouted from cracks in the pavement. Three cars huddled together at the front of the lot. Here and there along the face of the building, decorations still festooned some of the classroom windows.

Directly to the right of the front doors, a black-and-white sign read COUNTY RECORDS and beneath it DMV.

She stopped the car but made no move to get

166

out. 'I graduated from everything from here,' she said, as much to herself as to Randy. 'Grammar school, junior high, high school. You just moved from one part of the building to another. Mama said they bus kids from all over the county over to Hadleyville these days.' She smiled. 'Said the school was 'bigger than a Wal-Mart,' which is my mama's idea of real big.'

A skinny man in faded coveralls and a weathered straw hat came out of the building. He hurried down the dozen stairs, got into a silver Chevy pickup truck, and drove away. She heaved a sigh. 'Maybe you ought to . . .'

He helped her out. 'No way you get me in there,' he said.

She got out of the car and then bent and leaned her forearms on the window frame.

'Don't imagine I'll be too long,' she said.

'Do what you've got to do,' he advised. 'I'll be right here.'

As she turned to leave, a middle-aged woman exited the building. Like the gentleman before her, she moved quickly, as if this were but one of many errands on her to-do list. As she passed, she offered Alma a brief, uncertain smile before getting into a faded red Honda Civic and motoring off.

Alma rocked twice in the direction of the building but failed to move her feet. Again she leaned down and peered across the seat at Randy. 'I'm scared,' she said.

'Sounds about right to me,' Randy said. 'I'd have to say this scenario here ranks right up there on the stressometer.'

She stood with her hands on her hips, swayed once, and then, without another word, turned and walked away, mounting the stairs without the usual swing of her hips, and then pausing to pat her hair into place at the door before disappearing inside.

Randy got out of the car. He stretched and then stepped up onto the sidewalk, where he lounged against a built-in bicycle rack, thinking, if he heard furniture breaking or the sounds of screams, how he'd hustle up the stairs and lend a hand.

He looked out over the roof of the car, out to the flat farm country, brown and fertile and flat as a griddle, a jigsaw puzzle of greens and browns, as rows of trees crisscrossed the plowed land without regard for reason.

Although the school couldn't have been elevated above the valley floor by more than a hundred feet, the air was warmer and sweeter up here. Randy cocked an ear toward the building, but the place remained silent as cement.

Half an hour later, an old Jeep Wagoneer pulled into the lot. From the car's open windows rolled the plaintive strains of countrywestern heartbreak. The driver was young, sixteen at the most, and singing along. She got out, threw a metal smile Randy's way as she mounted the stairs. She was inside maybe ten minutes. She came out red-faced, holding a wad of paperwork in her right hand. Her braces glinted in the sunlight as she skipped down the stairs. She raised the paperwork and giggled from behind her hand.

'You Randy?' she asked.

He said he was.

'The lovebirds want you should come inside,' she said with an embarrassed grin.

She giggled a couple more times as she got back in the Jeep, turned the radio up even louder than it had been before, and drove off. Randy waited until the girl was all the way gone and then slowly made his way up the concrete stairway. He took a deep breath and opened the door.

The interior was dark and cool. The couple locked in a passionate embrace down at the far end of the room was not. Randy smiled. No wonder the little rodeo princess had gotten her knickers warmed up. Randy started their way. Made it to within ten feet before their mutual ardor managed to sense his presence.

Danny Leery had about half the curly brown hair he'd started out with. He stood about six feet tall, a lean guy with the look of an athlete. Excess nose and a pair of eyes set too far apart wouldn't allow him to be considered outright handsome, but he was goodlooking all the same, and probably would have looked better without her lipstick spread all over his face.

169

'He's not mad,' Alma announced.

'So I see.'

Danny Leery stuck out his hand and introduced himself. Randy took the hand and moved it up and down. The palm was callused; the grip was strong. Whatever Danny did in his spare time was something way more active than shuffling county paperwork.

'When's the wedding?' Randy asked with a wry smile. The minute it left his mouth he regretted saying it. Their faces went blank. Randy winced. He held up a hand and opened his mouth to apologize.

'We're gonna take it slow this time,' Danny Leery said.

Randy closed his mouth.

'Get to know each other again,' Alma added.

'You're off to a pretty good start,' Randy said. The three of them burst out laughing. The pair threw arms around each other and held on tight.

'We've got presents for you,' Alma said.

'What's that?'

'Come on,' said Danny, leading him across the worn vinyl floor. He pointed to a piece of tape on the floor. 'Put your toes on the line.'

Randy did as he was told. When he looked up, Danny Leery had his eyes pressed up against a set of camera lenses at the end of an articulated arm. He moved the focal point up and then moved in closer. 'Give us a smile now.'

170

Randy did the best he could. He stood where he was and watched as the other man pressed a few buttons, stepped back from the apparatus, and sat down at the nearest desk and began to type.

'What's your date of birth?' he asked.

Randy held up a finger, fished the wallet out of his hip pocket, and read the appropriate information. Danny typed it into the system. A minute passed.

'You really don't have a license.' He looked over at Alma and grinned. 'That sure makes things a lot easier.'

He pushed a final button and got to his feet. 'Alma says you can drive, that's good enough for me,' he said. 'I don't do road tests these days. Most of the kids around here been driving farm machinery since they could reach the pedals.' His eyes twinkled. 'Besides, the state's closing this office for good next Tuesday, finally moving everything over to Hadleyville.'

'What are you going to do?' Randy asked.

'If I want, I can move with the office, but I expect I'll just move over to full-time farming, like most everybody else around these parts.'

The machine whirred and spit out a piece of plastic. Danny looked it over and then handed it to Randy. 'Here you go, buddy.'

Randy thanked him. 'Now all I need is something to drive.'

They passed a furtive look. 'That's my part of

171

the present,' Alma said. 'You can have the VW. I'm not going anywhere anytime soon.' She and Danny exchanged toothy grins.

Randy wouldn't hear of it. Took five minutes of hemming and hawing before he reached in his pocket and gave her back the fifteen hundred bucks she'd paid for the car.

She ran outside, grabbed the title, and signed it over to Randy. Deal complete.

They left Danny to close up shop. He was going to run home and then be over at the Harris house in about an hour.

Outside in the car, she bubbled over. 'It was like it was yesterday, like we'd never been apart. Like the conversation just took up where we left it off.' She looked his way. 'You know what I mean?' she enthused. 'You know . . . like we'd never been apart.'

'No . . .' he said truthfully, 'but I'm hoping.'

She turned out onto School Street. A white van passed them going the other way.

'You know what he told me?'

'What?'

'He told me he knew I'd be back. That it was just a matter of time.'

They stopped at the Main Street stop sign. 'He said . . .'

Her jaw muscles rippled as an immaculate eighteen-wheeler rolled by, big chrome grill and bumper glinting in the sunlight, chrome bulldog leaning his pugnacious mug into the wind, shiny chrome pipes belching diesel smoke. JB HARRIS HAULING read the fancy paint job on the door.

'Holy Jesus,' she whispered.

'Is that . . .' Randy began.

'That's my papa,' she said.

CHAPTER 20

The raindrops were huge. Bob watched as they drummed the hoods of cars and exploded on the pavement. He chose his moment with care, waiting for a break in the solid line of traffic before stepping into the street. He crossed two lanes before a yellow cab was forced to slide to a stop in order to avoid hitting him. The horn blared. The Sikh screamed at him through the window. The roar of the rain pounding on sheet metal drowned the words. He crossed another lane, waited for a *Washington Post* delivery van to pass, then hustled to the far curb, where he turned and scanned the intersection for any sign of pursuit.

He didn't dawdle but instead moved quickly down the wide stone stairway and into the city park below, where he turned hard right twice and then sidled off into the sodden shrubbery. He placed his feet carefully, avoiding several piles of watery dog shit as he moved along. The overhanging trees shattered the rain to mist as he leaned against the balustrade and waited, sipping his coffee through a hole in the plastic lid and fretting about what could possibly call for a clandestine meeting on a day like this.

Two more sips and suddenly he wasn't alone. Ron Jacobson appeared from the maze of trees and bushes on his right. His raincoat was wet all over. The brim of his hat had begun to sag, allowing a steady stream of water to run onto his shoulder.

'What's up?' he asked, trying to sound breezy. 'This is as woodsy as I've been in years.'

'We've had two more hits on the name,' Jacobson said.

'He's dead. Remember?'

'Apparently, somebody doesn't know that.'

'Somebody who?'

'One is that woman from the group home.'

'She a problem?'

'Not as I see it.'

Horns blared. Engines raced. The hiss of traffic swirled around their heads. The temptation was to talk louder. Instead, the two men moved closer together and lowered their voices.

'And the other?'

'Northern Alabama.'

The words stopped his breathing. 'Really?' he said.

'Thurston. I've got people on the way.'

'This Wesley Howard thing has gotten pretty far afield.'

'Too far.'

'I don't like it,' Bob said.

'If more could be done, I'd be doing it.'

He considered the news. The coffee was tepid. He removed the lid and dumped it onto the ground. He pushed the plastic lid down into the cup and dropped it also. Immediately, he regretted littering. He'd started to retrieve it when Jacobson spoke.

'I had a thought,' Jacobson said.

Bob straightened up. 'Oh?'

'Walter Hybridge died last year.'

Bob frowned at the segue. 'I hadn't heard,' he said.

'Prostate cancer.'

Bob winced. In the past six months, much to his wife's chagrin, he'd canceled three appointments for a checkup.

'As you know Walter was in a position to . . .'

'Much like ourselves.'

'Yes.'

'And he's no longer around to defend himself.'

'And Walter was a careful man.'

'Very quiet and very careful,' Bob agreed.

'Not the type to leave anything one way or the other in his personal papers.'

'Not the type at all.'

'His papers went to Georgetown. I doubt they've created much of a stir.' He shrugged and a small storm ran from his coat. 'Probably more of a tax deduction than anything else.'

'And?'

'And there's no telling what might be in there.'

He considered Jacobson's words. 'You're not a nice man.'

'It's how we got to where we are today.'

'Could be very hard on his family.'

176

'Sacrifices sometimes have to be made.'

'Ugly.'

'Better him than us.'

'Amen.'

'I have a man in mind.'

Bob ground the cup into the loam with his shoe. 'Are you crazy? . . . We can't—'

'He's got a weekly column in the *Post* and a daughter with nasty habits.'

'But—'

'Very nasty habits.'

Bob rocked back and forth on his heels. He asked himself how far he would go to protect one of his children and felt marginally better about Jacobson's suggestion.

'What have you got in mind?' Bob asked.

'My friend with the *Post* column goes through Walter's papers.'

'And finds what?'

'Something damaging.' Jacobson threw a nonchalant hand into the air. 'Something suggesting Walter may have compromised himself.'

'Like you said . . . better him than us.'

The sound of voices pulled Bob's attention out toward the park. When he turned back, Jacobson was gone. He bent to retrieve his coffee cup. It was gone, too.

'Who?' Kirsten Kane listened carefully as the security guard read the names again. 'You sure it's me they want to see?'

177

She listened as he posed the question.

'That's what they say.'

'Ask them what it concerns.'

She dropped the phone onto her shoulder and waited. The guard came back on the line. 'Something to do with Harmony House.'

'Ah . . .' she said. 'I've got it. Yeah, all right . . . go ahead, send them up.'

By the time she got her desk into some semblance of order, they were standing in her doorway. They made an interesting pair, she thought. Couple of months in the gym and she would have been a middle-aged stunner. He looked like the last of the samurai, all stiff-necked and haughty in an outdated suit. They stood shoulder to shoulder as if leaning on each other for support. Kirsten wondered if they were sleeping together. They certainly were comfortable in each other's space; that much was certain. The rest of it she wasn't so sure about. Her instincts said 'probably not.' She motioned them in.

'Good morning,' she said. She gestured toward the pair of chairs flanking her desk. They seated themselves and then looked to each other as if to ask who was going first. The Willis woman took the lead.

'We were hoping . . .' she began. 'We were hoping you could help us with something.'

Kirsten spread her hands. 'I'll do what I can,' she said.

'Paul . . . Paul Hardy is still missing.'

Kirsten raised an eyebrow. 'One would think a seriously disabled man would have turned up somewhere in the system by now.'

Ken and Helen passed a telling glance. 'Tell her,' Ken said.

Helen looked around the room as if seeking a way out. She looked over at Ken, who gave her a curt nod.

'He's not disabled anymore,' she said.

'Excuse me?'

Helen straightened herself in the chair, took a deep breath, and then told her everything, starting with Paul getting run over by the Lexus and ending with him saying his name wasn't Paul.

'That's quite a story.'

'I'm worried about him,' Helen said.

Kirsten shifted her gaze to Ken Suzuki. 'What about you, Mr Suzuki? Are you worried about him too?'

'I'm with her,' he said with a smile.

Kirsten laced her fingers behind her head and rocked back in her chair. 'He's over twenty-one. He's not, as far as we know, wanted for anything. As far as I can see, Mr Hardy is entitled to be wherever he chooses to be.'

'He's a ward of the state,' Helen said quickly.

The younger woman thought it over. 'Interesting,' she said finally. 'As the person in charge of Mr Hardy, you would, of course, be "in loco parentis." As such, it would not only be your right to know of Mr Hardy's whereabouts, it would be

179

your legal obligation to do so.' She unlaced her fingers and rocked forward in the chair. 'We can declare him a missing person . . . the police will—'

'That's not what we want.' Helen said it in a voice she'd never heard before. Like she had another being in her chest somewhere. Little Miss Assertive.

Kirsten stifled a sigh. 'What did you have in mind?' she asked.

'We want to know if a person named Wesley Allen Howard was reported missing anywhere between . . .' And she ran a pair of dates by her.

Kirsten asked Helen to repeat the dates. She wrote them down on a small blue notepad.

'Nationally,' Ken added.

Helen watched as the younger woman began to doodle on the page, drawing deep dark squares around the dates, sending arrows this way and that. Her pencil work lasted long enough to be awkward. 'Why not?' she asked nobody in particular. 'It's a bit outside our normal sphere of influence, but I think I can get it done discreetly.'

'And this,' Helen Willis said, offering up a brown paper sack.

'What's . . .'

'It's a water glass. It's got Paul's fingerprints all over it. Can you run this through . . . you know, that national database thing?'

'IAFIS is an FBI operation.' She folded her arms across her chest.

'Does that mean you can't do it?' Helen asked.

180

Kirsten made a face. 'In case you haven't noticed, Ms Willis, the feds are not the easiest people in the world to do business with.'

'Can't you just . . .'

'When we need this kind of information, we go through the police department.'

'Can't we leave them out of this?'

'Maybe,' Kirsten said. 'I can't promise anything, but I'll try.'

Another awkward moment passed before they both took the hint and got to their feet. They shook hands all around. Kirsten Kane watched them walk off together.

After they'd been out of sight for a while, she picked the paper bag up by the edge, carried it across the room using only her fingernails, and deposited it in the bottommost drawer of the nearest file cabinet, after which she used the toe of her shoe to slide the drawer closed. Her phone began to buzz.

CHAPTER 21

His given name was Junior. Not something or other Junior, like the name was handed down or anything, because it wasn't . . . just Junior Blaine Harris of Airhart, Alabama. Thin as a rake and brown as a berry, he'd taken one look at his prodigal daughter standing on the front lawn and his eyes had filled with tears, as he'd swept her into his arms and twirled her round and round like they used to do so long ago, back in the days when she used to dance with her daddy, her tiny feet riding the tops of his boots as they'd listened to the steel guitar crying into the night while they cut waltzing circles in the rug.

For Randy, the tearful reunion felt as if it might rend him asunder. On one hand, he was glad to have been proved right, glad the love for a daughter had reigned over ancient animosities. Happy to have been part of last night's festivities, as the family had gathered to welcome home one of their own. Grateful for the pork chops and gravy, for the green beans and the mashed potatoes and the cherry pie. Grateful and better for all of it.

182

On the other hand, he was overwhelmed by a sense of being alone in the universe, of drifting through the darkest realms of space, without direction or motive, merely following the dictates of gravity and motion. His chest felt as if a solid block of ice was at his center. For the first time since throwing himself into the car, he was forced to make his own decisions as to where he was going and when. Problem was, he didn't have a clue.

Randy watched a squadron of crows feeding in the nearest field. Inside the house, Alma and her mother were chattering away, doing the breakfast dishes together. The squeak of the screen door pulled his eyes from the squabbling crows to the back stairs. Junior Harris had traded his jeans for a pair of battered coveralls, his cowboy hat for a green cap.

He sat down on the top step and pushed his John Deere back on his head. 'You're welcome to stay for a spell,' he said. 'We can always use . . .'

Randy thanked him for the thought. 'Time for me to move on,' he said.

They went silent then, basking in the morning sun, listening to the squawk and rustle of the birds. Junior broke the spell.

'Alma was talkin' about you this morning,' he said. 'Said you was out lookin' for your people.' He paused and fixed his gaze on Randy. 'That so?'

'That's about right.'

'She said all you got is these little chunks of

183

memory. Like nothing ain't connected to nothing else.'

'That's about right, too,' Randy admitted.

'Tell me what you remember.'

Randy eyed him warily. 'Why?' he asked.

'I been deliverin' chickens and such to this part of the country for thirty-four years,' he said. 'Ain't many places I ain't gotten to or roads I ain't been down.' He pulled his cap all the way off and ran a hand over his bald head. 'Last night when Alma was tellin' us about the things you remember . . .' He paused.

'Yeah?'

'Well . . . I thought maybe I had me an idea.'

'About what?'

'About where you might start lookin' for your folks.'

'Where's that?'

'In your dream.'

'Yeah.'

'What color's the sand?'

Randy closed his eyes. 'Yellow,' he said. 'Kind of thick and grainy to the feet.'

'Gotta be Florida, then. Probably the east coast of Florida. Only place with palm trees and sand like that.'

'You sure?'

'That's the only place I ever seen it.'

Another silence settled over the morning.

'She said you seen a tower.'

'Way out at the edge of the ocean,' Randy said.

184

'Only one big ol' tower anywheres in this part of the country.'

Randy looked up. They locked gazes.

'In your dream, which side is this tower on?' Junior asked finally.

'On the water side.'

Junior let go a chuckle. 'Left or right, boy?'

'Right.'

'Then you got to be someplace near Cocoa Beach. Someplace out on the peninsula there. That's for sure.'

'Why's that?'

''Cause what you're seein' there is the tower at the space center.' He waved a hand in the air. 'You know where they send up the rockets and such. And the onliest place you can see it from, where it's on the right and close enough to make out, is right there in the Cocoa Beach area someplace. If you was up north of the center, the tower'd be on the left.'

The door squeaked again. The sound must have meant something to the crows, who suddenly took to wing and flapped off over the brown broken ground.

Alma stepped out. She was carrying her laptop beneath her arm. She put her hand on her father's shoulder. They shared a tender moment.

'You tell him?' she asked.

Junior nodded.

'Papa knew right away,' she announced with pride. 'Soon as I told him what you said . . . he knew. Just like that.'

185

She retrieved her hand, stepped around her father, and walked down the stairs.

'Got something to show you,' she said to Randy. She opened the laptop, pushed a few buttons, and waited. 'Remember that list of people with that Howard name we downloaded.'

'At the ice-cream place?'

She nodded. 'Take a look at this.'

He walked over and peered at the screen. Names and addresses filled the space from top to bottom. She'd highlighted one of the notations. It read: *Wesley Allen Howard. 432 Water Street, Cocoa Beach, Florida. 32932.*

Randy read it three times. His body began to tingle. He began to stammer.

'Maybe it's just a . . . you know . . . a weird coincidence or something.'

'Could be, I suppose,' Junior agreed.

'You really believe that?' Alma asked her father.

'Nope,' he said. 'But I guess it's possible.'

She looked over at Randy.

'Me neither,' Randy said.

'That makes three of us,' said Alma. She pushed another button and the computer shut down. She uncoiled the maze of wires wrapped around her arm and piled them on top of the laptop. She held them out. 'Here,' she said. 'Take it.'

Randy didn't move.

'I don't need it anymore,' she said.

'Sure you do. You need to—'

'I'm starting over, and I don't need that thing to remind me of what a fool I was.'

'What am I gonna do with it?'

'Anything you want. You see a sign advertising wi-fi, you just pull up out in front and tune in. Nobody'll even know you're there.'

'I can't . . . I mean . . .'

She didn't give him much of a choice. She pushed the computer against his chest and let go. He caught the whole package in his arms. She stepped forward, wrapped her arms around him, and gave him a hug and a quick peck on the cheek. 'Good luck,' she said. 'Have a safe journey.'

'You too' was all he could manage to squeak out.

He walked over to the VW's open window and dumped the load down into his bag on the passenger seat. When he turned back, she was at the top of the stairs.

'Danny's gonna be right along,' she said. 'I gotta jump in the shower.'

'Take care now,' Randy said as she disappeared inside. Felt like somebody was squeezing his heart. He opened his mouth to say something else . . . something that would keep her there on the porch, but nothing came out.

Junior gave Randy a two-fingered salute and got to his feet.

'I want to thank you for whatever part you had in bringing our girl back to us,' he said. 'We wasted a lot of good years,' he said sadly. 'I'm just hopin' we can get some of it back.'

187

'I was just along for the ride,' Randy said.

Junior's narrow eyes said he didn't think so. 'Thanks just the same.' He held the open door in one hand. 'Careful driving, now.' He eased the door closed and disappeared inside.

Randy stood for a moment in the empty yard. Two fields over, the crows circled the cloudless sky. He got in. The little car started on the second try. He sat for a moment gazing at the house and then wheeled out of the yard, trying to kick up as little dust as possible.

Five minutes later, he found himself in beautiful downtown Thurston, Alabama.

He downshifted to third as he reached the middle of town. The empty storefronts seemed to accuse. The only two cars on Main Street were parked in front of the ice-cream parlor. He began to inch over the centerline, heading for an empty spot next to the other two cars. Black cars. Black Lincoln Town Cars. Two of them. The hair on his arms stood on end.

He braked to a halt, started forward again, and then changed his mind and turned the wheel as far as it would go to the left, cutting a tight U-turn and heading back the opposite way. He turned right on Crawford Street, drove three blocks up the hill, and turned right again, following Swezey Avenue all the way to the stop sign, where, like he figured, it T-boned into School Street.

By the time he completed the loop and stopped

188

at the stop sign, things had heated up at the ice-cream parlor. A pair of suits were stuffing the struggling old man into the backseat of one of the Lincolns while another pair were putting out the 'Closed' sign and locking the front door.

He didn't wait to see what was going to happen next. He gave the little car full throttle. As he sped along the two-lane blacktop, he had a vision. Must have been from a movie he'd seen sometime, a movie where a guy in a white space suit somehow managed to sever his tether to the ship and went floating off into the blank darkness of space. The last shot was of his face, twisted in horror behind the plastic face shield as he pinwheeled into the void.

CHAPTER 22

Memory rode the hot breeze, swirling bits and pieces of his past around his head like so many scraps of litter. Seemed like the farther south he drove, the more mileposts of memory he encountered. Batches of blue water covered with boats. His head swam from the effort of trying to make sense of it.

On two occasions, the crush of images had become so vivid he'd pulled off the road, easing the car onto the shoulder, where he'd closed his eyes and waited for the torrent to subside. The second time he'd fallen asleep in the driver's seat, only to be roused by a seriously annoyed Alabama state trooper, who admonished him about the dangers of sleeping on the side of the road, checked and rechecked his paperwork, and then grudgingly sent him on his way.

The DJ said it was 4:37 in the morning when he crossed from Alabama into Florida on the old highway just north of Monticello. He passed the green 'Welcome to the Sunshine State' sign just as the sun poked its first fiery glint over the horizon. On the radio now, some guy with a rusty

190

voice was singing about looking for the heart of Saturday night as Randy spotted the sign for the rest area, two miles ahead. Other than a quick stop for gas, he hadn't been out of the car since he left Airhart, and needed to take a piss for the ages.

As promised, the exit road materialized from out of the darkness. He veered off the highway, took the right-hand fork, and drove toward the back of the rest area. On the far side, half a dozen truckers were cooped for the night, their orange roof lights gleaming like teeth in the darkness. On his car's passenger side, a black Mercedes was the only vehicle in the lot. He brought the VW to a halt as far from the Mercedes as he could get and eased himself out onto the pavement.

He felt like the Tin Man, brainless and rusty at the joints. He windmilled his arms and twisted his torso back and forth as he waited for gravity to bring his legs back to life. Overhead, the carpet of stars had begun to slide beneath the dawn. The air was hot and moist. For reasons he couldn't put his finger on, this moment seemed more right than any he could readily remember. He walked around the other side of the car and grabbed his bag. Figured he'd clean himself up a bit, maybe change his shirt while he had the chance.

His back was stiff and his kidneys ached as he made his way up the path toward the cinder-block restrooms. A trio of soft-drink dispensers were chained to the front of the building. The red-and-white display panel on the Coke machine had been bludgeoned to plastic shards. The pay telephone had been torn from the wall and reduced to rubble.

The recessed light fixtures in the overhang had attracted a menagerie of insects, some crawling upside down across the oily stains, others driven mad by instinct, flying about the lights in endless circles of futility.

As he approached the door to the men's room, a sudden plaintive note rose above the drone and crackle of the insects. Randy took hold of the door handle; cocking his head, he listened, wondering whether the sound was in real time or something remembered . . . lately he was never sure . . . he wondered whether the urgency in the sound was his own anxiety or that of some third party.

He pulled open the door and stepped inside. A pair of figures struggled in the center of the floor. On top was a guy in his late thirties. His faded Red Sox baseball cap had fallen from his head and lay among the wadded paper towels littering the floor. His freckled pate was surrounded by a fringe of stringy hair. He had one knee on top of the other figure, pinning him to the floor while he whaled away with his free hand, smacking the writhing figure about the head and shoulders. 'You little bastard,' he grunted as he swung his fist. 'I'm gonna kick your fuckin' ass, you hear me?' When he swung and missed another couple of times, he

192

grabbed the collar of the smaller man's jacket and pulled him up to his knees, where he could get a better angle on his punches. That's when he noticed Randy standing in the doorway.

'You know what's good for you, my man, you'll get the fuck out of here,' he said.

'I need to take a leak,' Randy answered.

The guy let go of the collar and straightened up. As the loose jacket fell back into place, Randy could see now that the figure on the floor was a boy, mixed race, maybe nine or ten, bad chili-bowl haircut, deep olive skin, big brown eyes wide with terror.

Two things were immediately clear to Randy. One was that if anything were to get between himself and the urinals, he surely was going to piss all over himself. Two was the certainty there was no way he was leaving the kid with this lunatic when he left.

The minute his antagonist stepped toward Randy, the kid went scuttling across the floor like a cockroach with a meth jones, trying to put as much distance between himself and his attacker as could be managed in a ten-by-ten room. Randy watched as the kid crawled under the side of the nearest stall. He heard the snap of the lock and then watched the kid's feet vanish from view.

Red Sox straightened his shoulders and puffed out his chest. 'You hear me, asshole?'

'I heard you,' Randy said. 'But like I said, man, I *really* gotta take a leak.' He stepped around the guy and made his way over to the urinals, where he set the bag on the floor, hoping he could delay the inevitable for long enough to take care of business.

No such luck. Before he could even reach for his zipper, the guy punched him in the back of the head, sending Randy staggering forward, bouncing his skull off the wall, nearly shutting off his lights altogether, leaving Randy with intermittent strobe-light vision and just enough wherewithal to slip the next punch. Nearly blind, his head threatening to detonate, he lurched forward and threw his arms around the guy.

They stood, locked in their feral embrace, staring into each other's bulging eyes for a long second before the guy drew back his head and butted him in the face. Randy's ears began to roar like a blast furnace. He got a forearm in between their faces and pushed his elbow into the guy's throat. The guy danced backward with the rhythmic surety of a boxer and then lowered his head and charged, driving his shoulder into Randy's midsection, throwing him off balance and then forcing his quarry down onto the filthy floor.

On his knees now, Randy pawed at his own face, as if any laying on of hands would somehow end the roaring in his ears and restore his shattered vision. Red Sox grabbed him by the hair and forced his face down into the urinal, then slipped his arm across Randy's throat. Caught between a powerful biceps and a bony forearm,

Randy's throat was nearly closed. They struggled together, red-faced and shaking from the exertion, until, after what seemed like ages, Randy's oxygen-deprived muscles started to run out of gas and his neck began to bow, ratcheting downward a millimeter at a time until the tip of Randy's nose brushed the round deodorizer at the bottom of the bowl, gathering within him an adrenaline-fueled surge of revulsion sufficient to explode him upward with enough force to pull his face completely clear of the smelly receptacle.

Not for long. Red Sox quickly parlayed the chokehold into a half-nelson, bending Randy forward again, pushing his face down into the urinal. Randy gulped a rancid breath, reached behind himself, and grabbed the guy's ankle and pulled as hard as he was able. He felt the pressure on his neck lessen as the guy struggled to retain his balance. He pulled again and this time threw his weight backward, breaking the grip on his neck and sending his antagonist reeling across the room.

Randy stood still, gulping air. Adrenaline had cleared his vision. His head throbbed to the beat of his heart. He wiped his mouth with his sleeve just as the guy came at him again, on the run, like a linebacker trying to drive him through the wall.

Randy timed the rush and brought his knee up at precisely the right moment. The crack of his knee meeting the guy's chin ricocheted around the room like a whiplash; the click of his teeth coming together served as an echo.

The guy's legs gave. He was still trying to bear-hug Randy around the waist as the rest of him headed south. Randy pushed him off and stepped over to the side.

'Hey, man,' he started, '. . . no reason we got to . . .'

The guy was sitting on the floor with his tongue hanging out, leaning back against the wall next to the trash can and then . . . he was reaching inside his jacket for something . . . something black and . . .

Randy took a long step across the floor and kicked Red Sox as hard as he could, catching him a little farther beneath the chin than he'd intended, driving his lower teeth into his tongue and slamming his head back against the wall with a hollow thud.

And then, except for his own labored breathing, the room was silent.

Until Red Sox began to blow bubbles in the thick blood running from his mouth and down over his chin, *pip, pip, pip*, with every ragged breath.

From the look of it, the guy had very nearly bitten his tongue in half. Randy didn't bother to check further. Instead he walked over to the nearest stall and kicked open the door. The kid was standing on the toilet with his fist raised to defend himself.

'You better come with me,' Randy said.

'Leave me be,' the kid said.

'Okay,' Randy said. 'But you probably better not be here when . . .' – he gestured toward the floor – 'when this guy wakes up.'

Took the kid a minute to make sense of it. He jumped down from his perch, pushed his way past Randy, and approached the unconscious man on the floor the way the wary would approach a sleeping rhino. Satisfied that Red Sox wasn't going to be jumping to his feet anytime soon, the kid hauled off and kicked the guy in the chest. He was winding up for another field goal attempt when Randy pulled him away.

'Nah,' Randy said. 'That's not right.'

The kid jerked himself loose. 'Don't be talking to me about right, motherfucker. You don't know a goddamn thing about . . .' – he threw a hand at the unconscious man – 'that motherfucker there . . .' He was starting to cry.

'Like I said, kid, you probably better come with me.' He didn't wait for the kid to say anything but instead turned and walked away over to the urinals, where he unzipped himself and began doing what he'd come in there for in the first place.

The kid was buffeted between his fears. 'How'd I know you ain't some fucking pervert . . . ten miles down the fuckin' road gonna want a blow job . . . some kinky shit like that.'

'Not my style, kid.'

'My name ain't *kid*, motherfucker.'

'What is it, then?'

'Acey.'

'Nobody's named Acey.' Randy finished up, patted everything back into place, and turned toward the kid. 'Well?'

'My mama named me Achilles,' the kid said. He rolled his eyes upward. 'Now, what kinda crazy crack ho gonna name a kid a thing like that? See some dumb-ass movie on TV and name a kid some dumb-ass name like Achilles. Bitch out of her mind.'

Randy washed his hands in the sink, then washed his face. Twice.

'Everybody call me Acey.'

Randy dried himself with a stiff brown paper towel.

'Okay, Acey. I'm thinkin' we better get out of here.'

Acey looked down at the floor again. He shook his head. 'Dog. I'm telling ya, we don't want this crazy bastard following us. You maya got lucky wid him one time, but it ain't gonna happen twice.'

Randy retrieved his bag and started for the door. 'Take his car keys. Take his cell phone. That'll slow him down some.' He stopped. 'Matter of fact, take everything.' The kid was patting him down as Randy stepped outside.

The sun was a bloody welt on the horizon. The jagged silhouettes of palm trees darkened the flaming vista here and there as Randy stepped around the corner of the building and headed back to the car. One pace and he turned on his heel,

198

stepping back out of sight, just as the kid came bouncing out the door.

Randy stuck out his arm and stopped the kid's forward motion. He pressed his index finger against his lips. 'Cops outside,' he said. 'We're going to take the Mercedes. Like we've known each other for years.'

The kid nodded his understanding.

'Give me the keys,' Randy whispered.

Acey rummaged around in his assorted jacket pockets until he came out with a heavy set of keys attached to an electronic keypad. 'Green button opens the doors,' he said. Randy fished in his own pants pocket and came out with the VW key. 'Put this in his pocket,' he said to the kid, who snatched the key and hurried back inside.

Randy poked his head around the corner. Looked like they were waiting for backup. A pair of Florida state mounties had the VW covered. They'd used their patrol car to prevent a retreat and had assumed the combat position, arms resting on the top of their patrol car, guns at the ready.

Randy shifted the bag to his left hand and took the kid by the shoulder. Together, they stepped out into the hazy sunshine. As they came down the walk, the cops frantically waved them away from their line of fire, over toward the far end of the lot and the Mercedes. The pair turned and walked quickly in the specified direction.

As they approached the car, Randy opened the

doors and stood for a moment at the passenger door while Acey belted himself in, all parental-like. He dropped his bag onto the backseat, closed the door, and turned to the cops.

'Guy's in the bathroom,' he said. 'I was just gonna call 911.' The cops relaxed a bit. Randy went on, 'Looks like he's had some sort of fit or something. Bit his own tongue. Y'all probably better get a wagon out here.'

Randy stood still. He watched as one of the cops got on the radio. Watched as they loped up the walk together, guns along their sides. Minute they stepped out of sight, he slid into the driver's seat, slipped the key into the slot, and started the car.

'You fucking crazy?' Acey said. 'You know that man?'

'You do what I told you? You take everything?'

'Lessen he had it up his ass,' the kid said.

CHAPTER 23

Fifty miles disappeared under the tires before either of them spoke. Randy kept one eye glued on the rearview mirror and the other bouncing up and down between the speedometer and the road. Over in the passenger seat, the kid had looked like he was watching a tennis match, rotating his head back and forth like a bobble-head doll.

'You think they comin'?' he asked finally.

'No,' Randy said. 'They was coming, they'da been all over us by now.'

'You sure?'

'I've been driving the speed limit. Besides . . . your friend back there . . . he's got no ID at all. He's got the key to the VW in his pocket. Not to mention the fact that the first thing those cops are going to do is slap him on a gurney and get him to the nearest hospital. Assuming he wakes up somewhere along the way, he's still gonna have a hell of a time explaining himself with that busted-up mouth of his.'

The kid took it in. He allowed a narrow smile to form on his lips. 'That was smart, dog. That thing wid the key in his pocket.' He nodded his admiration. 'That was hella smart.' Randy felt the boy's eyes on the side of his face.

A minute later, Acey began to empty his pockets onto the console. First a black wallet. Randy picked it up and flipped it open. Florida driver's license. Chester D. Berry. South Miami address. From the corner of his eye Randy saw the kid set something else down. He adjusted the steering wheel and peeked down. His throat felt like Chester Berry still had him around the neck. An automatic. Nine-millimeter from the looks of it. He picked it up and hefted it in his hand.

'Where in hell did you get this?' he asked.

'Offin him,' Acey said.

'You know he was carrying?'

Acey gave him a 'damn you're dumb' look. 'Shit, yeah. Them assholes always packin'.'

'What assholes is that?'

Acey pulled what looked like another wallet out of his pocket. He held it up and allowed the case to fall open. Big gold badge. *Miami-Dade Police Department. Detective First Class. Chester Berry.*

Randy put both eyes back on the road and took several deep breaths, trying to still the rampant beating of his heart.

'You coulda told me the guy was a cop,' he said after he'd calmed down a bit.

'Ain't no real cop.'

'What kinda cop isn't real?'

'The pimp kind,' the kid said. 'Kind don't help people.'

'If he doesn't help people, what does he do?'

'He line himself up, dog.'

'What's that mean?'

'He's a rock cop, dog.' Acey looked disgusted. He banged his fist against the passenger window. 'Where you think he got this ride, dog? You think cops got the cheese to be buying a short like this?'

'How'd you end up with him?'

'It's a long story,' the kid said, turning his face away.

'I'm in no hurry.'

The boy continued to look out the side window. They were driving through a low forest, dwarf pines, palmetto, and swamp grass running off in all directions, as far as the gaze could follow. Dawn was done, traffic was picking up. From the corner of his eye, Randy watched the boy's reflection change from exasperation to embarrassment.

'My mama give me to him,' Acey said after a moment.

'Gave you to him?'

'She owe him money.'

'For what?'

'For rock, dog. What you think?'

'How was I supposed to know?'

'She's a rock ho. Ain't nothin' in a rock ho's min 'cept rocks.'

'So . . . what were you and Mr Berry doing in the restroom there?'

'You saw, dog. He was kickin' my ass, is what we was doin'.'

'For what?'

'For tryin' to jump out his fuckin' car.'

'Why in the bathroom?'

''Cause he doan wanna fuck up his car, man. Whadda you think?'

Randy processed the words and then asked, 'What was he gonna do with you?'

'Gonna take me up to Atlanta. Gonna sell me to this pimp he know up there.'

Randy had already decided not to ask another question, but the kid went on.

'Gonna have me work off my mama's freight.'

The fiery ball rising in the east forced Randy to swing the sun visor around to keep the left side of his head from melting. He reached for the air-conditioning, fumbled unsuccessfully with the controls several times before the kid slapped his hand away and did it himself.

The Mercedes was everything the VW wasn't: fast, luxurious, roomy, and responsive to the touch. He felt at home behind the wheel but didn't know why.

Randy asked, 'So where you headed now?'

The boy thought it over. 'Goin' to my auntie's, I guess,' he said.

'Won't she just call your mama?'

He made a face. 'She give up on that dumb ho sista o' hers years ago. I'm the only fool still hung wid that crazy bitch.' His lower lip began to tremble.

204

He set his jaw like a bass. 'Auntie Jean say anytime I get so's I can't deal wid it anymores, I'm welcome to crib wid her.'

'Where's your auntie live?'

'Port St Lucie.'

'I'll buy you a bus ticket first chance I get.'

The kid went through his pockets and came out with a big roll of cash.

'Gonna take me a fuckin' cab,' the kid said.

'That his?' Randy asked.

'Not no more,' he said with a flash of a grin.

'What else you got in those pockets? You got a sandwich in there somewhere? I'm hungry as hell.'

The boy laughed. 'Just this,' he said, waving a cell phone.

'Lemme see,' Randy said.

The kid handed the phone over.

'You don't want to be using this,' Randy said. 'He'll find your butt in a heartbeat, you start using his phone.'

Acey nodded his understanding. 'Smart,' he said.

Acey glanced down at the wallet, the cash, the badge case, the automatic, and the silencer. 'What about this shit here?' he asked.

Randy handed him back the phone and pointed at the glove box. 'Put it all in there,' he said. After the kid had shoveled everything inside, Randy bent over and locked it.

'So what's your story?' the boy asked.

Randy set the cruise control on sixty and settled back into the plush seat. 'What story?'

'The story where a couple of cops are bringin' serious heat on your POS back there. You seen 'em. They was roustin' your ass hard.'

'What's a POS?'

'A piece of shit,' dog. Doan fuck wid me. What's the deal?'

'It's complicated.'

'I got time.'

Randy smiled and then told him, sort of like the *Reader's Digest* abridged version. Took about five minutes. 'So lemme see I got this lined up,' the boy said. 'You doan know who the fuck you are.'

'More or less.'

'Mostly more.'

'Yeah.'

'All you got is the address of some crib in Cocoa Beach where this dude you think you might be . . . but you ain't sure . . . might fuckin' live.'

'Something like that.'

'Sheeeeet. You even more fucked up than me.'

'Are you capable of forming a sentence that doesn't include some form of the word *fuck* in it?'

'Why the fuck would I wanna do that?'

Randy threw a glance his way. The kid grinned. 'I'm just clownin' wid you, dog. Lighten up. Doan be getting brittle on me now.'

'Brittle, huh?'

'Where you goin'?'

'I told you . . . Cocoa Beach.'

'The address, dog. The address.'

'Four thirty-two Water Street, Cocoa Beach, Florida. 32932.'

The kid pushed a button on the dashboard. A panel slid upward revealing what looked like a small computer keyboard. The kid pushed some more buttons. A map and a set of directions shared the screen.

'There you go,' the kid said. 'Hundred eighty-one miles.'

'Wow,' Randy said.

'GPS,' Acey said.

'What's that mean?'

'On Star.'

'What's that?'

'Fucked if I know.'

CHAPTER 24

The ambient light flickered. Kirsten looked up from the deposition she was reading. The estimable Bruce Gill didn't wait to be invited in. He elbowed the door closed, crossed to the green leather chair, and plopped himself down. In general, if the D.A. wanted to see you, you were summoned to his office. Precedent for arriving elsewhere unannounced, while not unknown, was sufficiently unusual as to command Kirsten's undivided attention.

'What's up?' she asked.

He pulled a sheaf of legal papers from the pocket of his suit jacket and dropped them into his lap. 'You remember the Robbins case?' he asked.

She silently repeated the name to herself several times. When nothing came into focus, she said, 'Not really?'

'Me neither.'

'So?'

'So we . . . you and I . . . are being hauled before the state ethics board.'

'For what?'

'Jury tampering. Suborning perjury and hindering prosecution.'

'On this Robbins case?'

'Yup.'

'What's the Robbins case?'

'Remember . . .' He unfolded the document and peeked inside. 'Nineteen ninety-nine. The guy named Neil Robbins owned a pawn-shop. Guy who was using street people and junkies to commit burglaries for him.'

'Okay . . .' she said, nodding. 'I've got a glimmer. Guy was a real scumbag, as I recall. Identity theft. Lots of mailbox burglaries.' She slapped the desk. 'Feds tried to hijack the case from us.'

'Guy got out on appeal.'

'I hadn't heard.' She leaned forward and held out her hand. He made no move to hand the document over.

'Let me save you the trouble,' he said. 'The gist of the charge is that you and I took money . . .' She started to protest, but the D.A. held up a forestalling hand. 'Me in the form of illegal political contributions and you in the form of a direct injection into an offshore account.'

'In return for what?'

'In return for creating enough doubt and confusion to virtually ensure the case would be reversed on appeal.'

'Didn't we get him fifteen, sixteen years, something like that?'

'He did four months.'

'Wasn't Irving Reist his attorney?'

'Yup.'

'Irving's good.' She spread her hands. 'We don't win 'em all.'

His brow was knit and his face beginning to color. 'Where in hell did this come from?' He leaned closer. 'I don't need this crap in an election year.'

'Don't look at me,' she said. 'I was second chair. You made the case.'

'It was a good case.'

'That's the way I remember it, too.'

'It was also a damn good choice.'

'What was a good choice?'

'The Robbins case,' he said. 'Whoever's trying to bust our collective chops here chose a hell of a good case. Our witnesses were a bunch of winos and junkies. All of them with sheets; all of them willing to say whatever as long as the price was right.'

'And most of whom we pressured into testifying against Robbins.'

'Kind of people it's easy to pressure.'

'The case was solid.'

He looked at her with an unspoken question in his eyes.

'Not only all of that, but we resisted when the feds wanted to take over,' he said. 'Like we had some agenda other than just the law.'

'Wouldn't take a leap of faith to see it that way,' she admitted.

Not the answer he wanted to hear. 'Where in hell did this come from?'

'Don't look at me,' she said. 'I was just along for the ride.' She held up her right hand. 'Not to mention the fact that I don't have an offshore bank account. Hell, I've barely got an onshore bank account.'

The D.A. waved her off as if to say she was preaching to the choir.

A knock rattled the door. 'Yeah,' Kirsten said.

One of the pool secretaries entered. 'For you,' she said, handing over an oft-used manila envelope to Kirsten. On other days Kirsten might have been amused by the look on the girl's face when she realized who the other party in the room was, but not today.

Kirsten thanked her. They watched her disappear.

'If this is Morgan's doing . . .' Gill muttered.

Brent Morgan was a local personal-injury attorney who'd parlayed a series of earnest TV commercials and a complete absence of ethics into a multimillion-dollar practice and was the best bet to be running against Gill in the upcoming election. The courthouse rumor mill held that Morgan had a team of researchers electronically combing the incumbent's past cases looking for anything they could parade before the public in the next election.

'That would be a new low . . . even for Morgan,' Kirsten threw in.

She unwound the little red string holding the envelope closed and pulled out a sheet of computer paper.

'If that son of a bitch—' the D.A. began.

'Whoa, Nellie,' Kirsten said.

'Nellie who?'

'Talk about timing.'

He reached across the desk and snatched the paper from her hand. Under other circumstances, with other people, she could have taken offense. Bruce Gill, however, was used to being the big dog and generally expected a certain degree of forbearance regardless of the situation. Kirsten calmly sat back and watched as he read his way down to the bottom of the page.

'Timing indeed,' he said when he'd finished.

'You really think . . . ?'

He rattled the paper. 'Tell me about this,' he said.

Took about a minute to tell the tale of Helen Willis and Ken Suzuki visiting her office, of checking to see if any Wesley Allen Howard had been reported missing during the years in question.

'First the carrot, then the stick,' Bruce Gill said.

'Excuse?'

'They tried to bribe both of us . . . exciting new job for you . . . expanded national exposure for me . . .' He paused to be sure she was with him and then continued. '. . . aaaaaand when we didn't immediately jump on board . . .'

'This thing shows up,' she finished.

212

He got to his feet.

'As you know . . . I don't believe in co-incidences.'

'As *you* know . . . that makes two of us.'

'End of carrot,' he said. 'We had our chance to nibble and we didn't. Now they're gonna kick our ass.'

'All they're accomplishing is they're getting my attention,' Kirsten said.

His teeth were showing, but it wasn't a smile. 'You send the glass to IAFIS?'

She shook her head.

'Don't tell me you threw it away?'

She hesitated just long enough to make him sweat. 'Yeah, sure,' she said, levering herself to her feet and retrieving the paper bag from the file cabinet.

'Gimme that thing,' he said. 'It's about time we started getting a little more proactive around here.'

'Yes . . . I understand. Thank you.' Helen set the phone back on the desk.

Across the room, Ken Suzuki read the news on her face. 'Well?'

'Nothing,' she said.

'I'da thought . . . with all those names . . .' he began.

'Me, too.'

'What now?'

'I don't know.'

'Any word on the fingerprints?'

'No.'

'I guess that takes longer.'

She flicked a glance his way and then got to her feet and walked over to the sink, where she turned on the water as if to wash dishes. She hoped to hide her frustration, lest he misinterpret and think she was unhappy with him, which couldn't be further from the truth. He was a dear man. Always trying to put a good face on things whether he believed it or not. She turned her head and smiled at him.

'She didn't make any promises anyway,' he reminded her.

Helen turned back and fixed her attention on the sink, allowing the warm water to cascade over her hands, warming both her fingers and her soul, as if the rushing water could somehow wash the whole mess away. To Helen, the situation with Paul Hardy seemed like a fall from grace, as if everything that transpired prior to Paul's accident had been the golden days of innocence and everything that had happened since had become the slate-gray days of experience. Despite her efforts to find a silver lining, it seemed as if something valuable had been lost without anything having been gained in return. A single tear escaped from her right eye and rolled slowly down the side of her face.

Ken was at her side now. 'You okay?' he wanted to know.

She hugged herself and nodded the kind of nod designed to convey the opposite message, something more like wounded pluck or grit in the face of horror. He stepped in close and put both hands on her shoulders. She leaned into him, resting the side of her face on his chest. She could feel the rhythm of his breathing as she began to sob.

He put a hand around her head and pulled her to him. She went willingly, turning herself away from the sink and allowing her tears to fall onto his blue work shirt.

'I'm just so frustrated,' she said between sobs.

'I know.'

'I feel like I need to do something.'

'Maybe something will come from the finger-prints.'

'What if it doesn't?'

'I don't know.'

She threw her arms around his neck and began to bawl. Wasn't until she'd cried out her anger that she noticed how close to each other they were. How their usual chaste hip-to-hip embraces had today evolved into a full-frontal hug. She held on tighter and wondered something she had wondered before. About Ken and whether he was experienced in these matters . . . because she certainly wasn't. She wondered whether he would be able to guide a neophyte like herself. Whether her lack of experience would sour the experience or whether . . . She hugged him tighter, pushing her substantial breasts against his chest. Her sobbing subsided.

'It's okay,' he said in a strangled voice.

CHAPTER 25

Coupla minor problems. One . . . they came in from the opposite end of the street, so it looked way different. Two . . . it was daytime and the streetlights weren't doing their thing. Didn't matter, though . . . half an hour in, Randy snapped to it. This was his street of dreams. The same opulent suburban neighborhood he saw every night when he closed his eyes. The realization weakened his knees.

They sat on top of a weathered picnic table at the back of a little neighborhood park, diagonally across the street from 432 Water Street. The houses sat on double or maybe even triple lots. Four thirty-two was, like the others on the street, an enormous two-story, white with black trim. The roof line suggested a vaulted ceiling on the ground floor, with a bunch of bedrooms upstairs. A quick trip around the block had revealed the obligatory lanai out back. The maturity of the landscaping and the size of the houses screamed of the late fifties. Cocoa Beach, Florida. Your Tropical Dreams Come True!

Acey sucked on a cherry Popsicle. His lips and mouth were harlequin red.

216

'You scared?' he asked between slurps.

'Why would I be scared?'

'Scared don't need no "why," dog. You either scared or you ain't.'

'Maybe a little.'

''Bout what?'

'I don't know,' Randy said.

'Maybe you scareda dat blond bitch.' Acey referred to the leggy woman they'd seen collecting the afternoon newspaper a half hour back. 'Maybe you one of those guys like my ol' man . . . go out one time fo' cigarettes and doan nobody see your ass again.'

'I don't smoke.'

Acey wasn't going for diversions. 'You figure dat ho see you again after all this time, she gonna put an ice pick in you' fuckin' ear.'

'I thought we had an agreement about that word.'

'I'm workin on it, dog. Ol' habits die hard.' With that, he went back to scowling and slurping his Popsicle.

The air was hot and thick and wet. Without enough breeze to stir their fronds, the trees hung limp. Randy dropped his head into his hands. He still harbored a dull ache deep behind his forehead. The images of things past were coming thicker than ever now, sounds and faces and places blazing past the inside of his eyes, like shop windows seen from a fast-moving train.

An elbow to the ribs lifted his gaze. In the street,

a blue-and-white police cruiser rolled slowly by the Mercedes. 'Nosy mother-fuckers,' Acey muttered. 'Wanna make sure dere ain't no niggers hanging round.' He giggled to himself. ''Cept dey know for sure some nigger woulda pimped that ride first thing.'

An hour ago they'd disagreed about how and where to wait. Acey'd wanted to stay in the air-conditioned car, but Randy knew better. The Mercedes was the only car parked in the street. Neighborhoods like this didn't park cars in the street. Probably against community covenants and that kind of shit. Way Randy saw it, sitting in the car was an invitation to meet the local cops. To show ID. To answer questions regarding his relationship with Acey. None of which appealed to his sense of well-being. Instead they'd repaired to their present position, deep in the shade, three quarters of a block down from the car, on the opposite side of the street.

'Smart, dog. Hella smart,' the boy said as they watched the cruiser roll away. The whine and growl of a school bus brushed the words aside. They sat on the table and watched as half a dozen children disgorged themselves from the bright yellow bus.

The kids stayed in a chattering knot for a moment and then, in ones and twos, splintered off in the direction of home, leaving only a pair of blond girls standing on the sidewalk. Took a minute for Randy to realize they were twins. They didn't dress the same anymore. Matter of fact, they looked so different from each other Randy wondered whether they hadn't gotten together and coordinated the difference.

'About your age,' Randy said.

'Punks,' Acey retorted.

'Hey now.'

'SpongeBob backpacks.' The boy sneered. 'That's fuckin' gay.'

Randy resisted the urge to disagree. Instead he watched in silence as the girls walked the half a block to 432, where the blond woman met them at the door. In the surrounding stillness, Randy heard the door click behind them. A minute passed.

'Well, dog, you gonna do it or not?'

'Don't rush me.'

'This what you come all this way for, ain't it?'

Randy dropped his head into his hands again, massaging his temples with his thumbs as arcs of images lit up the inside of his head like signal flares.

'You okay?'

Randy looked up into the boy's brown eyes. 'You're right,' he said. 'I'm scared.'

'Doan worry 'bout it, dog. I been scared long as I can remember. Scared 'bout what that dumb ho gonna do wid me next. Scared some john gonna fuck her up more dan she already fucked up. Scared of the cops. Scared of the welfare people. I been scared of all dat shit my whole damn life.'

'Kid your age, that's not right.'

'Right got nothin' to do wid nothin',' the boy said. 'There's what is and what ain't.' He cut the air with his bare Popsicle stick. 'That's the whole show right dere.'

Randy kept his gaze pinned on the boy. Behind the bravado was . . . was something else . . . terror probably. He wondered how a kid this age had managed to lose all sense of the ideal. How his short life had managed to extinguish that flickering sense of fairness most people carry inside themselves forever. That instinctual scale of justice with which people persistently refuse to part, no matter how many times they've been told that 'life isn't fair' or they 'gotta roll with the punches' or any of the million other phrases designed to snuff out the eternal flame of how things actually 'should' be.

Randy slid down off the table. 'I'll be back,' he said.

'Good luck, dog,' Acey said as Randy walked away.

The sun was behind him as he crossed the street, stepped over the patch of grass separating the street from the sidewalk, where, for some reason, he thought of Shirley and all the odd funny things she had to say. He wondered how so much inner grace could have been contained in such an ungraceful exterior. He started to think it wasn't fair but cut himself off midthought with a bitter laugh.

Once on the sidewalk, he stopped walking and looked back at the park. He was barely able to make out Acey in the gloom of foliage. The boy waved him forward. He took a step. His head swam. He thought he might pass out.

A single electronic *whoop* broke the spell. Randy looked over his shoulder just in time to watch a private security vehicle slide to a stop. The passenger side window slid down. The uniformed driver leaned over far enough to look Randy in the eye. He was black as the Beach Commons security car and just about as shiny.

'Help you, sir?' The voice asked not so much if Randy needed assistance but instead tacitly demanded an explanation for his presence on the street.

'Visiting friends,' Randy said with a car salesman smile.

'Who would that be?'

'Four thirty-two Water Street.' Randy anticipated the next question. 'Wesley Howard.'

The guy pushed a few buttons on his dashboard computer, then looked up.

'Have a nice day, sir,' he said without conviction. The window slid up. The car drove silently off down Water Street. Randy stood and watched until the car turned right two blocks down and disappeared from view.

Over in the park, Acey was on his feet now, standing with his hands on his hips, poised and ready to run. Randy gave him a wave and received one in return. He watched as the boy climbed back on the table and sat down, then turned and continued down the side-walk to 432, where he mounted the small porch and rang the bell.

He was about to ring again when he heard the rattling of a chain followed by the snapping of a bolt. The door eased open. One of the girls held the door in both hands. She had what he thought were the bluest eyes he had ever seen. For a moment he wondered if everybody didn't start their lives with radiant eyes, only to have time and circumstance, little by little, dim the glow, to the point where the so-called windows of the soul came to function more like barricades.

'Is your mom or dad home?' Randy asked.

Opening her mouth to speak revealed a mouthful of clear plastic braces. 'I'll get her,' the girl said, running off toward the back of the house, her ponytail bobbing up and down as she half ran, half skipped around the corner. The sight tightened Randy's chest.

Her long graceful limbs suggested she was going to be tall, like her mother. He rubbed the back of his neck, trying to ease the growing knot of tension between his shoulder blades. The woman came around the corner alone.

Up close, she was prettier than she'd appeared at a distance, and although the girls had inherited her height and coloring, the similarity ended there. Her narrow features spoke of a Scandinavian background. The girls, on the other hand, were, to his eye, destined to a wider, more . . . more . . . He couldn't find the word.

'Yes?' she said.

Randy swallowed. Whatever he had imagined he was going to say at this most important moment burst from the thicket of his mind like a covey of startled birds. He waited for the feathers to settle, held up a finger, and managed a weak smile.

'I was looking for Wesley Howard,' he managed finally.

She turned her head and called over her shoulder. 'Wes,' she called. 'Wes.'

He watched the cords in her neck bow as she called out the name. Something in her tone set Randy's teeth on edge, as if a great distance existed between the woman and whomever she was calling to. One of the twins danced back and forth behind her mother.

Footfalls padded their way to Randy's ears. She looked over her shoulder again.

'Here he comes,' she said without a shred of enthusiasm. She stepped back from the door, allowing a thickset specimen to plug the gap. 'He was asking for you,' Randy heard her say to the man's back.

'Can I help you?' the man asked. He looked Randy up and down, like there was going to be a test on it later. He had the look of a boozer. Running to fat, red-faced, with one of those wide stippled noses that reminded Randy of a golf ball.

'Hey, ah . . .' Randy stammered, still smiling, 'I was

223

looking for a person named Wesley Howard . . . guy I was in the service with . . . I was hoping . . . that maybe you were . . .'

'Never been in the service,' the guy snapped. 'Wish I could help you . . .'

A muted voice in his head was telling him to watch the woman, to move his attention to the back of the stage, where the blond wife lingered stiff-legged and alert, and then yet another row back, where one of the girls skittered back and forth like a frightened fawn using the trees for cover.

Wes started to close the door. Randy stepped forward and put his face in the way.

The guy stopped the swinging door about an inch from Randy's nose.

'I don't suppose you'd know of anybody else of—'

'Lots of guys with my name. Good luck.'

Randy pulled his face back just in time to avoid getting his nose broken. He listened as the chain was put in place and the door bolted. The last image . . . the look in the woman's eyes in the second before the door closed spoke of something . . .

He turned away from the door, walked down the pair of steps, and retraced his route. Instead of crossing the street to the park, he meandered all the way to the next corner, past the Mercedes and all the way around the block, so's he could approach Acey and the park unseen. 'They was lookin','

Acey said as Randy sat on the table next to him. 'Lookin' fo' a fuckin' long time.'

'Huh?'

'They was peekin' out though the curtains. I seen 'em.'

Randy dropped his head into his hands. He ran his fingers through his hair.

'So?' the boy asked.

'Not the right one,' Randy said.

'What? Da bitch got her a new man. So what?'

'Her man's name is Wesley Howard,' Randy said.

'Shit,' the kid said. 'What we gonna do?'

Randy thought it over. 'Let's go to the beach,' he said.

CHAPTER 26

Junior Harris and his chickens had been right on the money. Randy found his dream beach in just under an hour. He'd started out south and worked his way north until the tower was just the right size. By the time he was certain he was in the right place, the sun was getting low on the western horizon. The sand was dull yellow and sharp to the feet as if some ocean creature had ground seashells in its gullet and then cast them up, half digested, onto the waiting shore.

What Randy had imagined to be a distracting hour of throwing a Frisbee on the beach had run into a few snags. First off, they had to go to three stores to find a white Frisbee. The first two stores had Frisbees all right, but none of them were the obligatory white. Second, Acey, despite having been born and raised in Florida, had never been to the beach in his life and had most certainly never thrown a Frisbee. Took Randy fifteen minutes to talk him into removing his sneakers and wiggling his bare toes in the sand. Another five or so to get him to dip a toe into the water, and then when he decided he liked the experience, another half hour to find and buy him a proper bathing suit.

And so, as the last of the sunset doused itself to gray, Randy had yet to throw his newly acquired toy, but had instead spent the past hour watching a kid getting a chance to be a kid, maybe, if he were forced to guess, for the first time.

He'd lounged in the rough sand watching the boy fight epic battles with the waves, marveling at the kid's energy and wondering what in hell he was going to do next. All he could think of was to get a room for the night and to get up in the morning and take Acey to his auntie. And then? And then what? He had no idea what came next. As of a couple hours ago, he was coming from nowhere and headed nowhere. The thought made him feel sick to his stomach.

To the west, out over the tops of the shops and hotels, the day had turned purple, and the transitory warmth of spring had bolted town with the light. The kid's teeth were chattering like castanets as the pair crossed the four-lane boulevard and hurried toward the Mercedes. As they approached the car, Randy pushed the button for the trunk, hoping he might get lucky and find a shirt or a blanket or something to help keep the kid warm until they got settled in a hotel room.

And there it was, a black wool blanket with matching fringe all the way around the edges, the kind of thing old codgers threw over their arthritic knees to keep warm. He reached in and snatched the blanket, snapping it like a whip to remove anything loose and along for the ride.

In a single motion, Randy settled the blanket around the kid's shoulders and reached to close the trunk. Two green gym bags, much like his own but bigger, rested in the center of the trunk. He reached out and touched the nearest bag, pushing down on the shiny fabric with the flat of his hand, expecting whatever was inside to give. Nope.

Whatever was inside was solid and square. Randy checked the street and told the kid to get in the car. The street was empty. Other than his lower jaw, which was still vibrating his teeth together, the kid didn't so much as flinch. Instead he bellied up to the trunk and peered inside. 'Oh fuck,' he whispered.

Randy's diaphragm froze. 'Something I should know?' he croaked.

'That pimp fuck in Atlanta . . .'

'What's his name?'

'Tyrone,' the boy said.

'What about him.'

'He sell a lotta rock.'

'And . . . you think what?'

'Sometimes—' He stopped, took a couple of breaths, and then went on. 'Sometimes he get his rock from that Berry motherfucker.' He pointed at the bag. 'I seen him usin' that bag before.'

'Seen who?'

'Berry.'

'With this Tyrone guy?'

'Yeah.'

'When was that?'

The boy turned away and didn't answer. Randy opened his mouth to question the boy further, and then had a lightbulb come on in his head. Only way the kid could know what transpired between Chester Berry and this guy Tyrone when they were up in Atlanta was if he'd been there himself. Like maybe this wasn't the first time he'd been used to pay his mama's crack bills. Randy's already queasy stomach rolled at the thought.

He reached for the bag and pulled back the long central zipper. Blocks of compacted white powder filled half the interior. Bundled in plastic wrap and sealed in freezer bags, the blocks emitted a vaguely medicinal odor, something like ether maybe.

The other bag was full of money. Hundreds, all banded up nice and neat into thousands, then those rubber-banded into ten thousands. Lots of them.

He took hold of the tab and pulled, but the zipper stuck. He leaned in and brought his other hand to bear. That's when he noticed each brick of cocaine had a stiff cardboard tag tied to it. He turned the nearest tag. Read the cramped script. *Property Room, Dade County Police.* A name, an intake date, a court date, a case number, the whole nine yards. He zipped the bag and slammed the trunk with a bang.

'Lotta bad motherfuckers gonna be lookin' for us, dog. Doan nobody be walkin' off'n Tyrone's coke and live to talk about it.'

Randy pushed the green button. 'Get in the car,' he said.

This time the kid did as he was told.

The Excelsior Palms Hotel was three blocks off the beach; a crumbling remnant of the Rat Pack period, it professed an Art Deco motif, which was accurate only insofar as one never looked closely at anything in particular, and thus never quite internalized the degree of decay present in nearly every object.

Acey had wanted to simply get dressed. Randy had to work to convince him of the abrasive nature of sand and that a shower was in order. Apparently, the warm water had loosened his thought processes. When he came out of the bathroom, his eyes were hard as gravel. 'They gonna kill our ass fo' sure.'

'Not if they don't catch us.'

The kid was shaking his head before Randy finished. His lower jaw was shaking, but it wasn't from the cold this time. There was panic in his voice. 'They gonna kill my mama.'

'Why would they do that?'

'Cause they know where she is, dog.'

'She didn't have anything to do with this.'

'Doan matter to these people, dog. They gotta send a message. "Nobody fucks wid Tyrone." Period. End of fucking story.'

'I thought you were through with her.'

'Fuck that,' he spat. 'She's my mama.' He was about to cry. 'These people . . . they can't find you . . . they kill everybody you know. They doan give a shit. They gonna keep killing people till dey get what dey lookin' for.'

'First thing in the morning,' Randy said.

The kid thought it over. 'First thing,' he said.

Randy looked him in the eye. 'First thing. We get you to your mama and we get rid of that car.'

'What about the rock and the cheese?'

'We find someplace to stash them. The dope and the money are all we've got to bargain with. They find us and we don't have them . . . it's . . .' He didn't want to say it out loud, so he let the thought peter out.

The kid's eyes narrowed. 'Smart dog. Hella smart. How you know all that shit? How come you always one step ahead of everybody else?'

Randy threw up his hands. 'I don't know. I just do.'

He walked to the window. Four floors down, the streetlights were on, and the neighborhood denizens had begun to make their evening rounds. Through the lattice of the iron fire escape, he watched as they exchanged furtive greetings.

He turned back to the room and walked over by the phone. He picked up the padded Guest Services book, thumbed his way to room service, and handed it over to the boy. 'Let's call room service and get us some dinner. I don't know about you, but I'm hungry as hell.'

He turned back to the window. It was the off-season. Things were slow along the boulevard.

A guy in a wheelchair was rolling himself across the deserted street.

A grotesquely elongated shadow on a palm tree fell awkwardly across the street. Randy rubbed his forehead and tried to get a handle on things.

No way Berry could have reported his Mercedes stolen, he decided. Not an eighty-thousand-dollar ride with the trunk full of stolen cash and dope anyway, which meant nobody knew what they were driving. So all they really had to worry about for the time being was Berry himself and the folks at the other end of the drug deal. As long as they didn't attract any attention to themselves, they should be good with the cops.

When he turned back toward the room, Acey was still staring at the room-service menu. 'You figure out what you want?' Randy asked.

The boy didn't answer one way or the other. He seemed to be staring at one particular entry. Randy smiled. 'Can you read?' he asked.

Acey shrugged and turned his face away.

'Can you?' Randy pressed.

'Not so good,' the boy admitted.

Randy held out his hand. The kid handed the menu over. Randy read it to him.

Spaghetti was Acey's choice. Apple pie with chocolate ice cream for dessert. Randy ordered a steak with french fries and a bottle of Heineken.

By the time Randy set the ravaged tray on the carpet outside the room, it was nearly ten and Acey was stone asleep.

Randy flicked off the TV. The Road Runner faded to a dot. The green-and-white stand-up card on the nightstand announced FREE WI-FI. He went to his bag, fished around inside, and pulled out the laptop. Another foray into the bag produced a handful of wires.

Acey began to snore lightly as Randy sorted his way through the maze of wires, and eventually figured out it was 'idiot simple.' Every wire only fit one receptacle. You couldn't fuck it up. Two minutes of button pushing and he had the mail program open. Big old long list of messages to Brittany. Nothing for Alma, which, Randy mused, was probably just the way she wanted it. The message on the top, though, was a bit more of a problem. *Paul/Randy*, it read. The sender was Hadleysweets@southeast.net. The subject line read . . . all caps . . . NAZI BASTARDS.

While he had resolved not to read Brittany's e-mail, this missive seemed both of an urgent nature and aimed at directly him, so he clicked at it until it opened.

Boy, do you ever know how to leave a trail behind you. I'm down at Hadley's using one of the house machines hoping you receive this message before the Nazis get to you like they got to us. About a half hour after you left, they were all over us like weevils. Whatever it is you got or know or did, these NSA dudes want you real bad.

Sorry to say but everybody here told everything they knew. Seemed like there wasn't nothing else to do. We talked about it afterward and everybody agreed if we had it to do over again we wouldn't tell them a damn thing. Hindsight's twenty-twenty I guess. We all wish we'd done you better, but as it is, you better get rid of that car as soon as you can. Best of luck in your quest. Alma.

P.S.: Danny says to tell you he deleted your picture from the system even before the Nazis got here, so they got no picture of you. That's something anyway.

P.P.S.: I guess we weren't who we thought we were either.

Take Care. Alma

Randy read it twice, then unplugged and shut down the computer. So it meant what? he asked himself. These guys were watching every e-mail anybody sent everywhere? Nothing . . . not even a simple Google inquiry sent from Buttfuck, Alabama, was safe from interception. The notion further boggled his mind.

After stashing everything back in his bag, he walked over to the bed and shook Acey's shoulder. The kid's eyes blinked open.

'I'm going out for a while,' Randy said.

'To that house, huh?'

'Yeah,' he said. 'Something about it . . .' He couldn't finish.

The boy marinated the idea. 'What if you doan come back?'

'You've got lots of money. Hit the bus station.'

His small brow furrowed. He seemed genuinely puzzled.

'Why you gotta go back there?'

Randy thought before he answered. 'It's all I've got,' he said.

'I can dig it,' the kid offered. 'It's like that wid me an' my mama.'

'I'm not gonna take a room key with me,' Randy said. 'That way . . . you know, if something happens, they won't know anything about anything.'

'Smart,' the boy said in the moment before his eyelids fluttered shut.

'Hey,' Randy said. The heavy lids opened wide. 'If I'm not here when you wake up . . . I'm not coming. You hear me?' Acey said he did. The look in his half-closed eyes said Randy had just joined the legion of fathers and uncles and Johns and Tommys and Bills who'd walked out of Acey's life on one pretext or another never to return. Randy stopped in the doorway.

'Hey,' he said.

The kid sat up in bed.

'I'll be back,' Randy said. 'You hear knocking on the door, it's me. Open up.'

His face said he didn't believe a word of it.

'Yeah,' the kid said. Randy turned out the light and eased the door closed.

The garage attendant pointed to the sign on the wall. 'No in and out,' he read.

Randy grimaced and handed him a twenty.

'A lot like my first wife,' the guy said with a grin.

CHAPTER 27

You get what you pay for, and in this case what the locals paid for was peace and quiet, so it wasn't surprising that, by ten forty-five on a Friday evening, Water Street was closed up tighter than a frog's ass, which explained why Randy parked the Mercedes at a Circle K convenience store half a dozen blocks north and walked into the neighborhood, because the way he saw it, he'd already gotten lucky with both the cops and the private security patrol, and another Mercedes sighting was surely going to attract more attention than he was looking for.

Rounding the corner of Burgess and starting down Water Street, he picked up the pace, walking quickly, making sure he didn't look like he was running. He was sure of two things. This time of night, tales of visiting friends weren't going to float, and whatever was going to happen for him tonight had better happen quickly.

He'd made this journey before; he was sure of it. He'd walked this same street at this time of night, and yet he was equally certain this wasn't his home.

'Home was . . .' He couldn't say. Someplace like this. That's all he was sure of.

The pictures were coming slower now, and had, for the most part, been replaced by a voice. The same voice he'd heard earlier this evening, the voice telling him to watch the woman as he'd stood in the doorway. The voice Acey had noticed the day before. *His* voice, Randy felt certain. The voice of the person he used to be . . . confident, street-smart, with an uncanny sense of what to do next. The experience was seriously schizophrenic, like doing a real-time voice-over for his own life.

A dull glow behind the drapes made 432 Water Street the only house on the block showing light on the ground floor. The faint illumination was secondhand, as if a light somewhere in the back of the house was on. Randy stood for a moment and listened. He thought he might have heard a hiccup of conversation but couldn't be sure.

Randy broke into a trot. The attached two-car garage blocked access to the backyard at the near end of the house, so Randy quickly cut across the lawn and checked the security arrangements at the far end. Better. A chain-link gate. Six feet high. Locked from the inside by nothing more than a thumb latch. The net of spiderwebs said nobody ever came this way. *Probably means they don't have a dog*, the voice-over said. *People with dogs would use the gate more often.*

He did a couple of knee bends, put his hands on top of the metal rail, squatted, and gave it all

238

the leg drive he could muster, propelling himself straight up, high enough to lock his elbows and then to throw a foot on top of the gate. From there it was easy. In one smooth move, he vaulted himself over the gate and landed gracefully on the other side. He stood still and listened. A car rolled by in the street. Must have had the window down. Something hot and Latin. Guy playing trumpet so high only dogs could hear.

The minute the music was gone, he heard the voices. Hers at first.

'How many times do I have to tell you? Don't you ever listen?'

Wes said something, but Randy couldn't make it out, so he began to creep forward into the yard. On the left, as he cleared the shrubbery, a gossamer lanai began to come into view, its delicate screened walls backlit by a light from the kitchen.

She was at the sink. He could hear water running. 'This guy was way too tall. They can't make people taller, can they?' Her tone said she wouldn't be surprised if 'they' could.

He inched forward. The weak fan of yellow light coming from the kitchen window did not begin to cover the backyard. He moved to his right and forward some more, moving away from the light, keeping even his shadow hidden from view.

The yard was huge; the untended acre was a graveyard of kiddie fare, as old toys bespotted the ragged lawn here and there like acne: five or six scattered lawn darts, a Big Wheels tricycle tumbled over on its side, a swaybacked swing set with a broken seat, a trampoline torn from the frame on one side, an abandoned kiddie pool turned upside down in the grass. On the far side of the yard, a long building ran nearly to the back fence. If the house had been grander or the building a bit bigger, it might have been called a carriage house. As it was, the structure must have been a work space or hobby room, something like that.

Randy crept forward into the yard until he could see the back of her head, standing under the kitchen light, leaning back against the sink with her arms folded tightly across her chest. Wes was nowhere in sight. From the next room over, maybe the dining room, Wes said something Randy couldn't make out. Whatever it was only served to anger her further. 'It was the voice, you idiot. I just thought I'd heard the voice before.' She waved a disgusted hand. 'I should never have said anything.'

And then Wes stepped into view. He was redder and sweatier than he'd been this afternoon. 'Sometimes with faces . . .' he was saying.

'Don't you hear me?' she pleaded. 'I never saw that guy before in my life. The face meant nothing to me. It was the voice I thought maybe I'd heard before. The Voice.' She spelled it out. '*V-O-I-C-E.*'

'I called it in,' he said.

Her voice rose an octave. 'You what?' She was halfway to hysterical. She stomped around in a circle.

240

'You just don't get it, do you?' she said. 'The minute anything's seriously wrong, this little charade is over.'

Anger tinged his voice. 'What about you?' he demanded. 'Don't think I don't know what's going on with you? Don't think for a second I believe all those "working late at the travel agency" stories you tell.'

'That's none of your damn business,' she said. 'Problems make us expendable. Can't you get that into your head?'

'We're supposed to call if there's a problem.'

'What problem?' She was right on the verge of yelling. She waved her hands like palm fronds in a hurricane.

'Guy freaked me out, I guess.'

'Freaked you out over what?' she demanded. 'It's not like he's coming back.'

'Sorry,' he said.

'How long ago?' she demanded.

'Five minutes maybe,' he said.

She didn't hesitate. She bolted from view. Wes said something inaudible to her back. A minute passed and then another before she burst out through the back door, carrying a load of paper-work in her arms.

Randy froze. He was in plain view. Only thing saved him was she was so intent on running toward the shop building that she failed to notice him squatting there on her lawn. Randy checked the kitchen window. Wes was gone to wherever Weses go. When Randy turned back, she was trotting

241

through the side door of the outbuilding. Inside the building, the light went on.

Randy knew for certain he couldn't stay where he was. When she came back, she'd be looking right at him. He hesitated and then ran headlong across the grass, hoping like hell she didn't come out right away, running toward the back of the shop building and then sliding into the area between the back of the shop and the wooden plank fence separating this yard from that of the neighbor.

He sidled in as far as the window in the center of the back wall and peeked into the shop. No sign of her. He pressed his face against the glass, trying to find her in the room . . . but no . . . all he could see were workbenches all around the perimeter. Cabinets for supplies and a nice big square drain in the middle of the floor for . . . for . . . except the drain grate had been removed, leaving a gaping black hole in the floor. His brain had just begun to work out the possibilities when she came climbing up out of the hole empty-handed. She grunted as she slid the grate back into place. After dusting her hands together, she double-timed it across the floor.

Randy stayed put as she doused the light and slammed the outside door behind her. He side-stepped over to the corner of the building and watched her hurry across the grass and up the stairs into the kitchen. He took a deep breath and thought about what he'd witnessed. Has to be one of those fifties bomb shelters, he thought to himself. Back when everybody was convinced nuclear war was inevitable and survival was just a matter of hunkering down and waiting for the dust to settle.

When the voices went suddenly quiet, Randy hurried back to the shrubbery at the corner of the house. He rested on his haunches, quieting his breath, and then in an instant, the Howards were back in the kitchen and back at it, harder than ever.

'You listen to me,' she growled. 'It wasn't in any of the house sale paperwork. If the Realtor had known about it, he'd have made a big deal about it. They don't know one damn thing about it. None of them. If it weren't for the girls playing in there, we wouldn't know it was there either, so just make sure you shut up.'

'Okay, okay,' he said.

The doorbell rang. Randy watched both of their heads swivel toward the front of the house in the half second before the gate rattled, just as it had when he'd jumped over a few minutes before. He grabbed the edge of the kiddie pool, lifted it from the ground, and rolled underneath, dropping the plastic and lying still in the dank grass.

He held his breath and listened intently. After a moment he heard footsteps and the squeak of a shoe as it approached his hiding place. The noise stopped. He hoped the outline of his body wasn't visible from above. The air beneath the plastic pool was rancid with mold. His nose began to twitch. He wanted to sneeze but forced himself to hold on. After what seemed like a week, the footsteps moved on. He waited, counted ten, and then lifted the edge of the pool just in time to see the back of a figure letting himself into the lanai, kicking around in the clutter of the place, and then, apparently satisfied it was empty, walking up the back stairs into the kitchen. The voices were louder now.

Wes was talking. 'It was nothing really. I just sort of overreacted. You know . . . this guy came to the door, you know, asking for Wes Howard, and I sort of freaked out. It was like—'

An unfamiliar voice asked, 'And you'd never seen him before?'

In unison, Wes and the woman said they hadn't.

'Do you recognize this man?' the voice asked.

A moment of strained silence ensued.

'Well?' the voice prodded.

'Hard to tell,' Wes offered. 'Might be.'

He must have stuck the picture in front of her face.

'Could be,' she said. 'It's really not much of a likeness.'

Randy began to sweat. What did they have? Some kind of drawing of him? How would they get something like that? These guys were scary.

'What was he driving?'

'He was on foot,' Wes answered. Another voice, probably the guy who'd come in from the backyard, said something inaudible. 'I didn't see a car,' Wes said.

Randy didn't hesitate: he rolled out from beneath the abandoned pool. His entire body was coated with sweat. He smelled like a foot-locker. The cool night air caused him to shudder as he double-timed it around the corner to the gate and let himself out.

CHAPTER 28

He must have stayed awake. The minute Randy's knuckles hit the door, bare feet started slapping on the floor inside the room.

'It's me, Acey. Open up.'

Nothing.

'Open the fucking door,' he growled.

The door opened. 'I thought we weren't using that word.'

Randy hurried into the room. 'Get your stuff. We're getting out of here.'

'Where we goin'?'

'I guess I'm gonna take you to your mama.'

The kid stood still. 'I tried to call her, but she don't answer.'

'Hurry,' Randy said as he zipped up his bag.

'I thought we was gonna stash the bag and shit.'

'No time now; hurry up.'

The kid sat on the floor with a thud. He pulled on his socks as Randy made a quick sweep of the room. 'Wassup?' he asked as he laced his shoes. 'You bring the heat back wid you?'

'It won't be long.'

'How come?'

Randy reached down and grabbed the kid by the shirt, hauling him to his feet. 'Let's roll.' The kid didn't move.

'Where's my bathing suit?'

'We don't need—'

'I want my bathing suit.'

Rather than argue, Randy dashed into the bathroom, pulled the wet suit down from the shower curtain rod, rolled it up in a towel, and hurried back out. 'Okay?'

'Okay.'

Randy dropped to one knee, looking the boy directly in the eye. 'So here's the deal,' he said. 'I left the car at a car dealer about three blocks from here.'

'Smart.'

'These guys are scary.'

'Wait'll you meet Tyrone.'

'Different kind of scary, Acey. These guys could find us on the moon.'

'What you sayin'?'

'I'm saying it might be better if I left you off downtown by the bus station. That way you could—'

'I ain't no punk.'

'I didn't say you were.'

'You said you'd take me to my mama's.'

'Might be better . . .'

The kid's eyes were hard as rivets. 'Might be better we got the fuck out of here.'

Inside of two minutes, they were out on the street, Randy with his Nike bag swinging from his hand and Acey with the towel tucked up under his arm, looking for all the world like a father and son on their way to the beach . . . at midnight.

Five minutes and Randy couldn't decide whether or not he was relieved to see the Mercedes still sitting there in the car lot with a paper sign tucked under the wipers.

NO CREDIT – NO PROBLEM, it read.

Acey liked it. 'Slick,' he proclaimed. 'You da shit, dog.'

They dashed for the car. Randy opened the doors, started around to the driver's side, and then suddenly slid to a halt. 'What?' Acey yelled, but Randy's attention was riveted to the back of the silver Cadillac Escalade parked next to the showroom door. The license plate was canted at a twenty-degree angle.

He smiled, hurrying across the pavement to the Escalade, whose license plate easily came off into his hands. One of those magnetic plates dealers use to ferry around unlicensed vehicles. He stopped at the rear of the Mercedes and placed the dealer plate over Berry's plate. When he turned back, Acey had removed the banner from the windshield and was strapping himself into the seat.

The multicolored pennants, strung from pole to pole in the yard, began to hum to the tune of a fresh breeze off the ocean. The silver streamers along the front of the dealership began to stretch themselves and spin. Overhead a pair of gulls dropped beneath the wind, swooping just above Randy's head as he jumped in and started the car.

He accelerated quickly over to the end of the lot and then slowed to a crawl, at the same empty display space where he'd entered earlier, easing one tire at a time over the concrete divider, gritting his teeth as the front of the Mercedes scraped hard on its way over, then repeated the whole process on the curb before finally making it to the street.

The midnight streets were deserted. From the look of things, a squall was brewing. The air smelled of salt water. The palm trees swayed like hula dancers. Bits of litter waffled through the air on the wings of the wind. Randy checked the mirror. Nothing. A thin mist began to hiss down upon the car.

Randy rolled up the windows and kept the Mercedes at the speed limit. The mist thickened; he put the wipers on intermittent. Acey was stretching his neck, trying to look everywhere at once, when, two blocks up, the white panel truck backed out in front of the car, blocking both lanes. No hesitation, no checking both ways, like maybe the driver wasn't used to traffic at this time of the morning. Randy braked.

'Hey,' Acey's voice interrupted his thought process. The kid jerked a thumb toward the rear. Randy checked the mirror. A silver-gray sedan was way too close to the back bumper for comfort. Worse yet, the car was full of guys wearing sunglasses at midnight. Randy's eyes narrowed.

He flexed his fingers around the wheel and then slowed even more. The panel truck hadn't moved. The door opened. The driver was wearing a dark suit. In his hand was a . . .

Randy put the pedal to the metal and veered left, bouncing up over the curb, barely missing a fire hydrant, cutting the corner on his way over the lawn, finding the far curb blocked, bumper to bumper with parked cars, cutting left up the sidewalk. All the way to the corner before finding a gap big enough to squeeze the car back into the street, airborne, landing with a crash and then turning hard left, going the wrong way on a one-way street with the headlights bobbing up and down a hundred feet back.

Randy floored the Mercedes. The big car leaped forward, growling as it gained speed. The road went on to the vanishing point. In the distance, traffic lights guarded the intersections. He checked the mirror.

Whatever they were driving didn't have the guts of the Mercedes. In less than a mile he'd gained half a block. They went airborne at the first intersection, coming down hard, losing something metal to the street. The first traffic light loomed in the distance.

Randy kept the car floored. They were doing eighty-five now. Ninety.

Up ahead on the arterial, cars crossed in front of them. Randy tapped the brakes, watching the intermittent flow of traffic, trying to pick out a spot where they could cross against the light . . . and then the light turned green and they were airborne again as the shape of the road sent them flying up and over the beam. Banging once and then a second time before regaining traction and tearing off.

Randy flicked one quick glance at the mirror. He'd lost some ground. The intersection up ahead suggested he was about to lose some more. He tapped the brakes again. The traffic was thicker now. A metro bus rolled by. A couple of cabs and then they were nearly there and a tandem eighteen wheeler was moving into view.

The driver saw him coming. The air horn tooted twice. Randy slowed the car. The guys in the sedan were twenty yards back now. The truck driver locked up the brakes. Clouds of blue smoke rose from the tires. Randy floored the big car.

Acey couldn't help himself. 'Ooh, ooh,' he was chanting as they entered the intersection on the fly, passing in front of the truck with so little to spare that the truck's bumper clipped the back of the car, sending it fishtailing down the road, its rear end swinging wildly back and forth . . . and then *bang* . . . the big-time *bam* as the pursuit vehicle slammed into the side of the trailer. And then silence as the scream of brakes went quiet and the Mercedes righted itself on the road and roared away from the steaming pile of debris littering the road behind them. 'You da shit, dog,' Acey breathed.

251

CHAPTER 29

'The Grove,' they called it. Thirty square blocks of misery that should rightly have been located in Tampa but which, through skillful manipulation of voting districts, remained technically part of Yrba City, a hundred and forty acres of filth whose sole raison d'être was to provide Tampa with a place to store those unfortunate trappings of post-industrial civilization deemed too dangerous, too carcinogenic, or too morally reprehensible to be contained within the borders of their fair city.

Acey's house was down at the end of Garber Street. The wrong side of the tracks of the wrong side of the tracks, only two potholed lanes of traffic from the railroad tracks themselves, located hard against a tire factory and an ice plant.

They were sitting in the Mercedes two blocks over, watching Acey's place from between houses. The building might have once been white . . . or maybe gray, it was hard to tell. Dawn was a couple of hours away. The place was dark. What appeared to be a blue blanket was tacked up across the front window. The gate hung from a single hinge.

'Place looks deserted,' Randy said.

'She doan get up till noon.'

Acey reached for the door handle. Randy put a hand on his shoulder.

'I'll go with you,' he said. 'Where can we leave the car and not attract any attention?'

Acey pointed out in front of the car. 'Over there,' he said. 'Round the odda side of the building.'

Randy dropped the car in drive and eased forward, bumping over the iron rails and into the dusty factory yard beyond. Acey directed him around the corner, into the employee parking lot on the far side of the ice plant, where Randy squeezed the Mercedes between a battered Ford pickup truck and the wall of the building. The fit was tight enough that they both were forced to get out the driver's side.

In the distance, a train whistle moaned. 'We better hurry up,' Acey said. 'These fuckin' trains go on forever.' Before Randy could comment on the language, Acey waved him off. 'I know, dog. I know.'

Randy followed the boy across the yard and then over the tracks. They crossed the sandy access road separating the house from the railway and crept around the back, where a narrow porch filled floor to ceiling with cardboard boxes ran the width of the house. The screen door was devoid of screens. Even from a distance, the place smelled of mold and sewage.

The screen door squealed on rusty hinges as

they let themselves in. The back door was open. Somebody had kicked it in, splintering the wood along the doorjamb. They walked into the kitchen together. The place was trashed. Torn to pieces by somebody looking for something. Acey started to cry. 'Mama,' he mumbled as they crunched their way across the floor, stepping carefully, avoiding turning an ankle on the debris-covered floor. Randy bent and whispered in the boy's ear. 'Where's she sleep?' he asked. Acey pointed up the narrow stairs on the right. 'Go see,' Randy said.

He stood in the hall, watching Acey pick his way up the stairway. He pushed open the door on his left. A bathroom. The medicine cabinet had been torn from the wall and now rested partially on top of the toilet. He could hear the sounds of Acey's feet shuffling through the refuse covering the upstairs floor.

Randy moved forward, stepping carefully, trying to avoid as much of the broken mirror and as many of the upturned nails as possible. Big old cast-iron bathtub with claw feet. No shower. He knew right away what the smell was . . . that metallic odor a bit like copper or maybe even steel. He stood still, holding his stomach in his hand.

An hour ago they'd stopped for breakfast. The scrambled eggs and toast that had tasted good now threatened to end up on his shoes. He swallowed hard and searched along the walls for a light switch, then groped around in front of himself until he found the string hanging from the light fixture. He swallowed a couple more times and pulled the string. Minute his eyes adjusted, he wished they hadn't.

His stomach heaved twice and then righted itself. He stood with his hand clapped over his mouth. She lay on her back in the bathtub, one oozing, fingerless hand thrown above her head. The other hand was hidden beneath her body, but Randy was willing to bet those fingers were missing, too. This was fairly recent. Within the past few hours anyway. In this climate, after four hours you were a science project.

The sound of Acey descending the stairs forced him to get a grip on himself. He tore the shower curtain from the rod and patted it down around her body, straightened up and pulled the string, sending the bathroom into darkness before stepping outside and closing the door.

Acey appeared at his side. 'She ain't there,' he said. 'Maybe she . . .' He reached for the bathroom door. Randy grabbed his wrist. He shook his head.

'No,' he said.

Acey read his eyes. He sobbed and tried to push his way past Randy, who held him at a distance. 'No,' he said again.

'Why you got to—'

'She's not coming back.'

Acey scowled.

'Not now. Not ever,' Randy said.

Acey shifted his weight from one foot to the other. Part of him knew what Randy was saying. Another part didn't want to believe it. Tears rolled down his smooth cheeks. He opened his mouth to speak and then started bawling. That's when the place lit up.

Headlights bounced to a halt outside the house, sending shafts of light here and there through rotten curtains, through every crack and cranny in the walls, creating a surreal world of light and shadows within the interior.

A movement to his right pulled Randy's eyes toward the back door. He watched the black guy in the parachute pants snap the curved clip into place with a wicked *snick*. The shape was all he needed to see. AK-47. The guy pulled back the bolt and leveled the weapon at the back door. Randy was off and running.

He snatched Acey off his feet and made a dash for the bathroom. The first volley of automatic fire tore through the house just as Randy flopped into the bathtub on his back, clutching Acey to his chest. He pulled the boy's head to his chest and closed his eyes. Wasn't until the first brief break in the gunfire that Randy remembered the corpse beneath him. The skeleton popped and cracked as it absorbed their collective weight. His stomach heaved as the slippery corpse tried to slide up the side of the tub, like it wanted to be on top. Randy rearranged his limbs so that wasn't going to happen and pulled the boy closer. A couple of her ribs cracked from their combined weight. Mercifully, the shooting began anew as another gun, being fired at right angles to the first, opened up and began to spit ammo through the walls. And then both guns at once, filling the air with the buzz of superheated metal, as the house first began to shake and then began to crumble from the fearsome onslaught of the cross fire.

Parts of the ceiling fell onto the backs of Randy's hands. Somewhere in the house a slug had cut through a water pipe. The sound of rushing water mixed with the pop of an exposed electrical wire. Then the toilet exploded and the sound of rushing water got louder in the seconds before the big cast iron tub began to vibrate from the volley of slugs tearing through the walls and clanking against its formidable sides, the power of the metal hitting metal pressing Acey and Randy deeper into the tub, setting them to using their hands to cover their heads and shield their ears from the terrible hail of gun-fire and the rain of debris falling from above, shards of wood and Sheetrock, bits of wire and glass and a veritable snowstorm of yellow fiberglass insulation filling the air inside the room like a blizzard. The firing went on and on. Acey held on tight.

And then . . . just as it seemed the roaring of gunfire might never end . . . it did. The car lights wavered and then bounced a couple of times before disappearing altogether.

They stayed put. Breathing. Waiting. Just in case.

Randy could feel the boy weeping. He hugged him tighter and stayed where he was.

'You okay?' he asked.

Acey said something but Randy's ears were still full of the sound of slugs hitting the bathtub. 'What?'

Acey said something else but Randy couldn't hear that either.

Randy lifted the boy high enough to clear the rim. Acey set his feet carefully amid the debris. Randy climbed out and stood beside him on the littered floor. He kept his body between the boy and the bathtub and looked around. The place was shot to pieces. Major portions of the ceiling had fallen. Sparks cascaded like fireworks in the kitchen where the overhead light fixture had been completely destroyed. Randy pushed the boy out into the hall and eased the door closed behind himself.

'Let's get out of here,' Randy said.

Acey reached up and took his hand. Together, they kicked their way through the debris covering the floor, out through the flooded kitchen to what remained of the back porch, where the roof had partially collapsed, forcing them to veer left toward the tracks or walk into a faceful of nails.

The cool morning air washed over Randy like a wave. He wiped his mouth with the back of his hand and came away with a wristful of sludge. The sight of Acey nearly caused him to laugh. The kid's head was covered with bits of insulation and

Sheetrock. He tousled the boy's hair but not much of the stuff came out. A train whistle sounded again, much closer this time. Two different car alarms were going off, and in the distance, the *whoop whoop* of a siren seemed to be moving closer. Randy looked up.

The car and the train were moving in opposite directions. Acey and Randy stood stupefied as the train came roaring toward them, its great single light sweeping the track in front of the engine. The red brake lights of the car flickered and then showed themselves for real. The car stopped.

'We gotta get the fuck outta here,' Acey said. He pointed after the car. 'Ain't no way out down there. They gonna have to come back.'

He was right. The car containing the gunmen had come to a stop and was in the process of turning around. The train came chugging past the headlights when the car was partially through the U-turn. A shout from the car floated their way. They'd been spotted. Randy grabbed the kid's arm. 'Let's go,' he yelled above the deep throbbing of the engine. They took off together, running hard toward the tracks.

Instinctively Randy turned his head toward the lights. The train was gathering speed. The car was bouncing at them with somebody hanging out the window. Wasn't until he saw the yellow flame of the muzzle flash that Randy realized somebody in the car was shooting at them. A slug buzzed by so close, he checked himself for blood.

259

Randy turned and scooped the boy into his arms, then turned again and ran for the tracks, ran for the patch of white light moving along in front of the engine. The engineer must have seen them coming. He tooted his horn twice and then repeated the warning as Randy approached the tracks, his legs burning from the strain of the boy's weight, his ankles threatening to roll over as his boots met the two-inch gravel and then one final lunge, stepping over the nearest track, so close to the front of the engine he could smell the grease, then getting a foot down between rails, before catching his heel on the far track, sending the two of them rolling head over heels down the far side of the grade. Randy groaned at impact and rolled over onto his back.

Acey got himself together first. He had Randy by the elbow, pulling him to his feet, 'Come on, dog. Come on,' he was panting.

Randy followed the boy's prompting and struggled to his feet. His head throbbed so hard he could barely see. His left arm, where he'd landed on the rough gravel, hung nearly useless at his side. The Mercedes was fifty yards away. They shuffled that way together.

As they approached the car, Randy shot a glance back over his shoulder. Acey had been right. The train went on forever. He threw himself into the driver's seat and started the engine.

'Go, dog, go,' Acey chanted.

CHAPTER 30

The Four Seasons Hotel offers two seating choices for lunch. For those of a romantic nature, the Pool Room offers a gurgling marble pool surrounded by a veritable forest of lighted trees, a nearly perfect setting for amour, improved only by the impeccable yet unobtrusive service. For those engaged in those more practical and power-oriented pursuits for which the hotel has become so justly famous, the Grill Room's legendary rosewood walls and soaring ceilings have beckoned moguls and machers for nearly a half century. More than sirloins had been devoured within its hallowed confines.

Every afternoon, the restaurant's gleaming brass door on East Fifty-second Street develops what owner Armond Arabelles likes to call 'a little limousine problem' as CEOs, managing partners, and all manner of political movers and shakers sit quietly and look out the windows as their drivers jockey through two blocks of 'limo lock.' Walk-ins are politely sent on their way. Regulars have their bills sent to the office.

'I'm going to list this lunch prominently in my expense column,' Jacobson said.

'Old friends catching up.'

'Why not? I don't get to New York very often these days.'

The waiter returned with their drinks. 'Good afternoon, gentlemen,' he said.

Jacobson ordered the civet-of-wild-boar appetizer. Pomegranate sauce on the side. Bob opted for the lentil-and-sausage soup. Entrées were bipartisan. They both ordered the roast turbot with root vegetables.

Bob took a sip from his glass of Talisker on the rocks. He'd been a single-malt aficionado since grad school days at Yale. Somewhere in the past he'd settled on Dalwhinnie as his Scotch of choice. That preference went unchallenged for nearly thirty years, until, two years ago when his wife, Christine, learned she had relatives living on the Isle of Skye, a discovery which of course prompted a visit to the venerable town of Carbost, a rust-tinged hamlet nestled among the rough slopes of the Cuillin Mountains and boasting itself as the sole distiller of Scotch on the isle. They'd hiked the broken ground, met the relatives, toured the Talisker distillery, and pretended to enjoy some of the most execrable food on the planet.

When they got back home, Bob suddenly found his preference in Scotch under fire. About the third time Christine demanded an explanation as to precisely *why* he preferred Dalwhinnie to her suddenly beloved Talisker, Bob had followed the party line of least resistance and switched his allegiance, exhibiting a chameleon-like ability to blend into the leaves, a long-nurtured talent which had served him so abundantly in the arena of politics.

'Didn't I just see you?' he asked Ron Jacobson.

Jacobson leaned forward and lowered his voice. 'Unfortunately so.'

'What's up?'

'The matter is rapidly coming to a head.'

'Really?'

'We always knew it was flammable.'

'Indeed.'

'I wanted to discuss with you . . .' He allowed the rest of the sentence to taper off as the waiter returned with the appetizers. He thanked the waiter and called him by name: Gino. He looked up from his food and commented on the quality of his appetizer; Bob reciprocated to the effect that his soup was likewise marvelous.

They ground away at the small talk until the four men in the next banquette said their good-byes and shuffled out. He checked the area. Satisfied no one was within earshot, Jacobson said, 'It may be time to implement our backup scenario.'

'Tell me.'

So he did. Starting with how they now believed Paul Hardy had managed to hitch a ride with a young woman named Alma Anne Harris, who at that time was in the process of quitting her job as a hairstylist and vacating her apartment for the purpose of moving back to her native Alabama.

Somewhere along the way, Paul Hardy had become Randall James.

'So?'

'So, it turns out the real Randall James is another of the residents at the group home where Mr Hardy once lived and they checked and found the real Randall watching the *Ultimate Fighting Challenge* in the home's TV room. Agents felt certain that Paul Hardy was using Randall James's identity.'

'Not much gets by these guys, does it?'

'Barney Fife could have figured it out.'

Jacobson went on about the wi-fi query from Alabama, the transfer of title on the car, and the assurance that no one on the Alabama end was otherwise involved.

'What else?'

'The Florida State Patrol . . .' he began.

'Florida.' Bob gargled a mouthful of soup. He dropped the spoon into the bowl and wiped his mouth with his napkin. 'Did you say Florida?'

Gino arrived with a gleaming silver tray. They smiled and nodded and thanked him for the service. When he was gone, they ate in silence.

'What now?' Bob asked.

'We hope for the best and prepare ourselves for the worst.'

Bob nodded his agreement. 'The turbot's excellent today,' he commented.

The lettuce was brown around the edges. Kirsten set the plastic container back on the counter and selected another salad from the array . . . and then another and a third and a fourth. They were all the same way. She could tell the guy behind her in line was losing his patience but was too polite to ask her to hurry the hell up. She grabbed two containers of yogurt and a white plastic spoon. Five sixty-five including tax.

The courthouse commissary was a weird place. Everybody treated it like it was a library and they weren't supposed to make any noise. The combined effect of the forty or so whispered conversations was akin to the prolonged hiss of a leaking tire, and so it caught Kirsten's notice when suddenly the hissing stopped altogether and the room fell strangely silent. She wiped her mouth with a stiff paper napkin and looked up.

Bruce Gill was smiling his political smile as he made his way toward Kirsten through the maze of tables, favoring those he recognized with a nod or a wink, stopping here and there to schmooze with several of the more noteworthy diners. Took him a full five minutes to cross the room.

'Slumming?' Kirsten asked.

'I like to think of it as keeping in touch with the electorate.'

He sat down in the chair opposite Kirsten. The

whispered conversations rose back to their normal level. All eyes were slanted in their direction.

'You ever been in here before?' she asked.

'Are you suggesting . . .'

'Have you?'

'No,' he admitted.

'So?'

'Margie said you were down here.'

'I'll have the brief for the ethics committee ready by tomorrow afternoon, say fourish,' she said as she peeled the foil seal from the second yogurt container.

'Take a look at this.' He slid an FBI document across the table at her.

'What this?' she asked around a mouthful.

'It's the IAFIS report on that water glass you gave me.'

'We got a hit?'

He checked the room and then bobbed his eyebrows up and down like Groucho Marx. 'Did we ever.'

It was obvious. He was going to make her read it on her own. He liked to do things like that. She put down her spoon, wiped her hands and mouth again, and picked up the report. She read it slowly, being careful not to miss anything.

'No shit,' she said when she finished.

'No shit,' he echoed. 'Can I quote you on that, Ms Kane?'

'The one who disappeared . . . right before the . . .'

'That's the one.'

'After all these years?'

'Yup.'

'This is a prank.'

'That's what I thought, so I ran them through again. They say the prints are no more than three months old.'

She checked his expression for irony and found none.

'I mean . . . where's he been all this . . .'

'On *Unsolved Mysteries.*'

She chuckled. 'I've seen it half a dozen times.'

'It's become folklore.' He made quotation marks with his fingers. 'Amelia Earhart, Jimmy Hoffa, D. B. Cooper, and our boy here. "Unexplained Disappearances."'

She thought it over. 'We get this wrong . . .' she began.

'We look like a pair of yodels.'

'*We* become folklore.'

'Think Geraldo Rivera.'

The thought caused her to shiver.

He interrupted her thoughts.

'I got us a continuance on the ethics hearing.'

'What's that got to do with the price of eggs in Tibet?'

He tapped his nose with his forefinger. 'I smell something here,' he said. 'There's a lotta juice being floated around. And it's all connected.'

'What makes you think that?' she asked between bites.

''Cause I had to pull out all the stops to get some bullshit ethics hearing postponed.' He had her attention now. His voice began to rise. Heads were turning their way. He leaned in and lowered his voice. 'I went to Billy, just like I always do.' Billy was the Honorable Speaker of the State House of Representatives William F. Crowley III, with whom Bruce Gill had been conducting mutually profitable business for the better part of twenty years.

'And he turned you down?'

'Flat. Just about told me to kiss his ass,' the D.A. whispered.

'Which means what?'

'Which means he's found himself a bigger, hairier ass to kiss.'

She finished her yogurt and dropped the spoon in the container. 'Round theses parts, Chief, there ain't no bigger, hairier ass than yours.'

'Exactly,' he said.

And then she got it. Somewhere in D.C. somebody was exerting a lot of pressure. Pressure whose upside promise was sufficient to make Crowley risk his long-standing relationship with Gill. Whatever it was . . . it was heavy. Crowley was no fool. If he was changing partners, the dance was a doozy.

'And you thought, what? . . . This . . .' – she gestured toward the fingerprint report on the table – 'you think this is all connected somehow?'

'How could it not be?' he asked.

Much as she disliked the idea, he had a point.

Either they were looking at some serious statistical unlikelihood, or the recent string of events was all, in some manner or another, connected.

'What do you need from me?'

'Make some calls, find out what in hell is going on here. Make damn sure we're not being duped. How come some dude who's been missing for years winds up in a home for the disadvantaged. How this guy mentions the name Wesley Howard and feds come raining all over our asses.' He shook his perfectly sculpted head. 'This is big-time shit here.'

What he meant was that this was big-time TV exposure – *60 Minutes, Evening Magazine* kind of stuff.

'Big-time shit,' he said again.

She stood up. He followed suit. 'Maybe not the best dining conversation I've ever heard,' she said.

CHAPTER 31

'Sit still,' Acey said. 'Ain't never gonna get this done you keep actin' like a bitch.' He dabbed antiseptic onto the topmost of Randy's wounds.

'Not a nice word,' Randy said.

'What's wid you and words? They just words, dog.'

'It matters.'

He daubed the wound quite a bit harder than necessary. 'Ain't nothin' but words.'

'I got an idea,' Randy said.

'Yeah . . . whassat?'

'Maybe you shouldn't refer to women as anything you wouldn't want somebody to call your mom.'

Acey stared a hole in the side of Randy's head, dropped the gauze on the bed, and walked over by the window, where he stood looking out at the bricks of the building next door. 'I got me an idea, too,' he said.

'What's that?'

'Maybe you oughta go fuck yourself.'

After a stop at an all-night drugstore for bandaging supplies, they were holed up in the

Whispering Palms Motel about fifty miles south of the Grove. One look at Randy and the desk clerk had demanded a hundred-dollar deposit on the room. Between the two of them, they ran the hot water out three times before they managed to wash all the debris from themselves.

'I was just trying to make a point,' Randy said. 'Sorry.'

'Fuck you.'

Randy went to work on his own shoulder, placing a sterile pad over the wound and then winding gauze over it to keep it in place until finally covering the whole thing with white surgical tape. He ripped the tape with his teeth and smoothed the end down.

'You seen her, huh?' Acey said out of the blue.

'Yeah,' Randy said. 'I saw her.'

'She . . . I mean . . . did they . . .'

'She never knew what hit her.'

Acey turned his way, trying to read his face. Randy hid behind a grimace as he shouldered himself into his last clean shirt.

'She always say that how she wanted to go.'

'How's that?'

'You know. Quick like. One minute you here. One minute you gone.'

'She got her wish.'

Acey sniffled and then wiped his nose on his sleeve. 'What she say? Live fast. Die young. Leave a great-lookin' corpse.'

'Fonzie.'

'Who?'

'Guy on TV used to say that.'

'Guy wid the motorcycle.'

'That's the one.'

'We used to watch that on the TV when I was little.'

'You're still little? '

Acey wiped his nose again. 'You remember when you was little?'

'No.'

'How far back you remember?'

'My memory's not like that,' Randy said. He could see Acey didn't understand, so he kept talking. 'There's no *before* and *after* in my memory. It's like everything happened at once. I have all these individual memories floating around in my head, none of which is attached to any of the others. I lack context.'

'What's that?'

'Context is who you are. It's the thing you filter everything else through.'

'But you doan know who you are.'

'Nope.'

'So you got no filter.'

'You got it.'

'Tell me one.'

'One what?'

'One of them things you got floatin' around inside yo' head.'

Randy thought it over. 'I'm good at math,' he said finally.

'How you know that?'

'I just do.'

'How you get good at math?'

'I don't remember.'

'I suck at math,' Acey said.

'How do you know?'

Acey made his 'damn you're dumb' face. 'School.'

'Probably the same way I got good at it.'

'But you doan remember school?'

'Nope.'

'That's fucked up, man.'

'Yeah. It is.'

'What we gonna do now?'

'We probably better get out of here,' Randy said.

Acey looked pained. 'We just got here.'

'Best we keep moving.'

'Wasn't nobody following us here, dog. We was careful.'

'They'll be along.'

'How they gonna find us?'

'I don't know, but they will.'

Randy stuffed the torn and bloody shirt into the wastebasket, picked up his bag, and headed for the door. Acey tagged along behind.

'I'm hungry, dog,' he said as they closed the door and started down the littered walkway along the front of the motel.

'Soon as we get up the road a ways, we'll stop and get something to eat.'

Acey kicked an empty Diet Coke can, sending it spinning off in front of them.

'What you gonna do after you get rid of me?'

'No idea,' Randy said.

Acey kicked the can again, sending it clanking end over end this time.

'You goin' back to dat house.'

'Maybe,' Randy said. He eyed the kid sideways, wondering how a nine-year-old could be so adept at reading his intentions. Of course he was going back to the house.

What had she called it? . . . *A little charade*. And something about the guy . . . how the dude kept using the name . . . like he was talking about himself in the third person or something . . . almost as if . . . Randy nearly missed a step on the sidewalk. He stopped walking. Acey kept going . . . as if maybe Wes Howard wasn't *his* name either . . . all of which made it possible that Randy was really Wes Howard after all . . . and then he heard her voice again . . . *it isn't like he's coming back*, she'd said. He who? Randy wondered.

Was she referring to him? Didn't sound like it, and how would she have any idea whether or not he was going to come back? And what were all those papers she felt a need to hide in the bomb shelter? And what was she . . .

The sight of the car scattered his thoughts. He kept walking as he found the keys and pushed the green button. Acey got in and was ready to go as Randy slid into the driver's seat and buckled up. Above his head, one of the buttons on the head-liner was blinking a blue light. On Star. Randy wondered whether it always blinked and he just hadn't noticed, or whether this was something new. He looked over at Acey. The look of terror painted on the kid's face froze the blood in Randy's veins.

Slowly he turned his eyes toward the front of the car. Chester Berry. The cop. Big old bruise running all the way across his forehead. Big black automatic pointed at Randy's head. Jaw wired shut so's his tongue could heal. He growled an order that sounded like: 'Gggowwwwdcar.'

'I think he wants us to get out,' Acey said.

'Stay put,' Randy said.

'Gggowwwwdcar,' louder this time. Chester Berry was waving the gun back and forth. 'Gggowwwwduckingcar,' he roared through a mouthful of gauze.

Randy showed his palms, then made like he was reaching for the door handle, instead dropping the Mercedes into reverse, crimping the wheel, and flooring it. A slug came roaring in the open window, passing so close beneath Randy's chin that it rattled his teeth.

'Hang on,' he said to Acey as the car rocketed backward. He heard two more shots and then another as he straightened the wheel and bounced out into the street. He dumped the car into drive and went speeding off in the direction of the ocean. In the rearview mirror, he saw Berry come out from between buildings, assume the combat position, and then change his mind, choosing instead to go ambling back out of sight.

Like he was in no hurry at all, Randy thought to himself. Like . . . like he could find us whenever he wanted to.

A minute later, the blue light began to blink. 'Shit,' Randy said out loud. He made two quick right turns and then squealed the car to a stop at the curb. The blue light blinked incessantly now.

He got out of the car, looked around, and there it was . . . right in front of his face, a little black square, no bigger that a matchbox, right at the junction of the roof and the back window. He hurried back, grabbed hold of it with his fingers, and ripped it from its magnetic mooring. He jerked until the wire broke and then threw the antenna in the street. He ran back to the driver's side and jumped into the car.

The blue On Star light was cold and dead. He turned to Acey. His exultation at finding how Berry had found them died in his throat. The kid sat staring straight ahead. Sounded like his breathing was labored . . . like he had a lot of congestion in his lungs . . . except the sucking noise wasn't coming from his mouth . . . it was coming from . . . Randy reached over and touched him. His hand came back warm and sticky. That noise again . . . coming from the bubbling hole in his chest.

'Oh, Jesus,' escaped Randy's lips.

CHAPTER 32

Landon Street was a zoo. The first 'shirt-sleeve' day of the year. Couldn't have been much more than sixty degrees or so, but after a tumultuous winter and early spring, anything in the vicinity of a warm day was greeted with unbounded enthusiasm.

Helen and Ken stepped aside and let a pair of baggy-pants skate-boarders thread their way up the sidewalk. Joggers wound their way through the crowded sidewalks, showing acres of pale skin to the crackheads and the junkies and the panhandlers who'd crawled squinting from winter dens and returned to their haunts along the avenue.

'I really think he was the best,' Helen said. 'I've always loved the old ones with Sean Connery, but this guy . . .' – she waved a hand – 'this guy was a dish.' She pretended to wipe sweat from her brow. 'Whatshisname . . .'

'Daniel Craig,' Ken filled in.

'I mean . . .' The hand across the brow again.

They'd just been to the new James Bond movie, *Casino Royale*. Something about Daniel Craig had pushed her buttons. Her breathing got shallow every time he came on-screen, which was about 99 percent of the time. At one particularly erotic moment, she'd leaned so far forward her Coke spilled onto the floor.

'It was good,' Ken said. 'More like the books than the others.' He made a disgusted face. 'None of the supertechnology crap. None of the toys. No giants with steel teeth. No foolishness like that.'

'How about an ice cream?' Helen asked.

Ken threw an arm around her shoulder, pulling her out of the way of another pair of skateboarders, whose noisy wheels ground over the uneven concrete like an oncoming train. She leaned against his chest and watched as the skaters propelled themselves through the crowd.

'Cherry Garcia?' Ken asked.

'Of course,' she said.

Walking through a crowd, holding each other close, isn't the easiest thing to do. They'd had to dodge this way and that and even come to a complete stop a couple of times before they made it to Ben & Jerry's.

'On me,' Helen announced as they slid through the door. 'You got the movie. I'll get the ice cream.'

Ken didn't argue. Instead, he sidled over to the only empty table and took a seat. The table was a mess. A deconstructed newspaper not only covered the table but was stuck to the surface here and there by what appeared to be ice cream residue.

Ken couldn't deal with that kind of clutter. While

Helen waited in line, he borrowed a wet rag from the busboy, wiped the table, and then began reorganizing the newspaper. By the time he had it reassembled, Helen was on her way to the table with a pair of ice cream cups. Cherry Garcia for her, vanilla for him.

Ken spooned ice cream into his mouth as Helen got settled in her seat. He pointed down at the blaring newspaper headline. HOPE FOUND?

'What about this whole missing-guy thing?' Ken said.

Helen was nodding. 'I only caught part of it this morning, so what? . . . The FBI has found this guy or something?'

'No,' Ken said. 'A confidential FBI source says they recently ran a set of prints through their system and the prints came up as his.'

'After all these years?'

'Could be the prints are that old, too.'

'Do they know where he is?'

'No,' Ken said. 'Just that his prints showed up.'

'Remind me about this Hope guy,' she said around a mouthful of Cherry Garcia.

'You remember . . . the astronaut . . . guy was scheduled to blast off on the *Venture* mission. Went missing the night before the scheduled liftoff. Big to-do over whether they were going to postpone the mission . . . then they decided to replace him . . . thing takes off okay, completes the mission in space . . .'

She poked the air with her ice-cream spoon.

'. . . and then the ship burns up in the atmosphere during reentry.'

'Killing everybody on board,' Ken finished. 'And, as far as I know, nobody's ever seen or heard from Adrian Hope again.'

'Isn't he supposed to have been in some way . . . involved?'

Ken waved a disgusted hand. 'All that's just conspiracy theory. All those TV shows and the stuff in the magazines . . . that's somebody making a buck. It's all bunk. Nobody's ever proved anything one way or another.'

'You never know,' she teased in a singsong voice.

'If anybody knew anything, they'd have sold it to the media by now.'

With the matter seemingly settled, they went back to the serious business of spooning ice cream into their mouths. Halfway through his nearest scoop, Ken turned the paper over. A gray inset box below the fold caught his attention. The head-line asked: GILL THE SOURCE?

According to staff reporter Wayne Fontana, unconfirmed sources within the FBI were now reporting that the fingerprints in question had been submitted for analysis by none other than Queen Anne County district attorney Bruce Gill, whose office was, at this time, refusing comment on the matter.

Ken swiveled the paper Helen's way. He pointed to the beginning of the insert. Helen leaned forward. Her spoon stopped halfway to her mouth.

280

She pulled the paper closer, read, then reread the article. She set her ice-cream cup on the table and looked up at Ken. 'No way,' she said.

'Be a hell of a coincidence.'

'That's crazy.'

'And the state never fingerprinted him?'

She made a rude noise with her lips. 'Are you kidding? Fingerprints cost money. The state doesn't spend money on *retards*.'

'The timing's right. He's been missing for nearly seven years.'

'I don't believe it,' she said.

Ken turned the paper back his way, put his index finger down at the bottom of the original article, and then started turning pages. He picked up the paper and held it close to his face. A moment later, he folded the paper into quarters and again turned it Helen's way. The picture was of a well-built young man holding a basketball. Late twenties maybe. Nobody Helen had ever seen before. The caption read: *Adrian Hope*. She looked at the hands. Her breath caught in her throat.

'Do you suppose?' she whispered.

'Let's not get ahead of ourselves here,' Ken cautioned.

'You're right,' she conceded. 'This isn't something we want to go off half-cocked about.'

'No kidding.'

They ate slowly, passing the newspaper back and forth as they spooned away.

Ken left a two-dollar tip. They sidestepped their

way through the crowded shop, back to the side-walk, where they crossed Landon, walked half a block, and started downhill toward Arbor Street.

They walked arm in arm in silence along the sun-dappled sidewalk. Helen wondered whether the silence was for the possibility of Paul turning out to be this Adrian Hope or something in the feel of the moment that merely discouraged dialogue.

They jaywalked across Arbor Street, stepping up over the high granite curbstones at just about the spot where Paul Hardy had been struck by the car. Inwardly, Helen winced and kept her eyes in front of her.

Three strides before turning up the front walk, the sound of shoes slapping on pavement pulled her attention toward the street.

Middle-aged and dumpy, he moved in their direction with uncommon speed and grace. He had his hand extended the whole time. 'Irving Jaynes,' he said as he approached. Energy seemed to ooze from his pores. He gave off the feeling he could sell iceboxes to Eskimos.

Baffled, Helen took his hand in hers. His hand was hard. His grip suggested strength. 'Helen Willis,' she said. She used her free hand to gesture toward Ken. 'This is my friend Ken Suzuki.' Ken favored the stranger with the smallest of nods.

'Just bought the house across the street,' he said, pointing at the seedy Tudor mansion which had been for sale for the past six months or so. 'Just wanted to introduce myself to the neighbors.'

Helen's breeding took over. She went all gracious and nice, welcoming him to the neighborhood, getting in her pitch for Harmony House. After exchanging pleasantries, she gave him several verbal cues to suggest the conversation was coming to an end. He didn't, however, get the message. He kept talking. How much he loved the city and the weather, his renovation plans for the new house.

It went on and on until Ken began to tighten his grip on her arm. She extended her hand again, intending to shake her way out of the conversation. With a mischievous look in his eye, Jaynes bent at the waist and kissed the back of her hand.

'My great pleasure,' he said.

They stood rooted on the spot, watching as their new neighbor hurried across Arbor Street and disappeared into the house.

'What kind of crap was that?' Ken asked when he was gone.

'What crap?'

'That hand-kissing stuff?'

'I thought it was elegant,' she said.

Ken's face looked like he had a bad taste in his mouth.

Helen stifled a grin. He was jealous. No doubt about it. She had the urge to giggle but suppressed that, too.

CHAPTER 33

Took forty minutes before the Pakistani doctor shuffled out from behind closed doors. The nurse at the desk pointed him toward Randy, who was sitting on the only bench inside the Trauma center. Randy would have met him halfway except he was handcuffed to the bench.

The doctor sat down next to him. He ran his liquid brown eyes over Randy's face, but remained silent. If he noticed the blood all over the front of Randy's shirt, he didn't let on. He put a hand on Randy's shoulder.

'I'm sorry,' he said. 'There was nothing we could do.'

Randy turned away. He rested his throbbing head on his cuffed wrist. The doctor started to speak, but Randy waved him off with his free hand. A minute passed before Randy heard the sound of the man's shuffling feet fading in the distance. A deep sob escaped Randy's chest. And then another, as they came more frequently, until he could hardly breathe. Took another few minutes to gain some measure of control over himself. He wiped his face with his free arm.

The cop wandered over. 'I called for a unit to take you down-town,' he said. He waited, but Randy stared off into space. 'I don't know what's going on here, mister, but I'm sorry for your loss,' he added. 'A boy that age . . . it's just not right.'

Randy broke out crying again, this time letting himself go; his shoulders shook as sorrow took charge of him, racking his body with spasms of grief. His head felt as if someone were pounding nails into his forehead. His stomach rolled once and then again.

'I need to use the john,' Randy said.

'We'll have a car here in an—'

'I think I'm going to be sick,' he said. Dropping his head down onto his manacled hand. Shielding the cop's view with his body, he stuck a finger down his throat. He dry-heaved several times. Did it again until he felt bile in his throat.

The desk nurse looked up from the pile of charts in front of her. She wagged a finger his way, opened her mouth to speak, but it was too late. The contents of Randy's stomach landed on the floor between his feet.

'No . . . no . . . no,' the nurse chanted. 'We can't be having that in here.'

She was on her feet now, moving out from behind the desk with the speed and grace of a woman half her age and a third her size. An orderly poked his head into the nurses' station. She pinned him in place with a thick brown finger. 'Get a mop and a bucket,' she commanded.

'I was just—' the guy stammered.

'I don't care what you was "justing" . . . you find a mop and a bucket and you get yourself back here and get this cleaned up.'

She used the same finger on the cop. 'Take him in there,' she said pointing to a door labeled STAFF ONLY.

The cop approached Randy from the side, careful to keep his well-shined shoes away from the puddle of puke shimmering on the floor. First he unlocked the cuff from the arm of the bench, then changed his mind and decided he didn't want his cuffs puked on either, removing them from Randy's wrist and stuffing them into the black leather case attached to the back of his belt.

He helped Randy maneuver around the mess and escorted him over to the restroom. He followed Randy in the door and stood with his arms folded across his chest, standing sentry as Randy braced himself, bent low over the sink, and puked again.

His dedication to duty lasted until Randy splashed water over his face, dried himself with a paper towel, and then began to undo his trousers. 'Sorry,' Randy said sheepishly. 'But I gotta . . .'

The cop winced. He crossed the room and tried the other door. Satisfied it was locked from the other side, he headed for the hall. 'I'll be right outside,' he said, stepping out and closing the door firmly behind himself. Randy waited a beat, then holding his pants up with one hand, he used the other to push the 'lock' button in the center of the handle.

He rebuttoned his pants and looked around. A rubber glove dispenser was attached to the wall. Three holes: small, medium, and large. A disposal container for needles and other sharp objects. Directions for how to properly wash one's hands. The cabinet along the far wall was filled with supplies: gauze, syringes, a blood-pressure cuff, tongue depressors, more gloves, a pair of scissors, several pairs of green scrubs, little green slippers, a stethoscope.

He grabbed the scissors and a couple of tongue depressors from the shelf and dropped to one knee in front of the other door. He inserted the sharp end of the scissors into the doorjamb, pushing hard, trying to get some purchase on the steel bolt. No luck. He tried again. No.

The door to the hall began to rattle. 'You okay in there?' the cop wanted to know.

'Not feeling too good,' Randy said.

'Let's go,' the cop said. 'Your ride's here.'

'Tell 'em to hang on.'

'Let's go, buddy. Squeeze it off.'

Randy tried the scissors again. This time the bolt moved. He tried to increase the pressure but slipped and lost his leverage. The bolt snapped back into place.

The cop rattled the door hard this time. 'Let's go.'

Randy wiggled the blade back and forth, hoping to make some sort of dent in the bolt, something the point could get hold of. The bolt moved again. This time Randy got his shoulder behind it; he watched as the bolt moved, millimeter by millimeter, until he could force the tongue depressor in the space between the end of the bolt and the doorjamb. The cop kicked the outside door. 'Let's go.'

'Gimme a break, man,' Randy wheezed.

Randy grabbed the knob with his free hand and pulled the door open. He stuck his head out into a deserted custodial corridor, scrambled to his feet, and took off running, all the way to the end of the space, to the green exit sign and the stairs.

CHAPTER 34

Bruce Gill lifted his chin, looked in the mirror, and made a final adjustment to his tie. He turned toward Kirsten.

'Looks great,' she said on cue.

He smiled, took a deep breath, and asked, 'You ready?'

'Backgrounds are us,' she said with a sneer.

He pulled open the door and then stood aside so Kirsten could precede him into the Queen Anne County press room. The roar of conversation rose considerably as they crossed the front of the room and mounted the dais.

The place was jammed. CBS, NBC, ABC, CNN, MSNBC, FOX, the BBC, the local affiliates, a hundred people packed into a room designed to hold twenty. From the look of it, another hundred were outside in the hall. The lectern was a forest of microphones as Bruce Gill gripped the wooden edges and gazed confidently out over the assembled multitude. 'Ladies and gentlemen,' he began. The roar of conversation dimmed as if it were on a switch. 'I'd like to say a few words and then, time permitting, answer a limited number of questions.' The cameras began to whir.

'In the course of a separate and ongoing investigation, my office made a routine request for a fingerprint identification from IAFIS' – he spelled out the letters – '. . . which, as most of you are aware, is the FBI's national fingerprint database.' The roar began to rise. 'Much to our surprise, the fingerprints were identified as those of one Adrian Hope. As you are also aware, Mr Hope has been missing since December fourteenth, 1999, when he disappeared from the Kennedy Space Center at Cape Canaveral, Florida, on the night before he was scheduled to captain the space shuttle *Venture* on a mission of scientific experimentation.'

Gill paused for effect. 'Adding to the mystery surrounding Commander Hope's untimely disappearance . . .' And then he went on and on about the tragic end of the mission and the years and years of hypothesizing and conspiracy theories which followed, burying the media in a blizzard of election-year sound bites.

Half a dozen hands were raised. Gill nodded in the manner of a parent with unruly children. 'Naturally, my office has taken every available step to assure that the fingerprints are genuine and not part of some elaborate hoax.' The dull roar raised itself to a full-throated rumble. 'The FBI crime laboratory assures us that the fingerprints were made sometime within the past sixty days.' He held up a hand. 'Apparently the age of the fingerprints can be determined by the amount of oil still clinging to the impressions.'

At this point, it sounded as if a small plane had landed in the room. 'Furthermore . . .' He waited for the buzz to subside. 'Furthermore . . . my office has obtained independent, firsthand cooperation as to when the prints were made and by whom.'

He pointed to the white-haired woman in the first row. 'Barbara?'

'Do we take it, then, that you have Mr Hope in custody?'

'You do not,' Gill answered quickly. 'To my knowledge, Mr Hope has no present and no pending criminal charges against him. Once again, as far as we know . . .' He let it trail off. Wolf Blitzer from CNN was next.

'Do you know where Mr Hope is at this time?'

'No . . . we do not.'

'Would you care to share this independent source with us?'

'Not at this time. As I said earlier, this is an ongoing . . .'

It went on and on. Kirsten hid a smirk behind her hand at the thought of tomorrow morning's headline. HOPE IS GONE!

Jacobson threw a five-dollar tip on the bar. Bob followed suit, drawing a 'thank you' nod from the bartender. As he shrugged himself into his coat, Jacobson cast a glance back over his shoulder.

Bruce Gill was still answering questions on the plasma screen over the bar. He grabbed the brass door handle and stepped out into the street.

The air was fresh and warm. In the city, the cherry blossoms were beginning to bloom. Jacobson lingered just outside the pub while Bob held the door for an entering couple and then stepped out himself.

'Nice,' he said.

'The weather?' Jacobson asked with a wry grin.

'All of it,' Bob said.

They began walking down the street together, heading east toward the river.

'I can't remember the guy's name. I think he was a famous writer or something.' Jacobson tried to recall a name. 'Anyway, this guy spent some time out in Hollywood, and when he came back he issued the famous pronouncement: "Nobody knows anything."'

'Golding or Goldman . . . something like that.'

Jacobson nodded. 'I believe you're right.'

'And you figure that's where we are?'

'Exactly.'

'The Florida situation needs to disappear.'

'It's already gone.'

'Really?'

'Our Mr Howard has been accounted for.'

'Oh?'

Mr G took care of things.

Bob stopped walking. 'After what happened?'

'He's still the best. He's been doing wet work

for fifteen years and never raised a ripple.' Before Bob could protest, Jacobson went on. 'Not only is he as interested in his own security as we are in ours, but he actually welcomed the opportunity to clean up after . . . after the last unfortunate circumstance.'

'I hate loose ends.'

'Look at this as an opportunity to clean one up.'

'But . . .'

Jacobson stopped walking. 'Look, Bob,' he said. 'I don't want to sound pontifical or anything . . .'

Bob averted his face and sighed. He felt blood rushing to his cheeks as he remembered how much he hated Jacobson's little lectures.

'You know . . . I think that's one of the hidden perils of success.'

'What's that?'

'You forget how you got there.' He waved a hand in the air. 'You forget about all the work and all the compromises it took, and after a while, you start feeling like you were destined to be where you are . . . like it was God's will or something that you be an undersecretary in the Defense Department.'

'Is there a point here, Ron?'

'The point is, Bob . . . you and I are where we are today because of what we did back then and for no other reason. Because we chose to ignore an engineering report.' He sighed. 'An overzealous engineering report.'

'I didn't do anything.'

Jacobson smiled. 'Because of what we *didn't* do, then,' he amended. Bob opened his mouth to speak, but Jacobson cut him off. 'I try not to delude myself that I was appointed to the highest civilian post in the National Security Agency because I was the most viable candidate.' He made a sweeping gesture with his arm. 'The trees were full of people who were at least as qualified as we were.'

'We didn't do anything,' Bob repeated.

'You must not be Catholic.'

'What's that got to—'

'The nuns back in grammar school spent a lot of time making sure we understood that *omissive sins* were the same as *comissive* sins.'

'I must have missed that lesson.'

'Point is . . .' He hesitated. 'Point is, we suspected the tiles weren't right. We had an engineering report to the effect that the tiles were a liability aaand . . .' – he stretched out the word – '. . . and we chose to ignore it.'

'Eight people died,' Bob whispered. 'Eight people.'

Jacobson kept talking, louder now. 'Accidents happen. Nobody was supposed to get killed.' He cut the air with his hand. 'At most we expected to lose a few tiles. Lost tiles would have meant a halt to the program. Nobody ever imagined the shuttle was going to spread itself all over East Texas.'

'Ten people if you count Howard and Barber.'

'Eight, ten . . . it doesn't matter, the point is, we were induced to look the other way.'

'Induced?'

'With promises of promotion . . . which . . .'

Jacobson was wagging a finger now. Bob wanted to break it off.

'. . . we have mined for everything it was worth. Ten years ago we were a couple of midlevel functionaries on a NASA project. These days we have everything . . . more money, more power, more perks than we could ever have imagined.' He swept his arm again. 'And all because of that choice we made.'

Bob thrust his hands deep into the pockets of his overcoat. His face was grim.

They reached the corner of Whitman and Bridge. Bob lived four blocks to the right. They stopped. Jacobson took up the thread.

'My friend is going to take care of Mr Hope once and for all.'

'Is that necessary?'

'Unfortunately.'

'How so?'

'There's another complication.'

'Oh?'

'*Our* Mr Howard . . .'

'Late of Cocoa Beach.'

'The same.'

'What about him?'

'At the very end of his tenure . . .'

'Yes?'

'. . . he claimed the woman had been keeping a diary.'

'Did he say where this item might be found?'

'He never got the chance. Apparently, he was quite distraught . . . babbling . . .'

'And?'

'Seems he made a move to escape and things got unfortunate from there.'

'And this diary hasn't turned up.'

'It was not among the personal effects.'

'What about the wife?'

'The wife and daughters have gone missing. They left Florida on a Greyhound bus the day before Mr Howard's tenure came to an end.'

'A bus to . . . ?'

'Fayetteville, Arkansas.'

Bob waited. He remembered how much he hated Jacobson's pregnant pauses.

'. . . where they never arrived,' Jacobson went on. 'Several passengers agree that they never reboarded the bus after a rest stop in South Georgia. The trail goes cold from there. She must have had somebody waiting.'

'Is that going to be a problem?'

'Not in any meaningful way. If she knew anything earth-shattering, we would have heard about it by now.'

'Something like that would have a great deal of prurient value even if she didn't know anything meaningful.'

'Yes . . . it would. And she didn't.'

'And you're thinking Mr Hope might be in some way . . .'

'He was in the neighborhood.'

'Two birds with one stone.'

'Hopefully.'

Bob stretched his arms out to the side and rolled his neck.

'It may be time to institute your Walter Hybridge idea,' he said.

Jacobson smiled. 'There were only three of us in project management. Engineering reports came directly to us. Walter was one . . .' – he craned his neck as if inspecting the street – 'and the other two are standing on this corner.'

'Unfortunate for Walter.'

'But good for us.'

'You'll keep me posted?' Bob asked.

Jacobson chuckled. 'From now on, you'll be able to read about it in the papers.'

'Grim tragedy in Florida.'

'Hope is about to go missing again.'

'And Walter Hybridge's papers?'

'A number of documents are about to surface. Documents that suggest Walter may have compromised himself.'

'Pity,' Bob muttered.

They shook hands and walked off in opposite directions.

CHAPTER 35

They were gone. He felt it the minute he jumped the gate and saw the backyard. The yard darts were missing . . . so were the broke-back swings and the pool and every other scrap of crap that was lying around in the grass when he'd been here last night. The yard was immaculate, like some neater, cleaner family had moved into 432 Water Street overnight.

Randy took two tentative steps forward. The lanai came into view. What just last night had been a jumble of toys and trash was now clean and empty. His heart sank. His skin tingled as he crossed the lawn, let himself silently into the lanai, and mounted the back stairs. He pulled off his T-shirt and wrapped it around his hand as he tried the back door. Wasn't even latched, let alone locked.

Randy pushed the door open and waited. The silence was cavernous. He climbed the trio of stairs and stood leaning against the kitchen counter waiting for his eyes to become adjusted to the darkness. His nose twitched. The place reeked of bleach.

A couple of minutes and he could make out the walls, which was fortunate because walls were the only things left in the house. The furniture was gone. The carpets had been torn from the floors and carted off. Every cupboard and drawer in the kitchen was empty. He opened the door at the far end of the kitchen. The garage was empty of cars and everything else people keep in garages. Even the trash cans were empty, hosed out . . . clean as a whistle.

He crept upstairs. Same deal. Nothing left at all. What had once been the master bedroom turned out to be the source of the bleach smell. So strong it made his eyes run. Dark blotches on the bedroom floor forced him to turn his eyes away. Randy's mind raced. Had they fled? Or had the woman been right? Was the charade, whatever that was, simply over? He returned to the kitchen and let himself out.

He crossed the lawn to the shop building and walked to the side door. Same deal. The place had been completely cleaned out. His eyes dropped to the floor, where long moon shadows crisscrossed the concrete. The grate was in place.

He crossed quickly and dropped to one knee. Lacing his fingers through the metal grate, he pulled hard and immediately fell over backward. The grate weighed about a third of what it should. Must have been aluminum or something.

The black metal stairs led nearly straight down. At the bottom, he found himself standing on a concrete slab. Poured-concrete walls hugged his shoulders. The black metal door in front of his face gave the impression he was about to enter a bank vault. He said a silent prayer and grabbed the handle, hoping they were holed up inside, sitting back eating Ritz crackers, drinking bottled water, waiting for nuclear winter to end, but once again, his instincts already knew better.

The door opened on silent hinges. He felt around the edges until he found a light switch. He was about to flip it but changed his mind, first stepping all the way inside, then closing the door, before hitting the lights.

What he had imagined to be a single room was, in fact, three separate ten-by-ten spaces. The vestibule, where he presently stood, doubled as a pantry; the walls were shelves and filled floor to ceiling with nonperishable foodstuffs, pork and beans to powdered milk.

To the left was a sleeping room. Six cots bolted to the walls. Every available empty space packed with supplies of some kind. A single overhead light cast deep shadows into the corners of each room. Tacked on the wall was a poster. AIR RAID SHELTER, it read. Randy moved in close. In the lower right-hand corner, the poster was dated 1959.

Directly in front of his position sat a table and chairs. A small sink occupied the right-hand wall. A curtained alcove contained a chemical toilet. But it was the table that commanded his attention. She hadn't bothered to hide it. It sat there on the table with an outdated can of green beans holding it down.

Randy walked over to the table and sat. Coupla hundred pages anyway. Looked like she'd been writing a novel by hand. He removed the can and turned the manuscript to face him. He read the top of the first page. Sounded like a message in a bottle. *I've been planning for this moment for years. If you're reading this, we've gone*, it began. Several cross-outs followed. One of the partially obliterated phrases had read, *or at least we tried to leave.* He took up reading where the corrections left off. *My name is Isobel Howard. I have lived in this house for the past seven years with my daughters, Tracy and Nicole, and a man whose real name I do not know.*

Randy thought he might have heard a noise upstairs in the shop. He held his breath and waited. When the noise did not repeat itself, he scooped the manuscript under his arm and started for the door. That's when the photograph fell to the floor facedown.

Randy bent to retrieve it. On the back, written in a woman's handwriting, *Wes* was all it said. He killed the lights.

CHAPTER 36

Memory's a funny thing. Everything transpires in the present tense. A second later, however, it's past tense and, as such, becomes immediately subject to both visions and revisions. Amazing how that happens. How the past and the present get mixed together into a stew of sights and sounds upon which we selectively attach the title 'reality' . . . meaning *that which actually happened* as opposed to *that which we made up about it later*, when 'in reality' we have no means whatsoever of keeping the 'real' and the 'imagined' separate from each other.

Fact is . . . human beings don't possess a feedback mechanism for that sort of thing . . . we have no way of knowing for sure what actually happened in a given situation as opposed to how we later edited it to suit ourselves, because *then* and *later* are sharing the studio apartment of our minds with nothing but a nanosecond of time sitting between them on the futon of memory.

Faced with this 'reality,' we take the only 'real' option left to us. We pretend that what we come into contact with through our senses is what is,

302

and that others who are prone not to see things precisely as we do need to pay more attention and maybe take a few notes. I mean . . . that's what growing up is all about, isn't it? Trial and error. That period of one's life wherein a person eventually grows into the role he's been playing.

So the current confusion as to how Randy whatever he called himself got into his present condition should be considered something less than surprising. All he knew for certain was that he wasn't Paul Hardy . . . Paul didn't exist at all, and he sure wasn't Randall James. He knew who Randall was. And he sure as hell wasn't Wesley Allen Howard either, a guy who had probably existed at one time but was presently missing and presumed . . . presumed what?

And so . . . it's safe to say Randy's head was seriously bent out of shape as he sat on the edge of that cheap motel bed and ran his fingers through his hair. Acey was gone. The Howards were gone. Felt like everything connecting him to the universe was gone.

He pushed the power button on the remote. Took the TV a full minute to come on. Black and white with a persistent roll. The tape loop of our lives: CNN. He sat there staring at the screen . . . trying to figure out what to do with the rest of his life, when this guy comes on the screen, hair helmet, hundred-dollar tie, the whole dog and pony show. In between rolls, the caption read *Bruce Gill, District Attorney, Queen Anne County.*

The hair on his arms began to rise. He groped for the remote, found it, and turned on the volume just in time for the picture to cut back to the talking head in the studio who was going on about how some guy named Adrian Hope, guy who once was an astronaut and had then disappeared . . . how he had recently been found . . . well, not exactly found, but about how his fingerprints had recently turned up on a routine fingerprint check initiated by this guy Gill, who claimed to have an unimpeachable witness who would swear the prints were genuine.

And then the first picture of the guy flashed on the screen, and in an instant, Randy knew. Not that he remembered anything. He didn't. He just knew. That was him. And then another picture of him, holding a basketball, and the tears began to roll down Randy's cheeks. Without willing it so, he got to his feet and kicked the TV over onto its back. The rolling stopped. He left it there, pointing at the ceiling.

What he knew for sure was that what came next was easy. After that, things didn't look so good.

CHAPTER 37

Whoever said 'power corrupts' was right on. Doesn't matter whether you get your power from a bottle or from a bullet, either way the seeds of corruption are sown and the beginning of the end is in sight.

For Chester D. Berry, the situation was exacerbated by his being a cop. Worse yet, he was a corrupt cop, one who'd been getting away with it for such a long time he couldn't imagine things turning out any other way. That's the problem with dishonesty. Getting away with rotten things gives a person all the wrong messages. It makes them arrogant, makes them assume deceit is within the natural order of the universe and that they're in charge of the local franchise.

All of which probably explained why Randy found Chester Berry in the very first place he looked for him. Why the key from his key ring still fit the back door and why he was sitting there in his underwear, big as life in his Barcalounger, with his dick in one hand and a strawberry milk shake in the other, hunkered down in the easy chair watching a porn video lyrically entitled

Buttman and Throbbin. You had to admire a man with taste.

He ground the silencer into the hollow behind Berry's ear and told him not to move. Not surprisingly, Chester wasn't good at following directions. Instead of doing what he told him, he dropped his dick and began to slide his hand down inside the chair, looking for something more substantial. Randy shot him in the top of the right leg.

The impact launched him out of the chair, down onto the floor, where he bellowed like an animal, rolling around with the injured leg pulled tight against his chest as he rocked back and forth over the strawberry-stained carpet.

Randy or Adrian or whoever felt around in the chair cushions and came out with the brother to the gun he was holding. Same make. Same model. Musta had a two-for-one sale down at the gun shop. He popped the clip and jacked the shell out of the chamber, tossing them in opposite directions before reaching down, twirling a handful of Berry's hair around his latex-covered fingers, and pulling him, kicking and screaming, back into his favorite chair.

Berry's breath came in ragged gasps. His face was the color of an eggplant.

Randy walked around to the front of him and sat down on the corner of the coffee table.

'You stupid fuck!' Berry screamed around the mouthful of sutured tongue. 'You can't kill me. I'm a cop. You kill me and—'

Randy hit him in the mouth with everything he had. Berry's bloodshot eyes opened wide. He made a noise like a horse. The force of the blow tilted the chair back a couple of notches. He brought both hands to his mouth. Thick red blood quickly covered his fingers. A high-pitched keening sound came squeaking out from somewhere deep in his chest. Randy watched his agony and felt embarrassed for him.

Several minutes passed before the sounds of his pain dropped a couple of octaves into something akin to groaning.

'Shut up,' Randy said. 'Open your eyes.'

Berry ignored him.

'Do what I tell you, motherfucker, or I'll hit you in the mouth again.'

The cop's eyes popped open. It was hard to tell what he was trying to say, but whatever it was started with an *N*.

'This is going to be a new experience for both of us,' Randy said.

Berry made some sort of noise Randy couldn't translate.

'As far as I know, this is going to be the first time I ever killed anybody.' Berry started rocking in the chair and screaming through the mess in his mouth. He was spitting blood all over himself. 'Fuck you, asshole,' he screamed.

Randy kept on talking. 'With my memory, I can't really be sure what I've done and what I just read about, but, you know, what the hell, I'll just have

307

to go with what I've got.' His stomach was tied in a knot. 'What we know for sure, though, is that this is going to be your first time to die.' Berry tried to claw his way out of the chair. Randy kicked him back into the seat. 'Barring, of course, such things as reincarnation and all that stuff.' Randy rolled his eyes and waved the thought away with his free hand. 'All of which is *way* over my head. Hell, I only found out who *I* was yesterday and I had to get that off the friggin' TV.'

He got to his feet, pointed the silenced automatic at Berry's right knee, and pulled the trigger. The kneecap exploded. The wall behind the chair was suddenly dotted with bits of blood and bone. A pink haze floated on the air. Berry looked like he was going into shock. Randy bent low, putting his mouth close to Berry's ear.

'That was for the lady down in the Grove. The one who gave you her boy so he could work off her rock habit with his ass. The lady Tyrone's boys cut to pieces because you didn't deliver the dope. I don't know her name and I sure as hell don't like what was going down with her boy . . . I just know she deserved better than she got.'

Randy took a step back. 'And finally, asshole . . .' Berry's chin had fallen to his chest. 'Open your eyes,' Randy said. No response. 'On the count of three, I'm going to smack you in the mouth again. Now open your goddamn eyes,' Randy yelled. 'One, two . . .'

He opened his eyes. The pain and fear were gone.

All that remained was the thousand-yard stare. Whatever he was looking at now was a mile away and visible only to him. Randy wanted him to know where the pain was coming from, but at that point, he was so worked up it didn't matter. He pointed the gun at Berry's forehead.

'And *this*, asshole . . . *this* is from a kid named Acey.'

He closed his eyes. Randy kicked him hard in the leg. The eyes opened again. 'You remember him?'

He nodded and opened his mouth.

He was trying to get control of his lips when the slug hit him between the eyes, sending the greater portion of his brain matter and nearly all of the back of his skull rocketing into the soft fabric of the chair, painting the ceiling above and forming a macabre halo of blood and brains on the leather behind his head.

Randy stood there on the carpet waiting to be overcome by remorse. Waiting to be bent double by a sick feeling in the pit of his stomach . . . the knowledge that he'd just killed another human being and that his life was never going to be the same, because he had taken that which only God had a right to give and take. He waited for the smoldering gut acid to eat its way through his innards, burning his tortured soul until his backbone melted and he fell among the milk shake and the smears of blood and bits of brain covering everything in the room. He closed his eyes and listened to the sound of his own breathing.

He stood with the gun hanging at the end of his arm and the mist of blood still hanging in the air . . . but it didn't come. Instead of remorse, he felt jilted. Like he'd been stood up for the junior prom. Besides which . . . it hadn't felt nearly as good as he had imagined it would. Not only that but he hadn't dragged it out for as long as he'd wanted to. The whole thing was over before he got a chance to 'carpe' the moment. His head throbbed and his mouth tasted of old pennies.

He dropped the automatic at his feet and looked around the room. Took a minute and a half to find Berry's pants hanging in the hall closet. Sure enough, the keys to the rental car were in one of the side pockets.

He went out the way he'd come in, backed the rental into the street, and pulled the Mercedes into the driveway. He emptied the glove box of his personal belongings, stuffing them into his pockets, popped the trunk and grabbed the bag full of dope, and then headed back inside.

He threw Berry's badge and wallet and car keys onto the kitchen table and then carried the bag of dope into the living room. He was looking for something dramatic. Something that couldn't be swept under the rug as cops sought to cover for one of their own, so he ripped one of the packages open and sprinkled it all over the stiff, then scattered the rest of the dope all over the room, dropping some of the bricks into Berry's lap and others down at his feet. Berry had lost all muscle control. The room smelled like a sewer. Berry was back where he belonged.

Randy held his breath and looked around. He checked the keys in his pocket. National Rent-a-Car. He had a wild thought about returning the car on his way out of town, but decided they'd find it in the airport parking lot on their own. He let himself out the front.

CHAPTER 38

Detective Sergeant Boyd Haase was what was once considered 'classically hand-some.' Unfortunately he thought so too. Too often, when Kirsten would turn to look at him, she'd find he'd beaten her to the punch and was already looking at himself . . . in mirrors, in shop windows, in anything reflective. It was, to him, like the world was one vast photo op, and he wanted to be sure he was ready, like he was always posing for some imaginary camera, chin thrust resolutely into the wind, steely gaze straight ahead, with a hint of a shoulder holster and a sardonic smile.

They'd dated for a while, dinner and a movie, that sort of thing, but in the final offing, they'd been unable to find any common ground they could plow in the upright position, and so, like so many others, he'd fallen by Kirsten's wayside.

'Hey,' he said in his most resonant basso profundo.

Kirsten looked up. 'Well, well. To what do I owe the honor of a visit?'

He shook his head. 'Does there have to be a reason for—'

'Yes,' she said. 'As a matter of fact, yes.'

He thought about arguing, but took another tack instead. 'You owe me.'

She rearranged her face into mock surprise. 'For what?'

'For running that name for you.'

'You didn't get anything.'

'I tried.'

'Sounds like the story of our relationship.'

'Now, now,' he chided.

'What's up?'

He wandered around her office, pretending to be on the horns of a dilemma. 'I don't know,' he said. 'This kind of reception . . . I just don't . . .'

She suppressed a growl. 'I'm buried, Boyd.'

He walked over and put one well-clad ass cheek on the corner of her desk. 'Must be tough,' he said. 'All that TV time over the Adrian Hope thing. All those interviews. All the—'

She cut him off. 'I'm just window dressing, Boyd. To me, it's nothing more than an unwanted interruption of my routine.'

'Gill sure loves it.'

'It's an election year.'

'Manna from heaven.'

'And then some.' She waited. Boyd Haase was one of those people who felt a great need to fill silence. As long as he was talking, he felt like he was in control. At least that was how it seemed to him. So all you had to do to find out everything knocking around in his head was to shut up and wait. Just wait until the screaming silence forced him to fill the void with words.

'Guess what I got this morning.'

'Spare me the guessing games.'

'An inquiry from the Bureau.'

'About what?'

'About that *inquiry* I made for you.' She was giving him nothing. 'The inquiry about a missing person named Wesley Allen Howard.'

She sat back in her chair. 'What about him?'

'I thought that would get your attention.'

'Why would you think that?'

'Come on, Kirsten . . . I was born on a weekend, but it wasn't *last* weekend.'

'What about this Mr Howard?'

'He's missing.'

'Missing how?'

'From his home in Cocoa Beach, Florida.'

'No kidding.'

'Along with his wife and a pair of twin daughters.'

'Was this Wesley Howard on the list of Wesley Allen Howards that we . . . ?'

He nodded. 'The girls hadn't been to school in a couple of days. Nobody was answering the phone, so the school sent one of their security officers over . . .'

'And?'

'And . . . the place was cleaned out.' He dusted his hands together. 'Everything . . . right down to the carpets.'

'No mention of it at school?' He shook his head.

'Nothing to the neighbors?' Same shake. 'Signs of foul play?'

He checked his reflection in the office door. 'You know the Bureau,' he said. 'They're not saying anything they don't have to.'

'Could be just a . . .' She couldn't bring herself to say the C-word.

The cop leaned in close enough for her to smell his breath mints. '*This* Mr Howard was a senior project manager at the Kennedy Space Center.' Before she could respond, he went on. 'The very same space center where your Mr Adrian Hope went missing lo those many years ago.'

Kirsten tried to look blasé. 'Interesting' was all she could manage in the way of repartee. 'So what have we got here?'

Haase went on. 'Neighbors say they moved in the dead of night.'

'It happens.'

'They'd been there seven, eight years.' He made a dubious face. 'Now all of a sudden . . .' He let it hang. He bent low enough to look in her face. 'So . . . what do I tell them?'

'Tell who?'

'The Bureau. They want to know what *we* know.'

'What *we* know is all over the news.'

'That's it? We tell 'em to watch TV?'

'That's it.'

'They're not going to like that.'

'I don't see as they've got a choice.'

He pried himself from his perch on the edge of

her desk, checked his reflection again, and headed for the door. 'Seriously. They're sending a team over this afternoon,' he said. 'What am I gonna tell 'em?'

'Tell them to come and see me,' she said.

He bent close again. She pushed him away.

'I was hoping . . .' he began.

'Hope springs eternal,' she said, and went back to her work.

Helen propped herself up on her elbow and looked around the room. Ken Suzuki kept house the way he did everything else, thoroughly, immaculately, as if somebody was keeping score somewhere and demerits were going to be handed out later. While her own living quarters were always awash in newspapers, magazines, and coffee cups, Ken's house didn't have so much as a pushpin out of place.

She moved her eyes to the right, to the other side of the bed where Ken lay sleeping, or trying to sleep maybe. Sleep came hard to people who weren't used to sharing a bed. They would both look a bit haggard, as if they hadn't been getting their rest, which, of course, they hadn't.

Not since that crazy moment at her kitchen sink yesterday. After James Bond and ice cream, when, completely out of the blue, without the thought ever having crossed her mind, she'd put the cake plate down in the sink, wiped her hands on her apron, and then put her arms around Ken's neck.

The Catholic part of her would have liked to say they'd fumbled, that they'd groped and grimaced their way through their first true experience of passion, due to lifelong purity and innocence.

Wouldn't have been true, though. Nope. Truth was, from the outset, they were a 'well-oiled machine.' Helen covered her mouth as she laughed at her unintentional double entendre. Any trepidations either of them might have had concerning their complete lack of experience had immediately been cast aside by their mutual desire. A chaste pressing of the lips quickly evolved into an open-mouthed attempt to swallow each other whole as they segued from sink to sofa, where it seemed like an instant later they were naked together and she felt his need before she felt him slide inside of her.

The Catholic purity-and-innocence thing reared its head again in that part of her and wished she might have suffered more, that her first experience might have merely been a prelude to better, more mature things.

That wouldn't have been true either. From that first moment, her passion had overflowed . . . and Ken . . . Ken was possessed, like *Rosemary's Baby* or something, a human dynamo, moving her this way and that for this experience and that, until he ran out of fantasies and Helen took him in hand and introduced him to a few of hers. Like Ken had said: If the sex got any better than it was, they'd need a doctor in attendance.

She lay in bed and mused on the idea that new love and its attendant throes of lust were most generally visited upon the young for a reason . . . because the young were the ones most able to weather the disruption of their life patterns.

Ken rolled over, facing away from her now. She started to reach for the bedside phone, resisted the urge, and smiled to herself. Whatever was going on at Harmony House would just have to take care of itself. Mrs Forbes and Mr Hallinan knew what they were doing. They knew where she was. They had a contact number. She pulled the sheet tight beneath her breasts and remembered something her mother used to say: 'The grave-yard's full of indispensable people.' Amen, she thought to herself.

The doorbell rang. Ken sat straight up in bed and checked the clock. Ten to eight, on a Sunday morning. 'Probably that Irving guy,' Ken muttered as he threw his feet over the side of the bed. He threw a mock scowl her way.

Helen laughed. 'He shadowed us,' she said.

'Guy needs to get a life,' Ken grumbled.

Irving . . . she couldn't remember whether it was his first or last name . . . the guy who bought the house across the street from Harmony House. Seemed like every time they went outside together, he was there, raking the yard, cleaning out the flower beds, coasting back and forth on the front porch swing. Any excuse to cross the street and make eyes at Helen. Although he'd never admit it,

Ken was seriously jealous. For her part, Helen was mildly flattered and genuinely amused.

She watched as Ken walked to the back of the bedroom door, to the hook where his *yukata* hung. Big blue-and-white koi swimming all over everything. He looked like a warrior as he tied the sash around his middle and pulled open the door. He looked her way, winked, and then closed the door behind himself. She listened to the sound of his bare feet on the hardwood floor.

Helen sat up, put her feet on the floor, and looked around for her clothes. The sight of her panties told her she needed to go shopping for something more enticing . . . not that Ken needed any enticing, but more as a matter of personal pride.

She carried her clothes and her purse into the bathroom. From her purse she drew a toothbrush and a tube of toothpaste. The way she saw it, they were nowhere near the leaving-things-at-each-other's-house stage of things, so she came prepared.

She was working up a good foam when Ken knocked on the bathroom door. She rinsed and then rerinsed before speaking.

'Yes,' she said.

'I think you better come downstairs,' he said.

CHAPTER 39

Randy was having an out-of-body experience, sitting in Ken's kitchen, where he'd been so many times before, only this time he was drinking coffee, shooting the breeze with Ken and Ms Willis, and watching an hour-long *CNN Special Report* about *himself*.

After the initial round of hugs and handshakes, Ken had gone back upstairs to get dressed. Feeling a need to relieve a somewhat awkward situation, Helen Willis had snapped on the TV. By the time Ken returned, they were hooked.

The TV rehashed the whole missing-astronaut thing, how the mission had nearly been scrapped only to be salvaged at the last minute. Went into detail as to what NASA engineers believed was responsible for the tragic reentry. Showed pictures of bits and pieces of the shuttle spread all over East Texas. They ran bios of the eight-person crew, interviewed surviving family members, most of whom had seemed genuinely dumbfounded about the sudden reappearance of Adrian Hope, while yet others had been angry . . . angry at having it all dredged up again, angry that Hope was alive while their loved ones weren't. On one hand, the attitude didn't seem any too charitable. On the other hand, Randy decided he didn't blame them a bit. That's when the words came creeping across the bottom of the screen. *BREAKING NEWS. BREAKING NEWS.*

Jump cut to a street scene. 'CNN correspondent Marcia Lockwood reporting from Cocoa Beach, Florida.' Randy choked on his coffee. There it was . . . halfway down the block . . . 432 Water Street. Police response vans had blocked the street off at both ends. Miles of yellow incident tape wound around 432 like ribbon on a package. '. . . a Cocoa Beach Police Department source, speaking on the condition of anonymity, has informed CNN that both the Federal Bureau of Investigation and the U.S. Secret Service are investigating the disappearance of a senior NASA project manager and his family from their home in the posh Beach Commons neighborhood of Cocoa Beach, Florida.'

A photo of the guy who lived at the house was inset into the screen. 'Wesley Allen Howard, thirty-nine, his wife, Isobel, and their twin ten-year-old daughters, Tracy and Nicole.' Three smaller insets beneath his picture. 'Neighbors have given the local police a description of *this* man . . .' Police artist drawing. Sinister looking. His general features but pretty generic. '. . . seen around the neighborhood over several recent days.'

Randy was still staring at the drawing when he felt their eyes.

'Not much of a likeness,' he said.

'Were . . .'

The voice-over was winding up. 'Recent developments surrounding missing astronaut Adrian Hope beg the question as to whether these events might be in some manner related. Citing the sensitive nature of Mr Howard's job as well as national security concerns, neither the FBI nor the Secret Service is prepared to comment at this time. This is Marcia Lockwood, in Cocoa Beach, Florida, for CNN.'

Cut back to the *Special Report*. They were working their way through the vast array of conspiracy theories surrounding his sudden disappearance. Randy turned to Ken and Ms Willis. The question was how much to tell them.

'Okay . . .' he began. 'Here's what happened after I left here.' He left Acey and his mama and Chester Berry and the drugs out of it. Other than that, he told it pretty much as he remembered it, for whatever that was worth. The way he told the story, it ended when he picked up the diary in the fallout shelter.

'What did it say?' Helen Willis asked.

He got to his feet and walked over to the floor next to the back door. He carried his Nike bag into the kitchen and set it on the counter. He pulled out the diary and handed it to her. 'Just read the first line,' he said.

She must have thought he meant *out loud*. '"*If anyone should find this diary please . . . My name is*

322

Isobel Howard. I have lived in this house for the past seven years with my daughters, Tracy and Nicole, and a man whose real name I do not know.'

Ken looked confused. 'So the guy on the TV . . .'

'Yeah.'

'He's not Wesley Allen Howard.'

'No.'

'And you're not Wesley either.'

'No.'

Randy fanned the pages of the diary and came out with the photograph.

'This, unless I'm mistaken, is the *real* Wesley Allen Howard.'

On the TV, Randy had been replaced by a weather bulletin. Big storm roaring in from the Pacific. High wind warnings. Flood watch issued.

They passed the photo back and forth a couple of times. Helen compared the writing on the back with the handwriting in the diary. 'Looks like her handwriting,' she announced. Randy told her he thought so, too.

'So . . . where's he?' Ken asked.

'Probably dead,' Randy said.

'Why?'

'Apparently he stumbled on something he shouldn't have stumbled on.'

'At the space center?'

'According to her, Wes went in for his orientation on the first afternoon they were in Florida and never came back.'

'So what did she do?' Helen Willis asked.

'She called the space center.'

'And?'

'Didn't she call the police?' Ken asked.

'Never got the chance,' Randy said. 'About five minutes after she called the space center, three men came to her house. Two stayed inside with her; one went out into the backyard with the girls, who were just short of three years old at the time.' He took a deep breath. 'They laid it out for her. Wes wasn't coming home. No explanation . . . just he wasn't coming home. She could either deal with it or die, just that simple. She and the girls could either carry on without him or they kill all three of them right then and there.'

'She should have gone to the cops,' Ken said.

'She was young and scared,' Randy said. 'She was terrified for her girls.'

'Where does the guy on TV come into it?' Helen wanted to know.

'About a week later, the same three guys show up with this new guy. They tell her he's going to be the *new* Wesley Howard. They can make any arrangement they want between the two of them, but as far as the outside world is concerned, they're just one big happy family. As long as the illusion lasts, they're alive. The minute anything goes wrong, they're dead.'

'I can't believe she went along with it,' Ken said.

'There's a final twist,' Randy said. 'A week passes. She's working her way up to going to the authorities when she gets a call from her parents.

They want to come down and help them move into the new house. She tries to head them off, but they're not having any of it. They pick up on the fact that there's something wrong and are coming anyway.'

'And?'

'And they never make it.'

'How?'

'They had a car accident on the way to the airport. The local cops investigate, think it was an accident, pure and simple, but she knows better.'

'Which means they're listening to her phone calls and that they're serious about killing all of them,' Ken said.

'Exactly,' Randy said. 'It also means that nearly everybody who knew the real Wesley Howard well enough to gum up the works was gone. Her whole support system was gone.' He pointed at the diary. 'You can read it for yourself. She figures she'll bide her time . . . wait for the right moment, and then get the hell out of there.'

'But it never comes,' Helen said.

'Their keepers are all over it. They appear to know everything. By now she's getting paranoid. She imagines there's one of them lurking behind every bush.'

'Can you blame her?' Helen blurted.

'The new Wes is a decent enough guy. He doesn't try to sleep with her. Treats the girls nice. Weeks turn into months. As far as the outside world is concerned, they're just Mr and Mrs Clean

White America.' He could see the questions in their eyes, so he kept talking. 'Over the years they get a dozen calls from people they knew way back when, but she fends them off with tales of being out of town and illness and such. You know how it is, you turn people down often enough, they stop calling.'

'Why?' Ken asked. 'Why the whole . . .' He searched for a word. 'Why the whole rigmarole of a new Wes and all that?'

'That's the question, now, isn't it?' Randy said.

'She never finds out? It's not in the diary?'

'Nope.'

'What about you?' Ken asked.

'I've thought about it,' Randy said. 'Carrying off the charade removes the possibility of the kind of investigation we were just watching on the TV. That way nobody has to explain what happened to Wes.'

Ken was nodding.

'Secondly, they've got a guy way inside a very secretive project. Somebody who can keep them in the project loop.'

'Why would that be important to them?'

He shrugged. 'All I can think of is some kind of internal power struggle maybe. Something like that.' He made serious eye contact with both of them. 'I don't want to be this Adrian Hope guy.'

'I don't blame you,' Ken said.

'I'm not looking for that much attention.'

'You can't . . .' Helen sputtered. She frowned. 'Can you?'

'I think maybe you can,' he said. 'I was Paul Hardy for seven years and there wasn't a problem. I spent the past week as Randy James and that worked.' He spread his hands. 'Why can't I be whoever I want to be?'

'Every reporter in the country is looking for you,' Ken threw in.

'Exactly,' Randy said. 'I mean . . . I wouldn't mind being Adrian Hope. He sounds like an interesting guy . . . if I could go back to being an astronaut . . . if I could remember any of the accomplishments that got me there . . . but I can't . . . I haven't got a history. If I knew what the reporters want to know, I'd call a press conference and tell 'em . . . but I don't . . . I don't have any idea what happened on the night Wes Howard disappeared, and as long as I don't, I'm a pariah . . . some kind of curiosity . . . some kind of . . .'

'The assistant district attorney,' Helen began. 'The one who ran your fingerprints through the FBI system.'

He winced. 'What about her?'

'She knows who you are. She knows about Paul Hardy.'

'They're going to figure it out,' Ken said. 'It's just a matter of time.'

CHAPTER 40

'You want to call who?'
'The person who gave me the glass,' Kirsten said.

'Why?'

'Because . . .' – Kirsten had to think about it – 'because I feel like the fingerprints were given to me in confidence.'

'How can evidence be in confidence?' Gill wanted to know

'Evidence of what? You said it yourself. There's nothing filed or pending. There's no crime involved here.'

'And they weren't given to *you*. They were given to this office.'

'No, Bruce . . . they were given to *me*.'

'And you work for *me*.'

He was getting angry. Kirsten worked on staying calm. 'You've got a press conference scheduled,' she said. 'I understand you want to have a nice big juicy bone to throw the press. I understand all that. The problem is that giving you the name is going to seriously disrupt the life of the person who gave them to me. The national media is going

328

to descend like locusts. Life as these people know it is going to be over.'

'Comes with the territory,' Gill snapped. 'If this person didn't want—'

'And what about Adrian Hope?'

'What about him?'

'What about his privacy?'

'He forfeited his privacy when he put himself in the public eye.'

'You sound like a paparazzi.'

'Make the call. You feel like you have to make the call, then make it.' He waved a finger. '. . . but I want the damn name and I want it now.'

'I'll call,' Kirsten said. 'But I'm not promising anything.'

Bruce Gill threw her his most baleful stare, the one he used to intimidate juries, and then turned and left the room without another word.

Kirsten sat still and rigid behind her desk as she watched him stalk down the corridor toward his office. He stopped to say a few words to Gene Connor, his private secretary, and then resumed his 'I'm pissed off and you better get out of my way' stomp toward the closed door at the end of the hall.

'I should never have come back here,' he said. 'I just didn't know where else to go. This is the only place I actually remember.'

'It's all just so . . . bizarre,' Helen said.

'I see that stuff on TV about how I came from

someplace in Wisconsin. I saw a woman this morning who said she's my aunt. She was talking about how I went to this college and that college . . . none of which I remember. It all sounds like somebody else's life to me.'

'It's still you, isn't it?'

'How can you feel good about something you don't remember?'

'What choice do you have?'

'The way I see it, I can live my life as Adrian Hope, go into seclusion and live like a hermit, or I can become somebody else and lead something like a regular life.'

'Maybe it will all come back to you one of these days.'

'And maybe it won't,' he countered. 'I can't spend the rest of my life waiting for something that may not happen.'

She put her face in her hands. 'Maybe you should go back to Wisconsin, see if maybe being there doesn't bring something up for you,' she said.

He pointed at himself. 'With this face?'

'You've got a point.'

'I'd be a freak, a curiosity. The guy who used to be . . .'

'Who would you like to be?' she asked.

The question stumped him. 'I . . . I really haven't had time to think about it. Just some Joe, I suppose. Somebody nobody ever heard of . . . you know . . . living a regular life maybe, something like that.'

The phone rang. Helen crossed the room and picked it up. She'd lost weight since the last time he'd seen her. 'Yes,' she said into the receiver, and then she listened and then listened some more. 'I understand,' she said finally. 'Yes. Thank you for calling. No, really, I understand.' She hung up.

She turned and looked at him. The news wasn't good. That much was plain.

'That was the assistant district attorney.'

'The one who ran the prints for you?'

'Yes. Her name is Kirsten Kane.'

'What'd she want?'

'She has a problem.'

'What's that?'

'Her boss . . . the district attorney . . .'

'Bruce Gill?'

'Yes.'

'I've seen him on TV a bunch of times. He always looks like he's enjoying the whole thing.'

'He's demanding she tell him where the fingerprints came from.'

'And?'

'And she's refusing . . .'

'But?'

'But she's not sure how long she can keep it up. She works for him, after all. Sooner or later she's going to have to give it to him.'

'That gets out and you're going to have a thousand reporters clawing at your door.'

'That concerns me.'

'That makes two of us.'

Ken came around the corner and into the kitchen. 'I gotta run down south,' he announced. 'One of my crews has run into some trouble. I'll give you guys a ride home on the way.'

Helen trotted upstairs to get her things. Randy pulled his jacket off the back of the chair, stuffed the diary back into his bag, and got to his feet.

Ken pointed at the diary. 'That's a bestseller, you know.'

'You think so?'

'Absolutely. That's big-time *Oprah* material right there.'

'She didn't know anything.'

'Does it matter?' he said. 'Helpless woman, living a lie for the sake of her daughters.' He leered at Randy. 'Bestseller stuff, I'm telling you.'

'What can I do for you gentlemen?' Kirsten asked.

FBI. Three of them. Two young. One older.

'Adrian Hope,' the older one said.

'What about him?'

'Do you know where he is?'

'No, I don't.'

The older guy looked her over, searching her for any sense that she might be lying to him. 'You're sure?'

She raised her hand like she was taking an oath. 'I have no idea as to the present whereabouts of Adrian Hope.'

'Where did the fingerprints come from?' the younger agent on the right asked.

'A confidential source,' Kirsten answered.

'We're going to need the name,' said the other younger guy.

'There are other considerations,' Kirsten said.

'Such as?'

'Such as the privacy of the people involved.'

'This is an ongoing federal investigation.'

'Is there a crime involved?'

The young guys looked to their leader. Kirsten felt a chill run down her spine. The older guy seemed to be having a discussion with himself.

'You're aware of the investigation taking place in Florida.'

'The family disappearance.'

'Indeed.'

'Then it shouldn't be any surprise to you that we want to know the source of the fingerprints.'

'At the risk of repeating myself, is there a crime in here somewhere?'

'Our technicians have been going over the house,' the older one said.

'Uh-huh.'

'Somebody went to a great deal of trouble to remove what appears to be a rather substantial collection of bloodstains from the master bedroom.'

Kirsten's stomach felt as if she'd swallowed a shoe.

'You're sure.'

'A single blood type.'

'And?'

'The profile matches Wesley Howard's NASA profile.'

Kirsten rubbed her temple with the fingers of her right hand. 'So what you're saying is that the man of the house . . . this Wesley Howard, was probably killed in the bedroom.'

'Exactly.'

'And the wife and daughters?'

'Gone.'

'How is all of this related to Adrian Hope?' she asked.

They exchanged glances again. The older guy took the lead. 'In the course of searching the premises, our agents made an interesting discovery.'

'What was that?'

'A bomb shelter.'

'Really?'

'The original owners had it built along with the house.'

'And?'

'And Mr Adrian Hope's fingerprints are all over it.'

CHAPTER 41

For once, the weatherman was right. Randy was standing at Helen Willis's picture window watching a hell of a storm roll their way. Ken had called to say he was going to be a while and not to expect him for dinner. Helen and Mrs Forbes were running all over the house making sure everybody had a flashlight and nobody had any candles.

Out over the rooftops, the sky was boiling, running over at the edges. Three miles distant, out over the bay, a gossamer curtain of rain danced along in front of the storm, anointing everything in its path. The trees in the backyard were beginning to sway; buffeted by the offshore wind, the tops seemed to be moving in all directions at once.

He'd never seen a sky quite like it before, almost like a Florida hurricane, purple at the center, running to a deep gray at the edges. A trident of lightning flashed on the horizon and then another higher in the sky as the storm rumbled his way.

He watched as the moving wall of turbulence swallowed the waterfront whole and began creeping up the hill in his direction. He checked the clock over the sink. Just before three in the afternoon and it was getting black as night. The trees were beginning to sway in earnest now. Anything loose became a prisoner of the wind. The lights flickered but stayed on. The slide of the elevator door announced Helen's arrival.

'You're all the rage downstairs.'

'They know I'm here?'

'Mrs Dahlberg. We're right over her room. She may be stone blind but she can identify a person's footsteps. She told everybody you were up here.'

'Shit,' Randy said.

'You know what Carman calls you?'

'What?'

'She calls you "New Face Paul."'

A volley of raindrops drummed the window, pulling both of their heads toward the noise. Dime-size hail bounced off the glass like bird shot. The front of the storm was no more than half a mile down the hill, swirling everything in its path as it worked its way inland. The intercom buzzed. Helen walked over to the call box.

'Yes?'

'There's a lady here.' Eunice's voice.

'Would you ask her for a name, please?'

Pause.

Another buzz. 'She says her name is Kirsten Kane.'

Helen looked over at Randy.

Buzz. 'She says it's important.'

'She already knows the story,' Helen said.

'But she doesn't know what I look like.'

'I'll go downstairs.'

'No,' he said. 'Tell Eunice to send her up.'

'You sure?'

'She's the only ally we have,' he said.

They stood in silence until the elevator door slid open.

She was tall for a woman. Somewhere right around six feet, he guessed. Beautiful face. Dark hair cut straight across the front. Sensible shoes. Soaking wet. Helen took her sopping raincoat and carried it to the bathroom. Her eyes searched the room before coming to rest on him.

She gave him a wan smile. 'The weather's terrible,' she said.

'And about to get worse,' he added.

'Are you . . .'

'Yes.'

Helen returned.

'Have you . . .'

'We've sort of introduced ourselves,' he said.

Kirsten gathered herself. 'I'm sorry to barge in like this,' she said.

'But I thought I owed it to you.'

'For what?' he asked.

'For the double dose of bad news I'm about to deliver.' She looked as if she was going to cry. 'My boss . . .'

'Bruce Gill,' Helen said.

'Mr Gill . . .' She shook her head in disgust and then looked over at Helen. 'The second I got off the phone with you, he had his secretary pull my phone logs. He knows the number I called. He's got a couple of researchers working on it right now. Within an hour he's going to know everything I know.' She looked back at Randy. 'I'm sorry,' she said. 'I never dreamed he'd sink that low.' She slapped the side of her head. 'I should have called from an outside phone.'

He told her not to worry. Spilt milk and all that. She went on.

'I spent the past hour dodging questions from the FBI. By the time I get back to the office, they'll have a federal material witness warrant for your arrest.'

'Witness to what?' he asked.

'They want to question you regarding the disappearance of a family in Florida.'

'The Howards.'

'They found your fingerprints in . . . in an air-raid shelter or something.'

'Do what you have to do,' he told her. 'You don't owe me anything.'

'I'm an officer of the court. They get a warrant and I'm going to have to tell them what they want to know . . . which is everything I know about you. Otherwise I find myself disbarred and on my way to jail.'

She pointed over at the TV. 'Gill has a news conference at four.' She checked her watch. 'Twenty minutes,' she said. 'After that, everybody is going to know about Harmony House and Paul

338

Hardy.' She took a deep breath. 'Another hour and he's going to know about the plastic surgery. Then the race is on for the first picture of the new Adrian Hope.' She waved a well-shaped arm toward the front of the house. 'That street out there won't hold all the reporters. There'll be photographers in the trees.'

'They can camp out there in the rain for all I care,' Helen said. 'Nobody says I have to let them in.'

'The FBI isn't going to camp out,' Kirsten said. 'They'll kick down the door if they have to.'

She looked at Randy. 'You've got to get out of here.'

CHAPTER 42

And then the rain arrived in earnest, blasting into the picture window with the strength of a fire hose, bowing the glass with its ferocity, whistling from some crack as a sudden gust of wind shook the house.

'Goodness,' Helen said. 'Was that an earthquake?'

'The wind,' Randy corrected.

And then another gust rattled the house to the rafters. From the floor below, several high-pitched cries seeped through the floor-boards.

'I've got to go,' Helen said quickly.

They watched as she trotted over to the elevator and disappeared.

He read the question in her eyes. 'Problem is, I don't know any of the things they want to know,' he said.

'What?'

'I don't remember anything before I woke up in the hospital seven years ago. I don't know what happened to Adrian Hope on the night before he was supposed to blast off. I don't know what happened to the Howard family or why.'

'You're serious.'

'Absolutely.'

'Nothing?'

'An image here, an image there,' he said. 'For a while there, it seemed like I might get my memory back. I started remembering random bits and pieces.' He shrugged. 'But that stuff stopped coming a few days ago.'

'What kind of images?'

'Oh . . . I can see myself sitting at a desk in a classroom. You know, one of those desks with the arm you can write on.'

She nodded.

'I can see out the window . . . out over this big expanse of snow.' He snapped his fingers. 'That's all.'

'That makes sense,' she said. 'You're from Wisconsin.'

'If they say so. In my mind, I'm not from anywhere. In my mind, Adrian Hope is just a name. At best, he's who I used to be.'

'Who are you now?'

'The jury's still out on that one.'

The lights flickered, went out for ten seconds, and then came on again. Sounds of commotion rose from the floor below. The screech of Shirley's voice caught his ear.

'Come on,' he said, heading across the room to the elevator. He slipped an arm around Kirsten's waist and let her precede him into the elevator car. Half a minute later, they were greeted by a scene of chaos. Shirley was down at the far end of the hall squawking at Eunice, who, for her part, was hollering back about how she'd stand anyplace she wanted. The lights flickered again. Screams of protest rose to the ceiling.

Helen shouted them down. 'Let's all go down to the TV room,' she yelled. 'That way we'll all be together.'

The notion was well received. Charles and Randall immediately went running down the stairs. 'Everybody bring your flashlight,' Helen shouted.

Carman was rolling Mrs Dahlberg toward the elevator. Dolores and Darl walked along with Shirley, waited for the elevator, and all rode down together. As usual, Eunice brought up the rear. She stopped in front of him and looked him over.

'I liked your other face better,' she said.

'Thanks,' he said.

'Let's go, Eunice,' Helen said.

Helen, Kirsten, and Randy stood on the second-floor landing and watched as Eunice flounced down the stairway in slow motion. 'Funny as it may sound . . .' he said when she was out of sight, 'but these guys feel a hell of a lot more like my family than those people I see on television.'

They descended the stairway three wide. 'Shirley thinks you're mad at her,' Helen said as they walked toward the back of the ground floor.

'I don't understand what she's saying anymore,' Randy said.

Helen stopped and looked at him. 'You're serious?'

'I don't know what happened, but it just sounds like noise to me now. It's like some switch got thrown in my brain.'

'She's going to be crushed.'

'I know.'

'You should tell her.'

He thought it over. She was right.

'I will,' he promised. 'First chance I get.'

As they turned the corner into the TV room, Eunice was trying to pull the remote control from Darl's hand. He could see in her face how she was hoping Darl would get agitated and give her an excuse to pop him one.

'Hey,' Randy called. They both turned his way. 'What happened to sharing?'

Helen settled the matter by snatching the remote from Eunice's hand. She hit the power button and channel-surfed to the local ABC affiliate. They were a minute or so late for the press conference. By the time Helen found the channel, Gill was already holding forth on the subject of Paul Hardy, about how he'd been found in a railroad car, about how he'd lived for seven years in a home for disabled adults. About the plastic surgery and Paul's ultimate recovery. Cut to a photo of the famous plastic surgeon Dr Lenville Richard and then back to Gill. The lights flickered; the TV quit.

The storm couldn't have been more than a block away now. The windows were shaking, bending inward from the wind. The volume of water dropping from the sky had rendered the panes completely opaque, like riding in the car through the car wash. The roar of the wind sounded like an airplane flying low over the house. The doorbell rang.

Randy said he'd get it. Without thinking, he took Kirsten by the arm and pulled her along with him. She came without a struggle. He looked out through the little telescope in the door. An older guy, but real lithe and fit looking, holding a huge plate of what looked like brownies before him on a platter.

Randy pulled open the door. The guy was a bit taken aback by the sight.

'Uh,' he stuttered, '. . . uh . . . is Hel . . . Ms Willis here?'

Behind him, Arbor Street was being thrashed by the storm. The trees bent like supplicants. Leaves swirled through the air. A black plastic garbage can was rolling down the middle of the street. A limb was down in the front yard. The trees groaned and cracked. Somewhere up the street something hit the ground so hard he could feel the impact tremor in his feet.

Randy took the stranger by the elbow and pulled him into the house. 'Come on,' he said. Kirsten followed along as Randy led him back to the TV room. Helen's shoulders slumped at the sight of him. 'Mr Jaynes,' she said. 'You shouldn't have. Really there was no need.'

She kept on at how he shouldn't have, but it

didn't matter. The brownies were a big hit. The assembled multitude made short work of what must have been thirty brownies.

Kirsten and Randy were standing hip to hip and neither of them bothered to move. On the other hand, Mr Jaynes had moved in on Helen. Randy could tell from her body language he was way inside her bubble. 'Watch him, he's making a move on her,' Kirsten whispered in his ear.

She was right, no doubt about it. This Jaynes guy definitely had the hots for Helen. Helen turned and looked at Randy as if he'd just pissed on the rug. That's when the lights went out and Kirsten leaned against his shoulder in the darkness.

CHAPTER 43

Looked like a prison break. Flashlight beams zipped around the walls and the ceiling for about five minutes, until everybody calmed down and got used to the idea that things were going to be dark for a while.

The storm settled over the house. The walls creaked and groaned from the power of the wind. The rain attacked the windows, sweeping across the backyard in ranks of silver soldiers, exploding on the grass, one following another in close ranks as the storm spent its fury on Arbor Street.

The joy of sitting in the TV room without the TV working was short-lived. Helen broke out the playing cards and the games. Half an hour later, the grumbling began in earnest. The house was starting to cool down. Dolores had her jacket on. Darl was playing poker with gloves. Eunice was cheating at dominoes.

'Everybody . . . everybody,' Helen sang out. Things quieted down. 'Everybody grab your flashlight.' Chinese fire drill. 'We're going to go upstairs to our rooms. It's warmer up there, and if the heat doesn't come back soon, the only place to stay warm will be in bed.' They stood up one by one. 'Let's put the cards and the games away before we go.' Grudgingly, they began to put things away.

A knock on the door. And then another, harder and more insistent this time. Helen looked at Randy through the darkness. 'I'll get it,' she said immediately. Anything to get away from Mr Jaynes. She was gone less than a minute. Her face was hard when she returned.

'We've got company,' she said. She jerked her thumb toward the front hall. 'I told them to go away.'

Randy hurried to the front hall and peeked around the window sash. Two remote TV trucks and counting. The curb was mostly full already. Seemed like every car had a logo. Must have been thirty media types braving the elements out there.

Kirsten cocked an eyebrow. 'The media,' Randy said.

She winced and walked away.

He followed. 'Problem?'

'I really shouldn't be here,' she said. 'It looks like I've taken sides.'

'Have you?'

She met his eyes. 'Of course not.'

Satisfied that things were cleaned up and put away, Helen wind-milled her arm.

'Let's go, bring your flashlights,' she hollered.

They moved slowly, dragging their feet as they mounted the staircase on the way to their rooms on the second floor. Eunice, of course, was last and loudest. 'I don't see why I have to go to my room . . . this isn't a prison . . . we . . .'

Randy walked over and checked the street again. Hoping . . . hoping for what? An additional twenty cameras? That's what he got. They were everywhere. Two-person teams. One with a microphone. Another with a camera. They were soaking wet and looking miserable. He smiled.

'We'll outlast them,' he said to Kirsten. 'The weather's on our side.'

They walked over to the window again, standing shoulder to shoulder, looking out over the front lawn as the media types jockeyed for position. CNN's team included a third guy whose job it was to hold an umbrella over the guy with the mike. Behind him, Randy could hear Helen coaxing everybody into their rooms.

Overhead, the wind roared, buffeting the eaves, threatening to tear the century-old roof from its moorings. And then suddenly it sounded as if a cannon had been fired. *Kaboom!* And then, swear to God you could hear the tree coming down, hear the volume of air the big black poplar was pushing before itself in the three seconds before it smacked into the roof, tearing through everything in its path, crushing century-old roof trusses like matchsticks, until, finally, after a series of bone-crushing starts and stops, it came to rest with its massive limbs poking down into the second-floor hallway. Splinters of wood and shards of glass rained to the floor. Several roofing tiles smacked onto the wet carpet at Randy's feet.

Randy ran for the stairway. The hall had been reduced to a crawl space. Helen Willis was on her hands and knees in the middle of the corridor. She had a cut over her left eye. Looked like a boxer. She was crawling his way. When she saw him, she stopped crawling and gathered herself.

'Everybody,' she yelled. 'Everybody open your doors.'

Heads poked into the corridor. 'Everybody get your warm jacket and your raincoat. Then come out into the corridor.' She wiped the blood from her eye, pulled her hand back, and was appalled by the sight of her own blood. No Mrs Dahlberg. No Eunice. No Carman. No Shirley. Randy ducked low and crawled under the trunk of the tree, all the way to Shirley's room at the end of the hall.

The doorjamb had buckled from the weight of the tree. He couldn't force it open, so he kicked in the panels. Shirley was sitting in her chair waiting for a rescue with her red down jacket spread across her knees. He crawled right up into her face and looked her in the eye. 'Since my surgery, I don't understand what you're saying anymore. I don't know why but it's true. I'm not mad or anything.' She nodded her understanding. He gave her a hug. 'Here's what we're going to do,' he said. 'I'm going to take you out of the chair and put you out in the hall. Then I'm going to fold the chair and pass it out. I'm going to carry you down to the landing and then come back and get the chair. Okay?'

She said it was and held her arms out to him.

And it was. Worked for Mrs Dahlberg, too, although he didn't have to kick in her door. By the time he'd finished with four trips up and down the hallway, his hands were alive with splinters and the rest of the crew was dressed and milling about the downstairs entrance area.

Helen's eyes were wide like a spooked horse. Kirsten was dabbing at the cut with the sleeve of her sweater. 'I called DHS,' Helen said. 'A bus is on the way.' She looked around. 'No Carman. No Eunice.'

As if to mock them, the tree shifted and dropped another foot. Everybody ducked and cringed. The rain was pouring in through the hole and running down the trunk of the tree in a long thin stream.

'Take them downstairs,' Randy said to Helen. 'I'll go looking for Carman and Eunice.'

She started to argue. 'Go,' he growled.

She went. He looked over at Kirsten. 'She could use some help,' he said.

Kirsten was torn. 'You be careful,' she said.

He promised he would be. The tree dropped another inch.

'Where's Mr Jaynes?' he asked.

They all looked around, bewildered, and then Randy headed back upstairs.

CHAPTER 44

Carman's room was directly beneath the largest section of the fallen tree. By the time the tree got to her room, it had expended most of its energy on the back side of the house. Took him half a dozen tries to kick in the lower door panel. He stuck his head inside the room and called her name. It was quiet enough to hear Helen talking to someone downstairs, telling them they were all right and waiting for a bus to arrive.

'Carman,' he yelled again. Nothing. He called again and thought he might have heard the smallest of voices, so he crawled inside the room, tearing out pieces of the fallen ceiling, clearing a path.

'Here' came to his ears as something less than a whisper. It occurred to him that Carman wasn't going to yell and scream, no matter what. She'd made a life being humble and keeping her mouth shut and wasn't about to be climbing up onto the radar screen now, not even to save her own life.

The room looked strange. Took him a minute propped up on his elbows to figure it out. At the

351

south end, everything had been crushed to dust. If she'd been at that end of the room when the tree struck, they'd have been picking her up with a squeegee. At the north, it looked like it always looked, neat and clean. The noise was coming from the bathroom. He once again had to break off and remove parts of the fallen ceiling in order to crawl in that direction.

The impact had flung the bathroom door wide open. Carman was bending over, peering out the bottom half of the opening. He could see her upside-down face as he crawled across the floor. She was smiling. Carman was always smiling. He used to wonder if she was having a good time or whether her face was just stuck in that position.

'New Face Paul,' he said when he got close. She smiled so hard her eyes closed.

'New Face Paul.' She repeated it three times before the wind returned in earnest, forcing them to hunker down in silence, waiting to see what might happen next.

When things calmed down a bit outside, he said, 'Okay, here's what we're going to do. Have you got a jacket or anything warm in this half of the room?'

'Downstairs closet,' she said.

'Okay then, we're going to have to be brave.'

'New Face Paul.'

'Give me your hand,' he said. She complied. 'Now careful coming through the hole. Some of the edges are sharp and splintery.'

Carman extruded herself through the opening an inch at a time. Outside in the hallway something heavy hit the floor. 'Okay,' he said. 'Good job. Now all we've got to do is crawl down the hall to the top of the stairs and then we're home free.'

'Home free,' she said emphatically. Randy took her hand and pulled her along behind until they cleared the doorway. The hallway looked like a deranged slalom course. The tree had crossed the house at a forty-five-degree angle. At their end, several of the larger branches had gone all the way through the floor, but still kept the trunk propped up. Down by the landing, the smaller branches had shattered on impact, allowing the trunk to fall nearly to floor level.

'Okay,' he said. 'We're going to get down on our hands and knees and crawl out of here. You ready?'

'New Face Paul,' she said.

'Follow me.'

In order to avoid the forest of limbs barring the way, negotiating the passageway required a zigzag path, crossing under the tree trunk several times, passes that became increasingly narrow as one approached the second-floor landing.

They moved slowly, taking one section at a time until they'd negotiated about three quarters of the way. The next-to-last place where they had to squeeze under the trunk was a tight fit. He had to grind himself down into the sodden carpet as hard as he could to inch his way beneath the tree.

He was directly beneath the hole in the roof. Above, he could see the sky, gray and angry, throwing a torrent of rain down into his face as he wiggled his way forward, the rough bark scouring his chest as he moved forward and came out the other end.

He motioned Carman forward. The wind was pushing her hair around. The fury of the storm frightened her. She didn't want to move. 'Come on,' he said. She caught the impatience in his voice and glued herself to the spot. He took a deep breath and modulated his tone. 'Come on, Carman. We're almost there.'

Once again she inched forward, crawling beneath the trunk on her belly. She stopped halfway through, right where it got tight. 'Can't,' she said. He didn't argue. Instead he grabbed her by the arms and pulled her through the opening. He didn't know why he was surprised, but she came through smiling.

'Just like that,' he said.

'Just like that.' Big smile.

The last section of carpet was a breeze. He put her in front of him and pushed her under the tree one last time. She came out standing on the far end. 'Just like that,' she said. He grinned at her.

'Just like that,' he repeated.

Randy rolled over onto his back and began to inch his way under the tree. He managed to force his head and shoulders through, then exhaled and held his breath as he wiggled his chest under the tree trunk. At that moment the trunk shifted downward, pressing against his chest with ungodly force, driving the air from his lungs with a strangled groan.

He couldn't move, couldn't breathe, couldn't do anything but wait. His vision began to cloud. The ache in his chest began to get cold and dull and the idea of closing his eyes and going to sleep became progressively more appealing.

'Come on,' he heard Carman say.

He tried to tell her he was stuck, but nothing came out. The blood rushing to his head seemed about to explode his skull.

And then she was next to him, looking into his eyes as his vision became dark and narrow. 'New Face Paul,' he heard her say, and then he felt her grab his hands and begin to pull. He wanted to help but couldn't muster the resolve.

Her efforts to free him threatened to pull his arms from the sockets, and then . . . he moved an inch . . . and then another as his sternum passed beneath the tree and his body got smaller. He gulped a mouthful of air and then another, before he was able to reach up and put his hands on the rough bark of the tree and lever himself forward until he was out from beneath the tree altogether and Carman was looking straight down onto his face.

'New Face Paul,' she said. 'Got to be brave.'

Randy pushed himself up onto his knees and then used the nearest limb to help himself stand.

He stepped gingerly over several branches, and next thing he knew, they were on the landing. Carman threw an arm around his waist and helped his shaking legs as they descended the stairs. Helen met them halfway. 'The bus is here,' she said.

'Go,' he said.

'Eunice?'

'I'll find her next.'

'Are you—'

'Go,' he said. 'Lock the door behind you.'

'They're taking us to the shelter at St Dominic's,' Helen said.

'We'll find you,' he assured her.

Carman turned his way. 'You find Eunice,' she said.

He said he would.

'The driver wants to go,' Dolores said. 'Come on.'

Helen and Carman hurried down the stairs. He heard Helen's voice giving instructions and then sat on the stair and looked out through the banister rails, watching as she pulled open the door and a thousand camera flashes exploded as she pushed her reluctant brood out the front door. The storm had quieted for the moment.

He stood up. His knees nearly buckled. Wasn't until then that he realized Kirsten was sitting beside him. 'You better hurry,' he wheezed.

'I can't go out there,' she said. 'Not with all those cameras.'

'It's not safe here.'

'I don't care,' she said with a gaze that made it clear there was no sense in arguing.

'Your job must be pretty important to you,' he said.

She looked at him like he was crazy. 'I am my job,' she said.

'No,' he said solemnly. 'No, you're not.'

CHAPTER 45

'She's not in her room,' he announced.

'You're sure?' Kirsten asked.

'Once I hacked my way through the door, I could walk around standing up. Believe me, Eunice isn't in there.'

He handed Kirsten the fire ax he'd commandeered from the case on the wall and then eased himself down from his perch on the tree trunk. She leaned the ax against the wainscoting and helped him steady himself.

'What now?' she wanted to know.

They walked around two corners into the parlor, the only room in the house unaffected by the hole in the roof. They sat down on the couch together. The wind had calmed a bit but the rain was still hammering the windows.

'I guess I'll start down in the basement and then work my way up to this floor, see if I can't find her.'

Kirsten got up on her knees and peeked out through the curtains. 'Street's still jammed,' she announced. 'Looks like the power company has showed up.'

Randy sat for a second and then got up on his knees next to her. Three or four police cruisers were doing their best to keep the street clear. The weather had driven most of the reporters to drier ground. Directly out front, a power-company truck's pulsing amber light bounced off the houses at regular intervals. A big thick guy in AG&E coveralls was coming up the front walk toward the door. He mounted the stairs and knocked on the front door.

Randy climbed from the couch and ambled over to the door. He cracked it an inch and peered out with one eye. The laminated power-company ID card carried the guy's likeness and his name. 'We're not going to be able to get you back online,' he said. 'At least not till this weather clears up and we can do a damage assessment.'

'Okay,' Randy said. 'They took the residents down to St Dominic's. We're just holding down the fort.'

'And you'd be?'

'James,' he said quickly. 'Randall James.'

The guy smiled and nodded. 'Probably a good idea,' he said. 'Keep folks from robbing you guys blind.'

He turned to walk away, but Randy stopped him. 'Hey,' he called. The guy stopped and turned around.

'You suppose you could get the cops to clear the street?' Randy asked. 'Tell them a transformer is about to blow or something?'

He thought it over. 'You know . . . that's a heck of an idea,' he said. 'Lemme see what I can do.' He gave Randy a one-fingered salute from his hard hat and walked back down the walkway.

Randy relocked the door and rejoined Kirsten on the sofa. 'He's going to see if he can't get the cops to clear the street.'

'What about Eunice?'

'I'm going to make one last sweep of the place,' he said. 'With Eunice, there's no telling where she might be. She doesn't do anything she's told to do. She might be anywhere. She might have gone out, for all we know.' He pointed toward the street. 'If he manages to get the street clear, we can maybe get out of here after that.'

'What if we don't find her?'

'Then we call Helen and see what she wants to do next. In the meantime, we hang around and see if maybe she doesn't show up.'

'And then we get out of here while the getting's good.'

'Right on.'

He picked up the flashlight and started back toward the kitchen, Kirsten hard by his elbow. The rain had begun to work its way through the ceiling. The carpet squished and sloshed beneath their feet. They searched methodically, every room, every closet, every cupboard, calling Eunice's name all the while. Nothing. After that, they headed for the basement and did the same thing. Still nothing.

Twenty minutes later, they were back on the sofa. The flashlight's batteries were beginning to fade. Outside, the street was clear. Randy poked his head out for long enough to ascertain that the cops had blocked it off at both ends.

The power-company van was out front. He looked around for the guy, wanting to thank him, but he was nowhere to be found. Randy closed the door and wandered back into the parlor. Kirsten had pushed the curtains back and was staring distractedly out into the street. She turned her eyes his way as he entered the room.

'You were right,' she said.

His face said he didn't have the faintest idea what she was talking about.

'About my job,' she said.

'A person is a lot more than a job.'

'It's easy to get caught up in it,' she said. 'Easy to use what you do as a . . .' – she searched for a word – 'as a balm for other parts of your life that don't work as well.'

'Nothing wrong with feeling good about yourself.'

She nodded. 'But your job shouldn't be a be-all and end-all.'

'No. It shouldn't.'

She considered the matter some. 'I'm thinking about resigning.'

'Why would you want to do a thing like that?'

'How can I work for someone I can't trust?'

'Who can you really trust? Be honest.'

'. . . what do you . . .'

'I mean *really* trust. No matter what. How many?'

They never got to the answer. A loud boom echoed throughout the house.

They held their breaths and waited. 'Must have been another part of the ceiling falling in,' he tried.

'You think so?'

'No.'

Without all the media lights out front, the place was pitch black. They moved slowly back into the main body of the house, following the dim yellow cone of light into the foyer. Ahead in the gloom, something on the floor stirred. He pointed the flashlight that way. It went out. 'Shit,' he said. He shook the flashlight. It flickered and then went out entirely.

Kirsten looped her arm through his as they crept across the floor. The flashlight flickered again. Long enough to make out a body on the floor. Randy kept shaking the flashlight trying to get a little light on the subject. No go.

They knelt on opposite sides of the body. It was splayed on the floor almost in the running position, as if the person had been treading air in the seconds before impact. Instinctively, they both looked up at the banister fifteen feet above their heads.

Carefully Randy lifted the head and turned the face his way. Eunice. She groaned and coughed a mouthful of blood. 'Better get an ambul . . .'

But it was too late. As Kirsten got to her feet, he heard a rustling of feet and sensed another form in the hall. And then a sound came . . . like the twanging of a spring.

He watched in openmouthed amazement as Kirsten grunted, threw both hands over her head, and then convulsed over backward, landing heavily on her shoulders and the back of her head. He looked right at the wires and still didn't get it.

The second twang of the spring and he watched, in one of those slow-motion moments, as the barbs crossed the six feet and plowed into his chest. Reflexively, he reached to put the stinger from his body and then the current hit him like . . . like . . . like nothing he'd ever felt before. He staggered but did not go down. The form in the darkness stepped forward as if to hand him something . . . a rod? . . . a scepter? A great blue spark arced through the darkness. Fade to black.

CHAPTER 46

He was humming while he worked. Show tunes. Gilbert and Sullivan, Randy thought. Using miles of silver duct tape to connect Kirsten to one of the rolling desk chairs from the office, winding it around her forehead, rendering her completely immobile.

Randy was already taped hand and foot, lying on his side on the wet carpet. He noticed Randy was coming around, pulled a Buck knife from the pocket of his AG&E coveralls, cut the tape securing Kirsten's head to the back of the chair, and then walked over to him.

The guy was as strong as he looked. He grabbed Randy by the arms and pulled him to his feet for long enough to slide the other desk chair under him with his foot and push him down into the seat. He kept humming as he taped Randy to the chair. Something from *The Pirates of Penzance*, humming away until he was finished and stepped back a pace to admire his handiwork.

Kirsten's eyes were closed but her chest was moving. Two streams of blood ran from her nose, rolling down over her chin before they disappeared into her blouse.

He bounced the knife in the palm of his hand. 'Okay, lover boy,' he said. His voice was pure New England, all filled with elongated *As* and dropped *Rs*.

'Just so you understand. This is quite simple. The only question is whether the two of you go easy or whether you go haaaad. Either way, the pair of you have to go. You just get to decide how.' He bent over Randy. 'You understand?'

Randy managed to move his head up and down.

'Good,' he said. He smiled. 'Smaaat call on clearing the street, by the way. It's going to make all of this so much easier . . . anyway . . . The first matter is the diary.' He placed the tip of the knife in the corner of Randy's eye. 'I'm going to ask you one time where it is. If I'm not happy with the answer, I'm going to take one of your eyes.' He put a little pressure on the tip of the knife. Randy's eye began to water uncontrollably.

'Now . . . where's the diary?'

Randy tried to talk through the tape. The guy smiled again and ripped the tape from his mouth. 'No noise,' he whispered. 'Now . . . where's the diary?'

'Over there by the front door,' Randy said. 'Under the table in that Nike bag.'

He replaced the tape over Randy's mouth and then walked over and retrieved the bag.

'Smaaat move,' he said. Once again he bent low

enough to make eye contact. 'Okay,' he said. 'Here's how it's going to be. I don't like to leave a mess if it can be helped. I'm going to wheel the two of you out of here and then we're going to take a little ride, and then it's all going to be over. If you make it difficult for me in any way, I'll cut both your throats right then and there. Her first and then you. You understand?'

Once again, Randy indicated he understood.

The guy straightened up and looked down at him. 'Twenty-four years,' he said. 'All that time . . . all those jobs and you're the only one ever walked away from me.' He smiled. 'Actually you rode away from it.' He shrugged. 'I always figured you fell off that railroad car and ended up unda the wheels.' He squatted down in front of Randy and looked closely at his face, 'You don't look nothing like you looked before,' he annnounced. 'You must lead a chaaamed life, my friend. I hit you haaad enough to kill three guys and all you do is go staggering off the catwalk, fall off, and land on the damn supply train.' He looked around as if searching for more of an audience. 'What in hell was I gonna do? I'm standing there with the other guy dead at my feet when you come blundering in. What . . . I'm gonna go off chasing you and that friggin' train? Just leave the Howaaad guy laying where he is?' He answered himself with a shake of the head. 'No way. I gotta finish up what I staaated.'

On the far side of the foyer, Kirsten stirred for

a moment, groaned, and then became still again. The guy stood up again.

'Only time I've missed,' he mused. 'Bothered the hell out of me all these yeaas and then what happens? It's like something out of a friggin' movie. All these yeaaas later and I get a chance to atone.' He slapped his own forehead. 'I mean . . . what are the chances? Here I am on my last job and I get a chance at atonement. How many times does a guy get do-ovaaas? I get to off the only guy I ever missed.'

He looked down at Randy as if expecting some kind of validation. 'I was thea to discuss offin' some guy namea Barber and outta the friggin' blue this guy Howard comes waltzin in when he was supposed to be long gone.' He shook his head. 'Both of youze just blundering in. Wrong place at the wrong time. Go figure,' he said, before turning and walking away.

Randy watched helplessly as the guy grabbed the back of the desk chair and wheeled Kirsten through the foyer. A minute passed before he came back for Randy. The wheels on the chair squeaked as they crossed the sodden floor.

The guy cracked the door and peered outside for a long moment. Satisfied. He pulled the door all the way open and then wheeled Kirsten out. He turned left on the porch and disappeared from Randy's line of sight as he wheeled Kirsten down the ramp. The rain was steady. The wind in the tops of the trees sounded like freeway traffic.

A moment later, they reappeared. Randy watched helplessly as he wheeled her up the metal ramp and disappeared into the back of the van.

Once he was out of sight, Randy struggled with his bonds, pulling for all he was worth, trying to free his hands, twisting, turning his wrists. He kept at it until he broke a sweat and his hands went numb. The tape had no give to it and he didn't have enough leverage to tear it. Something between a groan and a sob escaped his chest.

The guy reappeared, walking down the ramp, whistling now as he rolled down the rear door of the van and started Randy's way. He wiped his hands on his coveralls, and then the street lit up a little. A set of headlights was coming down the street at him. He held up a hand and shielded his eyes.

A black sedan pulled to the curb behind the power-company van. The circular logo on the door said FBI. The eagle held lightning bolts in its talons. Funny how things work. If anyone had asked Randy about his religious beliefs an hour ago, he'd have told them he was a nonbeliever, and now all he could think was, Thank God. Thank God. Thank God . . .

They came piling out of the car like clowns at a circus. They encircled him, leaning in close to intimidate. Randy watched as he pointed at the house . . . at the tree bisecting the roof. He kept talking. Randy could see the FBI's body language relax. Whatever the guy was telling them, they were buying it. No doubt about it.

368

Behind the duct tape Randy was screaming at Kirsten, telling her to wake up. As close as she was to the feds, any sound at all would surely attract their attention. 'Come on, wake up!' He tried to tip himself over but the chair wouldn't budge. He thrashed around, giving it his all, making adenoidal noises through the sticky silver tape.

Outside, the fake power-company guy was waving his hand and smiling and then pointing toward the south. The wind ripped through the trees, drowning Randy's pathetic attempts to call attention to himself. He was bellowing behind the tape but they couldn't hear anything except the freight-train rustle of leaves. One of the agents shook the guy's hand.

Randy watched in horror as the FBI got back into the car and drove off down the street. His captor stood rocking on his heels with his hands thrust into the pockets of his coveralls. He stayed that way until the feds passed through the barricade at the far end of Arbor Street and disappeared.

He moved faster now, hurrying up the steps. He smiled at Randy. 'Close one there, lover boy.' He grabbed the back of the chair. 'Wouldn't want to fuck up just as I'm about to enta a whole new phase of my life.' Randy threw himself violently from side to side, but the wide wheelbase of the old chair absorbed the shock instead of toppling over onto its side. 'Take it easy. Take it easy,' the guy chanted as he began to push Randy toward the door. 'Some you win, some you—'

The noise was hard to describe. Hollow but hard, like somebody planting an ice ax. The chair stopped moving. Behind him, Randy heard the splash of a body hitting the floor. Silence prevailed for a moment and then squishy footsteps approached from the rear. He held his breath and waited.

Eunice was a mess. Blood all over the front of her. One eye swollen closed. The odd angle of her right leg and the way she dragged it behind her said it was surely broken. She held the fire ax in both hands as she shuffled around in front of Randy.

'He pushed me,' she said before raising the ax over her head and starting it down. Randy closed his eyes.

CHAPTER 47

'He pushed me,' Eunice said again.

Randy cracked one eye, hoping like hell they hadn't died and gone to heaven together. Mercifully no. Eunice had used the ax to cut his left hand free. He breathed a sigh of relief, used the left hand to free the right and then both of them to untape the rest of him.

He got to his feet, gently took the ax from her hands, and made her sit down in the chair. 'Hang in there,' he said to her. 'I'll be right back.'

He dropped to one knee, fished around in the power company coveralls until he came up with the Buck knife, and then sprinted for the door, long-jumped the stairs, and was at the back of the power-company van in four long strides. Kirsten's eyes were the size of saucers. A sob caught in her throat at the sight of him.

He had her separated from the chair in less than a minute. She threw her arms around his neck. 'Hurry,' he said, pulling her up and out of the chair. Her legs were a bit shaky. He helped her up the stairs and into the foyer. The sight of Eunice snoring in the chair and the dead guy sprawled in a pool of blood stopped her in her tracks.

He sat her on the bottom step of the stairway and then made his way to the body on the floor. He'd thought of feeling for a pulse, but the up-close sight of the guy's head dispelled any such idea. Eunice had driven the hooked front part of the ax completely through the top of his skull, creating an open wound the size of a baseball through which most of his brain had now seeped into the carpet.

Randy patted him down, coming up with a thin wallet and a disposable cell phone and a plastic hotel key from the Vintage Gate Hotel. He rolled the guy up onto his side. He had a gun under his belt buckle. Randy left it there, pocketed the rest of it, and then hurried over to Kirsten.

'We gotta get some help for Eunice,' he said.

She nodded. Her eyes were locked on the guy on the floor.

'He's dead.'

She nodded again and opened her mouth to speak. Nothing came out.

'I can't be here when help arrives,' he said. 'You understand?'

She looked at him as if he were speaking Turkish.

'As long as the world doesn't know what I look like, I've got a chance of living something like a normal life. If I'm here when the help arrives, life as I know it is over.'

'What . . .' she began. 'What do you need me to do?' she choked out.

'I want you to sit right there until your legs get right. I'm going out the back way. As soon as you're feeling better, hustle down to the corner. Tell the cops what happened here. Tell 'em everything . . . just like it happened . . .' He waved his hand in the air. 'Get an aide car on the way.'

He bent over and patted her on the back. She threw an arm around his neck and struggled to her feet. She put her face close to Randy's and looked all the way to the back of his skull. 'You saved my life,' she said.

'Eunice saved your life,' Randy corrected. As if on cue, Eunice emitted a loud series of snores and snorts.

Kirsten grinned. 'The Lord works in mysterious ways,' she said.

'Something like that,' Randy offered.

'They're going to want to know what Adrian Hope looks like.'

'So maybe you're not much of a visual person,' Randy said.

She smiled again. 'I guess I can do that,' she said. 'I owe you that much.'

'Thanks,' Randy said.

She wagged a long finger at him. 'You can't run away from yourself, you know.'

'I don't want to be Adrian Hope.'

'But you *are* Adrian Hope.'

He shook his head. 'I'm whoever I decide I am.'

'That doesn't make any sense.'

'Sure it does,' he said. 'I've had time to think

about it. The way I see it, people spend their whole lives making themselves up. All they come into this world with is a name. After that, they pick and choose from the all the things they come into contact with . . . from the TV, from the movies, from their parents, their relatives, their friends, from everywhere.'

'Interesting idea,' she said tentatively.

'We reinvent ourselves all the time.'

'I've got a feeling I'm about to do exactly that.'

'How's it feel?'

'To tell you the truth, it's kind of exciting.'

'Why is it exciting?'

She thought it over. 'I seem to like a little subterfuge in my life.'

'You're a lawyer,' he said.

'This is different,' she said. 'I'm messing with *the authorities* . . . usually I *am* the authorities.'

Randy smiled. 'Who knows . . . you might get to like it.'

'I do like it,' she said. 'That's what makes me nervous.' She checked the room.

'I've never done anything like this before,' she said. 'I was always the good girl. Top of my class. Always knew the answers. I can't . . . I just can't believe I'm doing this.'

'Never?'

She thought it over. 'Once.'

He waited.

'I cut school.'

'Lordy be.'

'I went to downtown L.A. with Jonny Dobbs.'
'That's it?'
'We ate chili dogs at a place called Pink's.'
'Yeah.'
'He wanted to . . .' She shrugged. 'We were going to get a room.'
'And?'
'I chickened out.'
'So what happened?'
'He left me there.' She said it like after all these years she still couldn't believe it. 'I'd never missed a day before, so the school called home. My parents nearly killed me. I was grounded for months.'

Randy smirked as he walked over and retrieved his bag.

'Give me a five-minute head start,' he said, running toward the back of the house.

CHAPTER 48

The page fluttered down from above and settled on the desk in front of her. She picked it up, gazed uninterestedly at the drawing, and handed it his way.

'You dropped something,' Kirsten said.

He plucked the page from her fingers, rolled it into a tight ball, and dropped it into her wastebasket. 'This is a joke, right?'

'Excuse—'

'The likeness.'

'What about it?'

She'd never seen Bruce Gill quite this florid before lunch.

'I don't know who you think you're fooling here.'

'Fooling how?'

He paced back and forth across her office. 'Need I remind you that you're an officer of the court?'

She batted her eyes at him. 'Whatever do you mean?' she asked.

He bent and retrieved the poster from the wastebasket. He used the palm of his hand to smooth the wrinkled page out on the corner of her desk. His hand shook slightly as he held the drawing in front of her face. 'You're trying to tell me . . . you want me to believe that you spent the better part of two hours inside a house with Adrian Hope and this . . . this . . .' – he rattled the page – 'is the best likeness you can come up with?'

'It was dark inside.'

'This could be anybody. This could be my uncle Charlie.'

'You don't have an Uncle Charlie.'

He slammed his hand down on the desk, hard enough to rattle the window. Instinctively, everyone in the office turned to catch the commotion. 'I'm not kidding.' Gill pushed the words through flattened lips.

'Me neither,' she said.

He wagged a finger her way. 'I won't be humiliated by my own underlings.'

'Underlings?'

'That's right. You work for me, in case you've forgotten.'

'How could one forget working for someone such as yourself?'

'What's that supposed to mean?'

'That you're unforgettable.' She gave him the least sincere smile she could muster. 'What else?'

'I want a report,' he said. 'As long as you are in my employ, I will expected detailed reports of your activities.'

'As I've told you . . . the Bureau has forbidden me to talk about anything that happened while I was at Harmony House.'

'The FBI has no right to—'

'They're citing national security.'

'They *always* cite national security,' Gill bellowed.

'As a citizen, I believe it is my obligation to—'

'Don't start that shit with me.'

'Language, please.'

He rocked back on his heels. 'I expect a complete—'

'If you want to know what the bureau knows . . .' – she leaned forward in her chair – 'give 'em a jingle.'

He put both hands on her desk and leaned in so close she could smell the Tic Tacs on his breath. 'You damn well better decide whose side you're on here, missy.'

'Trust me . . . I've already decided.'

'So be it,' he said.

She kept her eyes glued to his. 'So be it.' She echoed.

'I only work with team players,' he said.

'Team players?' Her voice rose. '*Team players* . . . are you kidding me? You're talking to *me* about team players?' She tried to modulate her tone but couldn't manage it. Instead she got to her feet. 'The guy who went sneaking through my phone logs—'

'I don't have to sneak. I was fully within my rights to—'

'—sneaking through my phone logs in order to violate a confidence . . .'

'I guaranteed nothing,' Gill insisted at full volume.

'But I did!' she shouted. 'I guaranteed those people anonymity and you crapped all over me, so don't you dare speak of team players, or of loyalty or of ethics or of any of the finer points of professional people working together.'

Outside in the office, people were standing up in their cubicles. hands covering phone mouthpieces, jaws hanging. Had to be like thirty people standing there aghast, eyes wide, chins or chests, just in time to witness Bruce Gill as he stormed from her office, slamming the glass door for all he was worth, sixty bulging eyes looking in horror as the door disintegrated into a thousand shards of glass, sliding from the frame the way an avalanche comes loose from a landslide, with a low rumble at first, then the earsplitting crash, and finally an irregular series of smaller tinkles. Kirsten stood in silence, waiting for the last of the glass to fall onto the carpet. Took all her resolve not to laugh.

When Kirsten looked up. Gene Connor was walking her way. The sight of Gene Connor with a scowl on her face sent the gawkers scurrying back into their cubicles. The *click click* of keyboards began anew.

'Maintenance is on the way,' Gene said. 'In the meantime, let's get you set up in conference room three until the mess gets cleaned up.'

Kirsten allowed herself a small smile. 'Thanks, Gene.'

The older woman waved her off as if to say, *Think nothing of it.*

Kirsten began to gather her case files.

'You've got a call holding on line five,' Gene said.

Kirsten raised an eyebrow.

'He says his name is Jonny Dobbs.'

Randy hung up the phone and started across the street, mid-block and against the light, ignoring outraged horns, dodging traffic like a bullfighter until he reached the far curb. The Vintage Gate Hotel had seen better days. What had once been a sumptuous lobby had been renovated into a dozen cheap rooms, leaving only a registration desk, a pair of elevators, and enough room to turn around.

Randy pulled the bright red envelope from his pocket as he approached the desk. He couldn't remember the title, but he was sure he'd seen Humphrey Bogart pull this trick in a movie sometime. The desk clerk looked up from a girlie magazine. Randy held the envelope out. 'For Mr Landis.'

The guy eyed him. 'Which Mr Landis is that?' He sneered.

'Mr Gavin Landis,' Randy replied.

The guy plucked the envelope from his fingers. 'I'll see to it he gets it.'

Randy turned and walked back out the door.

No hurry, he kept telling himself. Mr Landis won't be coming back.

When he ambled back into the lobby two hours later, the desk was being operated by an older woman whose graying, tangled hair looked like it may never have been cut. Like it may have been longer than she was. Her blue eyes were filigreed red, red as the envelope waiting in the mail slot numbered 916.

'You guys have a parking garage?' he inquired.

She shook her head. 'Not no more,' she said.

He thanked her and crossed to the elevators. He pushed nine and then leaned back against the wall of the elevator car with a smile threatening to break out on his lips.

The ninth-floor hallway smelled of cabbage and dirty socks. Nine-sixteen was the last door on the left. No cabbage. No socks. Nothing anywhere in the room. He pulled the wallet from his pants pocket, sat down on the edge of the bed, and went through it again. California driver's license in the name of Gavin Landis. Social Security card. Folded-up copy of his birth certificate. MasterCard. Visa. That was it. Except for the ticket. Number one, nine, seven, three, three, nine. Didn't say what it was for. Just that whoever it was wasn't responsible for theft or damage. He walked to the window and looked down. The street was a shambles. Filled with heavy equipment and men standing around. Looked like new sewer lines were being installed. Half a block down, a blue-and-white neon sign blinked on and off and on again: PUBLIC PARKING.

Took Randy the better part of five minutes, leafing through the torn and tattered phone book, to come up with the number. 'Downtown Valet,' the voice answered.

'Would you please bring up one, nine, seven, three, three, nine,' he said into the mouthpiece.

'Five minutes,' the voice answered.

Blue Ford Taurus. Avis. Randy kept driving until he was out of the downtown core. Two blocks west of the rooming house he was calling home these days, he pulled to the curb on a run-down residential street and got out. He went through the car. Nothing whatsoever. Not so much as a pop top in between the seats. He popped the trunk. Two attaché cases, one bigger than the other. Eeeny meeny. He opened the one on the left. A trust deed lay faceup on the top of the contents. A hundred eighty-four acres and the buildings, someplace called Marlboro, Vermont. Randy pulled the deed aside. Gavin Landis's face peered up at him. Several trimmed photos. One of another guy. Landis's passport. The dates were valid. The physical data much like his own. And . . . oh, by the way . . . filling the lion's share of the case . . . what must have been something like several hundred thou in hundred-dollar bills. He closed the lid and reached for the second case. More money, he figured.

Wrong. More head shots of Gavin Landis. Scraps of plastic. What at first looked like a laptop turned out to be a little laminating machine.

Nestled next to it was a set of X-Acto knives and next to that a Leica digital camera no bigger than a credit card. The kit explained the power-company ID Gavin Landis had been wearing on his chest.

Randy replaced the deed, closed the cases, and set them in the street before slamming the trunk and walking away. He left the keys in the ignition.

CHAPTER 49

Half a block west of Keith's Lunch, Kirsten looked to her right and, for the first time since leaving the office, caught a glimpse of her reflection in a store window. The sight stopped her in her tracks. She brought the back of her hand to her mouth and laughed into her own flesh. She looked like Jackie Kennedy in mourning, black silk scarf covering her hair, sunglasses the size of hubcaps, a costume destined to attract considerably more attention than it could ever be hoped to avert.

She sighed, pulled the scarf from her head, removed the sun-glasses, and pocketed both. She'd chosen Keith's as a meeting place because it was about as far from the courthouse as a body could get and remain within the city limits, and because it was the social centerpiece of the neighborhood where she'd lived when she first moved to the city nine years before.

As usual, the place was jumping. Not only were all the tables occupied, but another dozen or so people circled the dining room like vultures, eyeing one another warily and waiting for a sign, any sign, that somebody was maybe giving up a table.

Randy . . . Adrian . . . her brain refused to give him a name . . . was over against the wall with his nose stuck in the menu. Behind the counter, Keith gave her a mock salute.

'Long time no see, girlie,' he called.

From most other people, being called girlie would have been unacceptable, but that's what Keith called women under a hundred. It was part of his charm. She smiled and waved as she sidled among the tables and sat down in the yellow Naugahyde booth.

He looked up from the menu and said, 'Hi.'

She leaned across the table. 'Are you crazy?'

He didn't answer.

'Calling me at the office?'

'It was the only number I had.'

'God knows who might have been listening.'

'That's why I didn't use my own name.'

She pulled a business card from her raincoat pocket, patted herself down until she came up with a fancy-looking fountain pen, and began to write. She passed it across the table to him. 'That's my home number,' she said. 'Use that.'

The waitress arrived at the table. Kirsten ordered a Cobb salad and iced tea, Randy a bacon cheeseburger and a Diet Coke. They sat in silence as the woman made her way back behind the counter and hung their order on the silver carousel over the grill.

'There's been nothing in the paper,' he whispered.

'No kidding.'

'The cops . . .'

'The cops never got there,' she said. 'After you left, I ran up the street like you said. The FBI was sitting there big as life. They just took over the whole thing. Kept everybody out of the house except their own people. Threatened me with every kind of federal crime imaginable if I said a word.'

'Could they make it stick?'

'Who knows?' she said. 'With this administration, anything is possible. The idea of civil rights doesn't seem to matter much to them. They could lock me up and not even have to meet habeas corpus standards.'

'Scary.'

She waved a manicured hand. 'Heck, they've still got Harmony House padlocked. What is it . . .' – she checked her watch – 'three days now.'

'Four,' he said.

She dropped her hand to the table with a smack. 'So they're sitting on it, and there isn't a damn thing anybody can do about it.'

'Any idea why?'

She stuck out her lower lip and shook her head. 'It's completely out of character. Usually the Bureau sweeps in, scoops up any glory that might be lying around, and then disappears before anything has time to go wrong. That's the only kind of behavior I've ever seen from them. I don't know what to say about sitting on something like this.'

'You been following that *Washington Post* stor—'

'Walter Hybridge,' she interrupted.

'Yeah.'

'Maybe it's got something to do with that.'

'How can that be?'

'I don't know . . . maybe it's—'

'The timing makes me nervous,' he said.

'That's it. It's like . . . like something Gill would do. Have a fallback plan. Something in his pocket that would divert everyone's attention away from him.'

He smirked. 'We're getting pretty conspiratorial here.'

Lunch arrived. They fell into silence for several minutes, munching away at their meals as the buzz of the café whirred around them.

'I want you to set up a meeting between me and the FBI,' he said.

She lifted half a dozen fries from his plate and dropped them onto hers.

'First off, they'll take you into custody as a material witness.' She devoured a french fry in two bites. 'Secondly, they'll know what you look like.'

'Let me worry about the second part.'

'What do they get out of this meeting?'

'I'll tell them everything I know,' he said. 'I'll give them her diary.'

She ate another fry. 'What's in it for you?'

'I want them satisfied I had nothing to do with any of this. I want to be left alone.' He held up a restraining hand. 'But I want to make sure you don't get yourself into any trouble here. You already went out on a limb for me.'

She laughed and waved him off. 'I'm already in a world of hurt. Don't worry about it.' She put down her fork and told him about that morning's confrontation with her boss. 'Either I'm going to quit, or Gill's going to fire me.'

'It'll be okay,' he said.

'No, it won't,' she said quickly.

Again, they ate in silence for a couple of minutes.

'They're going to want to know about Adrian Hope,' she said.

'I'll tell them what I know.'

'Which is zip.'

'Not quite,' he said. He leaned closer and told her what the killer had said in the moments before Eunice worked her magic with the fire ax.

'No kidding.'

'That's what he said.'

'You're saying he was hired to kill Howard.'

'Uh-huh,' he grunted around a mouthful of cheeseburger.

'So you want what?'

'I want to meet one on one at a location of my choice and I want a guarantee that I'm not going to be detained in any fashion. And . . .' He waggled a finger. 'It's got to be tomorrow.' He tore off the bottom half of the business card on which she'd

388

written her home number. He wrote a phone number on it and passed it to her.

'Call me there,' he said. 'Leave a message if you have to.'

'Why tomorrow? Not much lead time there.'

'It's gotta be tomorrow,' he insisted. 'Middle of the day.'

She shrugged. 'I'll see what I can do,' she said, liberating another handful of fries from his plate. She read the look on his face. 'They're not as fattening if I don't order them myself,' she said.

CHAPTER 50

Randy watched as the cab pulled to the curb. The driver reached over the seat and popped open the door. Before slipping into the backseat, Kirsten looked his way and smiled. 'I'll let you know,' she said.

'Thanks.'

The clouds had rolled in while they were at lunch. The air smelled of salt water. The slate-gray sky roiled like a cauldron as he hurried north toward the bus stop, three blocks down on Blundred Avenue. He thrust his hands deep into his pockets, turned up his collar, and bent into the breeze.

A block down, he suddenly felt as if he was having some kind of neurological incident. He slowed his gait. His fingers came into contact with something hard and he knew for sure. They weren't numb. They were vibrating. It was the disposable cell phone he'd taken from the man calling himself Gavin Landis. It was vibrating. He held his breath and eased his hand up and out as if the phone were a snake. The vibrating stopped. He took a deep breath. Waited.

The impending rain had cleared the street. Randy had the side-walk to himself as he hurried on. The Plexiglas bus kiosk had been tagged and vandalized until it was little more than a stall for urban livestock. He sat on the cleanest section of bench available. Waited.

The phone began to buzz again. He held his breath. The sound of the killer's voice bounced around his memory. He reached into his pocket, pulled out the phone, and raised it to his ear. Silence.

'Yeah,' he intoned in as close an approximation to the killer's voice as he could manage. He held his breath again. Again, nothing. He waited a full minute and then he used his thumb to break the connection. Another minute passed. The vibrating started again.

'Third time's the chaaam,' he said.

'I had expected to hear,' an electronic voice said.

'Things went a little haywhya.'

'Oh?'

'It's unda control.'

'You're sure?'

'I'm heea.'

A chuckle. 'So you are.'

'What can I do for ya?'

'Another job.'

'I'm retiyad.'

'Five times the going rate.'

Randy swallowed his tongue. Waited. 'I'm done,' he said finally.

'Half a million. Nonsequential bills. A little kicker for your retirement fund.'

A longer silence ensued.

'Who?'

The voice on the other end mentioned a name.

'That's a wicked famous name. Access is going to be a problem.'

'I'll bring him to you,' the voice said.

'Tell me about it.'

The voice held forth in great detail. He finished with, '. . . and, as per usual, I'll wire your fee to—'

'No,' Randy interrupted. 'I've closed down alla my regula channels.' He felt the tension from the other end of the telephone. 'Bring the money with you,' he said.

The voice cleared its throat. 'Nothing personal, but I had hoped we would never have occasion to meet again.'

'I undastand. You want the job done, then bring the money when you bring me the subject.'

After a prolonged silence, 'I'll be in touch with the details.'

Randy closed the connection.

The mess had been cleaned up. The shattered glass panel had been replaced. Took Kirsten a second to figure out why the scene seemed so odd. The glass was blank and shiny. Her name and job title were nowhere to be found. She'd watched the changeover process many times before. The painters usually arrived about five seconds after the glass was replaced. A not-so-subtle message.

Kirsten checked her messages. She had returned the phone to its cradle when the shuffle of shoes brought her eyes to the hallway, where Gene Connor was showing off a new suit, something-or-other rose the designer probably would have called it. 'He's at a deposition up at the Federal Building,' Gene said. 'He wants to see you at four-thirty.'

'Thanks, Gene,' Kirsten said. 'Tell him I'm leaving town for the weekend. If he'd like to chat, we can do it on Monday,' she said, gathering papers from her desktop and stuffing them into her briefcase. When she looked up, Gene was still standing there. Her eyes were telling Kirsten how poorly her message was likely to be received.

Asking, in her reserved way, if things were truly beyond repair. This was as close to schmoozing as Gene Connor got, and although she would never appear to be taking a side contrary to her employer, her face was darkened by clouds of regret.

Kirsten met her gaze. 'It's time, Gene,' she said. 'I'm not the person who started out here nine years ago.'

Gene smiled. 'You were a bit green in those days.'

'I was fresh from the vine,' Kirsten said. 'A lot of water's flowed under my bridge since then.'

'Perhaps if you—' Gene began.

'No,' Kirsten said quickly. 'It's time.'

Gene looked as if she was going to attempt another reconciliation. Instead, she squared her shoulders and smiled. 'You'll be a success wherever you go and whatever you do,' she said.

Kirsten felt her eyes beginning to well up. She tightened her jaw and swallowed. She met Gene's gaze. 'Coming from you, I'm going to take that as high praise indeed.'

'You should,' the older woman said. 'I mean every word of it.'

'Thank you.'

Gene Connor turned and walked back up the aisle. Heads disappeared in a heartbeat. The sounds of office work whirred above her measured footsteps.

Kirsten walked over and closed the door.

She pulled her center drawer open and riffled through a stack of business cards.

Finding the card she was looking for, she picked up the phone . . . stopped . . . looked around, and then pulled out her cell phone instead. She dialed, worked her way through three automated phoneservice menus until she finally reached an operator. 'This is Kirsten Kane of the Queen Anne County District Attorney's Office,' she said. 'Could you please connect me to Special Agent in Charge . . .' – she looked down at the card on the desk – 'Robert A. Moody,' she read.

CHAPTER 51

Apparently, torrential rain didn't improve the sound of bagpipes. The Highland Heritage Bagpipe Brigade's heartfelt rendition of 'Amazing Grace' sounded vaguely Egyptian as they marched up Seventh Avenue in the driving rain.

Both sides of the street were six deep with people, perhaps a few less than could have been expected in more hospitable weather, but an eager and enthusiastic crowd nonetheless. St Patrick's Day was seemingly impervious to the weather. Didn't matter that they could have gotten just as hammered yesterday or tomorrow, this was St Patty's Day and by God they were going to party, come rain or come shine.

Standing beneath Scofield's Furniture's faded red awning, the gentleman in the trench coat was not among the revelers. A pair of drunken college boys sloshed his way and offered him a cup of green beer. He smiled and waved them off. He watched as the pair disappeared back into the crowd. His face spoke of podiatry and indigestion.

When the garishly costumed leprechaun stopped at his side, he looked the other way, hoping to convey his disinterest in the proceedings and thus avoid any give-and-take. He kept his eyes glued on the Cleveland High School Marching Band as they pranced and postured their way up the street. The leprechaun didn't seem to be in any hurry to move along. The guy took a step to his right.

The oversize plastic leprechaun head bounced off his shoulder. He turned that way. The character had closed the distance between them. Whoever was inside was looking out through the smiling mouth. The jaunty green hat dripped water. The leprechaun carried a rough bag looped across his shoulders from which he suddenly pulled a white kitchen trash bag.

'Here,' he said, offering the bag to the guy in the trench coat.

The agent hesitated and then took possession of the bag. 'What's this?'

'It's her diary,' the leprechaun said. 'I found it in the bomb shelter.'

'And how did you know about the bomb shelter?'

He told him of spying on Isobel Howard.

'You know where she is now?'

'No idea.'

'Lady at the travel agency where Mrs Howard worked said she thought maybe Mrs Howard had some kind of love interest going on the side.'

Randy told him what Wesley Number Two had

said about not believing her stories about working late at the agency.

FBI shook the diary. 'How do I know this is legit?'

'Because I'm telling you so.'

The agent shook the bag. 'This going to clear up all my questions?'

'No,' The leprechaun said. 'She didn't know what was going on either.' He nodded his huge head at the bag. 'That's the story of the seven years she spent in the dark, living with some guy she didn't know.'

The agent sneered and started to speak. The leprechaun beat him to the punch. He related the story of the real Wesley Howard, of his disappearance and the subsequent substitution of a new Wesley Howard.

'Why would somebody want to do something like that?'

'I think maybe whoever it was had something else big going down and felt like they couldn't stand the spotlight right then.'

'Seven years is a long time.'

The leprechaun shrugged. 'Whatever the reason, I didn't have anything to do with whatever came down there.'

'Just a tourist, eh?'

'Something like that.'

'We found substantial amounts of Wesley Howard's blood on the floor of the Water Street house.'

'I don't think so.'

FBI raised his eyebrows. 'Oh?'

The leprechaun removed one of his enormous white gloves, fished a photograph from one of the pockets on the front of his plaid vest, and handed it over. 'Unless I'm mistaken, that's Wesley Allen Howard.'

'Our lab tells me the blood on the bedroom floor matches the security sample.'

'That's because the people responsible were in a position to see to it that the samples matched.'

'Can't be that many people with that kind of clout,' the agent commented.

'I'd bet money one of them was this guy Walter Hybridge I've been reading about in the papers.'

The fed's eyes betrayed him.

The leprechaun went on. 'I'd also be willing to bet that Hybridge is being set up as the fall guy.'

The fed remained silent.

'Interesting timing,' the leprechaun added.

A pair of beautifully appointed palomino horses preceded the FFA float down the street. 'Where do you come into this?' trench coat wanted to know.

'I told you. I don't.'

'Adrian Hope sure as hell does.'

'Howard's wife says he went to work and never came home. At first I thought he'd confided whatever he'd heard to someone else in the program. For a while, I thought it was Adrian Hope. But now I don't think so.'

'What do you think now?'

He related what the killer had told him. 'He said he was there making arrangements to kill some guy named Barber when Howard walked in on it.'

The other man's eyes told the leprechaun that the agent was familiar with the name.

'He said Howard was supposed to have left for the day. Once he got a look at Mr Mystery, he had to go. Said "I just blundered in" while he was taking care of Mr Howard.'

The agent abruptly changed the subject. 'Speaking of the unfortunate gentleman with the hole in his head . . .'

'I already told you everything I know.'

'He doesn't exist. His fingerprints are on file nowhere in the world. His DNA profile likewise. Amazing . . . huh? A guy could live that long and not leave so much as a footprint.' He pinned the leprechaun with his gaze. 'Nothing on his body but a shiny nine-millimeter automatic.'

'Really?' Randy felt the blood rising to his cheeks inside the plastic head.

'You know what's interesting about the automatic?'

'What's that?'

'Lab says it was the murder weapon in the shooting of a Wisconsin Teamster official way back in '73.'

'No kidding.'

'And also the murder weapon in the death of a captain in the U.S. Border Patrol. Happened in

Corpus Christi just last year. Aaaand . . .' – he stretched it out – 'also the possible murder weapon in a double murder in Cleveland back in '95.'

'Quite a time gap.'

'Quite a career,' he corrected. He waited for a long moment. 'And you don't know anything about any of this?'

'I don't remember a thing before I woke up in the hospital seven years ago, and most of that's real fuzzy because my brain wasn't working right.' The leprechaun anticipated his next question. 'All I had was this name floating around in my head . . . Wesley Allen Howard.'

'Which took you to Water Street.'

'Yes.'

The agent entwined his fingers and cracked his knuckles. 'Want to hear something funny?' he asked.

'I'm all ears.'

'Couple of the Water Street neighbors claimed to have seen our mystery man in the neighborhood.'

'Lately.'

'On and off for years.'

'You showed them a picture?'

'Of the stiff.'

'Gotta be a mistake.'

'You think so?'

Randy shrugged. 'Unless you've got a better explanation.'

The agent waved a nonchalant hand in the air.

'And, throughout this whole thing, you didn't hurt a living soul?'

'No.'

'What about a cop named Chester Berry?'

If he hadn't been leaning against the building, the leprechaun would have fallen to the sidewalk. 'Never heard of him,' he said.

'Not that the world isn't a better place without Chester Berry, mind you.'

'I'll have to take your word for it.'

'Interesting thing is . . .' He waited a beat. 'Your fingerprints are all over his car.'

'I stole it from him,' the leprechaun said, and then told him an abridged version of the rest area story, leaving Acey, the dope, and the money out of it.

'How'd he get his car back, then?'

'Musta had friends on the force.'

FBI nearly smiled. 'That it?'

The leprechaun thought it over. He reached inside the costume and came out with a prepaid cell phone. 'I took this off the nameless guy,' he said.

The FBI guy grabbed him by the shoulder.

'I got a call on it,' the leprechaun said.

The grip lessened. 'From?'

'He didn't give me his name.'

'A call regarding what?'

'He wanted to buy another hit.'

The fed let go. 'On who?'

'Robert Reese.'

The name brought the agent up short. He whistled. 'And how were you supposed to get close enough to a deputy cabinet minister to do the job?'

'That's what I asked.'

'And?'

'He's going to bring him to me.'

The FBI agent tried for nonplussed but came up considerably short. 'Where and when?' he wanted to know.

'He said he'd call back with that.'

The agent's jaw muscles rippled like a snake.

'That name I just gave you,' the leprechaun said.

'What about it.'

'He work for NASA seven or eight years ago?'

The fed's face stayed blank.

'Quid pro quo,' the leprechaun reminded him. 'You want to know when this thing's coming down, you better humor me.'

'Okay . . . yeah, he worked for NASA.'

'Which tells you who was on the other end of my phone call, doesn't it?'

'Pretty much,' the agent admitted.

'You want to enlighten me?'

'Not much,' the agent said. He checked the street in all directions. Sighed and then sighed again. 'The third guy in project management was Ronald Jacobson.' He looked around again. 'Who, in case you don't keep track of such things, is presently the deputy director for the NSA.'

'Sounds like Mr Jacobson is trying to tie up his loose ends.'

'Yeah . . . it does.'

The leprechaun tilted his oversize head. 'The Bureau's interest in this didn't just start, did it?' he asked. 'How long have you guys been looking into this?'

The agent rubbed the corners of his mouth with his thumb and forefinger. 'Before the shuttle ever went down.' He paused to let the news sink in. 'The Bureau got a call from an engineer . . . guy on the space program named Roland Barber . . . says he sent a letter up the chain of command saying the thermal protection tiles were likely to be a serious problem upon reentry.'

'Sent to who?'

'The guy said he sent it to project management. According to NASA's records, no such letter was ever sent or received.'

'So?'

'So we went through their records.'

'And found no such letter.'

He shook his head. 'Not until it appeared in this guy Walter Hybridge's papers last week. A copy, of course, but addressed to Hybridge.'

'Just so happens Mr Hybridge isn't around to defend himself.'

'Amazing, huh?'

'So . . . your engineer. That's all he did? Send a couple letters and then just let it go at that?'

'They transferred him. Next business day. To Iowa. Customer liaison to General Dynamics. That was a Tuesday. Friday morning on his way to the office, Roland Barber was struck and killed by a hit-and-run driver.'

Before the leprechaun could react, the agent asked, 'You want to guess who his replacement was?'

The leprechaun nodded his big plastic head. 'Wesley Allen Howard.'

'Touchdown,' the agent said.

'What now?'

'We'll take it from here.'

The leprechaun stepped in as close as the over-size head would permit.

'I can't just walk away here,' he said.

'You don't have a choice.'

'Sure I do. He's expecting me on the other end of the phone when he calls back with the details. You want my help, you're going to have to let me see this thing through.'

His lip curled. 'No way I could let a civilian get involved with this.'

'Remember . . . they've met before.'

The special agent's eyes wandered over him like wasps. 'How do you know that?' he asked in a strained voice.

'He said he'd hoped we – meaning him and Mr No Name – would never have to meet again.'

'We'll work around it,' the agent said quickly. 'You just—'

The leprechaun cut him off. 'Then you handle it without me.'

'I'll clap your ass in a federal detention facility.'

'Be that as it may,' the leprechaun said.

The agent set his teeth and looked away. When he looked back, his eyes were hard as stones. 'This isn't some damn game here, Mr Hope. This is a potentially dangerous situation.'

'I'm aware of that.'

'Ronald Jacobson has more potential deniability than practically anyone in the nation. He can refuse to answer questions on the basis that it endangers national security and there's not a damn thing anybody can do about it. You understand what I'm telling you.' He didn't wait for an answer. 'Jacobson could shoot you in the head in Macy's window and get away with it. You grasp what I'm telling you here, Mr . . . all he'd have to say was that the matter concerned national security or the war on terror or both and that would be the end of the inquiry.' He snapped his fingers. 'Just like that.'

The leprechaun twisted his plastic head a quarter turn to the right and then used both hands to lift the brightly painted bucket from his head. The two men stood eye to eye beneath the dripping overhang.

'These people stole my fucking life,' Randy said. 'This is identity theft . . . the real kind, not some unfortunate slob losing his wallet and having to stop all his charge cards. These guys side-tracked my entire life.' His voice rose above the din. 'They pushed me over onto a siding and left me for dead. I have no idea who I am, no idea of who I used

405

to be or how I got there. All I know for sure is I've got no intention of being this guy Adrian Hope and . . .' He shook his finger in the air. 'If I've got a chance to hang some trouble on the people who did this to me . . . well then, I'm goddamn gonna do it . . . period.' The agent started to speak. Randy cut him off. 'If Jacobson's got the kind of deniability you say he does, then you're going to need a smoking gun. You're gonna need to catch him in the act of paying me off.'

'Even that might not be enough.'

'All the more reason you need me.'

The agent looked Randy over. 'You and Mr Mystery are about the same size and body type.'

'Mustache . . . a change in hair color,' Randy said.

'Might work from across the street,' the agent admitted.

'And then you've got him.'

'Or he's got you.'

'I can handle myself.'

'So can Jacobson,' the agent. 'He goes down to Quantico and qualifies with a nine-millimeter. He scores better than most of *us*.'

'Well then, you and your guys are going to have to be Johnny-on-the-spot, aren't you?'

FBI leaned Randy's way. 'Has it occurred to you that you're a loose end, Mr Lucky Charms?' He didn't wait for an answer. 'About the time you kill

Reese and Jacobson kills you, he's fresh out of loose ends and free as a bird.'

'It's crossed my mind.'

'Okay,' the agent said, as much to himself as to Randy.

The Fort Harrison Drum and Bugle Corps were as crisp as their uniforms were soggy.

'When this is over . . .' the leprechaun began.

'Yeah?'

'I walk. No questions asked. No strings.'

'Okay.'

'You got a business card?'

FBI produced a gray leather card case, scribbled on the back of one, and handed it to the leprechaun. 'Day or night,' the agent said.

The leprechaun held the plastic head beneath his arm as he stepped out into the driving rain. '*Erin go bragh,*' he said before walking off into the melee.

CHAPTER 52

Kirsten Kane lost her grip on the cardboard box. It fell to the ground, spilling some of its contents. The framed copy of her Georgetown Law degree landed faceup on the front steps of her apartment building. She squatted and began to stuff the memorabilia back into the bursting box. Amazing how much crap one collects in nine years, she thought to herself.

'Let me help you there,' said a voice.

'I've got it,' she said, too engrossed in her own thoughts to pay any real attention to the would-be good Samaritan. She had replaced everything in the box when the voice spoke again.

'Looks like somebody's reinventing herself.'

And then she knew. She left the box on the sidewalk and straightened up.

'You quit or he fire you?' Randy asked.

'I quit *before* he could fire me.'

'How's it feel?'

'Weird. I haven't been unemployed since I was a sophomore in high school.'

He nodded. 'I know what you mean. I keep feeling like I ought to be doing something, except I don't have any idea what it is I should be doing.'

'I'm going to take my time,' she said. 'I'm not in any hurry to move on to whatever comes next.'

'Me neither,' he said.

'You going to continue your quest to find out who you are?'

'I already know.'

'Really?'

'I used to think that once I knew my name and my past history, I'd know who I was.' He laughed a bitter laugh. 'Turns out to be too corny for words. Turns out . . . it's not about having a name or a history . . . turns out who I am is inside of me, not something out there in the great beyond somewhere.' He waved a huge hand in the air.

'That's not corny.'

'Sounds like the last line of a bad movie.'

'It does not.'

'You don't think so?'

'No. I think it's great you found yourself.'

An uneasy silence settled over the street. He seemed to be having an internal discussion with himself. She reached for the box.

'I had an idea,' he said.

She straightened up. 'About what?'

'Reinvention.'

'Oh?'

'I was thinking Rome.'

'Rome?'

'I was thinking it might be just the place to . . .

you know, just the place to take stock before, you know . . . before moving on.'

'I've never been to Rome.'

'So why don't you come along?' he said.

Her jaw moved a couple of times before words came out of her mouth. 'You mean like . . . you and me . . . like . . . in Rome?'

'Yeah. Like that.'

'That's crazy. You and I hardly—' The rest of the sentence stuck in her throat. 'I'd have to think it over,' she said finally.

'There you go being sensible again.'

She grinned. 'It's in the blood, I guess.'

'Okay,' he said, picking up the box and handing it to her. 'Take care now.'

'You, too.'

He turned and walked up the sidewalk. She watched him go. He reached the corner of Franklin and Densmore and started to cross the street.

'Hey,' she called.

He turned.

'I thought it over,' she called.

He smiled and wandered back her way. 'I've got a spot of business to take care of before we can go.'

'Me too,' she said.

'A week or so,' he said.

'Okay.'

CHAPTER 53

Jacobson wasn't hard to spot, standing resolute and rigid on the street corner, exactly where he was supposed to be, diagonally across the street from the park. The guy had the prominent government official look down pat, not a bit like the kind of riffraff who would hire a hit man to kill an esteemed colleague.

The question was whether or not Randy looked enough like Jacobson's hit man to set things in motion. If not, the jig was going to be up before it ever began and Jacobson was probably going to be able to slide back behind his curtain of deniability.

Randy stood with his back to the thick concrete railing. He stretched and checked the street . . . a groaning garbage truck and two people walking dogs. The rest of the city was still asleep. The fake mustache felt like a caterpillar crawling on his lip. He wore a black Barcelino cabbie's cap and a pair of oversize sunglasses, from behind which he took Jacobson in, before removing the cap and running his fingers through his new ginger-colored hair in their prearranged signal.

Jacobson nodded back. The message was: 'He's there.'

They were on.

Randy watched as Jacobson turned and walked through the revolving doors. Randy held his ground for long enough to see the guy seat himself in the window of the second-floor coffee shop. The aluminum attaché case by his feet gleamed like a silver beacon.

Randy bumped himself off the banister and started down the stairs into the park.

Bob was miffed. These clandestine little meetings needed to stop. Not only was this get-together on short notice, but they were meeting in the same place they'd met once before, down beneath the stairway in Conroy Park, back against the retaining wall where he'd have to force his way through the shrubs, probably ruin his coat.

Jacobson was going to hear about this in no uncertain terms. This matter was supposed to be handled by now. Just as they'd planned, Walter Hybridge was taking the heat. His family was already issuing tearful denials on television. It was a done deal. What could possibly merit a meeting first thing on a Monday morning?

He leaned back against the wall. Above his head, the traffic rushed and roared as the city came to life. He wondered how many people were still suffering the lingering effects of St Patrick's Day, still a bit green around the gills as they

412

made their way back to their normal workaday worlds.

To make matters worse, Jacobson was late. Bob checked his watch again, sighed and stamped his feet to keep warm. That's when he caught sight of the feet sliding along the edge of the stone staircase, moving his way. Had to be Jacobson . . . and about damn time, too. A single large rhododendron bush separated them now.

Bob readied his verbal salvo. He opened his mouth as the hand pushed the bush aside and he stepped into the narrow clearing at the back of the flower bed. His body began to vibrate. He felt as if he must be emitting a humming noise. It wasn't Jacobson but a white-haired man in a trench coat, with a well-trimmed mustache and bright blue eyes. The man felt his panic and held up a restraining hand.

He pulled a leather case from his pocket. 'FBI,' he said.

Bob looked to his right. Another figure approached. Vaguely familiar. Bigger. Younger. Wearing a black wool cap.

'There's nowhere to run,' the white-haired man said.

'Do you have any idea—' Bob began.

'Please.'

'Has it suddenly become a federal crime to stand in a public park in broad daylight? What exactly do you imagine you're . . .'

The FBI agent was waving a photograph of what

413

was obviously a dead body. Bob recognized the corpse. His stomach churned. He looked away.

'Do you know this man?'

'Never seen him before in my life. Now if you will . . .'

The FBI agent gestured toward the photo. 'Ronald Jacobson hired this man to kill you.'

Bob felt his knees weaken. The contents of his stomach flipped over and threatened to spew from his lips. 'No one was supposed to get hurt,' he forced out.

The other two men looked at him as if he were speaking in tongues.

'The tiles . . .' he stammered. 'We were just trying to . . .' Bob looked from one man to the other. 'We just wanted to stop the program for a while, don't you understand?' Neither man seemed to have heard. 'It wasn't personal,' Bob insisted. 'It was about money. About appropriations . . .' he tried. When the men appeared not to comprehend, he went on. 'The generals wanted the space program stopped for a while so they could use the money for the war.' He looked for understanding. Finding none, he segued, '*We are at war, you know*,' he tried. The righteous indignation fell flat.

'Which generals?' the younger man asked.

Bob Reese began to stammer. 'I wasn't the one who—' He stopped himself. Sirens began to fill his ears. Above his throbbing head vehicles screeched to a halt. More sirens, whooping their

414

way, closer, louder, groaning to silence, and then the sound of voices followed by the slap of feet running down the stairs in the seconds before the sound of something metal, something on wheels bouncing his way.

'Mr Reese,' Agent Moody said. 'We're going to go through a little charade here for Mr Jacobson's benefit.'

'I . . . I don't understand . . . I . . .'

Another pair of agents pushed their way through the shrubbery.

Agent Moody gestured toward the pair of younger men. 'Please go with these gentlemen,' he said.

'It wasn't personal,' Bob muttered. 'We just wanted to . . .'

They took Bob Reese by the elbows and led him away. Randy and the FBI agent followed them out into the park. A cadre of agents was keeping gawkers at a distance as the ambulance attendants carried the gurney back up the stairs to the waiting aid car. Even up close, the bloodstains on the sheet looked real.

Agent Moody looked over at Randy.

'Go,' he said.

Randy recited the directions in his head as he walked along Beacon Avenue. Three blocks north. Left on Cavanaugh. Halfway down the block . . . just past the Gnu Deli Delhi, left into the alley, all the way down the end.

He checked his watch: 5:57 A.M. This part of the city was strictly business. Housing was virtually nonexistent. Nobody was on the street as he stopped at the mouth of the alley. Somewhere in the distance the roar of a truck rumbled to his ears. He took a deep breath and made it a point not to look over his shoulder.

The alley was long and dark, running, without interruption, for an entire city block. A collection of overflowing Dumpsters jutted out from the right-hand side of the alley. He kept as far left as he could, trying to keep his feet out of the stinking refuse and broken glass as he worked his way across the rough stones.

Halfway down the alley, Randy could make out a jagged silhouette standing at the far end. He hesitated as the figure stepped away from the bricks, into the center of the narrow confines.

He kept his hands in his pockets as he moved along. To his right the scurrying of rat feet made his skin crawl. He kept moving. The figure bent at the waist and set the attaché case on the ground.

'I had hoped we would never have occasion to meet,' the figure said. 'Nothing personal, I'm sure you understand.'

'Everything's personal,' Randy said.

The guy kept his right hand in his pocket as he gestured with his head toward the case. 'As promised.'

Randy stood still. Something about the guy set his nerves to jangling. Beneath the layer of

416

bureaucratic blubber, Randy could sense something . . . something . . . He squatted and groped for the case's handle, keeping his eyes glued on the dark shape and wondering where in hell Moody and the rest of the FBI were. The deal was done. Money was changing hands. They were supposed to be appearing about now. The roar of the truck drew ever nearer.

Without willing himself to do *so*, Randy found himself looking back over his shoulder, back the way he'd come, back in the direction the cavalry was supposed to be riding to his rescue just about now. Big mistake. Damn near his last.

Jacobson was quick. He had the silenced automatic out of his pocket in a flash.

All Randy could do was raise the case in front of his face. The slug came out of the barrel as nothing more than a loud hiss, a lead comet tearing through the metal, coming out the far side so close to Randy's face he felt as if he'd been branded on the cheek in the second before he threw the case at the guy and began to reel backward like a Friday-night drunk, flailing his arms as he sought to regain his balance. The guy blocked the case with his forearm and raised the gun again.

Randy dove behind the nearest trash bin as another hiss gouged a furrow in the brick closest to his face. He used every bit of his strength to propel the oversize metal container in a half circle, forcing the rank, rusted wheels across the littered surface until he thought his shoulder would surely break from the socket, staying low, angling the Dumpster across the alley sideways, filling the entire space with a ton and a half of metal-clad garbage. He cradled his aching shoulder, scrambled to his feet, and ran.

Ran toward the street in the seconds before the mouth of the alley filled with the diesel roar and the bright lights of the garbage truck whose groaning bulk filled the alley, leaving only inches to spare on either side. He heard a curse from inside the truck and then another as the red-hot buzz of another slug tore past his ear and smashed itself against the grille.

He ran. It was all he could do. He was still forty yards from the truck when the driver pulled himself out the window, climbed quickly to the roof of the cab, and scrambled over the length of the truck before dropping out of sight as another bullet smashed one of the headlights.

Unsure his aching legs could jump high enough to get up on the hood of the truck, Randy, in the time-honored manner of the pursued, went to ground, diving under the front bumper of the garbage truck, crawling beneath the roaring collection of pipes and engines and mufflers, using his elbows to walk himself forward faster than he would have believed possible.

Despite the throb of the exhaust and the scrape of moving parts, Randy could hear the slap of feet coming up the alley behind him, could sense the moment when his pursuer went high, scratching and crawling his way over the hood and up onto the roof and the top of the truck, moving much faster on his feet than Randy could manage on his bleeding elbows.

Whatever advantage Randy might have gained was gone. They arrived at the back of the truck in the same instant. As Randy flipped over onto his back and began to pull himself to his feet, his pursuer jumped down into the yawning mouth of the trash compartment. He was close enough for Randy to see the beads of sweat covering his face. The guy pointed the gun at Randy's face and smiled.

Trying desperately to get to his feet, Randy reached for the nearest piece of metal, sending the hydraulic compactor platform snapping upward with the speed of a freight train, crushing Jacobson's legs like matchsticks. The guy screamed like nothing Randy had ever heard before as Randy pulled himself to his knees, still using the handle to pull himself upright, the truck groaning and shaking as the compactor drum rose in the air like a massive metal moon.

The gun clattered to the ground. Jacobson was howling at the moon and shaking back and forth like a branch in the wind. Randy glanced over his shoulder in time to see Moody and his FBI minions arrive at the mouth of the alley. He grabbed the handle again. 'Which generals?'

Jacobson mumbled something. Randy pulled the handle. In his peripheral vision he could see

Moody holding his agents back. The crushing power of the truck pulled a full-fledged scream from Jacobson's lungs.

'Which generals?' Randy yelled again.

'Samuels,' Jacobson said in a high-pitched voice.

'Who else?'

Randy made a fake reach for the handle.

'Crane . . . Crane.'

Randy tweaked the handle. Jacobson went back to baying at the moon.

'Who else?'

Randy eased off on the power.

'That was it. Swear to God,' Jacobson wheezed. 'Swear to God.'

Moody was at Randy's shoulder now, pulling his hand from the handle and leading him out to the mouth of the alley.

'You recognize the names?' Randy asked.

Moody's expression said he wished he hadn't. 'Joint Chiefs of Staff,' he said. 'Both of them.'

CHAPTER 54

The late afternoon sun wore a smog halo as it splashed its last orange rays onto the ancient buildings. The worn paving stones of the Via Minerva seemed to glow from within. Behind the couple, the ancient dome of the Pantheon rose in the air like a brick-and-marble mountain.

Kirsten slid the front page of the *International Herald Tribune* across the table. 'Seems you've caused quite a stink,' she said.

He winced and pretended to ignore the page, sipping at his coffee until he couldn't stand it anymore and then sneaking a peek at the lead story about how a pair of resignations in the Joint Chiefs of Staff were being scrutinized by a Senate subcommittee whose charge it was determine the extent of possible military involvement in an alleged effort to undermine the space program.

While embattled NSA deputy director Ronald W. Jacobson was refusing to testify on advice of council, former undersecretary of defense Robert Reese was cooperating with the congressional investigation and was expected to testify in open session early next week. Recent allegations regarding the *Venture* tragedy . . .

He pushed the paper back across the table. 'Couldn't happen to a nicer bunch of guys,' he said.

Kirsten spread her arms and stretched. A yawn escaped from her mouth. She covered it with the back of her hand and apologized.

He smiled. 'Sounds like somebody could use a nap,'

She gave him a wolfish grin. 'Is that what they're calling it these days?'

He squinted into the setting sun. 'Let's head back,' he said.

By way of agreement, she yawned again.

Paul . . . Randy . . . Adrian . . . Gavin. He wasn't sure what to call himself these days. He threw a ten-euro note on the table and rose to his feet.

A sudden break in the traffic along the Via del Cestan revealed the army of feral cats who made their home in and around the Pantheon, skittering from sunshine to shadow and back in search of whatever tidbits they could find, constantly in motion like a fast-running river of fur winding in and around the foundations.

They strolled arm in arm along the narrow streets until they arrived at the Hotel Coronet, where they had been staying for nearly a month. As they mounted the three steps to the vestibule, a flash of yellow in his peripheral vision pulled his eyes back along the route they'd just traveled.

She read the concern in his eyes. 'What?' she asked.

422

'I thought I saw something,' he said.

A grandmother shepherded a pair of young boys along the street.

He rubbed his eyes. 'I'm the one needs a nap,' he joked as they stepped inside. Something in his voice told her the levity wasn't sincere.

The entire building had once been a private palace called the Doria Pamphili. Modern sensibilities and Italian taxes had reduced the once-proud Pamphili family to living exclusively on the sixth floor and leasing out the remaining space. Retail shops filled the ground floor. The Roman offices of the Associated Press occupied the second, while the Hotel Coronet did business on the fourth. Three and five were an eclectic collection of doctors, dentists, accountants, and bond brokers.

His name tag read *Vincenzo DeGrazia*. He manned the small registration desk of the Hotel Coronet. He was scheduled to leave at four, a mere fifteen minutes away, when he looked up from the desk to see the familiar couple now approaching him. Big, both of them. The man was a bruiser. She was tall for a woman but beautiful. Must be newlyweds, Vincenzo decided. The way they clung to each other.

'Aaah . . . Mr and Mrs Landis. Welcome back,' he said in his heavily accented English. 'I hope you enjoyed your day in Roma,' he said.

'Thank you, we did,' said Kirsten.

The man nodded pleasantly and cast a backward

glance toward the empty street. Before Vincenzo could muster up enough English to make further small talk, the man took her by the elbow and pulled her off down the hall and out of sight.

Room 43 was the third door on the left. The maid had pulled the curtains. The room was cool and dark. Kirsten excused herself and headed for the loo.

He waited to hear the snap of the lock and then walked over to the window. He pulled back the drapes in time to catch yet another flash of yellow as it disappeared around the corner.

He snatched a room key from the top of the desk, let himself out into the hall, and hurried back to the lobby. 'Mr Landis . . . What may I . . .'

Mr Landis hurried across the carpet, into the elevator, and was gone without a word.

Vincenzo shook his head. 'Americans,' he whispered to himself.

Mr Landis moved quickly now, stepping out of the narrow elevator, jogging across the foyer and out into the street. He looked both ways. Only the grandmother and the boys, carrying cups of gelato now close to their stained faces. One had chosen grape, the other what appeared to be raspberry. Nothing yellow anywhere in sight.

He stood in the street for a moment checking traffic before turning back toward the Hotel Coronet. He glanced up as he crossed the street. Kirsten stood at the window. The lines in her forehead were visible, even through the glare on the glass. He managed a wan smile and a halfhearted wave before disappearing inside.

Her dress was unzipped. She held a hanger in her hand but made no move to undress. 'Everything okay?' she asked.

He hesitated. 'I guess so.'

'That's not terribly reassuring,' she said with a small smile.

He walked to the window and gazed down into the street. 'Last day and a half' – he walked over and stood at her side – 'I had this feeling that somebody's been watching us.' He shrugged apologetically.

'That's it? Just a feeling?'

'No.' He looked away.

Her smile disappeared. 'What else?'

'Coupla three times . . . I've thought I've seen somebody . . .' He ran a hand through his ginger-colored hair. 'You know . . . somebody stalking us or something.'

'Man or woman?'

'Can't tell.'

'Who would be stalking us?'

'I can't imagine.' He paced across the room. 'Gavin Landis doesn't exist.'

'You're sure?'

'Positive.'

'Maybe it's somebody stalking Adrian Hope,' she said.

Behind his deepening tan, he blanched. 'Maybe we oughta go find out,' he said.

CHAPTER 55

The water running beneath the Ponte Umberto shimmered in the moonlight as the couple strolled slowly along, seemingly entranced by the current crawling beneath their feet. At the mid-point of the bridge, they stopped and looked down into the water together. Kirsten stole a quick peek back the way they'd come.

'You see it?' he asked.

'Back at the end of the bridge,' Kirsten whispered. 'Just for a second.'

'Good,' he said. 'I was beginning to wonder about myself.'

They stood by the railing, looking down into the ink-black water.

'You ready?' he asked.

The air around them seemed to tighten.

Kirsten nodded.

'All we want to do is get a look at whoever it is, right?'

'Right.'

'No confrontations. No heroics.'

'Trust me,' she said. 'I'm not looking for trouble.'

They'd talked it over as they'd dressed for dinner.

The Café Adriana was a half-hour walk from the hotel. Long enough to work up an appetite or walk off a dinner and, not coincidentally, just about right for ascertaining whether or not one was being followed. Their shadow had picked them up as soon as they'd left the hotel, casting something of a pall over what had otherwise been a terrific dinner at the Café Adriana, a small bistro in the shadow of the Vatican, where the sacred and the secular regularly came together to break bread. Took her a full minute to recall exactly what she'd had for dinner.

'I'm ready,' she assured him.

They ambled another twenty yards.

She took his hand in hers, moving closer to him now.

'I'm almost relieved,' she said.

'How's that?'

'I noticed.'

'Noticed what?'

'How you were all of a sudden way more uptight.'

'How's that reassuring?' he asked.

'I thought . . . you know . . . maybe it was us . . . like maybe you lost interest in me or something.'

'Anyone loses interest in rolling around with you should see a doctor.'

'Is that all?'

'Is what all?'

'Sex,' she whispered.

'Why do you always whisper that word?'

'Do I?'

'Every time. Like it's something shouldn't be talked about.'

'It's the last taboo, I guess,' she said.

They passed beneath the final ornate gold street-light on the bridge. Ahead, the brightly lit Piazza Della Rovere beckoned them forward. Instead, the pair turned sharp left and disappeared behind what must have been in medieval times some kind of watchtower, where the man now calling himself Gavin Landis stepped into the deep shadows and waited as Kirsten continued down the stairs talking to herself now, emoting as if they were still together and engaged in a lively conversation.

He held his breath and waited. Nothing. He sneaked another chestful of air and held it. Still nothing. He began to contemplate the possibility that he was mistaken. That no one was shadowing them. That the whole thing was a figment of his imagination. He shook his head in disgust and was about to follow Kirsten down the stairs when the sound of running feet sent him leaning back into the darkness.

Soft feet, feet whose tread was little more than a whisper. He listened as their pursuer hesitated at the top of the stairs and then began to follow the sound of Kirsten's voice as she rounded the lower corner and started to walk along the river.

He took a deep breath and stepped out to the top of the stairs. The interloper was nearly at the bottom step. He watched as . . . as . . .

428

she . . . it was definitely a woman . . . as she peeped around the corner. Whatever she saw sent her scurrying back the way she'd come, taking the stairs two at a time on long legs, until she finally looked up and saw the hulking figure at the top of the stairs.

She stopped dead. She looked behind her, where Kirsten suddenly appeared at the foot of the stairs, then upward again at the shadow towering above her. And then, in the near darkness, as the single streetlight dumped its pale cone of light directly onto her face . . . suddenly he knew. He'd seen the face before.

'Isobel' escaped his lips.

CHAPTER 56

The sound of her name froze her in place. 'I . . . I . . . please . . .' she stammered.

'You remember me?' he asked. When she didn't respond, he went on. 'I came to your house on Water Street. Remember?'

She stood transfixed, her jaw unhinged, staring up the stairs until the sound of Kirsten's high heels behind her pulled Isobel Howard's head around. She closed her mouth and looked from the man to Kirsten and back. Her knees quivered and then bent. She sat on the ancient marble stair and put both hands over her face. 'I don't understand,' she said finally. 'What have you done with Gavin?'

The question made his head spin.

'How do you know Gavin?' he choked out after a minute.

'He was . . . we were going to . . .' She looked around as if she were suddenly lost in the woods, and then her mouth drooped and she began to hiccup, and then, after a moment of sniffling, she broke out into full-fledged crying. 'I don't understand,' she wailed over and over from behind her hands. Kirsten walked up and sat beside her on the stair, leaning in close and whispering, soothing Isobel Howard's back with an understanding hand.

He walked down the stairs and sat on the step above the women. He put his hand on Kirsten's shoulder. She lifted her head and looked his way. Her eyes told him to wait. He took her word for it, trying in his mind to work up a scenario about how Isobel Howard could be linked with a professional assassin, a man with no name, no address, no connections, a man who didn't, for all intents and purposes, exist at all.

Nothing came to mind. He waited until the sniffling stopped.

'How do you know Gavin Landis?' he asked again. She looked up.

'After Wes disappeared . . .' She searched herself looking for a tissue. She came up empty and reluctantly wiped her nose on her sleeve. 'After Wes disappeared . . . Gavin . . . he used to stop by to check on me.'

'Check on you how?'

'You know . . . to make sure the little man-and-wife charade was working.'

'Why would he do that?'

'He was with security.'

'Security?'

'You know, for the space center.'

Kirsten threw a cautionary look his way.

'So?' Kirsten prompted.

Isobel Howard's shoulders began to shake. 'It went

on for years,' she hiccuped before breaking into tears. 'Gavin and I got to know each other. I stopped hating him. Started looking forward to his visits.' She knew how odd her story sounded. She made an apologetic face. 'The girls adored him,' she said by way of explanation.

'So?'

She looked away to ease the pressure and then began to talk, halting and hesitant at first, until the dam broke and the words flowed from her mouth in a torrent. You could tell she'd practiced the story in her head, over and over. She had her rationalizations down pat. About how she'd become fond of one of her keepers and how the feelings were mutual. How, when things had begun to fall apart, he'd helped her to escape. How he was supposed to pick them up and how, when he'd failed to show, she'd gone online and fed his name into the GDS system, which was what travel agents used for bookings, and lo and behold if his name didn't come up as having flown to Rome two weeks earlier. According to the GDS system, Gavin Landis was staying at the Hotel Coronet. She'd arrived the day before yesterday. She wouldn't say where she'd left the girls, just that it was something that Gavin had arranged.

She looked up at him with bloodshot eyes. 'Where's Gavin? Why are you using his name?'

'Because I can't use my own' was all he could think to say.

'I don't understand.'

'I'm Adrian Hope.'

She blinked twice and began to shake her head. 'You're not . . . I've seen pictures of Adrian Hope and you're—'

He interrupted, told her about the plastic surgery and the fingerprints. Isobel Howard looked to Kirsten for confirmation and received it.

'Where's Gavin?' she asked again. She read the look of pity as it passed between her companions. 'Please . . .' She began to weep. 'Don't say . . . Don't tell me . . .'

'I'm very sorry,' he said.

'It was in the line of duty,' Kirsten added.

'This can't be happening again. It can't.' The woman folded her arms over her knees and buried her face. Kirsten looped an arm around her shoulder and pulled Isobel Howard close. They sat huddled together as Isobel poured out the tattered remnants of her heart onto the cold stone below her feet. Kirsten kept up a steady whisper about the *real* Gavin Landis, if a guy who didn't exist could be considered real, about how he'd been working on his new life with Isobel and her girls when he'd been killed. How he'd surely have picked her up as planned if only it had been possible. The way Kirsten told the story Landis had been nothing short of a national hero at the moment of his untimely demise.

The man *now* calling himself Gavin Landis pulled out his wallet. He fished around inside and came out with a pair of keys. He selected one and returned the other to his hip pocket. He squeezed the silver key in his hand as he waited for Isobel Howard to regain some measure of composure.

She used her sleeve as a hankie and looked up.

'Nobody's looking for you anymore,' he said. 'Everybody connected to what happened to you and your husband is permanently out of commission.'

'You're sure?'

He said he was. 'Take this,' he said, proffering the key.

Her hand was clammy and cold as he pushed the key into her palm.

'Market Street Station.' He named the city. 'The locker number is on the key.'

'I don't . . .'

'There's a whole bunch of money in that locker. It's enough to start a new life. It was Gavin's money. He'd want you and the girls to have it.' She was about to lose her composure again. 'There's also a deed to a piece of property in Vermont. I'm guessing that's where he had in mind living out his days with you.'

The news ushered in another bout of sobbing from Isobel Howard and another round of whispered encouragement from Kirsten.

While she collected herself, he told her everything he knew. Everything Bob Reese was about to share with the congressional subcommittee. How Ronald Jacobson was approached by a couple of generals on the Military Oversight Committee. All the generals wanted was for project management to ignore reports that the heat tiles constituted a hazard. How Roland Barber wouldn't keep his mouth shut about it and needed to be silenced. How Jacobson was discussing that very matter with a professional hit man when Wes walked in. And then Adrian Hope came waltzing in when Jacobson and the killer were dealing with Wesley Howard. The rest, as they say, was history.

'Why the charade?' she wanted to know. 'Why take my life from me?'

'They didn't feel like they could weather a full-fledged investigation into Wes's disappearance right then. Not with Roland Barber about to meet his maker. Not with Adrian Hope turning up missing. Not only that, but putting a new Wes in place gave them a man on the inside of the program.'

She took several minutes to process the information. 'Who was . . .' She waved a hand in the air. 'You'd think I'd know what to call a man I spent seven years living in the same house with. I always thought of him as "it."'

'Reese says he doesn't know who the guy was and Jacobson's not talking,' he said. 'That part's going to stay a mystery, for the time being at least.'

For the third time, she used her sleeve as a tissue, then pushed herself to her feet.

'I'm going home to my girls,' she announced.

She opened her hand and looked down at the key. 'Thank you,' she offered.

'It's how he would have wanted it.'

'Does anybody but you know . . . you know . . . the farm and . . .'

'Just us,' he assured her. 'Anybody but you know about Gavin Landis?'

She shook her head.

'We'll just have to trust each other, then.'

They shook hands and then the three of them walked to the top of the stairs, where they said their good-byes. Kirsten and Gavin watched Isobel walk off in the direction of the bright lights and raised voices of the Piazza Della Rovere. She looked back twice before disappearing into the crowd. Kirsten opened her mouth to speak. 'Maybe we should have told her the truth.'

'What? That her beloved Gavin killed her beloved Wes and that the only reason he kept stopping by was he was trying to decide whether or not to kill the whole bunch of them.' He shook his head. 'Not me.'

'It was a story she could live with,' Kirsten said. 'That's all it takes.'